PRAISE FOR THE FIRST BOOK IN THE SERIES

'A gritty and steamy post-apocalyptic novel. Written with an intentionally rough and raw pen, where every scene feels packed with the potential for explosion, this is a bold and gratifying read for action, romance, and dystopian fans of all kinds, especially those drawn to the darker edge of genre-hopping romance.'

Self-Publishing Review

'Harley is an entertaining character with sharp wit, excellent dialogue, and a thirst to prove she doesn't need the protection of others.'

Independent Book Review

REVENGE
THE IRON FISTS

Margot de Klerk

Dedicated to my readers. Thank you for letting me take you on this journey.

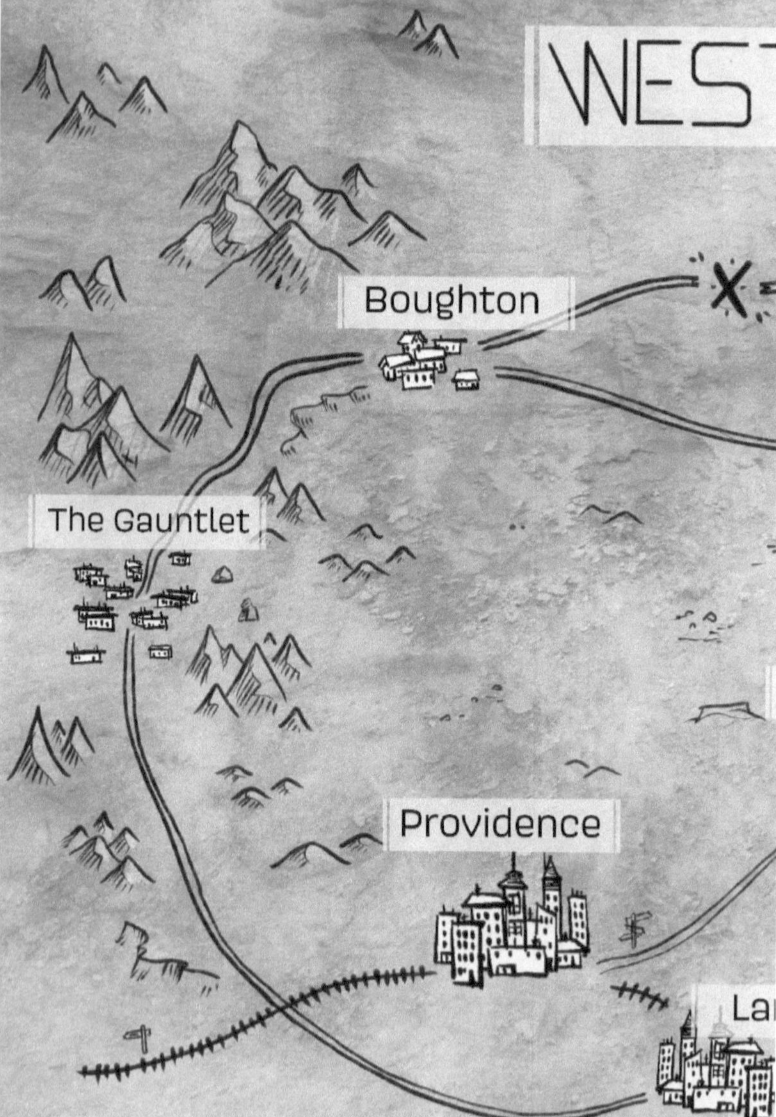

WEST
Boughton
The Gauntlet
Providence
La

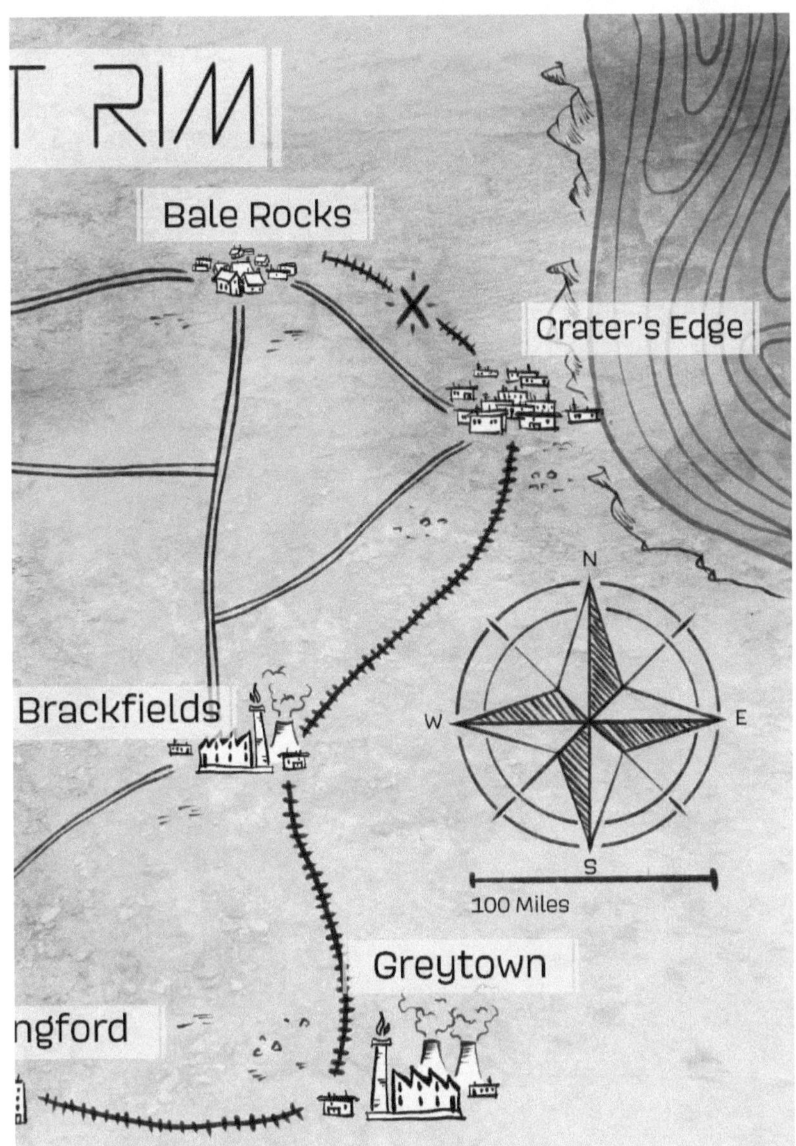

RIM
Bale Rocks
Crater's Edge
Brackfields
Greytown
ngford
N
W
E
S
100 Miles

AUTHOR'S NOTE

Dear reader,

Welcome to the final book in the series! Congratulations on making it this far—and thank you. From the bottom of my heart, thank you. I never, ever imagined that there would be people out there who would love my work enough to read four books in a series, and I am beyond humbled by the support I've received.

By now, you should know the ropes, but as a reminder: this is the fourth book in a (now!) complete sci-fi romance series. It cannot be read without the books before. Please also be aware of the following trigger warnings:

- Violence, firearms usage, and gang warfare
- Drugs
- Swearing
- Sexual content, including non-consensual sex, consent under duress, and sexual harassment
- Slavery

Thank you for sticking with me during this little adventure, and I hope you enjoy the final instalment of Harley and Bas's story.
Margot

'We should forgive our enemies, but not before they have been hanged.'
—Heinrich Heine

ONE

THE FIST CAME FLYING TOWARDS my face. I threw my arm up, already shifting my weight to avoid it—his forearm bounced off mine.

The crowd hollered.

Too close.

My opponent grunted, jabbing an undercut. I twisted, and his fist glanced off my shoulder.

Fuck.

Come on, Harley. Find his weakness.

He threw a volley of punches. I raised my arms. Block—block—*there!*

Seizing the opening, I slipped behind his guard and landed a punch to his solar plexus. He grunted. I followed it up with a swift kick to the knee.

My opponent staggered.

Gotcha.

I pressed my advantage with a flurry of rapid punches. He blocked two, but the third missed. He stumbled back a step, hitting the side of the cage.

Time to finish it.

A punch to the stomach doubled him over. An elbow to the face, and he sagged. He slapped the ground, yielding.

I took a step back.

'AND THE WINNER IS… SIERRA!'

The roar of blood in my ears was supplanted by the shouts and screams of the crowd. They loved it—of course they did. There were hardly any women who fought in The Arsonist, and I'd just won for the third weekend running.

I was on fire.

That is to say, Sierra was on fire.

Because that was my name now. Sierra Davidson. Sierra after my mother, and Davidson after, well, Harley-Davidson.

Ellery had laughed.

But it had worked. No one had realised that Sierra Davidson was Harley Benoit.

The ref hopped the railing, grabbed my arm, and pumped it into the air. 'WELL DONE, SIERRA!'

'SIERRA! SIERRA! SIERRA!' the crowd chanted.

I hated it all.

But I smiled, a big, airheaded grin. Sierra didn't need to have opinions; she just needed to win.

My opponent, a muscular guy with a perpetual scowl, stalked out of the ring. I pulled away from the ref and jumped down, accepting a towel from the towel boy, Lee.

'Well done!' Lee called over the music.

'Thanks,' I panted. Now that the fight was over, all sorts of aches and pains were making themselves known. Not that I was any stranger to the bruises; they'd become more or less a fact of life since Bas had started training me to fight in earnest.

Two months—in two months, I'd gone from dancer to fighter.

I wiped the rough towel over my face. 'Water,' I said.

'Here.' Lee pushed a bottle into my hands. He was young, definitely too young to be working in a place like The Arsonist. I figured him for about fifteen, and word on the street was that his father was one of the refs.

I was getting very good at listening to rumours.

For example, rumour had it that there was a member of the Iron Fists here tonight, watching. I'd heard the other fighters whispering about it whilst I was warming up.

So far, though, I'd seen neither hide nor hair of whoever it was.

I drained the water in one go and handed the bottle and towel back to Lee. 'Thanks.'

'See you next week?' he asked.

'You betcha.'

I headed for the bookie's table at the edge of the room, unwrapping my hands as I walked. Vinny had a hat pulled low and glared at me from beneath it as he doled out a wad of cash. Apparently being the only female fighter was a good money-earner—for me and the pub.

'Good going,' he said. 'Next time maybe don't drag it out so much, yeah?'

Drag it out? I could have snorted.

'Don't see you in there getting your butt kicked.'

'That's because I'm smart. I go where the money is.' He tapped the ledger. 'Same time next week?'

'Maybe.' I shot him a flirty smile, tucking my money into my bra. Old habits died hard.

Vinny smirked. 'Get yourself a drink. On the house.' He jerked his head towards the bar.

'I'm not in the mood for drinking.'

'Boss's orders, hon.'

Boss's orders? Why would the boss want me to get a drink?

Only one way to find out.

My bag was stashed in a locker in the back room. I pulled my jeans and shirt on, wrinkling my nose as they absorbed my sweat. *Ugh, gross.*

Once I was dressed, I made my way back into the main room.

From the outside, The Arsonist looked like a sprawling single-storey building. It was only those in the know who could access the secret basement room, where there was another bar and the fighting cage.

The dim, low-ceilinged room was crowded with people, all shouting their approval. The next fight was already underway, two tall, burly men locked in a clinch. I passed them and pulled out a stool at the bar, waving to Tania, the bartender. She sashayed over and leant her elbows on the counter.

'What you having?' She had to shout to be heard over the crowd.

'Whiskey.' One wouldn't hurt; my fight was over. But I certainly wouldn't have more than that. I needed my wits about me.

Bale Rocks was a very different place these days than the town I'd grown up in.

Tania poured two fingers into a tumbler and slid it to me. I took a sip, turning back to look at the room.

Forty people cramped into a space that fit thirty. The cage took up the middle of the room. The floors were plain concrete, as was the ceiling, and the whole thing was lit by bare bulbs. Heavy, driving music thumped over a struggling sound system. I'd never even met the boss of The Arsonist—why would he be giving me free drinks?

The whiskey had been watered down. I grimaced at the taste but drank it anyway. *Gotta show them you're playing along.*

That was the name of the game: playing along. It was inarguably the most frustrating thing I'd done in my life—I hadn't realised how much I needed action until I'd been condemned to inactivity. Weeks and months of it, filled only with fighting lessons with Bas and the occasional fruitless trip to gather information.

Patience wasn't my strong suit, that was for sure.

At least one good thing had come of it. In my boredom, I'd thrown myself into the fighting lessons with gusto, and I'd progressed much faster than Bas, or anyone else, had expected. Turned out I had a talent for punching men.

A slight smile tugged at my lips.

Who'd have thought?

The stool beside me scraped as someone slid into it.

'So, you're the one causing a stir down here?'

I turned my head so I could see the man out of the corner of my eye—and did a double take. Heavyset, with thick brown hair and a matching beard, tan skin, and biceps the size of my thighs. I knew this man, but he wasn't a member of the Iron Fists.

His name was Wilder, and he worked for the Black Hands.

My heartbeat picked up a notch, but I lifted my drink to my mouth and calmly took a sip.

Play it cool.

'I don't know about causing a stir,' I said. 'I'm just doing what I do best.'

'And what's that?' Wilder asked. He had a drink of his own, which he cradled between two beefy hands. What was he doing here?

'Knocking heads together.'

Wilder chuckled. 'Is that so? What if I told you someone I knew was interested in watching you knock heads together?'

My throat felt tight all of a sudden. 'I'd say he's welcome to come watch. I like an audience.'

'I'll bet you do.' Wilder gave me an appreciative once-over that left me wishing I'd worn baggier jeans. 'But he's not the sort to travel. He expects you to come to him, if you catch my drift.'

Triumph rushed through my veins, but I schooled my face to give nothing away. This was the moment I'd been waiting months for.

'And where would I find him?' I asked, my voice slightly unsteady.

Easy does it, Harley.

'Do you know where the old bottling plant is?'

I bit my cheek. 'I'm vaguely familiar.'

Wilder's dark eyes glittered dangerously. 'He'll be waiting for you there. Friday night, ten PM. Don't be late.'

I gripped my glass harder.

'Of course.'

Wilder smiled, sliding off his stool. 'Oh, and Sierra?'

'Yes?'

'Make sure you come alone.'

With that, he stalked off, vanishing down the hallway that led to the back rooms. I stared after him, unease making the back of my neck prickle.

Our entire plan had hinged on me attracting the attention of the Iron Fists. That, after all, was how you got an invite to fight in the bunker.

I had not expected the invitation to come from a member of the Black Hands.

What the hell was going on?

On the way home, I related the story to my chauffeur, a.k.a. Andrew Kade. The tall black man had been an unexpected but welcome addition to our little team. He was polite, almost perpetually in good spirits, but generally not obnoxious about it like Ellery was. In short, I enjoyed having him around. It helped that he took me seriously, something which had been in short supply in my life until recently.

'You're sure it was Wilder?' Kade asked as he navigated the Ellerys' battered truck towards the checkpoint. 'There's a few guys who look sort of like him.'

'Fairly sure.' I bit my lip. 'Who else is there?'

'Roswell, for sure. He's got the whole beard situation going on.'

I suppressed a grin, shaking my head. My neck and shoulders were getting stiff, though they had nothing on my abs and forearms. 'No, I definitely think it was Wilder. Roswell's not as big.'

'Hmm.' Kade nodded. 'So does that mean Jackson is commanding the Black Hands now? Or is Wilder trying to steal you out from under Jackson's nose?'

'Only one way to find out,' I said.

'When does he want to meet?' Kade entered the slow zone in front of the checkpoint, weaving between the concrete barriers. A soldier exited the guard house, rifle slung over his back.

'Friday, ten PM.'

We both fell silent, Kade's expression pensive. As the soldier approached, Kade rolled his window down.

'Evening,' he called.

'Destination?' The soldiers who'd been sent up from Brackfields were largely humourless, I'd noticed.

'Freetown.'

'Late for a supply run.' The soldier looked between us. I tried to look appropriately uninteresting, but his gaze settled on me anyway.

'We were delivering in town,' Kade said. 'It ran late. My apologies.'

The soldier grunted. I couldn't make out his face; most of it was covered by a brown buff, and a hat concealed his head. 'Papers,' he demanded.

I fished the bundle out of the cubbyhole and leant over Kade to pass them over. The soldier's gaze lingered on my face, but he took the papers and flicked through them without comment. I held my breath. The papers were forged—provided to us by Turner, Bas's contact. Every time we went through the checkpoint, I felt the same bubbling anxiety in my stomach.

Finally, he passed the papers back to Kade. 'Safe driving.'

'Thank you,' Kade said, a study in politeness. The soldier retreated and Kade rolled up the window, blocking the stiff wind that was blowing.

'I hate doing that,' I muttered as we rolled through the barrier. They'd finally got the permanent barrier up, run by electricity. Word had it they were now building a fence around the town, but given how little we had in the way of supplies up here, it was slow going. They had to bring everything from Brackfields.

Also, the Iron Fists kept shooting the soldiers whenever they ventured into the north side.

Safely out of town, we started the now-familiar drive through the wasteland to Freetown, the farming community ten miles north of Bale Rocks. I'd been pleasantly surprised by how welcoming they were: so long as we helped out with the work, we were welcome to stay. Seeing as there was no shortage of work, even in the dead of winter, we would probably be welcome to stay forever.

Which was our plan at the moment.

'By the way, listen.' Kade hit the button for the radio, and it buzzed to life.

'*… this is Crater FM, and you're listening to Before The Fall…*'

'You got it working!' I grinned.

'Laura helped. She's pretty good with fine-tuning stuff.' Kade grinned. A slow, deep track filled the car.

'Finally,' I said. 'I hate driving in silence.'

'You mean my esteemed company isn't enough for you?' Kade demanded.

'Oh come on, don't tell me you like driving in silence.'

'I happen to enjoy a good, well-stewed silence.'

I snorted. 'Well, in that case, I won't give you a play-by-play of my fight…'

'Oh no, come on, don't hold back the details.'

I grinned. 'Alright, alright.'

We occupied the rest of the drive dissecting my fighting tactics. Kade was incredibly athletic but didn't seem to enjoy fighting like Bas and Ellery did. Though he did find pleasure in discussing my fights.

'Wish I could sneak in and watch,' he said, not for the first time.

'Please don't. The last thing we need is you getting caught.' I bit my lip. We were already down one person—Theo. In two months, I hadn't heard so much of a whisper of where he'd gone. I'd even convinced Bas to drive me back down to Brackfields a few weeks ago to see if we could find out what had happened to him there, but it seemed like he'd vanished without a trace somewhere in between Dignity Jones's rest stop and Bale Rocks.

No car, no body, no clue.

And without any leads, I'd had to just leave off the search. It hurt my chest to even think about it.

I pushed the thoughts away.

'Are Bas and Ellery back yet?' I asked.

'Not yet. But I hope they will be soon. We need to come up with a plan for next weekend.'

Bas and Ellery had been working the slaver angle—a task I was not allowed to contribute to because, according to Bas, 'You have your job and I have mine.'

Ellery had laughed and told me Bas couldn't take me along because I'd distract him.

More inactivity, more frustration.

We reached the gates of Freetown. Their electricity ran entirely off generators and was switched off at eight-thirty sharp every night. The fights kept us out until after midnight, so Bas had asked one of the boys from the Jaeger family to wait up and let us in when we got back. When Kade flicked the headlights on and off, Micky popped through the gate, clutching a shotgun that was comically large on his gangly frame, and loped over to us.

Kade rolled his window down. 'Hello, Micky.'

'Hi, Andy,' Micky said shyly. He had a beanie pulled low over his face and a jacket four sizes too big for him swamped his frame. 'Hi, Miss Harley.'

'Hi,' I called back.

'I'll open the gate.'

He hurried back inside, and a moment later one side of the gate rolled back so that Kade could drive in. We stopped inside until Micky had closed it again, and then he climbed up into the back of the truck and knocked on the cab to let us know we could go. Kade dimmed his headlights and trundled slowly through the sleeping village, stopping at the bottom of the road to the Jaeger farm. Micky jumped off and waved to us, and we continued up the dirt track that would bring us to the Ellery farm. A single light flickered in the kitchen window.

Either Claire or Laura had waited up.

We parked and headed inside. Even after lights out, the house was blissfully warm. Laura sat at the kitchen table, a small electric lantern by her arm as she squinted at a pair of trousers she was mending.

'Hello, Miss Laura,' Kade said.

Laura set her work aside, blinking tiredly at us. 'You're back already? Gosh, what time is it?'

'Almost two,' I said.

She rubbed her eyes. 'Wow. Do you want something to eat?'

'Please.' Kade shrugged his jacket off and sagged into a chair at the large table. I poured us glasses of water and sat opposite him.

'How was your fight?' Laura asked as she brought plates of stew over to us. Leftovers had to be eaten cold, but food was food. I was always starving after the fights.

'Good, thanks,' I said as I tucked in. 'At least, I won.'

There had been a few moments where Bas would probably have told me I'd been sloppy—but Bas hadn't seen the fight, so he didn't need to know.

'Of course she won.' Kade grinned.

'That's great.'

'Yeah.' I munched another bite. 'No sign of the guys yet?'

Their cars hadn't been out front, but I still had to ask.

Laura shook her head. 'Just me and Claire.' She fiddled with her cuticles. 'Do you have any news?'

'I went by the Hawke and Tern,' Kade said. 'Turner hasn't heard anything from them. But they're not past their deadline yet. They'll be back.'

'I know. I just worry.'

'It sucks having to stay home and wait whilst they're off in danger,' I filled in. It was a feeling I was well familiar with, from years of waiting to see if Theo would come back from his latest adventure.

Theo—who had not come back from his latest adventure.

I swallowed, the food turning to rocks in my stomach. *Damnit.*

'At least you're out doing something!' Laura exclaimed. 'All I have is mending and… and farm work.'

'They're tough guys. They'll be back soon,' Kade said.

'Yeah.' Laura pressed her lips together, glancing away. She was scared.

I didn't blame her. Everything was different now.

'Let's get to bed,' I said. 'There's no use staying up and worrying.'

Laura nodded glumly. 'You're right.'

Maybe, but I didn't feel right. Worry was bunched like a hard knot in my chest, and not just worry for Bas and Ellery—who were who-only-knew-where right now—but for all of us. For the future.

We couldn't stay here forever; it just wasn't practical. This was a temporary fix.

At some point, we were going to have to make a choice: either take a stand against Jackson and win our way back into town… or abandon it and all of our friends with it.

And if Jackson was collaborating with the Black Hands now, then that day might come sooner than any of us expected.

TWO

THE OUTHOUSE WAS FREEZING. DAINTILY, I reached a single hand out of the steamy shower stall, snatched my towel, and wrapped it around myself.

There were many things nice about the farmhouse. The fresh bread, for one. The warmth of the kitchen. Drinking tea with the family at breakfast. It had all made me tremendously nostalgic for the before time, when my parents had still been alive and I'd still been a kid.

Then Laura had told me we had to shower in the outhouse. That had put a dampener on things.

It was frigid today, as well. Frost lay thick on the ground, and the sky was the colour of steel. I'd been up at the crack of dawn to milk the cows and spent the morning helping with repairs to a tractor. Those, at least, had been sweaty activities which had kept me warm.

I dried myself with rough sweeps of the towel, before pulling it around my shoulders and clenching it with one fist. With the other hand, already cringing, I grabbed the door and shoved it open.

Cold air rushed in.

Fuck, that's awful.

I snatched my jumper and yanked it over my head, then pulled on my jeans. Boots. Coat. *Phew.*

I'd survived.

Teeth chattering, I covered my head with the towel and headed for the flimsy wooden door that led to the garden. As I swung it open, barking erupted from somewhere ahead.

Dogs. One thing I was not used to having around. I'd never been a fan of big dogs, slobbery creatures that they were, but here I was having to get used to them. There were four on the farm. I followed the noise around the house and watched as Bas's car pulled up.

He was back.

He cut the engine and swung the door open. I opened my mouth to call out to him.

But my courage failed and I ducked back around the corner of the house instead. Peeping around, I watched as Bas strode to the back of his car and began pulling things out. Ellery drove up and stopped beside him.

Both back. Both able to drive, which was a decent sign that no potentially fatal injuries had been incurred.

Call out to him.

I bit my lip and slipped back around the house, letting myself in at the back door. I'd see him at lunch.

Halfway up the stairs, I heard doors swinging open upstairs. Laura came hurrying along the landing, followed by Kade.

'Did I hear cars?' Kade asked.

I nodded.

'Is it—' Laura's eyes shone with hope.

'Yeah, they're both back.'

'Brilliant!' She hurried past me, sprinting for the front door. Kade took the steps at a more measured pace.

'Where are you going?' he asked.

'My room. I need to finish changing.'

He shot me a sceptical look.

'It's freezing out there,' I added, crossing my arms. 'I'm not going out with wet hair.'

'Well, alright.' Kade shrugged. 'I'll let Bas know where you are, shall I?'

My cheeks heated. I unwound the towel from my head, letting my damp hair fall to hide my blush.

'Yeah, sure.' Swallowing, I passed Kade and headed for the room I shared with Laura.

It wasn't that I was avoiding Bas, precisely. It was just normal to have early relationship jitters.

Right?

I scrubbed the towel over my hair, trying to get as much moisture from it as possible, then exchanged my clothes for my warmest jumper and trousers. And thick socks. Ms Ellery, upon discovering that I had none, had dispatched me to the Yates household and instructed me to trade a few hours of repairs for extra pairs of thick socks.

To my surprise, they'd been quite keen to make the trade; the Yates had lost their oldest son in the military and needed the extra labour.

The barter economy in Freetown was quite impressive. No one seemed to ever pay for anything, yet everyone managed to get what they needed.

Finally, I had no more excuses to procrastinate. I headed downstairs and followed the exuberant voices to the kitchen.

'…bloody huge! I didn't even realise. We should go there for fun sometime.' Ellery was waving his hands; his cheeks were ruddy and his blond hair was greasy, but he looked happy. Seemed like it had been a good trip.

Bas, by contrast, was a study in seriousness—as always. His chestnut brown hair fell in his eyes. It was getting long. His green eyes jumped to the door, and for a moment we made eye contact. A soft smile crept over his lips.

'Harley!' Ellery shattered the moment. Bas looked away, back at the coffee he was boiling. 'Heard you did well last night.'

'Yeah.' I slid into the kitchen, sighing as the temperature instantly jumped from tolerable to toasty. 'I won.'

'And finally got approached by someone.'

'Wilder,' I said.

Ellery and Bas exchanged glances.

'Who's he?' Laura asked from where she was setting the table. I grabbed a handful of cutlery from the drawer and set about helping her.

'He works for the Black Hands,' Ellery said. To Bas, he added, 'You think that means Jackson's pulling support from the Hands?'

'I wouldn't put it past him.' Bas took the coffee off the stove. 'Hannover was there when we were arrested.'

'I thought that was a one-off, but I suppose it fits with his current ethos.' Ellery pulled a stack of mugs out of a cupboard, and we all converged on the table.

'So, tell us where you were,' I said, sliding in beside Bas.

'We went all the way to the Gauntlet!' Ellery said, leaning over to grab the coffee strainer. 'Helluva place. You wouldn't even believe it.'

'It's awful,' Bas said quietly.

I glanced his way. Up close, he looked tired.

'Must have been a long drive.'

He nodded. 'We stayed over a night in Boughton on the way back.'

'Did you find anything?'

'Maybe—' Ellery cut himself off as his sister approached, a heavy pot in her arms.

Claire slammed the pot down in the centre of the table, her lips pursed. 'Lunch is served.'

'Thank you,' Laura said, earning herself a scowl.

'Don't thank me, it's just my job.'

'Lay off, Claire,' Ellery grunted, grabbing the serving spoon. 'We're all pulling our weight around here.'

'No, you're off galivanting around the wasteland and expecting Mum and me to hold down the fort.'

Ellery sighed. 'Anyway,' he said, 'we staked out the Black Hands' compound. There's a *lot* of activity out there. Whatever they're planning, it's big.'

'That's bad, right?' Laura asked.

'Depends. If they're planning on going against the Iron Fists, we might be able to use it to our advantage. But we don't know yet.' Ellery scooped up a mouthful of soup.

'How'd you end up on the Gauntlet?' I asked. The Gauntlet was the road that ran north-south to Providence—but that was the extent of my knowledge. I'd only heard about it from patrons of the Kranikovska, never been there myself.

'Followed one of their trucks. Looks like that's where they're sending the slaves.'

I swallowed. It was easy to forget what the stakes were—my brain rebelled against the very idea. But I kept reminding myself anyway: the Black Hands were capturing people and selling them.

If nothing else, even if we never got to return to Bale Rocks, we had to stop them.

'They're not transferring all of the slaves out,' Bas said. 'There are too few being sent out.'

'What does that mean?' I paused, my spoon hovering over my bowl.

'I think they're escaping,' Ellery said. 'There was a huge ruck—'

'It's almost impossible to escape that compound without inside knowledge,' Bas objected.

'Someone could have helped them.'

Bas shook his head.

'Oh, come on,' Ellery wheedled. 'You heard them shouting—'They're gone!' Some of the slaves definitely escaped in the transfer.'

'We didn't see anyone.'

'Didn't you once mention there was a secret way in?' I asked.

Bas frowned. 'Yes, but it's unlikely they were using it. You can only find it if you know where it is.'

'And someone could have told them,' Ellery said.

'Doubtful.'

'We need a contact in the Black Hands' compound who can tell us what's going on,' Kade said.

'Too dangerous,' Bas vetoed immediately.

'Agreed,' Ellery said. 'Besides, who? None of us can do it.'

'I might be able to help,' I said. 'I mean, it was Wilder who reached out to me.'

'Absolutely not,' Bas said, his voice flat and dark.

'What? If I can get information out of the Black Hands—'

'What you're suggesting is insane, Harley,' Ellery said. 'It's one thing to be invited to the bunker, which we all know really well, and quite another to try and get into the Black Hands' compound. You'll get yourself killed.'

'Hannover will recognise you,' Bas pointed out.

'That will be a risk in the bunker, too,' I pointed out. 'It's not as though he never goes there.'

Bas pressed his lips together, glaring at his soup as though it had personally offended him.

'We can get to the bunker to back you up if we need to,' Ellery said. 'So that's entirely different.'

Was it, though? I was going to be in danger, anyway.

We lapsed into a heavy silence, each lost in our own thoughts. Mine mostly revolved around next Friday.

'We need a way to communicate,' Kade said.

'The radios aren't secure,' Ellery said. 'And they don't have the range we need.'

'Something else, then. Laura—you're quite handy with that stuff. Got any ideas?'

'Me?' Laura bit her lip. 'I don't know. I'm just good at cleaning electronics. It's not the same as building them from scratch. I don't think I could do that.'

Kade looked disappointed. Ellery scratched his head. 'It would be good if we had a way of talking. I suppose we could keep switching channels—'

'Too complicated,' Bas said.

'And we only have two radios,' Kade added.

Déjà vu struck me. I'd had a similar conversation to this before—with Theo, about tech. I swallowed against the pain that blossomed in my chest at the thought of my missing best friend.

'Kayla might be able to help us,' I said.

'Kayla?' Ellery asked. 'The woman who works at Krani's?'

'Yep. Her dad sells old tech. He has a shop on the west end of Busker Street.'

'That could work.' Ellery glanced at Bas. 'Thoughts?'

'Worth a try,' Bas said.

'We'll have to pay him,' I said. 'And his services aren't cheap.'

Ellery grimaced. We had people, skills, products to trade, but money? That was the one thing none of us had. I'd blown most of mine on our wild goose chase around the West Rim looking for Maddock.

'Let's worry about that after we've spoken to him,' he suggested.

'Alright,' I said.

As we continued eating, I found myself looking at Bas more and more frequently. He kept his gaze on his food, shoulders tense.

Since we'd arrived in Freetown, a gap had been growing between us. Every time he went away and came back, I felt it widen more and more.

Look at me, I willed him. *Smile at me. Tell me it's going to be okay.*

Bas finished his food and stood to clear his plate. 'I'm going to take a shower.'

He strode out.

He hadn't even looked at me.

I picked unenthusiastically at my food. Across the table, Laura shot me a sympathetic look. I scowled.

Was I that transparent?

I procrastinated over lunch, as well, helping Claire clear the table. If I spent long enough in the kitchen, Bas would have retreated to his bedroom by the time I came out.

I mistimed; I stepped out of the kitchen at the exact moment he stepped in from the garden. He had a towel over his hair and an armful of dirty clothes.

'Harley.' He slowed his footsteps, staring at me.

'I'll give you some space,' Claire said. Smirking, she scampered to the stairs, leaving me alone with Bas. *Damn.*

I stared at Bas.

'Hi,' he said in a husky voice that sent a thrill down my spine. I pushed the feeling away.

'Oh, you finally feel like speaking to me?' I asked.

Bas blinked, a stunned look crawling over his face. 'What?'

'In the kitchen. You barely even looked at me.' I crossed my arms.

'We talked plenty.'

'Yeah, about work. But not about—about *me and you.*'

Bas frowned. 'That's private. I don't want to talk *me and you* in front of the others.'

'That's not—' I shook my head. 'Don't take my words out of context. You know what I mean.'

'No, I don't.'

I glared at him. He was being deliberately obtuse. I was sure of it.

'How are you?' I snapped finally.

'I'm fi—'

'Don't you want to know how I'm doing? Hug me? Kiss me? It's like we barely know each other!'

'I don't like doing that stuff in front of other people,' Bas said. 'You know that.'

So he could step into the hall? And what about saying hello? That was hardly intimate.

'No, you're just angry that I went ahead with fighting, even though you didn't want me to.'

Bas's expression flattened out abruptly. 'I just got back. I need to sleep.'

Of course. Run away, then.

'Fine,' I snapped. 'I'm going to train. Enjoy your nap.'

I turned on my heel, heading for the stairs.

One of the old army buildings in the centre of Freetown held a gym. After changing, I jogged down there to do a workout.

My workouts had changed completely since we'd hatched our plan to put me in the cage, and with it, my body was changing, too. I was losing my lithe dancing muscles in favour of something else. I hadn't told anyone, but looking in the mirror was weird these days.

I didn't quite recognise myself anymore.

But it was a necessary sacrifice. I'd always loved dance, but the truth was, it wasn't my future. And I wouldn't have a future unless I got good at fighting.

Get in the bunker, find out what Jackson is planning, figure out how to stop the slavers.

What seemed like a simple three-step plan was, in fact, horrifically complicated. Bas only cared about the slavers. Ellery and Kade wanted their home back—and of course Ellery wanted his family to be able to freely trade with Bale Rocks again. I wanted to keep Savannah safe and find out what had happened to Theo. As for Laura, I had no idea. But we all wanted different things, and when I was in a bad mood—like I was now—all I saw were the cracks between us.

I purged my frustrations on an ancient punching bag.

Sure, Bas was tired. But he could have at least kissed me and told me he was happy to see me.

But was he happy to see me?

I honestly had no idea. I didn't know what he was thinking, ever.

We needed to talk, but there was hardly a moment of privacy around the farm, and somehow—through Bas's machinations—we hadn't been paired on any excursions so far.

He was avoiding me. I was becoming more and more sure of it.

Punch. Punch.

My fists smacked the cracked leather.

Maybe we should just admit that chemistry wasn't enough. We weren't good for each other—we never had been. It didn't matter how much we clicked in the good moments, if our relationship was ninety percent bad moments.

But I didn't want to give up either.

Punch. Punch. Punch.

Damnit.

Breathing hard, I leant my head against the punching bag.

I was exhausted. Every time I fought, it took me days to recover—and that was just from the muscle soreness. Forget the bruises, the scrapes, the niggling cut on my right arm that didn't seem to want to stay closed. Sure, injuries had been part of dancing, but this was different.

If I got injured, it would ruin my dancing. But if I died, I'd definitely never dance again.

So fighting it was.

I stepped back, rolling my shoulders, and readied myself to restart.

'You need to hold your hands higher.'

I jumped and spun around. Bas stood in the doorway of the small, dimly lit room. He'd changed into training clothes and his hair was dry, though he didn't look like he'd slept. I'd only been here an hour.

'I thought you were sleeping.' My voice came out stilted with poorly concealed hostility.

'I changed my mind.'

Bas stepped into the room. Slowly. Tentatively. Almost like he was afraid I'd blow up at him again. It made my heart hurt.

I put my hands down.

'I'd rather you slept. I know you're tired.'

'You need to keep training if you're going to fight in the bunker.'

A sinking feeling filled me. So he wasn't here to see me. It was just about training.

'I can train by myself,' I said. 'Don't worry.'

'Harley…' Bas stepped closer, shaking his head. He stared at me, mouth opening and closing. I crossed my arms—if he wanted to say something, he could say it. I didn't feel like helping him out.

'Are you okay?' he asked finally.

'Yeah, sure. Why wouldn't I be?'

'I missed you.'

Could have fooled me.

I looked back at the punching bag. 'It wasn't that long.'

'Six days.'

Yeah, I know. I can count, too.

I bit the inside of my cheek. 'Let's… let's just train.'

'Alright.'

Bas and I moved into the middle of the room. Training with Bas, at least, was familiar. He put me through my paces efficiently, his every blow precise and brutal. Within a few minutes, my skin was slippery with sweat, and my hair stuck to my face. I lifted a hand to scrape a lock out of my eyes, and Bas's next fist slipped under my guard and caught me in the solar plexus.

'Fuck!'

'Sloppy,' he chastised.

I took several steps back, gritting my teeth so hard my jaw ached.

'I wouldn't do that in a real fight.'

'Then you shouldn't do it whilst training,' he flatly.

I clenched my fists, then shook them out, forcing myself to relax. He was trying to rile me up. Why? Because he wanted to prepare me for anything I might face—or because he was angry with me?

You never knew with Bas.

It didn't matter. I wouldn't take the bait.

'Fine,' I said. 'Let's go again.'

Bas nodded sharply, and we resumed sparring. Every one of his jabs was precise and deadly. Didn't this guy ever get tired? Hadn't he just got back from a long trip? But it felt like I was the one who'd been on the move for the last week. My movements grew more and more sluggish, until Bas slipped beneath my guard again, chopping me under the ear. I stumbled and threw a desperate punch which hit his shoulder. He turned, arms moving too fast to track as he blocked my next blow and twisted my arm behind my back. I staggered back a step, trying to ease the pressure, but he drove me unerringly to my knees. I jabbed my free arm back and landed a blow against his chest. Bas's balance gave out and we both crashed to the floor.

His grip loosened. I tried to roll away, and pain exploded through my scalp. Groaning, I turned my head to the side. Bas's hand was gripping my ponytail.

'Ow,' I hissed. 'What the fuck? Don't pull my hair.'

'You need to cut your hair,' Bas said as he unwound his fingers. 'It's too easy to use it against you.'

'That's an illegal move!'

Bas shrugged as he climbed off me. 'People get away with much worse in the cage,' he said.

I rubbed my burning scalp. 'That doesn't mean *you* have to do it.'

'Or you could cut your hair.' He offered me a hand. I stared at it for a few seconds, fury swirling in my chest. Then I scrambled up— without his help.

'I thought our goal was for me to look feminine.' Wasn't that the whole point of what we were doing? Hardly any women fought in the cage—so advancing through the ranks as a woman would catch the right attention. That was what we'd agreed.

'You don't need long hair to look feminine.' Bas frowned. 'It's a vulnerability.'

'I'm not cutting my hair!' My voice came out whiny and shrill. I cringed. Moderating my tone, I continued, 'I like my hair.'

'Not everybody is going to follow the rules,' Bas said. He strode over to his bag and pulled out a water bottle to drink. 'And what will you do if they recognise you?'

'No one has so far.' I rubbed my scalp again. *Ugh, sweaty.*

'You've been lucky so far.'

I scowled at his back. Great, a new thing to argue about. It seemed like Bas had a never-ending list of critiques these days.

'No one is expecting me to be in the cage,' I said as I retrieved my own water bottle. 'We discussed this over and over—'

'That's not going to protect you for long, Harley.'

I gnashed my teeth. 'I'm not cutting my hair. You agreed before—'

'Before, it was only a hypothetical. We had no idea whether you'd be successful enough to get invited to the bunker.'

'Oh great.' My fury sparked up like a fire doused in gasoline. 'What you mean is that you didn't think it would be an issue because you didn't think *I'd* be good enough.'

'I never said that.' Bas frowned. 'Harley—'

'Spare me.' I grabbed my bag. 'You know what? I'm tired, you're tired. Let's just call it quits. Training today was a bad idea.'

I swung the bag over my shoulder.

'Harley!' Bas called.

'See you later.' I shoved my way out, rolling my shoulders, then put the bag across my body and broke into a jog.

This was the opposite of what I needed. It seemed like everything I achieved, Bas just found a way to make it… smaller. No success was big enough. Nothing I did was good enough to make him see I could do this.

He still believed I'd fail.

And he was constantly picking at everything I did, trying to mitigate that failure, ignoring the fact that he didn't *need* to.

Ugh.

My anger lent me speed, my feet pounding the packed, frozen dirt, and soon I was back at the farmhouse. There was no one else around. Collette—Marco and Claire's mother—would be having a nap, so the rest of us usually found somewhere else to be, or something we could do quietly for a couple of hours after lunch. As I crept up the stairs, Ellery's bedroom door opened, and he emerged, blinking sleepily.

'Oh, hey,' he said.

I locked my jaw. I didn't particularly feel like talking right now. I just wanted to wash up and then go hide in the kitchen or something.

'Hey,' I muttered.

Ellery frowned. 'Everything alright?'

I sucked in a deep breath, tamping my frustration down. 'Yeah, fine.'

'Have you seen Bas?'

'We were training together.' I jerked my thumb over my shoulder. 'He should still be at the gym.'

'Alright.' Ellery frowned intently at my face, as though he was trying to read my secrets in my eyes. I squirmed. Finally, he said, 'Look, cut him some slack, okay? What we saw in the Gauntlet wasn't easy for him.'

Instantly, I felt like the most rotten person on the planet. Cut him some slack—the opposite of what I'd done. Of course, it must have been hard for Bas, seeing the slaves there. It must have brought back all sorts of horrible memories. I hadn't even thought of that.

Shit.

'Yeah,' I mumbled. 'Yeah… I will.'

'Great.' Ellery shot me a grin. 'I'm going back to bed. I'm fucking exhausted.'

He trooped back into his room, leaving me alone in the hallway with my guilt.

Shit. I sucked. Bas wasn't the problem here.

It was me.

THREE

I SLOWED THE TRUCK, FIGHTING the steering to get it over to the side of the road. Finally, I pulled the handbrake up and cut the engine.

Made it.

In two months, my driving skills had improved quite a bit. However, it turned out there was a significant difference between driving Bas's four-by-four, which was well cared-for, and Ms Ellery's truck, which had more spirit than an entire schoolhouse worth of ten-year-olds.

Still, I'd made it across the wasteland, through the checkpoint, and to the west side of town, and I'd done it all with a glowering Bas sitting silently in the passenger seat.

I took the keys and opened my door, sliding down. Ellery hopped out the back, pulling his beanie off and running a hand through his mussed-up hair. He nodded to a shopfront beside where we'd parked. 'This the place?'

It looked much the same as the last time I'd been here: a wire mesh reinforced the insides of the windows, and the shop beyond was cluttered with all manner of gadgets. A cardboard sign was tacked inside the window.

NO GANGS – NO GUNS

'I'm surprised they let them keep the sign,' Ellery remarked.

'This is the Aces' territory,' Bas murmured. 'They might have made some kind of deal.'

'Kayla pulls shifts in one of their casinos,' I said. 'Maybe they let her dad operate because of that? But I don't think she'll rat us out. She's my friend.'

Ellery glanced at Bas; Bas nodded. My heart fluttered. He might have been annoyed, but he still trusted my word.

If only he trusted me that I could keep myself safe in the bunker.

I led the way to the door. No sooner had I swung it open then Kayla came racing over, a look of concern wrinkling her brow.

'Harley!' she snatched my arm and dragged me inside. 'In the back! Go!'

What the hell?

I hurried to the back and slipped into the workshop. Declan, Kayla's father, was bent over a table, using tweezers to pick apart some kind of device. He looked up at the sudden intrusion.

'Harley? What's happening?'

'Search me.'

I turned in time to see Kayla herding Bas and Ellery into the workshop.

'I'm just locking the front,' she told her father.

'Alright.' He crossed his arms over his beefy chest, surveying us. 'What trouble have you brought to my door this time?'

'We don't want any trouble,' I said. 'Just hoping you can help us.'

His lips thinned. 'We'll see. Have a seat.'

He moved to the large table in the middle and cleared the bench along one side so we could sit. Kayla popped back in a moment later, wringing her hands.

'Are you completely stupid? There's a kill-on-sight order for the three of you!'

'We know,' Ellery said.

'You *know*?' Kayla spluttered. 'But you brought Harley here?'

'I drove,' I said. Kayla's gaze jumped to mine. 'This was my idea.'

'Did anyone see you?'

'I don't think so.'

She scowled and slouched onto the bench opposite. Her father loomed over all of us.

'I don't typically help gang members.'

'We're not gang members anymore,' Ellery said.

'Once a man with a gun, always a man with a gun.'

'We don't have any guns either. It's tricky to get them through the checkpoint.'

For a moment, Declan and Ellery stared at one another in a silent standoff. I held my breath and crossed my fingers under the table. Then Declan jerked his head and held out a hand. 'Declan. You are?'

'Marco Ellery,' Ellery said, shaking hands. 'And this is Bas.'

'Right, and I take it you know my daughter Kayla.' Declan nodded to Bas, then sat opposite me at the table. 'What can we do for you?'

I glanced at Ellery and Bas. Ellery raised an eyebrow at me.

Right, then.

I cleared my throat. 'We're looking for a way to communicate.'

'Discreetly,' Ellery added.

'Discreetly,' Declan echoed. 'Any other requirements? What sort of distance are we talking here?'

Was it necessary to know this stuff? Once again, I was out of my depth. I looked at Ellery.

'Short distances,' he said, resting his elbows on the table. 'No more than a couple of miles. But it needs to be small. To pass a frisking. And Harley will be wearing it whilst fighting.'

Kayla shot me a surprised look. 'What the hell have you got yourself into now?'

'It's complicated,' I said weakly.

'You *don't* say.'

'The less we tell you, the better,' Bas cut in.

'Of course,' Kayla said, her tone neutral. It was one of the things I liked about her—Kayla was very strict about keeping things professional.

Declan wore a thoughtful look. 'Be that as it may, we can't help you without some kind of guarantees. Some of what I sell here is extremely valuable; I'd hate for it to fall into the wrong hands.'

'We're happy to comply with any of your requirements,' Ellery said, resting his hands on the table. '*After* you show us what you have.'

'That's not how this is going to work,' Declan said. 'Do you think I was born yesterday?'

'I think it must be pretty difficult keeping this place going with the army in town,' Ellery said levelly. 'They do have a habit of helping themselves to whatever they want. And the army needs tech for all sorts of things.'

Declan raised an eyebrow. 'The army is hardly the first to treat this town as their own personal surplus shop.'

Ellery pinched his lips together.

Declan leant forwards over the table. 'I've lived in this town over sixty years, you know that?'

'That's a damn long time,' Ellery said.

'It is,' Declan agreed. 'Long enough that I remember the time before old Sayle came into town, throwing his weight around and thinking he could run things here. Long enough that I remember how we used to do things in these parts. Long enough that I know change ain't always a good thing, if you catch my drift.'

'Change is inevitable though,' Ellery said. 'Things never stay the same.'

'No, but that doesn't mean we can't reject the changes that are bad for our town.'

'No,' Ellery said slowly, 'it doesn't.'

'So I'll ask again,' Declan said, tapping his fingers against the tabletop. 'What guarantee can you give me that this technology won't find its way into the hands of the Iron Fists?'

Ellery glanced at me. I nodded—I trusted Declan, and I was pretty hopeful he'd be able to rig something up for us. At the very least, he wasn't going to betray us.

'Alright.' Ellery leant forwards, resting his elbows on the table. 'I'm sure you've noticed that there have been a few… changes of management around the north side of town lately?'

Declan narrowed his eyes, darting a half-glance at Kayla. 'I'm peripherally aware.'

'Unfortunately, those changes have meant that we no longer have eyes and ears around town… and particularly in the bunker,' Ellery said. 'We want to change that.'

'I see,' Declan said. 'Any particular reason?'

Ellery opened his mouth—to give the information we'd agreed on. *We want to get rid of the army, and we think Jackson has cut some kind of deal with the mayor.*

'The Iron Fists and the Black Hands are collaborating,' Bas cut in. 'The Black Hands have been shipping slaves out of town to the Gauntlet, and we intend to stop them.'

So much for subtlety.

Ellery sat back, smirking faintly. Declan turned to Bas.

'And getting into the bunker will help you achieve that?'

'I know the man who is heading the operation,' Bas said. 'He'll be at the centre of the action. If he's working with Jackson, he won't let Jackson too far out of his sight.'

Declan nodded.

'Well, fine,' he said, clasping his hands. 'That, at least, is a goal I can get behind. And what of the army?'

'At the moment, we have no quarrel with them,' Bas said.

'But would you collaborate with them if your goals aligned?'

I held my breath. Bas was doing the talking. I knew what I'd say—*no*—but what would he say?

'Yes,' he said. 'Temporarily. But I doubt that's going to happen.'

Declan weighed that, his lips pursed, for what seemed like an impossibly long time.

'I can appreciate your honesty, at least,' he said. 'Fine.' He nodded my way. 'You do like to bring me interesting challenges. I take it you want to communicate inside the bunker?'

'That's the idea,' Ellery said, leaning in again.

'Alright, well, I've never been. However, I do know a little about the old world—if I may toot my own horn.' Declan smiled wryly. 'It was constructed by the military, or so they say, and if there's one thing that remains true about the military, both Pre- and Post-Crash, it's that they need ways to communicate. I take it your radios have worked down there in the past?'

'Yes,' Ellery said.

'Good. Then it's just a matter of making it secure. I have the gear you'll need.' He stood and strode to his chest of drawers, tapping each drawer with a long finger until he decided on the one he wanted. He opened it and extracted a tiny black device.

'Slots in the ear, like so.' He demonstrated. 'Should be discreet. You may want to take it out during the actual fights, but otherwise, I think it will go unnoticed.'

I nodded, eyeing the device. It was so small, I could hardly believe it was fit for purpose.

'The main difficulty is going to be keeping the channel secure. Do you have some kind of centre of operations?'

'We're using my house,' Ellery said uncertainly.

'The Freetown transmission station might work,' Bas said. 'If we can commission it.'

'We don't know how to do that though,' Ellery said. We'd looked at it when Bas and I had first arrived, but although there was no evidence of tampering, none of us knew enough to get it up and running.

'What kind of transmission station are we talking about?' Declan asked.

'It's Post-Crash,' Ellery said. 'Probably an old army base.'

'Camp Red Rock?' Declan asked. He turned abruptly and snatched a bundle of papers out of another drawer. Bringing them over, he spread a map out on the table. 'I had thought it was further northeast—now why did I never think of that?'

He indicated an area on the map, northeast of Bale Rocks, where I knew Freetown was. 'I take it the army base got subsumed into the fortification?'

'We're not sure,' Ellery said. 'It was a long time before I was born, in any case.'

Declan shot him an amused look. 'Yes, I'd say so. The army base was attacked by raiders from the north. In the end, it turned out to be more trouble than it was worth, and they relocated to the base they have now. Yes.' He nodded, more to himself than to us. 'Are outsiders allowed into Freetown?'

'Technically no,' Ellery said. 'But I'm pretty sure we could arrange to make an exception.'

Declan nodded, suddenly excited. 'If you let me in to look at that transmission station, I'll consider it payment for the earpieces—so long as I'm allowed to take anything you don't need.'

Ellery frowned and looked at Bas and me. I nodded. After a moment, Bas did too. 'Seems like our best option.'

'Alright,' Ellery said, holding out a hand. 'It's a deal.'

Declan shook his hand. 'Let me show you how these work, and then we can arrange a time for me to get out to Freetown.'

The men gathered around the other side of the table. Whilst they studied the earpieces, I pulled the map towards myself. It was marked with all sorts of features I'd never even known were there—ridges, lakes, even a forest. How had Declan got this much information about the area around Bale Rocks? He didn't seem like the type to go out bush-whacking. Maybe from the scavengers who brought him the tech he sold?

Kayla slipped around the table and joined me. 'Hey.'

'Hi,' I murmured.

'Come on.' Kayla jerked her head to the door. 'Let's leave them to it. I need to speak to you.'

'Alright.' I let myself be pulled away. In the main room, Kayla busied herself sorting through a box of scraps on the counter. I kept my body turned away from the windows, just in case. 'What is it?'

'What are you doing?' Kayla asked in a stern tone.

'Pardon?'

'Fighting? Getting involved with some kind of rebellion? You have no skin in this conflict.'

It was a question I'd asked myself a thousand times. She was right—I didn't have a reason to fight. I could have left. Even if Savannah didn't want to leave, I could have gone. And even if I stayed, I didn't have to go after Jackson. I could have let things play out.

Could have.

I couldn't even explain it to myself.

'I can't leave Bas and Ellery to fight this on their own,' I said lamely. 'It's my town, too.'

'Men with guns can fight battles,' Kayla said. 'You're only going to get stepped on.'

I swallowed. I understood where she was coming from, but the sentiment still hurt.

'I don't want to hide and let other people fight my battles for me.'

'But it's not your battle.' Kayla looked up from her box, her amber-brown eyes intense.

'No…' I struggled for words for a moment. 'It's… it's *our* battle. The entire town's battle. But… most of them can't… or won't fight…' The more I spoke, the more certain I felt. 'I can fight. And I'm willing. So… so I'm going to.'

'Huh.' Kayla stared at me, an odd look creeping over her face.

'What?' I felt self-conscious all of a sudden.

'Just didn't think you had it in you. You've always just… kept your head down.' She smiled, and her entire demeanour changed. She stood up straighter. 'Alright then. Well, as Daddy already said, we'll do what we can to get the army out of town. We're no warriors, but we make our contribution.'

I nodded.

'You should know that people have been sniffing around all over, looking for you.'

'I know,' I said.

'I won't ask what you did to annoy the Iron Fists,' Kayla added, smirking. 'You'd be better off not showing your face in the same place twice though.'

Don't come back, I translated. *Fair enough.* If I kept popping up here,

I'd put Kayla in a whole different kind of danger than just being harassed by the army.

I nodded.

'So if you have any questions, you should ask now.'

That was a valuable offer. I turned some kind of long, slender metal box over in my hands as I considered. I doubted that Kayla knew anything about the movements of the gangs or the mayor—and even if she did have insights into the Aces, she probably wouldn't share or she'd be risking her job. But there was one thing she might know.

'You wouldn't, by any chance, have seen Theo?'

Kayla shot me a sidelong glance. 'I thought you two were tight.'

'We are.' I swallowed against the lump in my throat. 'He… he was meant to meet me, but he vanished. Two months back.'

Her gaze softened. I knew what she was thinking, because I was thinking the same thing.

Two months is a long time in our world.

But I'd waited longer than that for Theo before. Maybe with anyone else, it would be a sure sign they were dead, but not Theo.

Not Theo.

I refused to give up hope.

'I haven't seen him,' she said finally. 'But I'll keep an ear to the ground for you. There is something that you might be interested in, though.'

She shot a furtive glance at the men before ushering me a bit further away.

'I don't usually gossip about Daddy's customers.' Her voice was low, barely a whisper. 'But there's been some rich, rich boys around town recently. Not the sort we usually see—you know, they can afford the working stuff. They don't need salvaged goods.'

I nodded, turning over a piece of metal in my fingers. It looked like a small fan, set in a case of some sort. 'Anyone I would know?'

'Diego Bartholomew.'

I glanced sideways, catching Kayla's eye. 'That's interesting.'

Diego Bartholomew had been at school with me. He was rich, aloof, and well-cushioned from the goings-on in town. There was no reason for him to get his hands dirty.

'We didn't sell him anything.' Kayla righted a few objects that I couldn't identify. 'We didn't have what he was looking for.'

'What was he looking for?'

'Medical tech.'

'Medical tech?' I echoed. I had no idea what sort of things that might include—my only experience with medicine was Savannah's work at the clinic.

She shrugged. 'Do with it what you will.' She took the fan from me, setting it back in its box. 'Like I said, Daddy and I don't want any trouble. But we won't cry if you get the army out of town, either.'

I nodded.

'I understand.'

Kayla smiled. 'Well then.' She straightened up. 'You should come by Krani's sometime. We miss you.'

'I miss you all too.' I followed her back over to the guys.

'If you come on my shift, I'll buy you a drink,' Kayla said.

Ellery turned my way.

'Get it working?' I asked.

'Looks like it. We're a go.'

'Great.' I tucked my fingers through my belt loops. 'One obstacle down.'

Just a million more to go.

I stared in the mirror, taking in my own features. Winter-pale skin, mud-coloured eyes, long brown hair.

Hair that I was about to chop short.

My stomach twisted itself into yet another knot.

I had always had long hair—it was part of my identity. Long hair was just practical as a dancer. It could be tied in a bun. It could be styled. It could drape seductively over your shoulders, giving indecent peeks at your breasts whilst you strutted your stuff on stage.

I'd never, ever considered cutting it.

Tears stung my eyes.

It wasn't just hair. It was a piece of me. And now, I had to give it up.

But then, it is just hair. Compared to saving people, what's a bit of hair? It will grow back.

I took a deep breath, blinked back the tears, and made the first snip. A lock of wavy brown hair fluttered to the ground. My chest ached.

I couldn't do it.

The next snip was worse. Each cut was slicing away a bit of my soul. I made a third, then stopped, tears trickling down my face.

God, I was weak. No wonder Bas barely wanted to look at me these days.

'Harley?'

I swallowed. *Speak of the devil.*

'G-go away,' I choked.

'I'm coming in.'

Fuck.

I dropped the scissors and scrubbed at my eyes with my sleeve. My nose was running, and I couldn't seem to stop crying. Bas swung the door open and stepped in, his boots loud on the tiled floor.

'Harley?'

He stopped, staring at me. I could feel his gaze like a physical weight on my shoulders.

'I s-aid go away,' I whispered, my words breaking on a hiccough.

'You're crying.'

Thank you, Captain Obvious.

I wiped my eyes again, gesturing to the sink. 'I'm cutting my hair. Isn't that what you wanted?'

'Damnit.' Bas strode over and grabbed my hand, tugging it away from my face. He pulled me against his chest. I resisted half-heartedly—in his arms, I'd find comfort. But right now, I didn't want it.

'Come on,' Bas said. He wrapped his arms around my shoulders. 'If you don't want to cut your hair, you don't have to.'

'I've already started,' I sniffed. My head fell against his chest. It felt fucking nice. He hadn't hugged me in ages. 'Besides, you're right. They might recognise me.'

'If they do, we'll deal with it.'

Who was this nice version of Bas, and where had he been a few days ago? But that was how it went. Sometimes we were in perfect harmony. Other days, we were at each other's throats. There was no rhyme or reason to it.

I wrapped my arms around his torso, squeezing tight. 'I hate arguing with you.'

'I know. I'm sorry.' Bas stroked my back. 'I'm just worried. It's no excuse.'

It was a terrible excuse, but I couldn't fault him for it. I was worried too. I wanted to lash out too.

I sighed.

'We're such idiots.'

'Mmm.' He ran his fingers up and down my back, a gentle touch that sent shivers through me. I looked up; Bas's expression had become focused in a way that made heat pool in my belly.

It had been two months, but we'd barely even kissed during that time. With so many people in the house, we barely had any time alone. And when we were alone, there were more important things to do, like training.

There were more important things to do now. Like cutting my hair.

I pulled away and picked up the scissors. 'Will you help me?'

'Are you sure?' Bas asked, meeting my gaze in the mirror.

No.

'Yes. You're right. It will be safer if I do.'

'Alright.'

He took the scissors, smoothed out my ponytail, and started to carefully cut beneath the hair tie.

'I'm going to look strange,' I said.

'You'll look just as beautiful as you always do.' Bas smoothed my hair down again.

'No. I've never had short hair. What if it looks awful?' Worry swelled in my chest. 'What if you don't like it?'

'I don't care about your hair, Harley.'

'It's part of me!' Tears welled in my eyes again. How could he not care?

'It's not an important part of you. Having short hair doesn't change who you are.' Bas set the scissors aside and turned me around. 'I like you because you're strong and resilient. You're a fighter. You never give up. None of that is going to change.'

'It might,' I said in a small voice.

'No.' Bas rolled his eyes. 'Come here.'

He took my chin between his fingers, nudging my head up. I met his gaze—such bright green eyes, so filled with certainty—then he closed the gap between us and kissed me.

Electricity jolted down my spine. Kissing Bas was like touching a live wire. My entire body came alive. I pressed into him, winding my arms around his neck. He ran a hand down my back, his other still cupping my chin. His mouth opened, and I tangled my tongue with his, tasting his toothpaste.

Breathing in the smell of his soap.

Fuck, it's been so long.

I broke the kiss, breathing hard. 'Anyone… anyone could come in.'

'I don't care.'

'But—'

Bas backed me up against the sink. I gasped as the cold porcelain hit my back. He'd hitched my shirt up without me noticing.

'Bas…' I gripped his shoulders. 'I thought you didn't want to… do stuff in public.'

He stared at my lips. 'I don't care about your hair. I don't care what you wear.'

'That… that's good to know.' I felt like I was fighting a losing battle against myself. We ought to stop this, but I wanted him to kiss me much more than I cared about getting caught. And Bas so rarely kissed me.

'Would you care if I changed my appearance?'

'No, of course not!'

'Good.' He brushed his lips against mine. 'I'm going to get a new tattoo.'

'What?' And why the fuck were we talking about this right now?

'Over my gang tattoo.'

'Oh. Okay then.'

'You don't mind?'

'No.' I was getting more and more confused by the second. 'Why would I?'

'Good.' Bas kissed me again—and this time was… *different.* He pressed into me like he was trying to weld us together. His lips covered mine. His tongue ravished my mouth. I could barely keep up. I clung to his shoulders as waves of *him* buffeted against my shores.

I felt warm all over. His erection dug into my stomach.

He dropped his hands to my top, fiddling with the buttons. 'I want to see you.'

'Pretty sure you've seen me without a top on before,' I mumbled. 'Pretty sure everyone has.'

'From now on, only me.'

'Yeah.' I'd have agreed to anything right then. 'Yeah, of course.'

I dug my fingers into the nape of his neck, his soft hair feathering over my skin. Lowering my other hand, I traced a line over his skin, just above the waistband of his trousers.

Tell me I can go further. Give me a sign.

I wanted Bas so badly, the desire felt like flames licking over my skin. I was hot all over. I couldn't breathe, couldn't think.

There was only him.

Bas pushed my shirt open and broke our kiss. He studied me for a moment, a serious, intent look on his face. Then he bent down, his breath brushing over my collarbone and electrifying my skin.

The door swung open. Bas sprang back, releasing me so suddenly that I stumbled and clocked my hip against the ceramic sink.

'Ouch!' I hissed.

'Oi, there you two are.' Ellery was smirking like the cat that caught the canary. 'What are you doing?'

'Nothing,' I snapped.

'Uh-huh.' His gaze drifted over us. Bas's hair was a mess, his shirt untucked. He also had a noticeable bulge in his trousers. I felt my cheeks heating up. I had to look just as bad.

'Right.' Ellery rolled his eyes. 'Please don't have sex in the showers. We all use this room.'

'We weren't—'

'Your top's open. I can see your bra.'

I buried my face in my hands.

'Would you prefer we use your bedroom?' Bas asked.

'Fuck off, man.' Ellery stomped past us. 'I'm taking a shower. I better not hear anything weird, capeesh?'

He shut the stall behind him. I groaned into my hands.

'Oh my God, let me die now.'

'I've caught him doing worse,' Bas said.

'That doesn't help,' I whined.

Bas just laughed.

FOUR

EVERY STEP FELT LIKE IT brought me closer to my doom. Step, step, step. I descended the stairs—Laura and Kade were chatting by the front door, waiting for me, and as one they turned.

'Harley, your hair!'

My stomach sank down to my toes. Those were exactly the words I'd been dreading.

Pasting a smile on my face, I turned to Laura. 'You like? I thought it would be more practical now that I'm fighting.'

'It's amazing! I never imagined you with short hair.'

Amazing. The compliment felt like a knife in my chest.

'Thanks,' I said weakly.

I hated it. My head was missing a weight I hadn't realised I was carrying around. The feathery ends of my hair kept tickling my neck and face. I'd plaited it tight to my scalp, partly because that would keep it out of the way in the fights, but mostly because I couldn't bear the constant reminder of how short it was.

'Are you ready?' Kade asked.

'Are you nervous?' Laura cut in before I could reply. 'I'd be terrified. I'm nervous for you.'

'I'll be okay,' I said, trying to ignore the nerves writhing like snakes in my belly. I had trained hard. I was as well-rested as I could get. I had the earpiece Kayla had given us, and I could call for help if the worst came to the worst. Whoever drove me there would be armed—we weren't going into town, so we didn't have to worry about getting it through the checkpoint.

I would be okay.

'You're made of much sterner stuff than I am.' Laura bit her lip and turned away.

I doubted it. I just had a much greater motivation to fix things. Bale Rocks was my home, and no one else was helping, so I had to.

I'd do the right thing for my home. Whatever that turned out to be.

'Is Kade taking her, then?' Ellery strode into the entrance hall, his heavy boots slapping the floor loudly.

'No,' Bas said, hot on his heels.

'I thought we agreed—' I started.

'It would be safer,' Ellery said. Kade was looking between all of us with an expression of unadulterated amusement.

'I don't care,' Bas said.

'Right, so if you two get caught, then we lose both of you. Is that how it is?' Even Ellery was smirking now. I had a sudden urge to bury my face in my hands… or maybe find a rock to hide under. *God.* Who knew relationships could be such a source of embarrassment?

'That's *exactly* how it is,' Bas replied.

'Right. So glad we cleared that up.' Ellery stretched and glanced at Kade. 'Guess you're taking the night off, then.'

'Is that wise?' Kade asked. 'I'm the only one of us who doesn't have a kill-on-sight order out.'

Ellery shrugged. 'The lovebirds have spoken. Who am I to argue?'

'Lovebirds?' I spluttered.

'No one,' Bas said. 'Let's go, Harley.'

Right. Clearly that was what we were doing. But then again, I didn't really mind. Bas's steady confidence in all things helped—except when it hindered, which wouldn't be tonight. Definitely not. We couldn't afford to argue tonight.

I cleared my throat. 'Alright.'

'Guess this is it then.' Ellery's smile melted off his face, replaced by a serious expression which sat oddly. 'Give them hell, Harley.'

'I will.'

'Remember, you don't need to win. You just need to show them you're worth taking a risk on.'

'I will.'

'Try to avoid anything that will cause a serious injury. Make sure you watch your surroundings—the bottling plant has all sorts of rubbish lying around. Don't trip.'

'I won't.'

The snakes in my stomach were twisting themselves into knots.

'We can't afford to be late,' Bas said.

Ellery nodded. 'Break a leg,' he said.

'Thanks.'

I headed for the door. Somewhere along the line, we'd stopped saying goodbye, and it really bothered me. I hated walking out the door and feeling like I'd never see them again, never speak to them again.

But that was the world we lived in.

Tonight, I couldn't do it. I spun around and hugged Laura—the closest to the door. She squeezed my shoulders. 'You'll be awesome,' she said. 'They're going to regret the day they crossed Harley Benoit.'

I laughed shrilly. 'I hope so.'

Then I hurried out the door before I said anything really soppy.

Bas jumped up into the driver's seat, and I pulled myself up next to him. We started driving into the darkness.

My ribcage felt like a vice around my lungs. I couldn't seem to catch my breath. I stared at the road ahead, fixedly, trying to control myself.

You're meant to be fighting tonight. You cannot be this keyed up.

Desperate for a distraction, I turned to Bas. 'I thought you didn't want me to fight,' I mumbled.

'I don't,' Bas said, his matter-of-fact tone belying the fact that we'd been arguing about this for weeks now. 'But here we are.'

'Here we are,' I agreed, my stomach twisting itself into another knot.

I knew that was Bas's way of saying he supported me—but it wasn't enough.

'Are you… still angry?' I asked quietly.

Bas sighed.

'No,' he said.

Something in my chest released just a little bit. 'Do you think I can win?'

'Of course.'

'But…' After everything he'd said, all the doubts…

'Harley, we wouldn't be here if I didn't think you could win.'

I glanced at him. Even in the darkness, I could see how his face was set.

'You haven't really shown much belief in me lately.' I couldn't help my tone coming out a bit snippish.

'Of course I believe in you!' Bas said. He sounded almost surprised. I swallowed as a pang of hurt jolted through my chest. After everything he'd said, how could he be surprised? 'It's not a question of belief. I just wanted you to consider every option before we put you in danger.'

'We agreed that this was the best option.'

'The best, yes, but not the only one,' Bas said. 'We could have found another way.'

I swallowed. The familiar irritation was rising in me. 'So you don't think I can do it.'

'I do!' Bas took a deep, loud breath. 'I do. But that doesn't mean I like it. You're going to be in there without any of us to support you—'

'I can take care of myself.' Tears stung my eyes, and I blinked them away furiously. I was meant to be a calm, focused fighter. Not an emotional child. 'I'd have thought I had proven that to you by now!'

'You have.'

'Then why—'

'I'm here, Harley,' Bas said. 'I'm here.' He slowed the car as we reached the gate, rolling the window down to sign to whoever was guarding it. 'I won't pretend to like it, but this is the plan. I'm on board.'

That had to be good enough.

But it didn't feel good enough. Doubt lingered under my skin like an itch I couldn't reach.

We rolled into motion again, passing the gates. Once we were through, I heard the *clank-clank* as they were closed again.

'Sorry,' I muttered.

'For what?' Bas asked.

'I don't know.' I stared into the darkness, my mind filling in the landmarks I knew were there: a burnt-out gas station with its faded blue sign. The stacked rocks and tattered sandbags where someone had built a long-abandoned defensive wall. The scraggly bushes that clustered around odd areas of ground that always seemed to be damp, even though it hardly rained.

'I don't want to argue,' I said finally. 'We always seem to argue.'

Bas dropped his hand to my lap and squeezed my knee. My heart caught in my throat. Bas wasn't too touchy-feely—usually I initiated casual contact.

'You'll be fine,' Bas said, his voice quiet.

I should have known he'd figure out what I was really worrying about. Somehow, Bas always did.

'I've barely been training for two months.' My voice came out as a fearful whisper.

Bas was silent. He navigated us off the farm track and onto a rudimentary road. The asphalt was pockmarked and had even broken away entirely in places, revealing the sand below. Finally, he said, 'When I first joined the Iron Fists, I didn't know how to fight either. Vaughn offered to teach me. He said he knew I'd be good at it, even before I started. Do you know why?'

'Why?' I whispered.

'Because it's in our nature,' Bas said. 'Some people are born fighters. Others are made fighters by life. But people like us have a quality that will set us apart from the others: we never give up.'

I bit my cheek. He was right, I hated giving up. But it wasn't some grand quality that set me apart. Stopping fighting had never been an option, because if I stopped, I'd disappear. Forces greater than me would keep eating away at my small world, until eventually it vanished, and I had nothing left.

'Sometimes I feel like giving up,' I said.

'But you don't.'

I didn't have an answer for that. We continued through the darkness. Bale Rocks was a glow on the horizon. Growing up, it had seemed like the brightest thing around. But now I knew that it was faint compared to Brackfields and Langford. We were barely a speck on the horizon.

We weren't important.

I wasn't important.

'It seems insane,' I said. 'Going up against the Iron Fists and the Black Hands all on our own.'

'That's what you've been doing since the start,' Bas said.

'Not really. I was just fighting for myself.'

'You're still fighting for yourself. Forget everyone else.'

I couldn't though. The stakes were so much higher now.

'What if I can't do it?' I asked.

'You'll find a way,' Bas said. 'It only takes one person to start a fire.'

'We're not starting a fire.'

'Not yet.' He steered around a rock that jutted out of the bumpy road. 'We still have to figure out what to burn.'

The bottling plant was located in an old factory district. Some of them had been defunct since the meteorites hit Earth. Others had worked in the years since then, some even in my lifetime, but most had been abandoned for one reason or another, looted for parts, fallen into disrepair. Because of the risk of Bas being seen, he couldn't stop anywhere near our destination, so instead he chose a spot in the shadow of the junkyard, where old cars got dumped once they were past repair.

'Careful you don't get mistaken for scrap,' I joked half-heartedly once Bas had cut the engine.

He chuckled. 'I'm not sure they'd even want this old beater.'

'You never know.' I reached out, my movements almost invisible in the darkness, and touched his arm. Bas turned and took hold of my wrist, lacing our fingers together. For a moment, neither of us spoke. Emotion whirled around in me, but I couldn't find the right words to express how I was feeling.

'You'll be fine,' Bas said.

'Thanks,' I whispered.

'If you need help, don't hesitate. Don't be a hero. Just call me.'

His gaze was steady. His eyes burned into me.

'I will.'

'Promise me.'

'I promise.'

Bas stared searchingly into my eyes. 'Okay,' he said, though I wasn't quite sure he believed me. We both knew I had a bad tendency to improvise. But I meant it—what I was about to do was bigger than anything I'd ever embarked upon before in my life. Bas was my lifeline. I needed to know he was on the other end of my radio.

'Have you got your earpiece?' he asked.

I touched my left ear. 'Yep.' It still felt weird, but I was getting used to it.

'If you can, take it out before the fight starts.'

I nodded.

'Like Ellery said, watch the ground. Debris at ankle height can—'

'I know,' I cut him off. We'd gone over this about five times yesterday, and Ellery had reiterated it today. 'Watch the ground. Don't trip. Count the people in the room so no one catches me unawares. Don't do anything reckless. I know.'

'Okay,' Bas said.

Silence fell again. We stared at one another.

'I'm going to kiss you,' he said.

'Please,' I muttered.

He cupped the back of my neck and pulled me close. I tilted my head, my nose bumping his cheek. Our lips met, and heat rushed through me. Bas gripped my shoulders, and I grabbed the front of his jacket to ground myself as he threatened to wash me away.

When he pulled back, he was breathing hard.

'Okay, okay,' I said between breaths. 'I have to... I have to go. Or I'm not going to.'

'Yes.' As usual, Bas seemed amused. I was starting to think he liked watching me lose my cool. 'I'll kiss you again when you get back.'

'I'll be gross,' I warned.

'You say that like it's a deterrent.'

My mouth dropped open as heat surged through me again. 'Oh.'

'Go,' Bas said. 'Win this for us.'

Sobriety returned. I took a deep breath and opened the car door. Cool air rushed in, chilling my heated cheeks.

'See you later.'

'Later.' He brushed his fingers against the back of my hand, before pulling away.

After the heat of the car, it felt very cold and lonely outside. I didn't have far to walk, but Bas's headlights quickly receded into the distance. Gravel, broken glass, and all manner of scrap crunched under my boots; I had to keep my torch on the ground to make sure I didn't trip over anything. Finally, the familiar shape of the bottling plant came into view, and my stomach snarled up again.

This was where I had killed Gabriel Tam.

The event that had started me down this path. I'd been trying very hard not to think about it this week, but now I couldn't avoid the memories that rushed in. Sprinting through the building. Fear closing up my throat. Gabriel's footsteps coming ever closer. A cold sweat broke out on my chest.

'Test, test,' a voice murmured in my ear. I almost leapt out of my skin.

'Bas?' I hissed.

'Good, it works.'

'We already knew it worked! We tested it earlier.' I rubbed my chest, breathing hard. Bas chuckled.

'I had to make sure. Break a leg.'

'Thanks.' He went silent. I took a deep breath, shaking off the panic. We'd tested the comms extensively, but it was still nice to know it worked. Declan hadn't had a chance to come out to Freetown yet, so for tonight my earpiece communicated directly with Bas's radio, mounted in the car. No one would hear our conversation except for us.

'I'm almost there.' My voice seemed very small in the darkness.

'Alright. I'll be listening.'

I had reached the fence that surrounded the bottling plant. It was too risky to continue talking to Bas—I'd blow the game before we even started if someone overheard me. With a heavy heart, I trudged around to the front gate and entered the grounds.

A light flicked on, shining directly in my eyes. I squinted, bringing my hands up to block it.

'Halt! Who goes there?'

'H—Sierra,' I said. 'Sierra Davidson.'

The light lowered, and I was able to see again. Wilder stood opposite me, his hand covering the torch.

'Had to make sure,' he grunted. 'Some people try to cheat. Come on.'

He turned and strode towards the open doors of the plant, the gaping maw of a giant beast waiting to consume us. I followed, my heart thudding against my ribcage. This was it.

Count the people.

That wasn't hard. There were three—Wilder, a man I didn't recognise, and a man I did recognise.

Shoulder-length brown hair, a scar cutting through his lips, and narrowed brown eyes. Dean Hannover.

Oh fuck. I had to tell Bas—but with all eyes on me, I couldn't risk using the earpiece. Instead, I schooled my expression to give nothing away. He *couldn't* recognise me.

'So, this is Sierra?' Hannover strode over, his gaze running up and down my body. I suppressed a shudder. I hated the way he looked at me like I was a piece of meat he was considering eating.

No, more like I was a toy, and he was a sadistic child deciding whether to play with me or break me.

'I'm Sierra,' I said.

'She's fought her way up at The Arsonist the last four weeks,' Wilder said.

'Very interesting.' Hannover smiled. I had a sudden, desperate desire to shower to get the feeling of his gaze off me. 'Well, we can't let an opportunity like that pass us by, can we?' His eyes sharpened. 'What do you want, Sierra?'

'Sir?' I asked, although the term of respect burnt my tongue.

'Why are you here? What do you want... from us?' Hannover prowled closer. The bottling plant was huge; he could have stood anywhere. But he chose to stand a scant foot away from me, studying my face. 'You wouldn't be here if you didn't *want* anything.'

Was he on to me? Standing this close, there was no way he wouldn't recognise me. My throat seemed to have closed up.

'I...'

Hannover raised an eyebrow. Mocking me. He was on to me. He was *definitely* on to me.

'We don't have all night, girl.'

No. I wasn't going down without a fight. Even if Hannover scared me silly.

I stiffened my shoulders and lifted my chin. 'I want to prove myself.'

'Prove yourself?' He laughed. 'Do you think this is a game, girl?'

'No.' With every word I spoke, my courage grew. 'I think it's an opportunity. A mutually beneficial one, if you let it be.'

'Mutually beneficial?' Hannover strode away from me, running a finger along a long-defunct conveyor belt. 'And what do you think you can bring us?'

A bullet in the head.

'A woman's touch,' I said.

All three men burst out into chortles. I met their gazes staunchly. 'I've been hearing all sorts of rumours,' I continued. 'Must be bad for business, all this... *negative* publicity.'

'On the contrary, I find a little controversy is excellent for business.'

'Is that why they're saying the cage has lost two of its best fighters?' I demanded.

Hannover stopped beside the stairs, his face in shadow. Tam and I had had our fight right above him—I pushed that thought away.

'Where do you hear that?' he asked.

'Around.'

I knew, of course, because Ellery and Bas were with me. But I'd never reveal that to him.

'Around,' he echoed. 'You're better informed than I imagined.'

'I don't walk into a situation without knowing the lay of the land first,' I said.

'So it is, so it is.' Hannover smiled, his eyes narrowing to slits. 'Very well. I have doubts that a 'woman's touch' will be as useful as you think it is… unless you plan to soothe wounded egos.'

I gritted my teeth.

'I plan on doing the wounding, actually.'

He chuckled. They were laughing at me. I could have spit nails, but getting angry wouldn't rescue this stupid situation. I hadn't realised I was going to have to talk my way in with *Hannover*, of all people.

'Shall we get to the wounding, then?' Hannover sang. 'Seems to be your speciality.'

'About time.'

Wilder snorted into his hand. I shot him a look. *Glad I amuse you.*

Hannover waved the third man forward; he was non-descript, with a shaved head, pale, almost ashy skin, and a compact build. He eyed me as though I was a particularly unpleasant species of rodent.

'You'll be fighting Donley here,' Hannover said.

Donley.

Ellery and Bas had given me a rundown of the main fighters and their styles, but I didn't remember them mentioning a Donley.

Damnit.

I nodded briskly.

'Begin,' Hannover said.

Wait, what?

No preamble, no rules, no marking out the fighting ring? Donley stepped in, and then his fists were flying. I blocked hurriedly, stumbling back. I wasn't ready—I wasn't even warmed up!

A fist hit my cheekbone out of nowhere. I staggered as pain jolted through me. *Shit.* I had to do something. I blocked the next blow and threw myself forwards, jamming my boot into his knee. Donley staggered. *Gotcha.* My elbow met his ear, and I pressed forwards, going for his solar plexus—

Donley grabbed my arm, grunting as he twisted. He swept my legs out from under me, and I stumbled. My shoulder wrenched as I fell, and I cried out in pain.

Fuck!

I rolled away, gravel digging into my ribcage, and scrambled up, rolling my shoulder. It throbbed in protest.

I'd never caught a serious injury in a fight before. I realised suddenly that I had been coasting until now. This fight was nothing like the ones I'd faced at The Arsonist.

Focus.

Donley and I circled one another like wild animals. I'd landed the first blow, but he'd drawn first blood—metaphorically speaking. I needed an opening, but there were none.

So I'd have to create one.

Quick as a flash, I darted in and threw a jab at his stomach. He dropped his hands to block, and I brought my other—injured—arm in to punch him in the face.

I connected, *hard.*

His teeth grazed my knuckles. His head flew back. I went in for my next strike, a sloppy jab to the abdomen again, which he parried, as I dropped to one knee and grabbed his legs, throwing my head into his stomach and knocking him backwards.

He sprawled with a grunt, but his hand gripped the back of my shirt and brought me with him. I landed awkwardly, half on, half off him. His hands went to my shoulders to shove me backwards. I jabbed in between his arms, striking his chest, then his chin. His head snapped against the concrete.

'Enough.'

Donley and I both froze. Glass crunched as Hannover strode over to us. I scrambled up and took a step back—into the shadows. My limbs shook from adrenaline.

'I've seen all I need to.' Hannover's gaze grazed over me. I suppressed a shiver and stood up straighter. 'I think you'll fit in very nicely.' A dangerous smile split his face. 'Very nicely indeed.'

'Thank you,' I said breathily.

'We'll do a trial run next week. Where do you want to be collected from?'

'C-collected?' I echoed.

'You won't be able to walk into the bunker, girl. Someone will have to show you the way.'

Oh. Yeah, that made sense. I calculated quickly. Whoever dropped me would want to be near an access point, in case they had to get into the bunker on short notice. But it also had to be discreet.

The station.

But I couldn't tell them that—it would look suspicious.

'Would here work?' I asked.

Hannover nodded. 'Very well. Come here at ten PM next Saturday. We'll send someone to meet you.'

FIVE

THE BRUISES LOOKED FRIGHTFUL in the light of day.

Donley had caught me in all sorts of places with his snappy punches and sharp elbows. I was black and blue across my ribcage, my forearms, my face. Worse, my muscles ached, and the shoulder he'd wrenched throbbed in time with my heartbeat.

'Could be worse,' Ellery assessed after examining my shoulder. 'It's not dislocated. Setting a dislocated shoulder hurts like a bitch.'

'Woohoo,' I muttered.

'There's not much we can do for you except give you ice for the bruises. But if you're badly in pain, you could speak to Reynolds when you meet Declan to look over the transmission station. He has medical training.'

'I'm meeting Declan?' I lowered the towel full of ice I had pressed to my face. 'How come?'

'Bas has arranged a meeting with Turner, so we have to drive into town,' Ellery said.

'Turner?' My heart quickened. Turner was their contact who was helping stop the slavers. 'I want to come.'

'You can't,' Bas said. I turned to look at him. Predictably, he was scowling. He'd looked furious since he'd seen my bruises this morning.

'Why not?'

'Because we're meeting at the Hawke and Tern. You said yourself that Hardwick likes to lurk there. If he sees you like this'—Bas jerked his chin at my face—'our whole plan will be blown apart.'

Damnit, he was right.

Hardwick was another loose end I'd left lying around, waiting to trip me. I could have cursed myself for how careless I'd been—between Hannover, Hardwick, Maddock, Briggs, and Tam, it was a wonder I'd survived this long. Sitting with Ellery and Bas and actually making a plan had taught me very quickly that there was no room for carelessness when you were fighting for your survival.

'Ugh.' I put the towel back against my cheek. 'Will you at least try and look in on Savannah whilst you're there?'

I hadn't laid eyes on my sister in two months, though not for lack of trying. Unbeknownst to me, when Bas and I had been arrested by the Iron Fists in a blaze of glory, Savannah had been standing just down the street. She had watched me be arrested. And now she was furious. I'd risked going to the clinic once and our flat twice, but all I'd got for my trouble was her staunch refusal to speak to me.

'You handle your life, I'll handle mine,' she'd said.

What *handling* she was doing, I hadn't managed to find out.

'We'll try,' Ellery said. He glanced at Bas. 'We should probably get going.'

Bas nodded. I bit down on a scowl. He'd hardly said a word this morning, and I had a feeling that he was angry at me again.

Even though I'd done what we'd planned.

Even though I had won the fight.

I pushed myself up out of my seat. 'I'm going to take a shower,' I said. 'I probably shouldn't meet Declan looking like someone put me through a meat grinder last night.'

Ellery grinned. I headed out, fetched my things from the room I shared with Laura, and then made my way out into the backyard. The sky was the colour of flint, an ominous purple-grey that said it was probably going to rain soon. Ms Ellery would be pleased.

'Harley.'

I turned. Bas was climbing down from the back porch, doing up his jacket as he went. I crossed my arms, but stayed where I was, waiting for him to reach me. He swooped in and kissed me—all teeth, tongue, and an odd, bristling tension that I could feel in his shoulders when I grabbed them.

'What was that?' I asked when he pulled back.

'Are you alright?'

'Of course. You asked me that earlier.'

'Not when no one else was around,' he said.

'What, you think I lied to Ellery?' I dropped my hands off his shoulders, annoyance brewing in my gut. 'Why would I do that?'

'No. I thought…' He trailed off, frowning. 'I was just worried. I didn't realise you'd see Hannover last night.'

'None of us realised that,' I said. 'But it's fine, right? It doesn't seem like he recognised me, and I got what we wanted. I'm in.'

'With the backing of the Black Hands.' Bas shuffled his weight from foot to foot, closing and opening his fists. He looked like a guilty child. I grabbed his hands to keep them still.

'I'm not going to become an evil slave-taking murderer just because I have the temporary backing of the Black Hands,' I said.

'I know.' Still holding my hands, Bas leant in and kissed me again. This time was softer, more tender. When he pulled back, he stared at me.

'What's going on?' I asked. 'You're acting weird.'

'I don't like seeing you with bruises,' Bas said.

'Kind of an occupational hazard.'

'I know.' His eyes darted back and forth, as though he was trying to memorise my face. 'I never told you last night… Well done.'

'Oh.' Surprise flooded me, displacing the confusion and negativity. He hadn't said; he'd been pleased, for sure. He'd been worried. We'd analysed Hannover's behaviour, for the most part. But he'd never said well done.

'Thank you.'

'You're welcome.' Bas wormed his hands out of mine. 'I have to go. Ellery's waiting.'

I nodded. Bas turned and loped off towards the house, leaving me staring after him. Suddenly, everything seemed brighter. The sky was less ominous, the trees were less brown. Even the prospect of having to navigate the freezing cold bathroom didn't bother me as much.

Bas was proud.

I continued to the showers with a bounce in my step.

The week flew by without me even noticing. There was always something to do on the farm, and with Bas and Ellery in and out monitoring the clinic for Turner, that something usually fell to either Laura, Claire, or me to do. At least the busy work kept me from worrying about how much time Bas was spending in Bale Rocks— flirting with the constant danger of the Iron Fists noticing him. It also kept me from worrying too much about my upcoming ordeal.

Fooling Hannover in the darkness of the bottling plant was one thing; surviving the bunker would be quite another.

But inexorably, between training, tending animals, and making deliveries into the centre of Freetown, the week did pass. My bruises faded, and the swelling in my shoulder went down. Declan and Kayla managed to fire up the transmitter station and connect our radios. On Saturday, I plaited my hair tightly and put on the clothes Ellery had scrounged up for me.

'I look like I'm joining the army,' I complained as I came down the stairs.

Kade grinned and saluted me.

With Ellery on comms, that left Bas and Kade. They'd both be coming with me tonight, ready to extract me if anything went wrong. Although the plan was for nothing to go wrong because we had no idea if they'd be able to pull me out safely. It depended. Everything depended.

Our plan was insane.

'Ready?' Bas asked.

I took a deep breath. 'Yes. Let's go.'

Because we weren't entering the checkpoint, we'd risked taking Bas's car. There was a chance that it would be recognised, but that was balanced out by the fact that it was much faster than the Ellerys' truck—which would be useful if we had to leave in a hurry. Bas's car was also much better at off-roading.

I flicked the radio on as we left Freetown, and the comforting, husky voice of the DJ filled the car.

'This is Crater FM radio, and I'm Barty, wishing you all the best for your travels tonight.'

A slow Pre-Crash rock song came on. My throat and chest felt like they'd seized up, like a snake had bitten me and the venom was slowly paralysing me.

'I won't have to fight tonight, right?' I asked. I knew the answer, but I needed the reassurance.

'No,' Bas said. 'They won't risk it. You could still be injured from last week, and they'll want you to be fresh and on form.'

'First fight is the most important,' Kade agreed. 'It'll decide where you fall in the rankings.'

'And how much people are willing to bet on you,' Bas added.

The thought of people betting on me was beyond weird. But then, in some ways, it was no different to men shoving money into my top when I danced. They were paying for a false luxury—the idea that they might have some temporary ownership of my body.

No, no different at all.

I smoothed my hands over the baggy cargo pants I was wearing. We were nearing the old industrial sector, and with it, my drop-off point.

'Remember,' Bas said as we approached the junkyard, 'you need to orient us underground. The station is east. The compound is west. The bottling plant is due southwest.'

'I won't forget,' I said nervously.

'And don't contact us unless the benefit outweighs the risk. Try and take note of who's there—either names or descriptions. Who's talking to whom, and who might be a potential in for us. Not just as an ally— blackmail is also an option.'

'I know,' I said. We'd gone over all of this earlier today.

'Watch out for Hannover and Jackson. Don't let them see you from close.'

'I know,' I repeated.

'Bas,' Kade cut in. 'She hasn't forgotten.'

Bas stopped the car and cut the lights, plunging us into darkness.

'Of course not,' he said. In the darkness, his voice was grim. I realised suddenly that the reminder was as much for his benefit as for mine.

'I'll be fine.' I leant over and pressed a kiss to his lips. He stroked my cheeks and hair, before cupping my face.

'Don't take any risks,' he said. 'Promise me.'

'I promise.'

'I mean it. I know you can handle yourself. But we need to be cautious. This is much more dangerous than entering The Arsonist.'

'I know.' I tried to make my tone serious, not irreverent, but it was hard when he was telling me things I already knew.

'And Bas has a much broader definition of 'risk' than the rest of us,' Kade quipped.

Bas turned to glare into the back of the car.

'If you can't handle it blindfolded with your hands tied behind your back, don't do it,' he said. His voice softened. 'I… I can't lose you.'

My breath caught in my throat. What the hell could I say to that?

'You won't have to,' I croaked.

'I know.' Bas kissed me once more, then reached past me to open my door. 'Go. You can't be late on your first night.'

'Alright.' I slid out of the car. 'See you later.'

And so it began. I strode off towards the bottling plant. *Southwest entrance. Due southwest. Same direction as the town.*

That the tunnels were identified by compass directions was just one of the facts Bas had taught me about the bunker which I would be expected to remember. And my brain already felt stuffed full of fear and anticipation—how much more could it hold?

A few minutes later, I reached my destination. The bottling plant remained unchanged from the previous weekend. My footsteps crunched over the rubble as I approached the door. Where was my escort?

Ca-clank!

I jumped and whipped around. A man was standing in the shadows. He snorted.

'So, you're our new recruit?' He pushed off the wall and sauntered towards me, flicking a torch on as he approached. 'Bit jumpy, aren't ya?'

I ground my teeth together. He'd scared me deliberately. I lifted my chin and flicked a dismissive gaze over him. He was younger than me—probably around twenty. Scraggly hairs adorned his chin, his blond hair was combed to the side, and his clothes fit poorly.

'You have soot on your jacket,' I said.

'What? Where?' He twisted around to look at his back, before realising that I couldn't possibly have seen it. Straightening up, he shot me a glare.

'You think you're funny?' he snapped.

'I'm hilarious,' I said.

'Whatever.' He stalked towards the factory entrance. 'I'm Tyler. They asked me to show you the way in.'

'Sierra.' I followed him, my curiosity rising rapidly. I'd expected to be driven to the station, but we were walking inside. There was no way he'd parked in the building.

There was an entrance to the tunnels in here—I'd even used it before, back when I'd first danced in the bunker as a teenager—but it had been sealed off for years.

But why else would we be heading inside?

I got my answer a moment later. In the second large chamber in the bottling plant, Tyler approached a large grate in the corner, which seemed to cover some type of service hatch. The manhole cover which had once concealed the hatch had been removed. Tyler heaved the grating up and gestured down a steep flight of metal stairs, into the dimly lit tunnel below.

'Ladies first,' he said in a mocking tone.

I rolled my eyes. Haha, kids these days were *hilarious*.

It was strange walking down the narrow tunnel from the bottling plant. I hadn't been here in years, and it felt at once familiar and foreign. The floor was scuffed, and a number of the lights had stopped working. On the walls, the many people who had walked this passage—Iron Fists members and fighters for the most part—had painted their names. *Jasper was here. Kaleb v Will Ma 19/03.*

I found my name with Posy's.

Harley B <3

Posy best dancer 4ever

She'd made me write it. I hid a smile as Tyler and I strode down the passageway, our footsteps echoing. It was a long walk—in my memory, it had seemed shorter.

'Not many girls fight in the cage,' Tyler said.

'Can't think why,' I muttered.

'Why do you wanna, then?' he asked.

My boots thumped against the floor. 'To prove I can.'

'You're going to have to fight really well. No one will go easy on you.'

'I wouldn't prove much if they did.'

My answers were unnerving him. His eyes danced around the hallway, looking anywhere but me.

'Aren't you worried?' he asked eventually.

'I wouldn't be here if I was.'

We lapsed into silence, accompanied only by the thump of our boots and the hum of machinery in the walls. And, at least in my case, my swirling thoughts. I wouldn't have to fight tonight. Bas, Ellery, and Kade had all agreed: no one ever fought on the first night.

But this was the ultimate test. There would be people there who knew me—plenty of them. Any one of them could recognise me.

Stick to the plan, I reminded myself. *Just stick to the fucking plan.*

By now, Bas would have looped around to the station, and he and Kade would be taking up their position by the secret entrance that we'd used to leave after Maddock had killed Sayle. Assuming everything had gone smoothly on their end—which I had to trust, just like they had to trust that I could fulfil my role.

Sure enough, not twenty yards later, my earpiece buzzed.

'In position,' Bas said tersely.

'Copy that,' Ellery replied.

My tongue burnt with the need to answer, but I refrained. I couldn't risk it with Tyler right beside me.

The tunnel brought us into a large chamber with a reinforced steel door. I had never seen that door shut since I'd been going to the bunker—unlike the other doors, this one sealed with a wheel that locked and unlocked it.

And it only closed from the outside.

Just like in the olden days, I felt a strange chill on the back of my neck as I passed through it. What had the Pre-Crash civilisation feared so badly that they'd thought they'd need to seal themselves into the bunker?

I didn't really want to know.

Inside, Tyler led me through the familiar maze of passageways until we reached the office. Carlos awaited us inside.

My first test.

I smoothed my trousers down. I looked as unlike myself as I possibly could: short hair, loose-fitted clothes. A far cry from my slinky dance outfits.

'This is Sierra,' Tyler introduced.

'Oh, right. The new kid.' He frowned at me. 'You want to fight? You know people break bones in that cage, right?'

I fought the urge to roll my eyes.

'Maybe I'll break a few bones.'

Carlos scoffed.

'Yeah, your own.' He shook his head and offered me another look, this one much more considering. 'Where'd you learn to fight?'

'A friend taught me.'

'Must be some friend.' He squinted at me again. I held my breath. Finally, Carlos jerked his head. 'You'll be in the circle. Tyler will sort you out. Try not to distract any of the fighters, yeah?'

Prick.

But I was no longer a dancer who had to kowtow to Carlos's moods. I could talk back now.

'If they get distracted, it'll be their fault,' I replied. I tossed my head, but with my short hair plaited to my scalp, there was no hair to toss. My stomach seemed to curl in on itself, but I kept my smile in place as I walked away.

I wasn't going to show any weakness, especially not in front of Carlos.

The circle felt totally different now that I was there as a fighter. Before, I'd always been on the outside looking in—even when I'd been able to enter the circle, I had been an outsider.

Now, I was one of the fighters. I sat with Tyler and his friends, drinking and enjoying the camaraderie. I didn't have to deal with gropey guests, or dodge Carlos's glares when I tried to watch the fights. The biggest danger was Hannover, who lurked like a wicked shadow on the far side of the circle, near where Jackson was sitting in the VIP area. It almost seemed like he was playing bodyguard to Jackson.

More like ensuring he gets a return on his investment.

Whatever Hannover was doing collaborating with Jackson, it was entirely self-motivated. Of that much, I was sure.

To my surprise, the fights quickly began to drag. When I wasn't emotionally invested, I didn't really care to watch them that much, and I found myself fidgeting and observing the room instead. Jackson lounged on his sofa like a throne. A steady stream of Iron Fists came to speak to him, each one stopping in the VIP area briefly to deliver their message before moving on. There were a fair few people I didn't recognise, but Bas and Ellery had predicted that: Jackson would have promoted his friends through the ranks and weeded out those who— like Bas—were solely loyal to Sayle, rather than to the Iron Fists.

There were also quite a lot of new faces amongst the fighters, including the group I was sitting with. That didn't surprise me either; with the upheaval going on in town, there were probably a fair few people who appreciated the security the gangs provided.

My gaze slid back to the VIP area as a tall, red-faced man entered. He murmured something to Hannover, whose face twisted in a sneer. Jackson, on the other hand, stood, a delighted look on his face. Something was happening. I squinted at the man, trying to memorise his features. Hopefully, Bas would know him.

The red-faced man left, and Jackson waved Hannover into the VIP area. Jackson seemed… excited, I decided. He gesticulated, and his face was crinkled in a smile. Hannover, meanwhile, was harder to read. Could I get closer?

Around us, cheers erupted. I flicked a glance to the cage in the middle. One of the men had the other in a rear choke. But even as I watched, the man on his knees managed to break the hold. The fights were picking up.

A good moment to slip away.

'Washroom,' I murmured to Tyler, standing up.

'You need me to show you where it is?' Tyler asked.

'No, I remember.' He'd shown me the changing rooms on the way in.

I edged away, making for the back hallway but keeping an eye on Hannover. He was still talking to Jackson, his gaze sweeping the room periodically. Suddenly, the whole room exploded into cheers. The fighters milling in the circle all lurched to their feet, and I lost sight of Hannover.

I turned to the cage—both of the fighters seemed to be on the ground, but I couldn't tell what was going on. I had to make a choice: try to spy on Hannover, or use this moment to slip away into the back and have a nose around. Both risky. Both with a potential reward.

Which to choose?

'Out of the way!' Someone shouldered past me. I stumbled and whipped around, ready to deploy a few choice caustic words—but they died on my tongue. It was the medics, heading to the cage, but I only had eyes for one of them. I barely caught a glimpse of her, but I'd recognise her anywhere: brown hair in a tight ponytail, an expression of grim determination on her face, and a shapeless white coat.

It was Savannah.

SIX

OH FUCK, OH FUCK.

I darted into the back rooms and let myself into the first unlocked room I found—a janitor's closet. As soon as the door was shut, I pressed the button on my earpiece.

'Savannah's here.'

'What?' Ellery demanded.

'Savannah's here! My sister! She's here!'

An odd silence ensued. 'Savannah is there,' Ellery repeated.

'That's what I said!'

Every time I spoke to him, our risk of discovery increased. He needed to get it, and he needed to get it *fast*.

'Shit,' Ellery said. 'What's she doing there?'

'I don't know, but… I—I have to speak to her!'

'Woah, no wait. Are you sure it was her?'

For fuck's sake, what wasn't he getting? 'Yes, I'm sure. She was with the other medics.'

'You're sure you didn't misrecognise her?'

'Ellery, she *looks the same as me*,' I snarled. 'Would you misrecognise yourself?'

'Alright,' Ellery said. 'But there's nothing we can do.'

'Damnit—'

'Harley, focus.' Bas's voice cut across our conversation, calm and steady. 'Savannah can take care of herself, remember? *Don't blow your cover.*'

'I can't—' I gasped.

'We can go and find her tomorrow if you want. But you *cannot* speak to her today. No matter how much you want to. Do you understand?'

He was right. It hurt like knives stabbing my chest, but he was right.

'I understand.'

'Good. Tell me what you see.'

'I'm in a broom closet,' I muttered.

A quiet snort came over the channel; I realised it must have been Kade.

'Can you talk?' Ellery asked. 'Will you be missed?'

'I told them I was going to the washroom.' I gave them a brief rundown of what I'd seen so far—the fights, Hannover and Jackson, the red-faced man, Savannah.

'So it's business as usual,' Ellery surmised.

'I don't like how close Hannover is to Jackson,' Bas said.

'No, that collaboration can't mean anything good,' Ellery agreed.

'It's more than that.' Bas's voice was quiet. 'It seems like Hannover is expecting something to happen.'

'Expecting us?' I asked, alarm creeping into my voice. 'I really don't think he recognised me.'

'Maybe,' Bas said. 'But he could be expecting Jackson to double-cross him as well. Hannover is notoriously paranoid.'

'If Jackson double-crosses Hannover, that will be good for us,' Ellery said. 'Best case, it takes one of them out—'

'—and the other consolidates their power,' Kade put in.

'Even so, keeping one enemy where we can see them is easier than two,' Ellery said.

'Worst case scenario, it leads to a war,' Bas said. 'Or Hannover getting his hands on even more power. Getting control over the army.'

Silence ensued. I hadn't even thought of that possibility, and it wasn't pleasant to imagine at all. Hannover was bad enough with only the Black Hands at his disposal.

'We stay the course,' Ellery said abruptly. 'We can't plan for every contingency. Harley, continue keeping an eye on Hannover and Jackson, and report their moves back to us. If anything comes up, we can adjust.'

'Got it,' I said.

'And forget about Savannah for tonight. If she got into the bunker, someone has to be helping her. They'll help her get out again.'

'Yeah, but who?' I asked.

'We'll worry about that later.'

I felt as though I'd swallowed rocks. Leave Savannah to the tender mercies of the men who frequented the bunker? I couldn't do it. Never.

But I had to.

I forced a deep breath into my aching lungs. 'Alright,' I said. 'I'm going back out again.'

'Break a leg,' Ellery said.

They went silent. I switched off my microphone and stepped out into the hall.

'Harley!'

I jerked my head in the direction of the fierce whisper. Someone took two strides towards me and shoved me back into the cupboard.

'It is you! I thought—Oh my God, are you crazy?'

'Posy?' I said, recognising my assailant. Short black hair, a shapely face, and dancewear. My best friend from back when I'd worked in the bunker. I stepped back, a metal shelf digging into my shoulder. 'What are you doing?'

'What are *you* doing?' Posy banged the door shut. 'Have you gone insane? Harley! They're out to kill you!'

She threw her arms around me and squeezed me tight. I cringed as the shelf stabbed into my back. Finally, Posy pulled away, staring at me. 'What the hell is going on?'

'How did you know it was me?' I pushed off the shelf and rubbed my shoulder.

'Of course it's you. What, you think because you changed your hair I wouldn't recognise you?' Posy rolled her dark eyes. 'I've seen you naked, darling.'

A shrill laugh burst out of my chest. *Shit. Shit!* Bas was going to kill me.

'What the fuck are you doing?' Posy repeated. 'No, wait.'

She opened the door and stuck her head out for several seconds, before pulling it back in. 'No one in sight. Okay, tell me.'

'I can't.'

Posy rolled her eyes. 'Let me guess, you're spying on Jackson? I know you're the reason why Ellery and Bas bailed. Gianna told me.'

Gianna—I'd forgotten Gianna. Posy's girlfriend, who was a member of the Iron Fists. Had she been there the day we'd escaped their compound? What else did Posy know?

I scrubbed my hands over my face. 'Look, I'd love to tell you everything, but—'

'Who do you think I'm going to tell? I'm just a dancer.'

'I can't put the others in danger like that.'

'The others?' Posy snorted. 'Where I'm standing, *you're* the one in danger. They sent you here.' She looked me up and down. 'To *fight? You're* going to fight?'

I tugged on one of my plaits. *Shit.* What did I do? I couldn't tell Posy the truth, but I hated the idea of lying.

And she'd recognised me. If she could, there would be others who did, too.

I turned away, gritting my teeth as I stared at the cleaning supplies. Finally, I took a deep breath and turned back.

'Jackson and Hannover are planning something,' I said. 'I'm here to find out what.'

Posy's artfully painted red lips dropped open.

'Are you serious? You have gone insane.' She shook her head.

'I can handle it.'

'You…' Posy shook her head. 'You're serious. You really plan on… on infiltrating the gangs, and what? Taking Jackson down? Are you going to take control of the Iron Fists?'

'For now, we just want to know what he's planning.'

Posy shook her head again. 'And this?' She gestured me up and down. 'Do you really plan on fighting?'

I hesitated. *Yes. No. I don't know.* Part of me wanted to, but the other half was afraid.

'I will if I have to,' I said.

'My God.' Posy shook her head. 'You've gone crazy. Fucking hell. Why? You have no skin in this fight. Just leave.'

'I can't.' I clenched my fists against the familiar feeling of helplessness that rose up in my chest. 'Savannah's here, and—'

'Savannah could go anywhere,' Posy said. 'So could you. What, don't any of the boys want to drive you to Crater's Edge? Typical men—'

'That's not it,' I said, possessed by a need to defend Bas. 'I want to stay.'

'This isn't your fight.'

'But this is our town!' I burst out. I didn't have the words—that was the trouble. All I knew was that I needed to do this, but I didn't know why, and I couldn't explain it. 'I have to fight.'

'And get yourself killed?'

'At least I can fight,' I said. 'Others aren't so lucky. They—they're taking slaves.' I shouldn't have said it, but suddenly it felt worth the risk. 'The Black Hands are taking slaves in town. I can do something about that. About all of the danger and—'

'You do want to take the gangs down.' Posy's eyes widened so far I could see the whites all around her dark brown irises. 'Christ.'

'I… That's not…' It was, though. It was the thought that had been in the back of my mind, and I knew Bas was thinking it, too. The Black Hands could not take over the town. If we had to destroy them, we would.

'I have to get back,' I said instead. 'I can't be missed.'

Posy set her lips in a grim line.

'And you have to promise not to tell anyone,' I added. 'Please.'

'I won't tell.' She stared at her hands. 'And I can distract anyone who looks likely to… to recognise you. But that's it. I'm not helping otherwise.'

'I understand.'

'And don't do anything stupid. I actually like you. Don't you dare get yourself killed!' She looked up, her eyes glimmering with tears. 'Be careful.'

'I will, I promise.' I grabbed her hands, squeezing them gently. Posy had lovely hands, small but incredibly strong. 'You promise me, too.'

'I promise I'll be careful.' She offered me a watery smile, before composing herself abruptly and pulling her hands away. 'Right, you'd better go first. I'll follow a few minutes behind.'

'Alright.'

'Let me check the coast is clear.'

Posy stuck her head out again. A moment later, she withdrew. 'Go, quick.'

'Thanks.'

I eased past her. As I slipped out the doorway, I thought I heard her mumble, 'You fucking idiot.'

I smiled. *Typical Posy.*

SEVEN

AFTER OUR LAST DISASTROUS TRIP to the NCC clinic, we weren't going to take any risks this time. Bas and Ellery both loaded up with every weapon they could carry, and we drove in through the north side to avoid the checkpoint.

It was alarming.

I had only been back to the north side of town once since we'd been arrested by the Iron Fists—during an acrimonious attempt to try and speak to Savannah two days after returning to Bale Rocks—and a lot had changed. The roads were pockmarked with holes, glass windows had shattered, many of the businesses were now boarded up. The residential buildings were shut tight, and most of the ground- and first-floor windows had been boarded over as well.

'What happened here?' I asked.

'The Iron Fists resisted the army's takeover,' Ellery said. 'This is the result.'

I swallowed. Somehow, hearing there had been fighting on the street and seeing the damages weren't the same thing. All of a sudden, the violence felt so much more real.

All three of us were silent as we made our way through the deserted streets. The atmosphere in the car felt heavy, like a physical weight was pressing down on us. Finally, Bas turned into a side street and parked a discreet distance along. Although we were more vulnerable on foot, we'd all agreed that the car was a liability—too likely to be recognised. The best bet we had was to leave it and walk the last few streets on foot.

Even so, as I climbed out of the car, I reached for the small knife Ellery had scrounged up for me. It was a comforting weight on my hip.

You can do this.

I took a deep breath. 'Let's go.'

We didn't have far to walk, but every distant shout, grumble of engines, or bark of dogs made me jump. I kept my hand on my knife and checked every alley and doorway that we passed.

Finally, we reached the clinic. It, too, had changed. The chain-link fence that had surrounded it had been reinforced with a mixture of plyboard and sheet metal, with barbed wire on top, and new gates had been fitted. The army definitely wasn't taking any chances here.

Fortunately, we didn't have to get in. We'd timed it so we'd arrive when Savannah left work—all we had to do was wait and hope we didn't get caught.

'So, why?' Ellery asked as we took shelter in an alleyway. 'Why would a charity doctor—and reputed do-gooder—decide to become a medic for the Iron Fists?'

He and Bas both looked at me. I stared at my hands, and then at Bas's. He was checking his weapons methodically—but I knew better. It was a nervous tic. I'd first noticed him doing it when we'd been in Langford together. He'd been doing it more and more as the days and weeks went by.

'Harley?' Ellery prompted.

I forced my gaze away from Bas's long fingers.

'I don't know. Maybe Talbot asked her to do it?' It was the only idea I had at the moment. I had always disapproved of Savannah's relationship with Greg Talbot, and it wouldn't surprise me at all if he'd dragged her into trouble.

But what could he hope to gain from it? That was the mystery. There was nothing Savannah could achieve in the bunker that Talbot couldn't have done himself, was there?

I was missing something.

'There she is,' Bas said in a low voice.

I turned, my breath catching in my throat. Savannah had just emerged from the clinic gates, along with a woman around the same age as her—elegant, with straight brown hair, olive skin, and a willowy figure.

'That's Nina Clairmont,' I whispered. 'The woman with her.'

'Markus Clairmont's daughter-in-law?' Bas asked.

I nodded. Markus Clairmont was—at least so far as we knew—the NCC contact with the Black Hands and their slaver ring. Or that was what we suspected. Proof was a little thin on the ground these days.

As we watched, Nina climbed into a waiting car. Savannah waved goodbye to her, then turned and set off for home.

'Let's go,' Ellery murmured.

It hurt to let Savannah out of sight, but I forced myself to follow my friends down the alleyway, past rubbish bags that were piling up high, and out onto the next street. We cut down the road and reached the corner at the same moment that Savannah did. She stopped dead, reaching for her belt—and then recognised me.

'*Harley!*' she hissed, her eyes going wide.

'Hey,' I said weakly. 'I need to talk to you.'

Savannah jerked her chin up. 'No thanks.' She continued walking, her boots clomping on the ground.

I followed her. 'Savannah, come on!'

'No.'

'We need to talk.' I darted in front of her, and she ground to a halt.

'Well, I don't want to talk!'

'I saw you at the bunker last night.'

Savannah set her jaw and marched past me. 'I'm not interested, Harley.'

'I saw you. I know it was you.' I followed her. 'You were with the other medics. What are you doing, Savannah? You know it's dangerous.'

'You're one to talk. You go there all the time.'

'The only reason I ever did that was to keep us safe!' I raked my fingers through my short hair. 'Look, please can we just discuss what's going on? You're my sister. I want you to be safe, and—and I miss you.'

Savannah's expression softened a tiny bit. 'Fine,' she huffed. 'Let's talk. What do you want to talk about?'

'I...' I glanced around. 'We should get off the street.'

We were in the Iron Fists' territory, and the last thing I wanted was to get recognised whilst I was out with Savannah. That would put both of us in danger.

'Where?' Savannah demanded. 'We're not going back to the clinic.'

I glanced around. Where could we go? A bar or café, maybe? I didn't know this part of town well.

'I know a place,' Ellery said, heading across the road. I hurried after him, and he led us down a small alley and up to a sturdy steel door with a broken lock.

'Come on,' he said. 'In here.'

'Here' was a restaurant, abandoned, but not yet looted. A layer of dust covered the floor and metal tables, and we left boot prints and scuff marks on everything we touched. The ceiling sagged on one side. We stuck close to the counter, which bore a stack of chipped enamel plates beside a stained chafing dish.

'This should do us,' Ellery said. 'Bas?'

Bas swept through the back door. I heard him thumping through the back rooms, and a moment later he returned.

'Clear,' he said.

'Alright.' I turned to Savannah. 'What—Why—' For a second, I couldn't find words. 'What's going on?'

Savannah gestured harshly to Ellery and Bas. 'I don't want to talk with them around.'

Ellery sighed loudly. 'We'll keep a watch outside. Shout if you need us.'

I nodded warily. To be honest, I wanted Bas and Ellery to stay. Savannah and I would be less likely to say anything we'd regret with them there. On the other hand, I needed her to be willing to talk.

'Fine,' I muttered.

They filed out, the door banging shut behind them with cloying finality. I turned to Savannah; she was standing near the closest table, clutching the back of a metal chair with a white-knuckled grip.

'Savannah...' My brain had gone blank. What could I say?

'I was looking for you,' she snapped. 'Alright? You just vanished, and I thought they'd have answers.'

Her words hit me like a fist to the chest, driving the air out of my lungs. This was my fault?

'But...' I said, but no excuse occurred to me. 'I...'

Savannah narrowed her eyes. 'What, no grand excuses?'

'I didn't mean to...'

'You were just gone!' The words seemed to wrench out of her with violent force. 'And I didn't know where you were!'

'I'm sorry! I—I looked for you before I left, but you weren't there!'

'Looked for me?' Savannah shook her head. 'You couldn't have left a note?'

'I thought they'd search the flat!'

'Sure,' she scoffed. 'You could have found a way, but no. It was a grand adventure, taking off with your friends into the wasteland, and you didn't want me tagging along.'

'That's not true.' I grabbed hold of the counter, needing something to keep me up. 'I would have taken you—I wanted you to be safe.

That's all I've ever wanted.'

'Safe.' Savannah rolled her eyes. 'I'm perfectly capable of keeping myself safe, Harley. How many times do I have to tell you? I don't need you around to do it.'

'But…' I stared at her furiously, desperately. She looked different, somehow, but I couldn't tell how. Something had changed.

'I'm sorry,' I said meekly. Hot tears sprang into my eyes. 'Theo was supposed to—'

'Oh, Theo,' Savannah hissed. 'Sure, that's how it is. Theo was supposed to tell me? Well, he didn't! That's what you get for putting your faith in gang members.'

'He was supposed to come back for you, but something went wrong!'

'I don't care,' Savannah said. 'I don't need you sending people to babysit me. I can make my own choices in life.'

'What, like working at the bunker?' I swallowed. 'You don't need to keep going there—you know where I am now.'

'Oh, that's rich.' Savannah rolled her eyes. 'You're back, so I must fall in line, is that it?'

'I'm not saying—'

'Yes, now you're back. You walked back in as though nothing had changed. As though you hadn't been gone for two fucking weeks, as though I had no reason to worry, as though I didn't get harassed by gang members trying to find you.'

'I didn't mean for any of that to happen!'

'But I must stop going to the bunker now, because you're back, and that's your territory, right?'

'No,' I floundered. 'It's not like that.'

'Of course not.' Savannah pushed off the table. 'Because I don't have to listen to you. I don't have to stop doing anything. And most importantly, I don't have anyone to share rent with now, so I'm the one having to work two jobs to support myself.' Savannah turned and marched to the door, but then she stopped and faced me again. 'Thanks for the help, Harley. I guess that's what I get for expecting you to pull your weight.'

She walked out. I stared after her, feeling like someone had shot a hole in my chest and I was bleeding out onto the floor.

That hadn't gone how I'd expected at all.

Savannah had changed completely.

I got it now. She was different. And it was my fault.

In low spirits, I climbed back into the car. Bas had brought it around whilst I was talking to Savannah.

'That bad, eh?' Ellery asked.

'Don't tell me you couldn't hear.' He'd been eavesdropping from the alley the entire time.

Ellery snorted. 'Excuse me for trying to sympathise.'

'She's… she's a…' I trailed off. Anger warred with hurt, and I couldn't bring myself to say what I was really thinking.

'Don't let it get to you,' Ellery said. 'You've known Savannah forever. Claire and I have our differences, too, but when it comes down to it, we'll stand by each other.'

'I don't think Savannah is much like Claire,' Bas said.

I stared at my hands, my stomach churning. 'I tried so hard,' I whispered. 'The only thing I *ever* wanted was for Savannah to be safe and happy.'

'It's not on you to make people happy,' Bas said. He turned the ignition, and the car came to life beneath us with a grumble. 'We can only make ourselves happy.'

'She's my sister!'

'She's her own responsibility.'

'Bas,' Ellery cut in, exasperated but fond. I turned to look at Ellery. I hadn't expected understanding from him—but it was more than welcome.

'You get it, right?'

He grinned. 'Siblings are hard,' he said. 'We're meant to love 'em, but how can we do that when most of the time we want to hate 'em?'

I smiled weakly. 'I don't know what to do,' I admitted.

'Nothing,' Ellery said firmly.

'I can't just—'

'Yes, you can,' he interrupted. 'Because Bas is right about one thing: Savannah is her own responsibility. She's made her choice. You've made it clear that she has the option of coming to you if she needs help. But she has to choose that. You can't make her do it.'

I sighed. He was right, of course. 'I hate doing nothing.'

'You can't focus on Savannah and the Iron Fists. You'll spread yourself too thin,' Ellery said. 'We'll keep an eye on Savannah—we're watching the clinic anyway. And who knows? Maybe we'll get an opportunity to show her we're on the same side.'

I grimaced, turning back to the front. It was a horrible plan. It sat all wrong. I'd spent so much of my life looking after Savannah, that letting go—*now*, of all times—felt like tearing a chunk out of my own flesh.

'Fine, but if she needs help, promise me you'll help her. Please.' I clenched my hands over my knees. 'You know I'd do the same for your family.'

'Of course,' Ellery said.

I glanced sideways at Bas.

'You could let my family burn. I wouldn't care.' A wry smile slid onto his face. 'But I promise.'

'Thanks.'

We lapsed into silence for a few minutes. I wrestled with my feelings—I felt all keyed up, but I had nowhere to direct the restless energy. I couldn't afford to lose my temper though, not with Bas and Ellery.

'Seeing as that's sorted, can we discuss what else we saw today?' Ellery asked.

'What?' I said.

'Nina Clairmont being picked up in a fancy-shmancy government car,' he said.

'Oh.' I thought back. Now that I was thinking about it, the car had been rather shiny, with blacked-out windows. 'Do you think that means something?'

'Hard to say,' Ellery said. 'It could mean something. It could mean nothing. Seems like it's worth following up, though.'

'It'll be risky to tail her,' Bas said.

'Kade might be able to do it,' Ellery said. 'He's the least known of all of us. The real issue is the cars—there are just too few about in town to mistake that you're being followed.'

'Theo used some kind of a tracker on Hannover's car.' A pang went through my chest. I swallowed and stared determinedly out the window. 'He got it from Declan.'

'Maybe we need to pay him another visit,' Ellery said.

'He won't be so generous a second time,' Bas mused as we turned onto a rundown street. We were in a pretty bad part of town. Even before the army had taken over, this wasn't an area I liked to come to. In fact, we were only streets away from where Bas had once saved me from being raped.

I shuddered. It had been months, but I didn't think I'd ever be able to remember it without feeling sick.

A vehicle cut in front of us, and Bas hit the brakes so suddenly that I slid forwards in my seat.

'The hell?' Ellery demanded. 'It's an empty fucking road.'

I jerked up straight, feeling as though I'd been electrified. 'That's Theo's truck!'

'What?' Ellery exclaimed.

'It is! It definitely is!' I cried. The colour was right—dark grey, almost black. The stickers on the bed—even the letters he'd painted over the space where the license plate was meant to be:

7H30

'Follow him,' I said.

Bas gunned the engine, closing the distance between our cars. Theo swung around a corner, heading for the western end of town, and Bas gave chase. Thank God we were in his car, not Ellery's truck—we'd never have kept up in the old banger. As it was, Theo gave us a run for our money as he took another corner and a hair-raising speed.

'What's he doing?' Ellery asked.

'It's not Theo,' Bas said.

'It has to be.' My hands were shaking with adrenaline. 'It's his truck.'

'He knows my car. Why would he run from us?' Bas asked.

'I don't know, but there has to be a reason.' I couldn't entertain any other possibilities. It had been so long that I'd lost hope of finding Theo. This had to be the answer. Gripping my knees, I added, 'Can you cut him off?'

'I can try.'

Theo vanished around another corner, and Bas followed him. We were heading south on one of the main arterials, and he was forced to slow down to accommodate the cars and vans using one of the few north-south roads that wasn't blocked by a checkpoint.

'If he crosses the river, you might be able to head him off by Striker Passage,' Ellery said.

Bas didn't reply, too focused on weaving around parked vehicles. A man stepped out from behind a van, carrying a stack of boxes, and Bas veered into the middle of the road to avoid him. A moment later, we reached the bridge and hurtled across it. I had seconds to take in the rushing river far below as Bas accelerated to close the gap between us and Theo.

The south of town was bustling compared to the north—the fighting between the Iron Fists and the army clearly hadn't made it this far, and people were going about their business as usual. There was far less damage to the buildings. It also meant that we had to slow down to avoid people and cars. Theo, obviously having the same thought, hung a right onto a quieter road.

Bas followed, pushing his car as fast as it could go. We were gaining on Theo—gaining—gaining—

He swung into a side street and braked sharply enough that Bas almost rolled into the back of him. Bas slammed down the brake, and I was thrown forwards toward the dashboard.

'Ack!'

I righted myself. Up ahead, someone sprang out of Theo's car.

But it wasn't Theo.

The figure was too bulky, too old, all wrong.

But that didn't mean I didn't recognise him. In fact, I knew him all too well.

It was Rhett.

The good-for-nothing drunk who'd helped us get into Brackfields Military Base. Someone I had sincerely hoped I'd never have to see again.

He'd driven north with Theo. He'd been in the car with Theo the last time I had seen my best friend.

Damned if I was letting this opportunity pass me by.

Rhett sprinted into an alleyway. I threw my door open, fumbled my seatbelt off, and hurtled after him.

'Harley!' Ellery hollered, but I didn't turn back. I had to catch Rhett.

I reached the alley. He was already vanishing around the corner. He certainly hadn't been this fleet-footed the first time I'd met him! I threw myself after him, rounding the corner and putting on a burst of speed. He skidded around the next corner.

'Rhett!' I snarled, reaching for him, but just missing his brown overcoat.

He was doubling back to the road. I chased him, hoping that Bas had stayed in the car.

Just as Rhett reached the mouth of the alleyway, Bas appeared. The two of them collided, both stumbling backwards.

'Oi, mind yourself!' Rhett shoved past Bas, but Bas grabbed him by the collar and threw him against the wall.'

'Get off me!' Rhett roared.

I jogged up to them, panting.

'You,' I snapped. 'What the fuck are you doing here?'

Theo had said he was taking Rhett north, but I'd never imagined that meant I would find Rhett hanging around Bale Rocks.

'Where's Theo?' I added.

Rhett laughed nervously. 'Thought you weren't welcome in these parts anymore. What was it? Harper, right?'

'Harley,' I snarled.

'Oh, that was it.' He pointed at me and snapped his fingers. 'Harley, that's right. Like the motorcycle.'

I ground my teeth together.

'Well, Harley,' Rhett tipped an invisible hat, 'nice to see you and all, but I gotta be off. Places to see, people to be, and all that.'

He turned towards the main road. Bas stepped in his way.

'I don't think so,' I said. 'You're driving Theo's truck.'

'Is that so? You must be mistaken.'

But he was obviously nervous. He shuffled his weight and peered around Bas.

'I'm definitely not mistaken,' I said. Anger was twisting in my chest. 'That is Theo's truck. Where's Theo?'

'Haven't the faintest. He leant me the truck—'

The anger took over. I grabbed him by the arm and shoved him against the wall. 'You're lying!'

'Oi, get off me!'

I pulled my hand back and balled my fist. 'Where's Theo?'

'You cracked, girlie?'

'Tell me, or I'll knock your teeth out!'

I leant my weight against his neck, and he gagged. 'Alright, alright.'

Loosening the pressure, I glared at him. 'Talk.'

'He's dead.'

Time stopped. My heart stopped. I couldn't move, breathe, think. I couldn't hear over the roar of blood in my ears. I couldn't do anything.

Theo could not be dead.

'You're lying.'

Rhett rolled his eyes. 'Why would I lie? We drove straight into it—idiots with guns everywhere. They shot him straight through the window. I barely got out of there alive.'

'You!' The roar in my ears became deafening. 'You barely got out of there alive?'

I lurched backwards and reached for Bas. He had his gun in his hand—I snatched it and turned it on Rhett's head.

Rhett paled. 'Oi, there's no need for that!'

'You think I give a shit if you got out of there alive?' I snarled. 'YOU LEFT THEO!'

'He was dead. I ain't a fucking medic.'

'You—' My vision tunnelled. I clicked the safety off on the gun. 'He helped you, and you *left* him!'

'He was dead,' Rhett repeated. 'Get over it. It was months ago.'

'*Get over it?*' I repeated shrilly. 'IT SHOULD HAVE BEEN YOU!'

I jerked the gun up, aiming straight between his eyes. Rhett's gaze darted all over the place. A hand landed on my shoulder.

'Harley,' Bas said, 'he's not worth it.'

'Don't—don't you fucking dare—'

'That's right, girlie, listen to your boyfriend,' Rhett said.

'Fuck you!' My hands shook and my eyes blurred with tears. *Do it, just shoot him.*

Bas wrapped a hand around my wrist. 'He's not worth it. He's a worm. Leave him.'

'No.' A sob burst out of my throat. 'I have to—I have to—'

Bas eased the gun out of my hand and pulled me into his arms. 'Shh.'

He was warm, and so, so steady. I tucked my head into his neck, and he rubbed my back.

'Aw, how sweet,' Rhett mocked. 'Guess Theo was right. You're not cut out for this life.'

Bas's hand tensed on my back. I whipped away from him, spun on my heel, and planted my fist in Rhett's nose. Pain exploded up my arm. Rhett bellowed in agony.

'YOU FUCKING BITCH!'

I hauled back, but before I could punch him again, Bas grabbed my arm.

'Harley.' His voice was low and steady. 'It's okay.' He tugged me behind him and levelled the gun on Rhett. 'Leave, or I'll shoot your knees out.'

'Fucker.' Rhett stumbled backwards away from us, never taking his eyes off Bas. 'You're crazy. Everyone in this town is fucking crazy.'

He spat on the ground, then turned and sprinted away. Bas kept the gun on him until he was around the corner. Then he turned to me.

'Let's go,' he said quietly and led me away.

EIGHT

I YANKED THE NEEDLE THROUGH the thick fabric of my jeans, my fingers aching in protest. I'd been at it for what felt like hours, but had made almost no progress on my pile of mending.

Instead, my thoughts circled, pulling me away from the task at hand.

Theo.

Theo was—

Don't think about it.

I smoothed the thread out and started pushing the needle through the edge of the patch I was sewing down. Mending was boring and annoying, but at least it kept my hands busy, if not my brain.

It was my fault. If only I'd asked him to come with us to Langford.

Then you wouldn't have Bas.

Maybe. But I would have Theo. Theo would be alive. My best, my oldest friend.

Fuck.

A hollow, yawning chasm seemed to have opened up in my chest, aching constantly. Hungrily. It sapped my emotions and pulled at my thoughts, forcing them down pathways I didn't want to tread.

It was my fault.

I forced the needle through the denim again, my eyes stinging.

'Are you sure you don't want me to help?' Laura asked. She was sitting on the opposite side of the room, methodically folding laundry. She'd been talking to me in that same gentle, kind tone all afternoon—as though I was a frightened stray dog—and I hated it.

'No thanks,' I muttered. 'I'm good.'

'Maybe you should speak to Bas.'

'No thanks.'

Bas was the last person I wanted to speak to right now. For all I liked him, I knew exactly what he would say.

'*Compartmentalise.*'

No fucking thanks.

I yanked on the needle. Stupid thing was stuck.

'I just think you'd feel better if you spoke to him,' Laura said softly.

I would feel better, if she only left me alone. Unfortunately, I couldn't exactly throw her out of the room we were sharing. And I couldn't leave the house, because a dull, icy rain was falling outside.

'I'm busy,' I said, my tone too terse, too vulnerable.

'I'm only trying to help,' Laura said.

Help someone else.

I yanked the needle furiously—and the thread snapped.

Shit.

'Damnit, I hate mending.' I threw the jeans down on the bed.

'I'll do it.' Laura stood and approached me.

'No!' I snatched the jeans and needle again. 'It's my stuff. I can repair it myself.'

'Harley—'

'For fuck's sake! Please leave me alone!'

'Alright, alright.' Laura backed off, her hands raised. 'I'm just worried about you.'

'I don't need you to worry about me. I'm perfectly capable of taking care of myself.'

'Fine.' Laura's lips twisted. 'I just thought—Well, in case you'd forgotten, I actually know what you're going through.'

I stared at her. Hurt shone in her eyes. I had forgotten—but it came back to me now. Laura had lost her husband to gang violence in Crater's Edge. The gaping chasm widened. Everyone was just fucking dying, and there didn't seem to be a thing I could do about it.

'That doesn't mean I want to bond over it,' I snapped.

I jumped off the bed, dumping my jeans back on the pile of stuff I needed to mend. 'I'll do that later. I'm going to train.'

'I am sorry,' Laura said.

I scrubbed my hands over my trousers, anger frothing in my stomach. I swallowed hard. Whatever I said to her in this mood, it would come out wrong.

'I just need to be alone for a bit.' I let myself out of the room before she could reply.

Downstairs, I pulled my boots on and headed out into the rain. It was as sharp and cold as a needle, cutting straight through my clothes, my flesh, straight down to my bones. Within minutes, my fingers were numb and my teeth were chattering. But I kept jogging until I reached the gym and let myself in.

It was my fault that Theo was dead, and the only option I had to make it right was to train even harder—*fight* even harder. I would have to take down the people who had killed him.

I had to.

I threw myself into my drills harder than ever. Every punch I threw at the bag, I imagined crushing my enemies' faces. Every kick, I imagined cracking their skulls. I trained with fire and fury as the sky darkened outside and the rain pounded on.

'Harley.'

I fell back, turning to the door. Bas stood there, his wet hair dripping trickles of water over his neck and face.

'Go away,' I snapped. 'I want to be alone.'

Bas stepped closer, shucking his damp jacket. 'I'll train with you.'

'No thanks.'

'Please.'

I couldn't hold his gaze. His green eyes were too intense. Too understanding.

'Fine,' I muttered. A good fight would wear me out at least.

Bas approached, and we took up positions opposite one another. I didn't bother waiting for a signal; I rushed him, throwing a furious punch at his chest and following it up with a jab—Bas parried effortlessly. Slipping behind my guard, he wrapped his leg around mine and tripped me.

I hit the mat, too shocked to even sprawl properly. That had been way faster than I'd expected.

'What the fuck?' I panted.

'You can't fight with your emotions,' Bas said. He held out a hand to help me up. I slapped it away.

'If you're just here to tell me to compartmentalise—' I cut myself off; I couldn't think of a good threat.

'I'm not,' Bas said. 'Take a breather and try again.'

Scowling, I hauled myself up and marched over to my stuff to grab a drink. 'I don't need you to patronise me.'

'I'm not,' Bas said.

I studied him. He seemed perfectly relaxed. I couldn't read him at all. What was his game? Did he think he was going to distract me or something?

I ground my teeth together and dropped my water bottle back on top of my bag. 'Let's go again.'

'Alright,' Bas said calmly.

I stepped back in and began my offensive again. This time, I took it slower, timing my jabs properly. Still, Bas put me on my back in a remarkably short time.

'Again?' he asked as he helped me up.

I nodded.

We fought for what felt like hours, and soon enough my body started to ache as badly as my heart. Bas had a way of finding tender spots, and he pummelled mine until I was ready to collapse and it felt like a physical effort to keep my fists raised. He put me on my back again and again, until finally, I gave in.

'I have to stop,' I said. 'I'm one giant bruise.'

Bas held out his hand, tugging me to my feet. 'Feel better?'

'I…' *No,* I wanted to say, but something gave me a pause. I certainly wasn't worse. And I hadn't thought of Theo in over an hour.

'I don't know,' I muttered finally. 'Was that your plan? To pummel the grief right out of me?'

'No.' Bas quirked his lips up in a tiny smile. 'Sometimes you just need to hit someone.'

'Yeah.' Without warning, tears welled in my eyes and flooded down my cheeks. I gasped in a breath, pressing my hands to my eyes to try and stem the flow. But it was useless. As though a dam had burst, suddenly, I couldn't hold the tears back.

'Shit, sorry.' I turned away, scrubbing my face with my sleeve.

'It's okay.' Bas wrapped his arms around my shoulders and pulled me into his chest. 'It's okay, Harley.'

'It's not,' I sobbed. 'It's—He was my best friend. For years.'

'I know.'

'He can't be gone.'

'I know.' Bas squeezed me tighter, as though he could crush the misery out of me. I leant against him. Bas was steady and strong, and he seemed to weather everything like a rock buffeted by wind and rain—unmoved.

The opposite of me, really.

Why couldn't I be more like him?

'I'm going to kill them,' I whispered.

'I know,' Bas repeated.

'You do?' Surprised, I pulled back so I could see his face. He gazed at me solemnly.

'Of course,' he said. 'I'd expect nothing less.'

'Oh.' Sometimes, I felt like Bas knew me better than I knew myself. Like he'd reached the obvious conclusion long before I even started on the path towards it. Of course, I'd get revenge because I owed it to Theo. 'You're not going to try to stop me?'

'No one can stop you when you put your mind to something.' Bas reached out and traced his finger over my damp cheek. 'Just promise me one thing.'

I leant into his fingers, and he cupped my cheek. 'What?'

'Be smart,' he murmured. 'No revenge is worth losing yourself. Not even this.'

I bit my lip and turned away, staring at the window—and beyond it, the steady pelt of cold winter rain. Theo hated winter—he'd always get antsy during the winter months. Restless and reckless. Whereas I had put my head down and got on with it, just like I did during spring, summer, and autumn. Just like I did about everything.

'I'm not sure how much there is left to lose,' I said.

'There's always more left to lose,' Bas said. Something in his voice made me look at him. He was frowning, and his eyes contained a deep, bottomless sadness.

'Who…?' I swallowed, unable to complete the question. I was under no illusions that I knew everything about Bas's life. But I never knew how to ask—it always felt like the wrong moment.

'I had a friend.' Bas caught my hand and tangled our fingers together, turning my hand so he could study the callouses that were developing from my training—replacing the old ones from dance. 'Vivianne.'

The name caught me by surprise, and the pang of jealousy was worse. It was unthinkably shallow to be jealous of any part of Bas's past—even the smallest thing that brought him joy should have made me glad. But I couldn't help where my mind had gone.

'Was she—I mean, were you…'

'No!' Bas's eyes widened. He shook his head hurriedly. 'Not like that. But… when I escaped, she was meant to come with me. I…'

His gaze slanted off towards the ground, and in a voice filled with self-recrimination, he finished, 'If I had just *left*—That was what she wanted. 'Just go, just get out.'' He shook his head. 'But I wanted my revenge. I wanted to see the look on his face—And they killed her. Shot her. Because she was weaker than I was. Couldn't run as fast.'

I swallowed, my throat suddenly blocked by a lump the size of my fist. I felt guilty for even thinking of being jealous—how horrible must it have been?

'Hannover?' I asked softly.

Bas looked up. 'No, Moriarty.'

My eyes met his, and for a moment, we were perfectly in sync. Both filled with regrets about past decisions. Both willing to do anything to make it right. His hand still held mine; I squeezed it gently.

'It wasn't your fault,' I said.

'Nor was Theo your fault.'

I bit the inside of my cheek. If only I could believe that.

'Thank you,' I said instead. 'For telling me.'

'I'll tell you anything you want to know,' Bas said. 'I don't have any secrets from you.'

'What will you do if you see Moriarty again?' I asked.

Bas's green-green-green eyes glinted.

'Shoot him,' he said. 'And this time there won't be any mistakes.' I could barely stand to meet his gaze; it was so intense. 'He knows. He doesn't show his face around me. But eventually he'll slip up, and I'll be waiting.'

I'll be waiting.

Bas was waiting for Moriarty. And I was waiting for Jackson. He'd slip up, too.

And I'd be waiting.

The bunker throbbed like the beat of a giant mechanical heart. Lights flashed, music thrummed, the floor vibrated beneath my boots. My own heart pounded in time with the angry rhythm as I braced my weight against a punching bag to steady it.

Tyler landed a deft combo on the bag that sent shudders through my body.

'Nice!' one of his friends called—Paulie, another young guy who kept shooting me glances whenever he thought I wasn't looking. Both of them were fighting today, but I got to watch from the sidelines. Again.

'Eh, I've seen better,' I said.

'Pfft.' Tyler rolled his eyes. The lights turned his blond hair blue, then green, then red. 'As if. You're all talk because you haven't been in the cage yet. That'll knock the ego right out of you.'

'I'll knock the ego out of you.'

I shouldn't have responded, but I just couldn't resist. I was filled with restless anger, which had nowhere to go. I was dying to fight someone.

Bas hadn't wanted me to come tonight, but I had insisted. He thought my emotions would cloud my judgement, but the truth was that I'd never been more focused before in my life.

I was ready.

'Sure.' Tyler laughed. 'You're angry tonight, aren't you?'

With effort, I dialled my irritation back. 'I just want to get on with it. I hate waiting.'

'I'm sure they'll put you in the ring next week,' Paulie said. 'Jackson's playing it safe with newcomers these days.' He leaned in. 'He's worried about profits, you know. Bets are down since Sayle—'

'Paul!' Tyler hissed.

Paulie rolled his eyes. 'C'mon, man, she'd have to be an idiot not to notice.'

'We're not supposed to talk about it!'

Paulie groaned. 'Whatever, whatever. I'm gonna get a drink.'

He slouched off, leaving Tyler and me alone in the training zone. I cast around for a new topic. 'Tell me about the medics. Are they legit?'

'Uh, yeah.' Tyler shrugged as he started to remove the wrappings from his hands. 'They fix up plenty of stuff. There's a new girl—she's particularly good, but she likes to lecture people. Dunno why she's here if she thinks we're so dumb.'

A thrill ran through me. He meant Savannah—he had to.

'Search me,' I said. 'Money, maybe?'

'Could be. Rumour has it Jackson pays them good. That's how he got the Clairmont guy, anyway—he's the top dog over at the NCC clinic. But they say the NCC doesn't pay shit, so the docs come here instead.'

'Why wouldn't the NCC pay their doctors?' I asked. 'They're the only ones we've got.'

'"Cos the NCC doesn't care about us?' Tyler asked, raising an eyebrow. He dropped his sweaty wrappings on top of his bag and picked up a water bottle instead. 'Where you from, anyway, that you don't know this stuff? Everyone knows the NCC clinic barely has two pennies to rub together.'

'Uh.' Where was Sierra from? No one had asked me that before. 'South side of town. I haven't been to the clinic in a while, I guess.'

Tyler squinted suspiciously at me. *Fuck. Smooth, Harley.*

Finally, he looked away. 'You're where the money's at, now. Jackson has the distillery, and so long as the Iron Fists have got that, they run the town.'

What would Sierra ask? Playing dumb, I said, 'What about the army?'

'Dunno. Word on the street is that Jackson's calling the shots. But no one knows.' Tyler shot me a glare. 'These are dangerous questions, Sierra. You're better off sticking to fighting.'

I'd spooked him. *Damnit.*

'Sorry,' I said. 'Just curious. I don't really want some hack stitching me up.'

He snorted. 'There's no hacks here. Jackson wants the best—he gets the best. C'mon, let's go watch the next fight.'

'Alright.' I sighed and followed him to the other side of the circle. So far, my attempts at getting information had fallen woefully short. The questions continued to pile up, but I hadn't found out any answers yet.

The night seemed to crawl by. I watched one fight after another, but I couldn't find it in myself to care who won or lost. Finally, Tyler went up to fight, and I took the opportunity to slip off into the back rooms. If I couldn't find anything out from Tyler, I'd go looking back here.

I crept down the echoey, dimly lit halls, my boots thumping softly. Had it always been this eerie back here? Or was it because I knew the stakes if I got caught snooping?

Jackson and Hannover wouldn't be forgiving, that was for sure.

Hurried footsteps sounded out behind me, and I darted into a narrow service hallway, holding my breath as someone passed by. Close—I needed to be more careful.

A few corridors later, I reached the office. I tried the door.

Locked.

Damnit, that was annoying. Where else could I try? I heard footsteps and hurriedly backed away from the door as Carlos marched around the corner.

'You, girl, what are you doing here?' he demanded.

Fuck.

'Uh… toilets,' I muttered.

Carlos's eyes narrowed. 'You're in the wrong part of the building for that.' He pointed back the way he'd come. 'Third left, right, then left again.'

'Thanks.'

He sneered. 'Get going.'

I hurried off without argument. *Damnit.* Today wasn't going at all as I wanted it to—I'd have nothing to report when I got home, and another week would go by with no results. Grinding my teeth, I swung into the main hallway and almost walked into someone.

'Sorry—' I caught sight of the person's face and immediately stumbled back a step. It was Hannover.

'Sierra.' A mean smile spread across his face. 'Settling in well, I hope.'

'Well enough, thanks,' I bit out. I stepped sideways, hoping to make my escape—Hannover was the last person I wanted to be up close and personal with. He followed me.

'That's good to hear. I know it can be hard, watching but not being part of things—'

'It's fine. I understand.'

His smile got even bigger. I straightened up, biting my tongue. I couldn't risk tipping him off that anything was amiss.

'Well, I'm glad.' He took a step closer. I resisted the urge to step back, even as he invaded my personal space. 'I have it on good authority that things are going to change for you very soon, though.'

'Oh?' I could barely think with him so close. My head swam.

'Absolutely.' Abruptly, he walked past me, landing a slap on my bum. Then he was gone, leaving me standing there, staring unseeingly down the hallway. I took several deep breaths to steady myself and get my heart back to a more normal pace.

It would not be an understatement to say I hated being close to that man. He reminded me of a snake—something about him just screamed danger.

I knew what he was capable of. He'd hurt Bas, and he would hurt me if he found out who I was.

I rubbed my butt. Just his touch made me feel dirty. Ugh.

Better get back.

I set off down the hall, forcing Hannover out of my mind.

'Well?' Ellery demanded as we walked in. He was waiting just inside the door when we entered the farmhouse.

'Well what?' I asked. I felt wrung out and miserable, and I wasn't in the mood to play word games.

'You didn't report anything. Did you find anything out?'

'Markus Clairmont is working at the bunker, and Tyler thinks Jackson is controlling the army.' I pushed past him and headed for the kitchen. 'Is there food?'

'Tyler thinks what?' Ellery pounded after me, followed by Bas and Kade. I led my entourage into the kitchen, where Laura was bent over the stove.

'Hi, Harley,' she called. 'How was it?'

'Awful.' I threw my jacket over the back of a chair and slumped down.

'I'm just heating some soup.' Laura shot me a sympathetic smile, which I pretended not to notice. I wasn't in the mood for sympathy, either. I wanted to be doing something. Taking action.

Avenging Theo.

Not sitting around.

Unfortunately, that was all there was to do now, and all there would be to do for the rest of the week until I could go back to the bunker and try again.

'The mayor controls the army,' Ellery said as he sat across from me. Bas slid into the open seat beside me. 'So if Jackson is controlling the army, that means he has to be controlling the mayor, too.'

'The mayor wouldn't be that stupid,' Laura objected, glancing over.

'Yes, he would,' I disagreed. 'He partnered with the Black Hands and let them take slaves from in town. How is this any different?'

'Point,' Ellery said. 'He probably doesn't see a difference. Especially if the Black Hands and the Iron Fists are working together now. To him, they're probably one and the same.'

'Could Jackson call on the army in a fight, though?' Kade asked. 'They've been fighting against the Iron Fists.'

'I thought the point of the army was to get rid of the gangs.' Laura plonked a pot down in the middle of the table and brought the electric lantern over from the counter so we could see. I reached for the ladle and set to serving myself.

'He doesn't want anyone to know he's in control,' Bas said darkly. 'Jackson would take a loss in order to keep up his public image.'

I turned to him. 'Why does it matter? If he's in control?'

'Because if word got out that the mayor was corrupt, there might be a push from Providence to replace him,' Ellery said.

Providence—the capital of the West Rim. It wasn't a place I thought about often. It had always seemed so far away, distant from our small-town way of life. But now that I'd been to Langford, I had closed that distance somewhat. And suddenly, the big, bright city that I'd only ever heard of seemed much closer.

Too close.

'Can they do that?' I asked.

'They're probably not about to march over and force us to hold a vote.' Ellery snorted. 'They'll just shoot him and put a new candidate in place.'

'Oh.' My stomach squirmed. A new mayor didn't seem like an entirely bad idea—our current one sure wasn't anything to shout about—but then again, we didn't want anyone from out of town running the show. And now was the worst time for a change of leadership. The situation in Bale Rocks was fraught enough already.

'They'd never get away with it, though,' Laura said. 'The people would revolt.'

'They aren't exactly revolting right now,' Ellery pointed out.

'Some of them are!' Laura protested. Ellery shot her an incredulous look. 'Some of them *are!*' she insisted. 'Maybe they're not waving guns around, but that doesn't mean they aren't fighting back!'

'Alright,' Ellery said. 'But whatever they're doing, it's not driving the army out either. Harley, pass the bread.'

'Sure.' I stood and reached across the table. Bas's hand ghosted across my bum, and I jumped, almost sending the breadboard tumbling to the floor.

'What are you doing?' I glanced at him with a flirty grin. Bas held something up, tucked between two fingers.

A note.

'What is that?' I asked.

'It was in your pocket.'

'Huh.' I handed over the breadboard and took the note from Bas, unfolding it. And froze.

TA, 11:30 PM Tues. DH

'What is it?' Ellery asked.

'I...' Wordlessly, I held the note out. He snatched it.

''TA, 11:30 PM Tues. DH,'' he read out. 'The Arsonist, eleven-thirty, Tuesday. DH?'

'Dean Hannover,' Bas said grimly. I didn't have to glance at him to know what his face looked like; his voice echoed the same feeling of dread that was seeping into my own chest.

'You sure? Could be Hasselby.'

'He's William,' Kade said.

'Huh.' Ellery frowned. I ran through all of the people I knew in the bunker to no avail. It was pointless. I knew full well what had happened—the strange and creepy conversation with Hannover. The butt slap.

''I have it on good authority that things are going to change for you very soon,'' I muttered.

'Huh?' Ellery asked.

'That's what he said to me.' I looked up from my plate. 'Hannover. It was Hannover. He must have slipped the note into my pocket when he passed me.' Better not to tell them about the bum-slapping incident. Bas would hate it.

'When did he say that?' Bas asked.

'I ran into him in the hallways—I was trying to snoop, but I ran into Carlos so I had to go back. And then I bumped into Hannover.'

'Alone?' Bas asked sharply.

I nodded meekly. 'He didn't try anything. He was just his usual creepy self.'

'That rules out literally nothing,' Ellery muttered.

'He asked me how I was settling in, then mentioned things were going to change. I thought he meant that they'd be letting me fight— but he must have mentioned this.' I nodded to the note. A horrible thought dawned on me. 'He knows who I am.'

'I thought you said he didn't recognise you,' Laura said.

'He must have.' The more I thought about it, the more convinced I became. Hannover wouldn't care about Sierra. But Harley—Harley, he knew very well. And he'd manipulated me before. I buried my face in my hands. 'Shit. He played us. Shit.'

'He knew,' Ellery mused. 'He knew it was you—from the start? Did he recognise you at the bottling plant, or was it someone at TA who tipped him off?'

'Could be either,' I mumbled.

'You have to pull out,' Bas said.

'What?' I jerked around to stare at him. 'No way!'

'The plan's a bust,' he said. 'You'll never get anything now.'

'That's not true,' I said. 'We don't know why Hannover let me in—and he's offering to meet me.'

'You're not going.'

Fury rushed through me. *Oh no you don't.*

'Are we back to making unilateral decisions, then?' I asked sweetly.

'It's too risky. Whatever Hannover wants, it will be bad for you.'

'I'm not saying I'll do what he wants,' I snapped. 'But we can at least hear him out—he's in the thick of things. He knows things we don't. And we've been looking for an in—'

'This is not an in,' Bas insisted. 'Hannover's as likely to shoot you as he is to help you. More likely, in fact.'

'I can look after myself,' I said. Were we really going over this again? After everything? 'I'm not going to go in blindly trusting him.'

'Why would Hannover even want to meet you?' Ellery cut in.

That brought me up short. 'I have no idea.'

I glanced at Bas. He was frowning into his soup. 'He has to have something planned,' he said.

'But what?' Kade asked.

'I don't know what his angle is,' Bas said. 'He benefits the most from maintaining the status quo.'

'It could be a grab for information about what we're planning,' Ellery said.

'I doubt he considers us a threat.' Bas shook his head. 'We only got Harley into the bunker by his grace—'

'Hey!'

'I'm not saying you're not skilled,' he said. 'But Jackson might not have let you in. Hannover probably recognised you.'

'I was winning that fight,' I reminded him. 'Besides, that's an argument to *go* to this meeting. If we pull out, Hannover will think we're scared.'

'If we go, Hannover will know we're desperate,' Bas replied. 'And you'll be in even more danger.'

'He doesn't say I have to go alone,' I said.

Bas frowned. Ellery turned the note over to check the back. 'She raises a fair point,' he mused.

'Hannover cannot be trusted,' Bas said. 'Last time you saw him, he was going to kill us.'

'Time before that, we were going to kill him,' I said.

'Point,' Ellery said.

Bas glared at him. 'You go if you're so keen on it.'

'Or we all go,' Ellery rejoined. 'Safety in numbers, and all that.'

'There's no safety from Hannover.'

'He reached out to us, though,' I said. 'Not the other way around.'

'So he's in control,' Bas said.

'He wants something,' I said. 'That gives us power.'

'We don't know what it is,' Bas replied. 'And even if we did, it's not wise to give Hannover what he wants. He'll screw us over.'

'So we don't let him,' I said. The more I thought about it, the more I wanted to go. Hannover might make me sick, but I could face him with Bas by my side. And this opportunity was huge. It would take our plan from a mere spark to a full flame. Hannover loved to play both sides—so he might be willing to reveal things about Jackson and the mayor that we'd never find out otherwise.

Bas shook his head. 'Have you ever heard the story of the frog and the scorpion? Hannover is the scorpion, Harley.'

I gritted my teeth. 'I'm not an idiot. I'm not going to let him ruin our plans. I just want to see what he wants.'

'I can't support that.'

And there it was, plain, for everyone to hear. A fist seemed to close around my heart. He said *I can't support that*—but he meant *I can't support you.*

I can't trust you.

I picked up my spoon. 'Sometimes you have to do things you don't want to do in order to make things right.'

'That's not how I do things.' Bas stood abruptly. 'I'm going to bed.'

He walked out of the kitchen, leaving us in an uncomfortable silence.

'I'll speak to him,' Ellery said quietly.

'I'm going to go,' I said. 'If Bas doesn't want to be involved, I respect that. But I'm tired of sitting around and waiting. And I'd rather keep Hannover where I can see him.'

Ellery frowned. 'You don't know Hannover like Bas does,' he said.

'That doesn't mean I can't make this decision,' I said. I leant over the table and picked up the note, then refolded it and put it in my pocket. 'I'm the one who goes to the bunker every week. I'm not letting Bas make decisions for me.'

'Alright,' Ellery replied unhappily. 'Like I said, I'll speak to him.'

We left it at that, but the whole thing weighed heavily on my conscience. I needed Bas on my side like I needed to breathe.

I didn't know what I'd do if I lost him.

NINE

BY MIDDAY THE NEXT DAY, a gloomy atmosphere seemed to have descended on the entire house. I had expected that there would be fractures between us—God knew Bas and I had butted heads enough already—but I'd never expected this.

I had always thought we'd find a way.

We were *meant* to find a way.

Instead, I found myself constantly vacillating between competing thoughts. If I spoke to Hannover, I might get important insights into what was going on behind the scenes in our town. But if I did so, Bas wouldn't forgive me. If I didn't go, I missed that opportunity. And Hannover might decide I was no longer valuable and cut me off from the bunker—or worse, put a bullet in my head.

And then there was the thought that lurked in the back of my head, needling me in my soft spots.

Theo.

I owed it to him to solve this. Speaking to Hannover might give me the opportunity I needed to do that.

But Bas would never forgive me.

I was back where I started. Like a broken record, the thoughts replayed: as I helped out in the barn, as I showered, as I cooked lunch, as I trained in the gym. Again, again, again.

I couldn't escape them.

In the end, I was going to have to make a decision, and I would have to face the consequences alone.

Bas avoided me the whole of Sunday, which made the whole conundrum worse. If even the mention of going had him avoiding me, I just knew that if I went the fallout would be epic.

That evening after dinner, Ellery cornered me.

'Can I speak to you?' He shot a smile at Laura over my shoulder, before turning back to me with an uncharacteristically serious look.

I sighed. 'Yeah, okay.'

'Let's go out on the porch,' he said.

We trooped out the back door and onto the porch. A collection of mismatched chairs was scattered around a firepit. Ellery lit a lantern and sat on a bench, gesturing for me to sit cater-corner to him.

'I spoke to Bas,' he said in a low voice. 'Look—I know this isn't what you want to hear, but I don't think you should go.'

I sighed. 'Of course.'

Ellery shuffled his weight. 'Bas is my best friend. I've known him for almost three decades.'

'I know,' I said. 'But this could be our only chance—'

'Chances are made, not bought,' Ellery said seriously. 'Bas is afraid of losing you, and he's right. You have no idea what Hannover's done to him.'

'I know plenty.'

'Do you?' Ellery snapped. 'I was the one who helped get him out. You know that? You've known him, what, six months? I was the one who saw him when he was malnourished and scared and flinched every time someone touched him. Not you.'

I tensed my jaw until my neck ached. He was right, but it still felt like a blow. There were parts of Bas that I would never have access to, and again I felt that irrational jealousy. Bas might have shared the surface-level details of what had happened to him, but I was under no illusions that he wasn't holding most of it back. Whereas I was pretty sure I'd trusted him with all of my secrets by now.

'Bas isn't the only person at risk here,' I said. 'I'm the one in the bunker.'

'We're all equally at risk, and we all have an equal say,' Ellery said. 'And both he and I are against this.'

'And what if Hannover does know something that could help us?' I was snatching at straws—I didn't have a hope of convincing them. But the more they fought it, the more I wanted to do it. I had to know why Hannover had reached out to me, of all people. I had to know what he was planning.

We were back where we'd been months ago, when I'd first told Bas about the slaves in the NCC office, and he hadn't trusted me.

'And what if he's planning on shooting you on sight?' Ellery responded. 'Or worse, leading you along and then betraying you at the worst possible moment?'

'But why do you think I can't plan for that?' A slow, cold anger was rising in me. Not just anger because they were disagreeing with me, but a dangerous, vengeful wrath that had been growing in me for years and years now. 'You know what the trouble is?' I asked bitterly. 'You never trust me. Not you, not Bas. Every decision I make has to be questioned twenty times over. Every bit of trust I gain, I have to fight tooth and nail for. Why? Is it because I'm a woman? Because I was never a gang member? Why don't you think I'm capable?'

'You're perfectly capable, Harley,' Ellery said in a placating voice. 'But this is bigger than just you.'

'Bigger than just me,' I spat. Suddenly, I'd had enough. 'This is bigger than all of us, Ellery. It's our town. Thousands of lives… You know what? Fine, you can stay here and play your long game. That's what you think is right. And I'm going to do what I think is right.'

I pushed off the bench and headed for the door.

'Don't do this, Harley,' Ellery said. 'We'll find another way.'

'I'm tired of looking for other ways,' I said. 'People are dying. Being sold. And I have to stop it. Even if it means talking to people you don't like. You either trust me—or you don't. But you can't control me.'

I let myself in the door and headed upstairs, my heart pounding in anger. I felt oddly light, as though I'd finally gotten something off my chest that had been weighing me down for years. I was tired of people withholding their trust in me whenever I did something they didn't like—if I did that to Bas, he'd be furious. He had been furious for exactly that reason in the past.

And now he was going to learn that he couldn't control me any more than I could control him. He'd either have to accept my decisions or… or we'd both have to move on.

My heart hurt, but I'd do what I had to do.

No one said anything more about the topic, and we all kept ourselves busy with our own tasks for the next two days. I made arrangements to be able to get in and out of the main gates on Tuesday night, and after dinner, I quietly took the keys to the truck from their hook by the front door. Laura went to bed early, but I changed into jeans and my boots, then slipped downstairs and out into the frigid night air.

And stopped dead.

Bas was leaning against the truck.

'Ellery told you.'

I shifted my weight back onto my heels, staring up at him. My stomach was dancing the tango.

'No,' Bas said. 'I just know you.' His tone was dead. No emotion, no affection.

I swallowed.

'Bas…' But I couldn't come up with anything to say to him. It was as though I'd used up all my words on Ellery on Sunday night, and now I had none left. 'I need to do this,' I said weakly.

'You don't,' Bas said. 'Hannover is the last person you need anything from.'

'I'm not about to trust him.' We were rehashing the same lines we'd already said, but it was as though I couldn't help myself. 'I just want to know what… what he knows.'

'You're impatient,' Bas said. 'But this isn't something you can rush. You'll get yourself killed.'

'I don't want anyone else to die.' I stared at my feet, scuffing my boot against a tuft of grass that stuck up out of the frozen mud.

'This is about Theo, isn't it?' Bas didn't sound surprised. The name made my chest ache.

'What would you do if… if it was Ellery?' I muttered.

'I'd talk to you,' Bas said.

'I did talk to you!'

'Yes, but you didn't listen.'

I swallowed and finally glanced up at him. He stared at me unwaveringly.

'I have listened to you,' I muttered. He made me feel small, and that annoyed me more than anything. 'You don't listen to me.'

Bas's lips twisted. Abruptly, he jerked his head towards the car. 'Get in.'

My jaw dropped. 'What?'

'We're going to meet Hannover.' For the first time since I'd found him waiting for me, Bas sounded angry. I rubbed my hands against my thighs.

'But I thought you didn't want to.'

'I do listen to you, Harley. You want to do this. So we'll do it.'

'But—' I swallowed. 'But you don't want to.'

'No, but I'm not letting you do it alone.' Bas's expression was grave.

'Hannover will betray you, Harley. When he does, who's going to pay the price for that?'

My chest ached. 'Me.'

'No, I will.' Bas reached out and pried the keys out of my hand. 'I'm not letting you expose yourself to him. We've gone down that path before.' He stared me right in the eyes. 'Together or not at all, Harley.'

I relinquished the keys, and he unlocked the car.

'But this isn't what you want.' *Just let it go,* I thought desperately. But somehow I couldn't. Because as much as I hated fighting with Bas, him giving in to what I wanted was somehow even worse. 'I don't want to make you do something you don't want to do.'

Bas swung open the passenger door before turning to look at me. 'Then what do you want?'

'I…' I dug my fingernails into my palms. 'I don't want us to fight.'

My voice came out smaller than I'd intended.

'You were determined to go and see Hannover.'

I stared at him, uncertainty and need twisting up in my chest. My eyes stung suddenly, and a lump seemed to have lodged in my throat.

'You're really not going to stop me?' I asked.

Bas shot me the tiniest of smiles. 'No one can stop you when you put your mind to something.'

He stood back, holding the door open, and his face said *it's your decision* and *I trust you.*

Trust.

I took a deep breath. 'Are you sure? I can go alone.'

'No. If you go, I go.'

Of that, he sounded absolutely certain. And I wanted him to go with me more than anything—I'd feel safer with him there.

'Fine. Let's go.'

Bas nodded. Then he held something out to me. I took it from his palm—it was the earpiece I had been wearing to the bunker.

'Marco will back us up,' he said. 'Just in case.'

I bit my lip against a smile that threatened to engulf my face. Typical Bas. He thought of everything.

'Thank you,' I said.

'Don't thank me yet.' Bas gave me a hand up into the truck. 'We have to survive the night first.'

'I know.'

Bas shut my door and rounded the truck to climb into the driver's seat. My stomach squirmed like I'd swallowed a tin of worms as we made our slow way out of Freetown and into the wasteland. Bale Rocks was a distant glow on the horizon.

I felt a burning need to clear the air before we met Hannover—like this might be the last chance we got.

'Bas…' I cleared my throat.

'Yes?'

I stared out into the night, searching for words. 'How do you manage to forgive me every time?'

Bas was silent, focused on navigating us around the scrubby bushes and rubble. Finally, he said softly, 'There's nothing to forgive.'

'But I…'

'…made a hard decision, because that was what you had to do,' Bas said. 'That's the world we live in. One day, I might have to make a hard decision. Will you blame me?'

'Maybe. I don't know.' I swallowed. 'I don't think I'm as forgiving as you.'

'I don't think forgiveness is the right word,' Bas said. 'Flexibility. Plans change. There are a lot of variables. People do unexpected things. We have to adapt, or we get left behind.'

'I wouldn't leave you behind,' I murmured. 'I want this—us. More than anything.'

'One day you might,' Bas said. He slowed as we reached the road. We were headed for the north of Bale Rocks. 'There are aspects of me that you might not like as much as you think.'

'That's not true,' I said, unease boiling in my belly. Bas was principled and strong. I couldn't imagine anything about him that I'd dislike that much. 'I like you for who you are.'

'You don't know everything about me.'

'You'll tell me when you're ready.' I remembered the spur of jealousy I'd felt whilst talking to Ellery. But that didn't matter. It was irrational and spontaneous. It didn't define our relationship. 'I'm not worried.'

'Maybe you should be.'

'Do you want me to be?' I could make out the shapes of the buildings ahead of us. I wanted this conversation to be over—I regretted starting it.

'No. Yes.' Bas hesitated. 'I want you to be realistic, Harley. Hannover—'

'I am realistic!'

'Sometimes, but not about me. You only see one side of me.' He glanced my way, his eyes shiny and black in the low light. 'Hannover basically raised me from age ten,' he said. 'We're not as different as you might think.'

A chasm opened up in my chest. 'That's not true!' I exclaimed. 'You're nothing like him.'

'Dangerous. Ruthless,' Bas said. 'We can both look a man in the eye and shoot him.'

I shuddered. I'd seen Bas do that to Briggs.

'That doesn't make you like him,' I said. 'You're kind. You protect people. Hannover hurts them.'

'Me protecting you is what hurts you, Harley.'

My mouth dropped open. I'd never thought about it like that.

'But—'

'Sometimes,' Bas spoke over me in a dark tone, 'I think I'd rather hurt you. I'd rather lock you up, knowing what it would do to you. I'd rather keep you safe and have you hate me than risk losing you.'

I dug my fingers into my thighs.

'But you haven't.'

'I want to.'

'But you haven't.'

Bas shook his head. 'You're not listening.' Frustration coloured his words. 'I'm not a good person, Harley. I try—so fucking hard. I try to be worthy of you. I try to let you make your own decisions. But underneath, I'm just not a good person. And Hannover can push me over the edge. He knows what buttons to push—and he will push them. He'll try to drive us apart.'

'So we won't let him.'

Bas laughed, a dark, bitter sound. 'You're so sure,' he said. 'How? Where does that certainty come from? How can you know me better than I know myself?'

'I know you're a good person. If you were a bad person, you wouldn't have helped me all those times.' I struggled to push the words out around the lump in my throat.

'Bad people are capable of doing good things,' Bas said.

'But you're not a bad person!' My voice cracked. I sucked in a breath. Bas said Hannover would drive us apart—we hadn't even spoken to him yet and he was already managing. 'I trust you,' I said firmly. 'I don't want to fight.'

'And if I do something you can't forgive?' Bas asked.

'It won't come to that.' I knew what Bas was capable of.

'And if it does?' he pushed.

'Then I'll stop you. Or I'll help you.' I reached over and touched his knee. 'We're in this together.'

Bas scooped my hand off his leg and squeezed it. 'I hope I don't make you regret that.'

Bas parked around the corner from The Arsonist, but close enough that if we had to make a quick escape, we'd probably make it back to the car. Even so, I was uneasy. We were inside the checkpoints, and with the current lay of the land, Hannover had more friends here than we did. We couldn't bank on things going well.

Bas had snuck a gun in, and I had a knife, but how much would that help against Hannover?

Before we left the car, he did a mic check.

'Marco, come in.'

'You're clear,' Ellery said, his voice crackly over the earpiece. 'Position?'

'Just parked around the corner from the TA. We're moving in now.'

'Good. Keep me updated.'

The line went silent. I glanced at Bas. 'Ready?'

He nodded.

We walked the last few hundred yards and entered the pub. As it had been when I'd been coming here for the fights, it was crowded, cheerful, and a bit dilapidated. Smoke hung beneath the low ceiling, and people were crowded around standing tables and at the bar. I skimmed over the groups of workers drinking away their salaries, retirees playing bridge in dark corners, and businessmen making illicit deals.

'No Hannover,' I muttered.

'Let's check the back.'

Bas wound through the room and down a narrow passageway, into the back bar. Like the front room, this one was chock full of people. Most of the tables here were seated, and the frosted windows let in orange light from the yard. Right behind here was where I used to live.

A pang went through me. That old life might not have been much, but it had been safe and comfortable. I missed it.

'There,' Bas murmured, nodding into a corner. I looked over—at first glance, I almost missed Hannover, lurking in the shadows. He brought a pint glass to his lips and winked at me over it.

My stomach churned.

'Okay. Let's… let's get drinks.' I grabbed Bas's hand, mostly for my own comfort, and headed for the bar.

It seemed to take far too short for the bartender to serve us up our cheap beer, and I felt Hannover's eyes on me the entire time. I was giving him time to prepare; I wished suddenly that we'd thought to arrive first. He would have his witty repartee ready, and my mind was blank.

I grabbed the slippery, condensation-covered glass and led the way over to Hannover's table.

'Hannover,' I said through stiff lips.

'Welcome.' He waved a hand to the chair opposite. 'Sorry, I wasn't expecting you to bring company.'

I pressed my lips together. Bas borrowed an unoccupied chair from the next table over.

'So,' Hannover said as I sat. 'Harley. Or do you prefer Sierra these days?'

'Harley's fine,' I said before I could stop myself. 'I wouldn't want you to get confused.'

Hannover's lips twisted into his characteristic mocking smile. 'I see your sense of humour remains undiminished despite the present circumstances.'

'Why would it be?' I asked. 'Things are swell. The streets are safer than ever, the gangs have lost their foothold, and—'

'—and you decided to join the fights in the bunker as a… marketing ploy?' Hannover raised an eyebrow. 'Planning on selling a new fashion line, maybe?'

'Maybe I'd be good at it.' I pursed my lips, as though I was actually considering it. Beside me, Bas shifted uncomfortably.

'Get to the point,' he hissed at Hannover, his words almost lost in a swell of laughter from the bar.

'Oh, come now,' Hannover said. 'The game is half the fun.'

'No, it's not.'

Bas was ruining my game, as well as Hannover's. I bit my cheek.

'Oh, fine,' Hannover sang, brushing a lock of hair back from his face. The action pulled his jacket open enough that I could see his gun.

A deliberate warning. *Play my game, or it will be your last.*

'I had been wondering where you'd frittered off to, actually,' Hannover said. 'It can't be easy having a price on your head from two sides.'

Was that a warning, too? I leant back, cataloguing the other people in the bar. Were any of them Black Hands, here to support Hannover? Impossible to say.

'On the contrary,' Bas said flatly. 'It doesn't bother me at all.'

Hannover laughed. 'I suppose it wouldn't. You must be used to it by now.'

Bas stiffened. Under the table, I could see his hands opening and closing into fists. 'What do you want?' he demanded.

'I can't imagine Harley is enjoying life on the run too much,' Hannover said.

He was doing exactly what Bas had predicted: trying to drive a wedge between us. Did he really think it would be that easy?

No, he was probing for weaknesses. And when he found one, he'd dig his nails in.

Time to move the conversation along.

'I can't imagine you brought us here just to express your concern,' I said.

Unexpectedly, Hannover nodded.

'Quite so.' He leant forwards, resting his elbows on the table, and leered at me. I had a sudden urge to check if he could see down my top.

I resisted.

'And?'

'I propose an alliance.'

I coughed. *He what?*

'No,' Bas said.

'Is that a joke?' I asked. 'After everything? You can't possibly expect us to say yes.'

There was no way Bas would ever work with Hannover. And Hannover had to know that.

But Hannover smiled.

'You think I don't know what you're doing, Harley Benoit? You're not one to take things lying down.'

There was a note to his voice on the last two words that I didn't entirely like. It turned a statement of fact into an innuendo that made my skin prickle.

'I'm not taking anything from you, lying down or otherwise,' I said. Hannover laughed.

'It seems to me you're not in a position to negotiate,' he said. 'But then, I'm starting to think you like being the underdog. You certainly have a talent for turning a situation to your advantage.'

Hannover and I had totally different reads on my abilities—but I certainly wasn't going to dissuade him of that notion.

'There's no chance of us working with you,' I said. 'There's no way we could ever want the same thing.'

'So certain,' he mocked. 'But I think we want exactly the same thing.'

Uneasiness filled me, and I had to resist the urge to squirm. I glanced at Bas out of the corner of my eye. He was frowning.

'What do you think that is?' I asked.

Hannover steepled his hands under his chin. 'The situation in town has become difficult, wouldn't you agree? One might even say that the Iron Fists' power has gone to their heads,' he began.

He was being deliberately vague, and it made me want to gnash my teeth in irritation.

'If you're asking us for a deal, you'd better start telling us what you want from us,' I said flatly. 'You want to put a bullet in Jackson's head?'

'He wants us to do it for him,' Bas said. 'And then take the fall, whilst he sneaks out the back and avoids all consequences.'

Of course that was what he wanted. The moment Bas said it, all the pieces slotted into place. It wasn't the first time Hannover had tried to set me up to carry out an assassination for him, after all.

Hannover raised both eyebrows. 'Can you blame me for exercising caution? We are not necessarily amongst friends.'

The back of my neck prickled, and I darted a furtive glance around the room. No sign of anyone watching us. But that didn't mean they weren't.

'Even if we did want Jackson out,' I said, 'that doesn't mean we'd work with you.'

Hannover's expression shifted from serious to calculating, his eyes narrowing. 'But I can offer you something you want more.'

He nodded to Bas.

Bas stared stonily at him. 'What do you think I want?'

Hannover leant in, his gaze hungry. 'This is bigger than just Jackson; he's only the first domino that will make all of the rest tumble. When the time is right, I can make sure you're in the right place to take the shot on your father.'

I tensed, turning to stare at Bas. He was frowning.

Revenge. The one thing I knew kept him awake at night. The thought that haunted him when no one else was around.

'That's not worth partnering with you for,' Bas said coldly.

'Isn't it?' Hannover asked. 'Men more powerful than us have already decided your father's fate. Would you *really* want to hand the privilege of pulling the trigger over to someone else?'

No.

My stomach squirmed like it was full of snakes. Hannover had never meant to pry into my weaknesses—he'd known all along that I would bring Bas to the meeting, and he'd had his arguments prepared. *Damnit.*

'If this is a negotiation, you're going to have to offer more than the promise of a 'maybe',' I said tersely. 'As far as I can tell, you're getting everything you want out of this and making us do all the work.'

Hannover's gaze jumped to me, a smirk drawing his lips up. 'There would be other benefits, naturally. How long has it taken you to infiltrate the bunker? How little have you learnt so far? I can give you the information you need—'

'More empty promises,' Bas interrupted. I glanced at him; he seemed to have pulled himself together somewhat. 'Let's go, Harley. There's nothing in this for us.'

'You're going to pass up your chance?' Hannover asked.

'As long as my father dies, I don't care who shoots him,' Bas said. A single glance at him told me all I needed to know. He was tense, his fists clenched in his lap. Lying. 'If I were out for revenge, I'd shoot *you*.'

Hannover laughed. 'You'd like that, wouldn't you, boy?'

A dark look crossed Bas's face.

'Don't call him that,' I snapped. Hannover continued to chuckle. I stood, anger rushing through me. 'No deal,' I said. 'You need to learn to read the room, arsehole. I don't work with people who insult my partner.'

Partner. The word felt wonderful in my mouth. Throwing it at Hannover felt even better.

I shouldn't have said it, though; revealing our connection gave him power over us.

A mocking smile crept over Hannover's face. 'Oh, is that how it is? My apologies, I didn't realise I owed you congratulations. When's the wedding?'

'If there is one,' Bas snapped, pushing himself up so suddenly that his chair almost toppled backwards, 'you will not be invited.'

He turned to me. 'Let's go, Harley.'

I nodded and turned. Coming here had been a massive mistake. But at least now we knew what Hannover wanted, even if Bas's predictions had all been correct. I grabbed Bas's hand, and we walked away.

'Jackson's sitting on a force stronger than you can possibly imagine.' Hannover's voice was soft and deadly.

Bas ground to a halt. I took another step before I realised that he had frozen.

'What?' he asked quietly, turning back to face Hannover. I gripped his hand harder.

'Haven't you ever wondered what the military wants with our washed-up backwater town?' Hannover's voice was quiet, but somehow it still cut through the ambient chatter of the bar. 'We're hardly a high-value target.'

A conversation Bas and I had had long ago wormed its way into my memory. High-value targets like Brackfields were protected. Bale Rocks wasn't important. What was the army doing here in such high numbers?

I let Bas tug me back to the table.

'If you know something,' he growled, 'tell us now. No more messing around.'

'I don't know.' Hannover leant back and licked his lips. 'Seems to me you're content to be on the losing side.'

'We don't need to know what force Jackson controls to kill him,' Bas said. 'We only need one person in the same room as him with a loaded gun.'

'Are you sure it will be that easy?' Hannover asked. 'I seem to remember a situation rather like that where things didn't go exactly as you planned.'

He was talking about Bas's attempt to shoot Moriarty. I could hardly believe he'd said it so blatantly.

Bas ripped his hand away from me, and slammed Hannover against the wall, gripping the older man's neck. Every muscle in Bas's body was tense, his expression a well of fury deeper than I'd ever imagined. Hannover looked completely unbothered. In fact, he smiled.

'Careful, careful,' he said.

Around us, the room had gone totally silent. I could hear the warbling strains of the radio, which had been hidden beneath the chatter. A glass clinked. I looked around; everyone was watching us, and one man was reaching for a weapon under his jacket.

'Bas,' I said quietly, 'he's not worth it.'

Bas stepped back, rubbing his hands against his trousers.

'You watch yourself,' he said in a low voice that sent a shiver down my spine.

'And here I thought you didn't want revenge,' Hannover murmured.

'You'd regret making me change my mind,' Bas said.

Around us, the chatter was starting to resume. But not everyone was as at ease as they had seemed earlier. We were surrounded by enemies.

'We should go,' I said.

Bas kept his gaze on Hannover. 'I don't make the same mistake twice,' he warned.

'Famous last words,' Hannover replied. 'You need me much more as an ally than as an enemy, Sebastian.'

He stood, dusting himself off. 'You'll change your mind. And when you do—'

'We will not,' Bas snapped.

'—when you do, I'll be waiting,' Hannover said. 'You know where to find me. After all, you can have your revenge on me, or your father, Sebastian. But not both. Pick your battles.'

'I choose you.'

'That would be a very poor choice.' Hannover smiled. He stepped towards us, and I suddenly noticed something that I'd missed the last few times I'd seen him: he was limping. Something was wrong with his right leg.

He glanced down at it, then met my gaze and smiled. 'As a gesture of goodwill, I'll give you the first one for free. Next week, on

Wednesday, find a way to be on the square at four in the afternoon. Jackson is going to put on a show, and you won't want to miss it.'

He stepped past us, his injured leg dragging as he made his way slowly to the exit.

TEN

'IT'S A TRAP,' ELLERY SAID. 'It has to be.'

'We've already established that,' Bas snapped. He'd been on edge the entire drive home, and now paced the family room, exuding the same kind of energy that I imagined a lion in a cage would give off. 'But what's his goal? What can he possibly achieve on the square?'

'Publicly exposing us?' Ellery asked.

'Why would he want to?'

'Revenge?'

Bas shook his head in frustration. 'Hannover doesn't care about revenge. He's solely motivated by personal gain.'

'Fine.' Ellery pressed his fist against his mouth as he thought. 'So what does he stand to gain? Jackson goes after us, and Hannover can carry out… whatever he's planning whilst everyone is focused on us?'

'Assuming that exposing us is his goal,' Bas rejoined.

'True, true.' Ellery sat back, considering. Bas continued to pace.

'It probably isn't. Hannover is too good at the long game,' he muttered.

'But what's the long game here?' Ellery asked.

Bas turned at the window and started to pace back across the room. 'He'll give us what we want in the beginning. Lure us in. We don't trust him right now, and he knows that.'

'We're never going to trust him,' Ellery objected.

'Not trust.' Bas paused in the middle of the room, tapping his fingers against his thighs in frustration. 'A false sense of security, maybe?'

'Or cementing the alliance,' Ellery said. 'Give us something, just to sweeten the deal.'

I sat by, watching the two of them bounce ideas back and forth, a glass of whiskey clutched in my hands. There was something fascinating about the way they worked together. They were completely in sync, and I could tell they had known each other for years. Had Theo and I ever looked like that?

I didn't think so.

'So then he's not planning anything?' But even as he spoke, Bas shook his head. 'Hannover doesn't work that way. There's a reason he wants us on the square. Everything he does has an angle. Ten angles.'

'Maybe we're looking at this wrong,' I said.

They both glanced my way.

'Hannover said Jackson was planning something,' I continued. 'Maybe he wants to make sure we're there so we stop it happening.'

'Because he wants it to be stopped without it looking like he was involved?' Ellery asked.

'Could be,' Bas said. 'In which case, we shouldn't go.'

'But if we don't, we won't know what's happening,' I said. 'And Hannover will be a step ahead of us.'

'But we'll be alive and safe,' Bas countered.

'If that's our goal, why don't we all just stay here?' I met his gaze, challenging him with my eyes, refusing to let him look away. 'Just stay here, safe, and let the town burn.'

Bas stared at me.

'She has a point.' Ellery shattered the moment. 'It's not as though Mum wouldn't let you stay here forever. She fucking loves you.' He waved at Bas. 'Likes you better than me, I reckon.'

Bas rolled his eyes. 'There are different levels of safety.'

'There are,' I agreed. 'If we stay here, we're safe today, and tomorrow. If we get Jackson out, we're safe forever.'

'Or we're dead.'

'We have each other,' I said. 'We can find a way to get weapons in. Ellery will be on comms. We can get through this.'

'You are a never-ending fountain of confidence,' Bas said, but there was a sulky, childish note to his voice that told me he wasn't really fighting anymore.

'I try.' I stood and grabbed his hand. 'We face it together.'

Bas pulled a face. I bit my lip to suppress a giggle. I'd never say it out loud, but he looked like a five-year-old who didn't want to eat his vegetables. A moment later, the look was gone. 'Together,' he murmured.

Then he stole my glass and downed the contents. *Git.*

Before we could make our decision about the square, I had to survive another Saturday and another trip to the bunker—and this time, I had to do it knowing Hannover was watching me.

Just the thought made me shudder.

'They'll almost certainly make you fight tonight,' Ellery coached as he drove me over. Bas had a meeting with Turner and had very reluctantly ceded the escort job to Ellery. It had taken a lot of kisses to convince him, and I was still a bit giddy. 'If they leave it too long, people will think they aren't confident in you.'

'Any ideas on who they'd pit me against?' I asked.

'I'm guessing they'll ease you in. Someone good, but not too good. Probably a well-known name. Someone who fights every week.'

'Huh.' I ran through the options in my head. That eliminated all of the big-ticket fighters, but there were still a lot of candidates.

'It's probably going to be someone you know,' Ellery warned. Gravel crunched beneath the wheels of the car as we turned off the road near the junkyard. 'You'll have to be careful not to give yourself away.'

'I can do it.' Acting was a major component of dancing. If there was one thing I could do, it was keep a straight face.

'I'm not doubting.' He grinned at me through the low light. 'I'm not giving you kisses for good luck.'

'No thanks.' I couldn't help but smile. Somewhere along the line, working together so closely, Ellery and I had come to an equilibrium. I liked it. We felt more like friends than we ever had before. 'Hey, Ellery? Thanks.'

'For what?'

'Driving me?' I shrugged, trying to act casual. 'For being supportive? For helping me work things out with Bas?'

'You're good for Bas, you know that?'

'You think?' I bit my cheek, the familiar doubts swirling in my chest.

'Yeah. He's more relaxed now.' Ellery nodded. 'I think he's good for you, too.'

'It doesn't bother you? I know we…' I hesitated. '…had… something. For a while.'

'I blew that,' Ellery said. 'I can admit that. Anyway, things have changed now, right?'

Right. I had Bas. Ellery and I had grown apart.

'We're good now, right?' he asked suddenly.

'Yeah, we're good.'

'Great.' He leant back. 'You should go. Break a leg out there, yeah?'

'Thanks.' I opened the door. 'See you later.'

'See you. Give 'em hell.'

I jumped down and headed into the darkness. By now, the route to the bottling plant, and from there through the tunnels, had become familiar. Tyler still met me in the factory. It didn't surprise me; in fact, I was certain the order had come from Hannover. He knew who I was, and he didn't trust me.

No surprises there.

We made our way down the long corridors and finally ended up at Carlos's office. I'd been worried that he would be suspicious of me after my attempt at prying the previous week, but he was all business as looked me up and down.

'You're on the roster for this week. Diego Bartholomew. Tyler can point him out. He ain't a pro, but he moves fast. Don't fuck around, got it?'

'Yes, sir.'

Inwardly, I was cursing.

Diego. I was fighting Diego Bartholomew.

Of all the bad luck.

It wasn't just someone I knew personally—it was someone I had known for years. Diego and I had attended school together. He would almost certainly recognise me.

Fuck.

Was that Hannover's plan? To blow my disguise out of the water? But how would that benefit him at all?

No, this was just bad luck, plain and simple. And there was nothing for it but to power through.

'Anything I should know?' I asked stiffly.

Carlos eyed me thoughtfully. 'He likes to run his mouth. Maybe you should punch him in it early on. Keep the brat quiet.'

Tyler snickered. I smiled carefully. 'I'll keep that in mind.'

Carlos nodded sharply. 'You have an hour. I suggest you go warm up.'

'Sir.'

Tyler and I headed for the door.

'Diego,' Tyler said as we headed for the changing room. 'Wish I could fight him. I never get any good matches.'

'I'll swap,' I said.

'You can't.' Tyler scowled. 'Higher-ups won't let you. Anyway, you wouldn't actually swap. You're in it for glory, just like everyone else.'

You don't know how wrong you are.

I'd much rather be facing some no-name idiot than Diego in the cage—even if he didn't recognise me, I knew Diego's brand of wit all too well. And he'd always been talented at riling up my temper.

Damnit.

Nothing to be done about it, though.

'Glory's for men.' I tossed my head. 'Let's go warm up. And you better tell me all his weak spots. I want to knock this guy on his arse.'

My confidence was all feigned, and by the time my hour had passed, what little confidence I had managed to scrounge up had deserted me. This was *very* different to fighting in The Arsonist—there were hundreds of people, bright lights, nowhere to hide… All eyes would be on me.

'You should go,' Tyler said eventually, grabbing a towel and wrapping it around his neck. 'You're almost up.'

I nodded, too tense to respond properly.

'Good luck in there,' he added.

I nodded again.

'I'll be over there watching.' Tyler retreated, leaving me to face my fate alone. I checked my hand wraps, straightened my shorts and vest, and headed for the cage.

The noise of the crowd seemed to get louder as I approached. The lights blinded me. My vision narrowed, as though I was walking through a tunnel, and at the end of it… was my opponent. Diego Bartholomew, a wiry man with brown skin and curly brown hair—and a perpetual smirk on his lips. The smirk broadened as I stepped up beside him. A ref joined us and ran through the rules, but I hardly heard a thing over the roaring in my ears.

This was it. In a minute, I'd step into the ring and fight.

Oh God.

This was a huge mistake.

Could I still back out?

But the ref held up the rope and waved me forwards. I climbed under it and straightened up, stumbling a little. The lights were too bright. The crowd was too loud.

Diego followed me in, sauntered past me and took up his spot. All I could see was his smirk.

'… SIERRA!'

Screams filled the room, drowning out the roar of blood in my ears. I shook my head. I'd missed my introduction completely. I shuffled to my spot opposite Diego.

No matter how badly I wanted to run, I was committed now.

Abruptly, the crowd hushed. A pregnant pause took over the room, and my fingers tingled with anticipation.

Any second now, the fight would start.

I dropped into a ready position.

And then Diego's mouth moved.

'Harley Benoit.' His lips curled in a smirk. 'I thought I recognised you. You should not be here.'

I jolted in shock, almost losing my balance. *Oh fuck, oh fuck.* It was my biggest fear realised — and there was nowhere to run. I had to fight.

'Keep your gob shut!' I hissed.

'I'm not going to go easy on you because you're a girl.'

Abruptly, the panic evaporated. How many times had I heard that line? And how many times had the blind fury filled me that rose in my chest now? Fury at men who thought that they could mock me for being female.

'I'm not going to go easy on you because you're a sexist prick,' I retorted.

Diego's smirk only grew. He dropped into a fighting stance, and above us, the bell rang.

The fight was on.

He'd done me a favour — he'd washed away my panic and replaced it with raw anger, and the anger lent me clarity. I took a deep breath to centre myself. Fight now, worry later. I couldn't afford to give Diego the chance to take the upper hand, so I darted in and threw the first punch.

It landed, my fist thumping against his solar plexus. He doubled over, and I took a step back in surprise. Had I really just—

Wham!

I staggered as his fist came out of nowhere, striking the side of my jaw. He followed it up with a sweeping kick, and I stumbled and hit the deck with one knee. *Shit!* I rolled away and scrambled up, narrowly dodging his next blow.

He was fast. And focused. His next punch slipped beneath my guard and caught me in the kidneys. I retaliated, but only brushed the side of his arm as he blocked me faster than I'd expected. We traded blows, and he pushed me back step by step until my back hit the rope. Diego came in for his next jab—and I lashed out, catching him beneath the ear.

The screams of the crowd cut through my focus. Diego stumbled, and I went for a trip, but he twisted, and my grip slipped. We both fell, and he managed to roll away.

I scrambled up, breathing hard.

'You're good for a girl,' Diego said in between pants. 'Who taught you? Ellery?'

'Guess again,' I sneered. I threw another jab, hoping that he'd be off-guard, but he blocked it. Damnit, how was he anticipating my every move? I'd thought I was good at fighting, but Diego was solidly proving me wrong.

He launched a volley of punches, and I found myself being pushed back again. Desperate, I threw a sloppy kick at his knee, and somehow it managed to find a vulnerable spot. He stumbled. I jabbed him in the abdomen and went to my knee, trying to execute the same move I'd used to bring Donley down in my test fight, but once again, I couldn't hold Diego. I had to get him on the ground—it had to be his weakness, or he wouldn't be trying so hard to stay standing. But he rolled away before I could go in for a finishing blow, and when I tried to punch him, I caught his elbow right in my chest.

'Ah!' I grunted, throwing my arms up. Diego backed off and clambered to his feet. I stood as well, less steady than I'd been before. My arms ached, and I was struggling to catch my breath. Usually, I closed fights faster than this.

I looked him up and down. Where to strike next? What hadn't I tried yet?

'Giving up?' Diego mocked.

'Not on my life,' I hissed. I stepped in, jabbing fast. He blocked the first—the second slipped through, and I landed a glancing blow—I dropped down, firing off an overhand punch, even as his jab went over my head, then I grabbed him and drove my shoulder into his stomach.

This one landed. Diego hit the ground and I sprawled on top of him, immediately going for an elbow to the face. I felt his teeth dig into my skin—I went in for a second one—I had to finish it now before he managed to claw back the advantage—

'I know what happened to your boy Theo.'

I froze.

Diego's fist caught me straight in the mouth—pain erupted in my jaw as I tasted his flesh and the metallic bite of blood—

Fuck.

His thighs wrapped around me, and then he flipped us. I squirmed, but my focus had shattered. I couldn't remember how to get free. I tried to roll us, but he was in the dominant position, and he was too heavy. His fist slammed into my face, and my head crunched against the floor.

Tap out.

But I couldn't. Not yet. I managed to worm a knee free and force it into his gut. My fist flew up and glanced off his cheek. Diego grunted. He was tired too, and I could fight back. I could.

Another punch—this one he blocked. He leant his weight against my neck, and I choked.

'I know what happened to Theo,' he hissed.

'You—you can't get me with that,' I spat with my last breath. My vision was blurring. 'I know… he's dead.'

'Are you sure?'

The entire world crumbled. An explosion could have gone off right next to me, and I wouldn't have noticed—it was just me and Diego and my blurring vision.

'What do you mean?'

'If you want to know what happened, tap out,' he said.

I was losing anyway. I tapped the ground, one, two, three.

Diego drew back, and the screams rushed in. A moment later, I was being pulled to my feet, the ref talking at me. I shook my head, trying to displace the ringing. Breathing hurt my throat.

'…kay? Okay?' He shoved me out of the ring. 'Straight ahead. A medic will meet you.'

Someone pushed a towel into my hand. I wiped my face as I walked, and the towel came away streaked with blood.

I was injured?

I felt nothing. My brain was divorced from my body, occupied by a single circling thought that drowned out every other sensation:

Theo might be alive.

I had to speak to Diego. Now. But I looked around and couldn't see him. My feet had carried me all the way to the back rooms, and at that moment hands descended on my shoulder.

'Harley! Harley? Are you okay?'

I turned and stared blearily into Savannah's face. Her eyes were blown so wide I could see the whites all around her brown irises.

'Sierra,' I managed. 'I'm Sierra.'

'What?' She shook her head. 'You're concussed. Come on.'

'I'm not.' I dug my heels in, but Savannah dragged me down the hallway and into a room I'd never been in before: white walls, metal desk, doctor's chair. This must be where they patched up injured fighters.

'Sit.' She pushed me down on the chair and shone a light in my eyes. I flinched away.

'I'm trying to check your reactions—Harley, keep still!'

'Sierra,' I repeated.

'Harley!'

'You have to call me Sierra, Sav. That's what they think my name is. Weren't you listening when they introduced me?' I leaned away from the light. 'I'm not concussed, God damnit.'

'That's exactly what you'd say if you were concussed.' Savannah shook her head and gripped my shoulder. 'Stay still. I'll be done in a sec.'

She shone the torch at me again. I scowled at her but let her finish my test. Finally, she declared, 'Your eyes are reacting normally. How many fingers am I holding up?'

She raised her hand.

'Three,' I said, thoroughly annoyed. 'I'm not concussed.'

'I have to check. You took quite a few blows to the head.' Savannah marched to the desk and rifled through a bag, coming back with a pack of wipes. 'What the hell possessed you to join the fights? And using Mum's name?'

'I needed a name I'd remember,' I said. Experience had proven that I was bad with aliases. 'And no one knows that's Mum's name.'

'I know.'

'I didn't expect you to be here,' I reminded her.

Savannah tore open a foil packet. 'Hold still.' She gripped my face in one gloved hand and scrubbed at it with a wipe. I held still, feeling rather like a chastised child.

'You're lucky,' she declared after a few moments. 'Doesn't look like you've lost any teeth.'

'I don't see you checking Diego over like this,' I grumbled.

'Someone else can worry about him.' Savannah stepped back, and her eyes skimmed over me. 'Any other aches and pains?'

'Not until tomorrow.' I crossed my arms. 'Can I go now? I need to speak to Diego.'

'Not even a thank you.' Savannah glared at me. 'How could I forget how rude you are?'

I forced myself to take a deep breath. 'Thank you,' I muttered. 'But this is important. Diego knows what happened to Theo—'

'Theo, Theo, Theo.' Savannah rolled her eyes. 'So Diego knows you're here too? What's the point of the fake name, then?'

'He only recognised me just now.' I gritted my teeth. The pain was starting to set in as the adrenaline wore off. My lip throbbed where I'd cut it. 'The Iron Fists will kill me if they find out who I am. I told you before. You have to keep this a secret.'

'Don't fight again,' Savannah said.

'This isn't a negotiation,' I hissed. 'I'll die if you expose me, and so will you!'

Savannah glared. I met her gaze full-on.

'You are such a stubborn idiot,' she snapped. 'Fine. Diego will be in the next room down.' She pointed. 'Getting treated as well. Go speak to him, seeing as you don't want to speak to me.'

'I do!' I snapped. 'I came to the clinic to speak to you, and you told me to fuck off.'

'You came to the clinic to shout at me because I wouldn't do what you want.'

'Well, what the fuck are you doing now?' I yelled.

Savannah's mouth dropped open, and for a few moments we both just faced each other, breathing hard. Finally, I said, 'I'll come by the clinic again. When?'

'Not the clinic.' Savannah looked down at her shoes, studying them as though they were the most fascinating thing on Earth. 'My next day off. Thursday. Please… please don't bring your boyfriend.'

That rubbed me up the wrong way. Bas was important to me—and it wasn't as though Savannah had room to complain.

'You still dating Talbot?' I asked.

'He won't be there,' she said, her voice suddenly becoming firm and uncompromising. 'I won't speak to you if you bring anyone else. Come alone. You can meet me at The Arsonist.'

'I'll pick you up,' I said. I didn't want to have any more private conversations in the pub—if I went there too often, I'd risk getting recognised. Or someone might accidentally link Savannah to Hannover, which would put her in danger. 'We can talk in the car.'

'You can't drive,' Savannah said.

'Yes, I can. My boyfriend taught me.'

Her lips twisted, and for a second I thought she would cry. Then the look was gone.

'Fine,' she said. 'Three PM on Thursday outside The Arsonist. Now go.' She jerked her chin at the door. 'I need to prepare for the next fight.'

That was an excuse—I couldn't imagine what she might need to prepare; she had everything she needed right here. But I had to catch Diego before he could weasel off.

'Alright,' I said. 'See you soon.'

Savannah watched me out the door. I took care not to show any pain, but my chest ached, and my throat burned. I really hoped I hadn't cracked a rib. I was going to be black and blue tomorrow, for sure.

I could hear voices through the door to the next room, so I leaned against the wall to wait. Not a minute later, Diego stepped out.

'Thanks, doc,' he called over his shoulder. Turning, he caught sight of me. 'Hullo, *Sierra*.'

'Diego,' I said coolly. 'I did what you asked. Now talk.'

'Ah-ah. You know how it works, kitten. You scratch my back... I tickle yours. Scratching comes first, darling.'

That nickname. I hadn't heard it in ages, but it brought the anger right back.

'I'll scratch your face off!'

Diego laughed. 'Sure you will, baby. I tell you what. You ain't here alone. I want to know who's backing you and what they're planning. In return, I'll tell you about your boy Theo.'

'No way! I already gave you what you want. Now tell me what you know.'

Diego laughed. 'Kitten, kitten, kitten. So impatient.'

I took a step towards him. 'You think just because I lost I can't paint the walls with your guts—'

'Ah-ah-ah!' Diego wagged his finger at me. 'That would not be conducive to getting the information you want.'

I ground my teeth together and glared at him. I was itching to punch him—but I just knew he'd hold this over my head forever.

I stepped back.

'What do you want?'

'I already told you: information,' he said smugly. 'You're not operating alone. Someone taught you to fight.'

My annoyance warred with my need to know. I had to, had to, had to find out what Diego knew about Theo. I couldn't pass this chance up. But, on the other hand… I couldn't betray my friends. I needed time.

'We can't discuss that here,' I said.

Diego raised an eyebrow and glanced pointedly up and down the hall. 'No one's listening.'

I couldn't take the risk.

'We'll meet in town,' I decided. 'Wednesday. Five PM, on the square.' That would allow me to deal with Diego and Hannover on the same day.

'I can't do Wednesday,' Diego said.

'What, rich boy got too busy a schedule?' I asked. 'You decided your terms; these are mine.'

It was a pointless powerplay, really. He had the upper hand, and we both knew it. But to my surprise, he caved.

'Fine,' he said, with visible reluctance. 'I'll meet you outside Krani's at five on Wednesday. Don't be late.'

'Believe me, I won't be.' I strode off, my head held high, and my heart racing in my chest.

Finally, I might get some answers. Finally.

ELEVEN

I SPENT THE NEXT FEW DAYS in a state of heightened anxiety. I was practically vibrating with tension.

Diego knew something about Theo, and I had to know what it was. Was he alive? The thought was too painful to entertain for long. If I let myself feel hope, and it got dashed again—

I couldn't take it.

Instead, I focused on something I could control: our plan for getting onto the square.

'We're going to have to get through the second checkpoint,' Ellery said. His voice was somewhat muffled as he crouched and rifled through a toolbox. 'The main problem is that we'll be on foot, which means we can't get any weapons in unless we can hide them on us.'

'They'll frisk us,' I said. 'Especially if I'm there. They never miss a chance to frisk the women.'

'Maybe we should leave Bas behind.' Ellery smirked at me over his shoulder. 'Wouldn't want him to punch anyone.'

'Har har,' Bas grouched. He was leaning against a workbench on the side of the garage, his arms crossed over his chest. 'I can control myself.'

'Even if a bunch of soldiers are pawing all over Harley?'

'Yes,' Bas said stonily. I grinned at him, and his statue-like façade cracked for just long enough to let the hint of a smile out.

'You just want to be at the centre of the action,' Ellery said. 'And so does Kade. What are we meant to do? Put Laura on comms?'

'Why not?' I asked. 'No reason why she couldn't do it. And we might well want Kade backing us up on the square.'

Ellery fell into pensive silence, before disappearing around the back of the truck to tinker. For a while, only the sounds of metal on metal filled the garage.

'Fine,' his voice drifted over to us. 'I can show Laura how to use the comms. But that doesn't solve the problem of the checkpoint.'

'What we need is a contact in the army who could get us through,' Bas said.

'What I need is a sunny beach holiday in one of those Pre-Crash resorts.' Ellery's head appeared over the bed of the truck. 'Equally as likely to happen.'

But it wasn't. The realisation slammed into me.

'I know someone in the army.'

They both turned to me.

'Beg your pardon?' Ellery asked.

'Not directly,' I added. 'Benny. The weapons check at Krani's. His brother is in the army.'

Ellery raised an eyebrow and glanced at Bas.

'Do you know his brother's name?' Bas asked.

'No.' I grimaced. I'd barely paid a lick of attention to Benny the entire time I'd worked with him. Why was I so self-centred? The only reason I knew of his brother was because he'd told the soldiers when they'd given me trouble at the checkpoint.

No, wait, he had mentioned a name.

'Savage,' I said.

'Must be his surname,' Ellery said.

'That won't be enough,' Bas said. He turned to me. 'Would Benny help us?'

'How would we get a message to him?' Ellery asked. 'Unless you happen to know where the guy lives.'

'I don't.' I shook my head. My mind, though, was racing ahead. 'I don't, but I know who could get a message to him. Kayla.'

'Huh.' Ellery tapped his fingers against the back of the truck. 'That might just work.'

Nerves were high in the car as we drove into town on Wednesday. I was riding with Bas, and Kade and Ellery were in the truck. Kayla had come through for us, and she'd assured me that Benny would too, but even so, I couldn't help but imagine the worst-case scenarios.

They took all our weapons and we were defenceless against Hannover. They saw Bas's gang mark and shot him on sight.

We got separated.

Hannover killed all of us.

Hannover killed Bas and I had to figure out how to go on alone.

The only person I'd ever cared this much about before was Savannah. Just the thought of losing Bas made me feel as though a heavy weight was crushing the air out of my lungs.

No. I couldn't think like that.

I reached over and switched on the radio, fiddling with the dial until I found Crater FM. Then I fixed my gaze on the passing wasteland. It had been a while since I'd driven through this area during the day—the last time was when we'd come to see Savannah.

Would Savannah be there today?

Probably not. She had work.

As we drove, I started to notice the first signs of spring. The nights were still cold, but during the day it was getting warmer. And with the warmth came the weeds, growing out of all the cracks and crannies in the wasteland. Soon, they'd take over, and we'd have a carpet of green for a few brief months before the long, hot summer set in and the plants all died off.

The first checkpoint was no problem. Between Claire's mechanical abilities, Ellery's tinkering, and Laura's sewing skills, they had managed to rig a secret compartment in the back seats of Bas's car, where we'd hidden our weapons. After a routine check, we were in. The second layer of checkpoints surrounded the centre of town, and we'd be entering via a familiar access point—on Prospect Avenue, where I used to live. Bas pulled his car into the same side street we'd used when we came to meet Hannover, and once he'd cut the engine, he touched his fingers to his earpiece.

'Comms check.'

'Got you loud and clear,' Laura responded brightly. 'Position?'

'We're leaving the car now and proceeding on foot to the central checkpoint,' Bas said. 'Romeo, come in.'

'That call sign is not sticking,' Ellery grouched.

Someone sniggered. I bit my lip against a grin. We'd had a great deal of fun picking call signs last night—mine was Fennec, Bas was Fossa, Ellery was Lynx, and Kade was Pronghorn.

Not that that stopped us from teasing Ellery just a bit.

'It's *not*,' Ellery insisted. '*Lynx*, reporting in. We're through the western checkpoint.'

'Sure, whatever you say, Romeo,' Laura replied cheerfully. 'You're behind target.'

'There was a queue at the checkpoint. I'm only five minutes behind.'

'Percy and the Aces seem to be making trouble on that end,' Kade added. 'The western checkpoint is much better fortified than the eastern one.'

'Good to know,' Bas said. 'We're moving out now. Going dark.'

'Let me know when you're through the second checkpoint,' Laura replied.

Bas pulled his earpiece out. I passed him mine, and he slid them both into a secret pocket in the lining of his jacket. Then we retrieved our weapons and headed out.

Everything hinged on whether or not Benny had managed to get a message to his brother. If yes, then we'd get through. If no…

We'd be arrested.

I forced the thoughts out of my mind. I had to stay alert as we walked. If Hannover was right, and Jackson was planning something, then we weren't the only people sneaking weapons into the centre of town today. The square was going to be crawling with gang members.

How are they all getting in?

I added it to the mental list of questions I had for Hannover. If nothing else, I was going to get answers out of this sick partnership. I'd string him up and beat them out of him if I had to.

My thoughts seemed to be taking more and more violent turns lately. I clenched my fists, letting my nails dig into my palms.

Get a grip, Harley.

The checkpoint came into view as we rounded the corner, and I forced myself to relax. Show time.

We strolled up to it, nothing more than a couple out for a walk—in tactical gear and armed to the teeth.

'Halt!' A soldier descended from the guard hut. That was new, as was the boom that now blocked the road. There was also a large sign.

VEHICLE ENTRY ONLY WITH OFFICIAL PERMIT

An ominous feeling swirled in my stomach. I hadn't been to the centre of town in months now—and I wasn't looking forward to discovering how things had changed.

We slowed our steps as the soldier approached, his rifle held at the ready. He was covered from head to toe—helmet, armoured vest, heavy boots. The only part of him I could see was his eyes. *Intimidating.*

He stopped about five yards away. 'This is a weapons-free zone,' he called out. 'Hands where I can see them.'

We lifted our hands.

This was it. I held my breath.

'I'll be needing your papers,' the soldier said. 'Put 'em on the floor and back away.'

'We've been cleared already,' Bas said.

That earned us a frown. 'I'll be the judge of that. Names?'

There hadn't been time to come up with elaborate cover stories. All we had to go on was the story and names Kayla had given us.

'Simon and Hannah Jones,' Bas said.

The soldier made a hand signal to the guard hut. A moment later, a second soldier appeared. Unlike the first, he'd taken his helmet off, but a buff covered his nose and mouth. He was handsome, with hawklike eyes and brown hair that stuck up in tufts. Raf Savage, Benny's older brother.

'Jones,' Soldier One said. 'Says they've been cleared.'

Raf skimmed his eyes over the clipboard he was holding. 'Purpose?' he asked in a bored tone.

'We're running security for a small caravan—they've put us up in the bunkhouse on Leeside Street,' Bas said. 'Should all be on the form.'

It wasn't. In fact, everything Bas had said was a code. Raf's gaze flickered over our faces, then back to his clipboard. I thought my heart would burst right out of my chest. My arms were starting to ache.

'Got you,' Raf said. To his colleague, he added, 'I'll search them. Cover me.'

Soldier One nodded and jerked his head to Bas. 'Wait by the wall. Keep those hands up.'

Bas stepped away, and Raf approached to pat me down. His hands passed over both my knives and the handgun Ellery had loaned from one of his neighbours, but his expression never flickered.

'You're good,' he said. He searched Bas next, with the same professionalism, before backing away.

'Straight through the barrier, and don't dillydally,' he said.

'Thank you, sir,' I replied. A bit of politeness probably wouldn't hurt.

Raf's eyes crinkled. As we passed him, he murmured, 'Benny sends his regards.'

I couldn't afford to respond to that, so I marched past, tense and uneasy. I didn't relax until we were out of sight of the checkpoint. Finally, I risked sliding my hand into Bas's.

'I'm so glad that worked.'

'That was the easy part,' Bas replied, tangling our fingers together.

I really hoped he was wrong, though somehow, I suspected that he'd prove exactly correct. Hannover's words were still lingering in the back of my brain—he seemed to believe we would change our minds about working with him, and it bothered me that I didn't know where that certainty came from.

Because as far as I was concerned, the opposite was true. Bas and I would never work with him.

We left the checkpoint behind us, and as we approached the square, I found myself cataloguing the changes. The centre of town was dirtier than it had ever been before. Rubbish was piled in alleyways that used to be clear. I spotted a man hunkered down in a doorway. Several businesses that had been there all my life seemed to have closed.

At least there were no bullet holes here, no sign of the fighting that had occurred in the north of town—just drudgery. We passed several people going about their business, and all of them had a harried, stooped look to them, as though they were carrying the weight of the world.

I reached out and took Bas's hand. He squeezed my fingers.

'In here,' he murmured, tugging me down a side street that was relatively clear. A pile of blankets occupied a doorway, and I eyed it suspiciously. There was probably a person under there, and I didn't want to disturb them, but neither did I want them to overhear us.

'Let's go down the other end.' I tugged Bas past the doorway until we were a safe distance away. He pulled out our earpieces and passed mine to me.

I slotted it into my ear. Bas did the same.

'Fossa, reporting in,' he murmured. His codename.

'Got you,' Laura said. 'Position?'

'We're past the checkpoint.'

'Alright. Romeo's on his way. He'll meet you soon. South side of the square.'

'Got it,' Bas said.

'Good luck,' Laura replied.

We exited the alleyway and passed by Doleman's—the greengrocer Savannah and I had often bought food from. It was still open, but the shelves outside barely held any fruit or vegetables, and the shelves inside looked discomfortingly bare. Was the army holding up food deliveries? Or was this something else? Bas tugged me past, and a few minutes later we reached the square.

There was a surprising number of people milling about. The daily market was in operation, but the stall keepers seemed to be closing up. One man was pulling the canvas cover down on his stall, and two women were packing their wares into crates. A van pulled away, tooting at us to get out of its way.

We passed the fountain in the centre of the square and approached the Kranikovska. It stood tall, reassuringly familiar, with its dark brick façade and dirty moulding around the windows. Several people milled on the stairs leading up to the door, all of them wearing sturdy black tactical gear.

Security.

And as I watched, a familiar figure stepped out through the doors and approached one of the guards: tall, blond, weedy.

Evander Hardwick.

I hadn't seen him in a long time, and I was honestly better off for it. The sight of him now sent a shiver down my spine, and I turned my head away, afraid he'd notice me.

'Harley?' Bas asked.

'Hardwick's here,' I murmured. 'On the steps.'

Bas skimmed over the men assembled there. 'The blond one.'

I nodded.

'If he's here, then that means the mayor is probably coming,' I said.

Bas frowned.

'Why would Jackson meet the mayor out in the open?' I added.

'We don't know for sure that Jackson is going to be here in person,' Bas said.

'True.' I cast a glance around the square. Townspeople were starting to filter in. More importantly, there were men standing in the alleyways. As I watched, I caught the wink of light on metal. A rifle.

'Armed guards blocking the exits,' I murmured.

Bas nodded. 'I count at least fourteen,' he said.

'Who do you think they work for?' My neck prickled, and my shoulders were tense. This felt a lot like a trap. If Hannover wanted us cornered, he'd done an excellent job of it.

'Probably the mayor,' Bas said. 'If there's an event on, they'll want to make sure no one can snipe him.'

He nodded to a building on the northwest side of the square. 'There's someone on the roof.'

I squinted. Another armed guard, by the looks of it.

'Why would Hannover want us to watch the mayor's event?' I mused.

Bas frowned and tugged me towards the south side. 'This might have been a mistake.'

I was inclined to agree, but we couldn't leave. I had to meet Diego afterwards.

'Let's meet Ellery and see what he thinks,' I said.

There were more armed guards on the south side of the square, and up close I decided they were the mayor's security team. I didn't recognise any of them, in any case. They watched us rather too close for comfort as we found a doorway to wait in. It felt like ages before Ellery and Kade finally came into view.

'There is a *lot* of security around town,' Ellery said in a low voice as he joined us. Unlike Bas and me, he was dressed inconspicuously, in jeans and a jacket, with a cap pulled low over his face.

'Too much,' Kade agreed. He, too, was in street clothes. Their cover was that they were new to town and looking for work.

'We should leave,' Bas said. 'This is a trap.'

'We're here now,' I said. 'We may as well stay and find out what's going on.'

'I agree with Harley,' Ellery cut in. I glanced at him. 'I don't think this is a trap,' he said. 'I heard the soldiers on the eastern checkpoint wittering about some event that a bunch of them got pulled in for. Hannover's not going to pull anything with this many guards around, anyway.'

'This is exactly the kind of chaos Hannover would enjoy,' Bas said.

'Let's follow the plan,' Ellery said. 'We all know the code to fall back. At the first sign of danger, you can give the order.'

'How do you plan on getting between the guards?'

'We can always go inside,' I said. 'Krani's will hide us.'

'Krani's will hide *you*,' Bas said.

'You're with me.'

I met his gaze. He sighed. 'Fine. But be careful.'

'Always.' I squeezed his hand, before pulling away. Bas shot us one more warning look before heading off. Ellery watched him as he went back the way we'd come.

Our plan was to split up and cover all angles: Bas up high, Kade on the south side, covering the main access road, and Ellery on the entrance from Prospect Avenue—the other major access road. I was supposed to stay near Krani's. Given that a crowd was starting to form near the fountain, my job would be the easiest. All I had to do was blend in.

'Don't be a hero,' Ellery said. 'If the signal goes up, you head straight for the rendezvous point, got it?'

I nodded.

'Be safe,' Kade said.

'Yeah, you too.' Ellery headed off in the same direction Bas had gone. I nodded to Kade and took off for the centre of the square, leaving him to find his position.

Showtime.

By now, the square had filled up with people. I wove between mothers clutching their children by the hand, construction workers who'd just got off shift, haggard businessmen in their second-hand suits, and an assortment of workers who'd obviously been coaxed out of the local businesses to beef up the crowd. I caught sight of Anna and Benny and veered away to avoid both of them. As I ducked around a mother herding a group of children under five, I bumped into someone and took a step back.

'Sorry—'

'Harley?'

My mouth dropped open as I stared, stunned, at the short black woman with voluminous curls piled on top of her head. A woman I hadn't seen in ages but had missed like I'd miss my own limbs.

'Brenda,' I spluttered. 'What are you—'

'Harley, it is you!' she hissed. She grabbed me by the upper arms. 'What are you doing here? Where have you been—oh my God, your *hair*!'

Her voice grew louder and louder, and I winced.

'Brenda, shh,' I muttered. I glanced around urgently, but no one seemed to be paying us any mind. 'Keep it down. No one can know I'm here.'

Brenda shook her head, her curls bouncing.

'I can't believe you're here,' she hissed. 'W-we thought you were dead!'

Tears welled in the corners of her eyes. *Shit.* Emotional stuff was not my forte.

'I'm sorry for worrying you. I had to leave town for a while.'

'Why?' Brenda dashed the tears away. 'Couldn't you have left a message?'

Abruptly, she yanked me into a hug, her arms crushing the air out of my lungs. 'I was so scared,' she hissed.

'I'm sorry.' I had to swallow; my throat felt all blocked up. 'I didn't mean to worry you. I just…'

I couldn't tell her the truth. That would only scare her even more. But what lie could possibly capture everything that had happened?

'Things got complicated,' I mumbled.

Brenda squeezed me harder before she finally drew back. 'Your life has always been complicated,' she said fondly. 'When did you cut your hair?'

'Oh.' I reached up and brushed my fingers through the short ends. It was becoming a strange sort of nervous habit—every time I did it, I felt a cocktail of frustration, regret, hope. 'Yeah. It's… more practical.'

'It suits you.' Brenda smiled. 'I love it.'

'Thanks.' How many times had I heard that now? But I couldn't seem to see what they saw—when I looked in the mirror, I only saw what I'd lost.

I shook my head. The crowd jostled around us, making way for a large, black vehicle that had just driven onto the square. I leant in to speak to Brenda.

'Do you know what this whole thing is about?'

Brenda nodded. 'The mayor is giving a speech—all the local businesses were ordered to close. Rocky asked me to come see what was up.'

Rocky was Brenda's boss.

'Do you know what the speech is about?'

'Haven't a clue.' Brenda shrugged. 'It'll be more of the same, won't it? We've had two government officials into the garage to reassure us that the army is here for our protection already this month.'

That was new. I'd have to tell Bas later.

The vehicle had reached the steps of the hotel by now. I had to crane my neck to see around the crowd. Ellery's voice came over my earpiece.

'What's going on?'

'I don't have a clear view,' Kade said. 'I'm moving.'

'Fossa?' Ellery prompted.

'I have visual,' Bas said. 'Someone has just arrived. Looks like security is moving off the steps.'

'The mayor will be inside the hotel,' I said. Brenda shot me an odd look, but I ignored her. 'He usually is.'

'Do you have line of sight?' Ellery asked.

'No. I'm moving.'

I started to squeeze between people.

'Harley!' Brenda grabbed my wrist. 'Where are you going?'

'To get a better look. Come on.'

'Fennec, who are you talking to?' Ellery asked.

'Brenda. Don't worry; I can handle it.' I slipped around two men who were bundled up in thick coats, and suddenly I had a clear view. The car was stopped right in front of the steps, next to a second one which I hadn't noticed arriving. As Brenda stepped up beside me, the first vehicle pulled off. There were two men behind the second one, their heads together.

'Has anyone got a clear view?' I hissed.

'Negative,' Ellery said.

'Car is blocking them,' Bas said.

'I'm—' Kade broke off. 'Shit. Security. Going dark.'

Ellery cursed down the line, but we couldn't worry about Kade, because at that moment the second car rolled towards the edge of the square, leaving me with a clear view of the two men and the bottom of the steps.

The first was Jackson, wearing a long leather trench coat, his bald head shining in the watery sunlight. The second, I didn't recognise. He was an unusually tall man, with broad shoulders and a sturdy build. He had a thick thatch of black hair and incredibly, unhealthily pale skin. Sickly. His shoulders were hunched, bunching his heavy coat around his neck and upper body. He took the stairs at a slow pace, and I noticed that he was heavily favouring his left leg.

I could recall the faces of almost everyone I met, and I had never seen him before in my life.

'Who is that?' I asked.

'Who's who?' Ellery asked.

'Guy on the stairs.' Jackson had reached the top and taken up a casual position against one railing.

'I still don't have visual. How many people are there?'

'Two at the moment. B—Fossa?'

Silence.

'Fossa, come in,' Ellery said.

Bas was silent, but as I listened, I could pick out heavy breathing in a shaky rhythm.

'Bas,' I said quietly, 'who is it?'

'Moriarty,' he said. 'That's Moriarty.'

The leader of the Black Hands was here?

'Moriarty's here?' Ellery hissed. 'Shit, that's—Fennec, pull back. Don't get close to him.'

'Why?' Even as I said it, I was pushing closer, weaving between the crowd. Brenda dogged my heels.

'He never leaves the compound,' Ellery said. 'What's he doing here?'

'Harley, pull back,' Bas said suddenly.

'No way!'

Straight ahead, the hotel doors swung open, and the mayor stepped out. He struck an unimposing figure: squat and balding, with a weak face and posture. Certainly, he was an uninspiring presence compared to Jackson and Moriarty, who both dwarfed him. Two men followed him out, and I recognised both of them as well: Richard Godfrey, an overweight man with curly blond hair, who ran the biggest real estate company in town, and Rochester—Bas's father.

I swallowed.

'Rochester's here,' I reported. 'And so is Godfrey.'

My legs tensed with a sudden need to run. I had a bad feeling about this. What had Hannover said to Bas? *Men more powerful than us have already decided your father's fate.*

The only person in the Black Hands more powerful than Hannover was Moriarty, and Moriarty was here.

And so was Hannover. I noticed him suddenly, lurking in the shadow of the steps.

'Hannover's here.'

'Harley, back down,' Ellery said. 'You're too close.'

'He can't see me,' I said.

'If things go wrong—'

'Ladies and gentlemen!' The mayor's words cut through the square. 'Thank you all for coming today. I know that… the situation has been difficult…'

He paused to consult a piece of paper in his hand.

'…recently. However, it is with greatest pleasure that I announce that today our town will be entering a new era of peace.'

The restless feeling began to coalesce in my body. There were no good reasons I could see for him to be talking about peace with two gang leaders standing beside him.

What has he done?

'Beside me stand several preeminent members of our society. Some of them have been long-time allies. Others have fought many battles to stand here today. Today, all of us will be closing a deal that will see an end to the fighting. As of today, we stand together for Bale Rocks!'

Hesitant applause rose around me, but I had no will to celebrate. I grabbed Brenda's hand, gripping it hard.

'Who are they?' Brenda whispered. 'You know everyone in this town.'

'Leader of the Iron Fists, leader of the Black Hands,' I murmured. 'And a bunch of rich old men. If I tell you to run, run. Okay? Don't wait for me.'

'But…'

'Don't.' I squeezed her hand. 'I can take care of myself. You have to get home for your boys.'

Brenda nodded, her body tense.

'Today marks the end of the divisions in our town.' The mayor stepped forward to the edge of the steps, waving Jackson and Moriarty over. The two gang leaders approached more slowly. 'Let us shake hands, to symbolise our union going forward.'

In front of him, Moriarty and Jackson clasped hands, shaking briefly. A glance passed between them. They broke apart, and then each of them shook hands with the mayor. The mayor passed his microphone to Jackson.

'Thank you.' Jackson's voice was low and rough, carrying across the square like a winter wind. 'I look forward to a fruitful collaboration.'

The mayor nodded eagerly. Then his eyes widened in shock, and he looked down.

CRACK!

Distantly, I heard Ellery and Bas swearing and shouting warnings, their voices mingling together over my earpiece, but none of it registered. The only thing I could focus on was the bloodstain growing across the front of the mayor's brown suit jacket as he keeled backwards and collapsed at the top of the stairs.

TWELVE

THE CRACK OF THE GUNSHOT seemed to echo around the square. No one moved. No one spoke.

No one even seemed to be breathing.

Then, all at once, the square erupted into chaos. I was jolted this way and that as people fled in every direction, most of them covering their heads as though bullets might rain down from the rooftops at any moment.

'Harley!' Brenda cried, yanking my hand. 'Come on!'

Movement atop the stairs caught my eye. I dug my heels in.

'Wait!'

Jackson had turned to Godfrey. None of the remaining men on the stairs seemed concerned—either about being shot or about the body at their feet. I watched them exchange words, far too quiet to hear over the racket of the crowd.

'Fennec, come in!' Ellery said urgently.

'Lynx—not now—' I sidestepped around a mother who was corralling her children. Jackson held out a hand, and Godfrey shook it.

Jackson and Godfrey.

I'd been wrong all along.

Thud! I stumbled as someone crashed bodily into me.

'Oof.' I grabbed someone's shoulder to steady myself, and a man in overalls shot me a doleful glare. 'Sorry!'

I seemed to have lost Brenda. I whirled around, trying to find her, but there was no sign of her amidst the pandemonium.

'Harley, come in!' Ellery repeated, callsigns forgotten. 'Bas, Kade? Anyone got visual on—'

'I'm here,' I interrupted. I wheeled around, trying to plot an escape route. Panicked crowds were bottlenecking around the nearest alleyways. No one seemed to be able to get out. 'Where are you?'

'West side. Where are you?'

'Still at the front. We were wrong—'

'That's not important right now,' Bas interrupted. 'Get out of there.'

'I'm heading for Lynx.' I dived into the crowd and was immediately submerged in a maelstrom of flailing limbs. 'Jackson wasn't working with the mayor,' I continued. 'He was working with Godfrey. I saw them shaking hands.'

It was all so obvious now. Jackson had planned this all along. All he'd needed was to get rid of Sayle so he could become top dog. Then he'd used the relations he'd been nuturing with Godfrey—the new faction that Rodney had mentioned to me months ago, that I'd completely forgotten about—and Moriarty to cement his coup. Now the mayor was gone, and Moriarty and Jackson were in charge.

Men more powerful than us.

Godfrey would be the next to fall; there was nothing stopping Jackson from taking him out now.

No, there was: the army. How was he going to get around the army?

I burst out of the crowd again by the fountain, and I climbed over the rim and marched straight through the empty basin.

'LADIES AND GENTLEMEN, ORDER!' The loudspeaker cut through the noise of the crowd.

I froze. All around me, people were grinding to a halt and whipping around in a panic. And I was exposed, alone in the fountain. I sprinted to the edge and climbed out, and for a moment, standing on the rim, I could see over everyone's heads.

Godfrey held the microphone.

'No one needs to panic,' he continued. I jumped down, squeezing between a group of women who were clinging to one another, and carried on making my way towards Ellery. 'Everything is under control.'

Yeah, but whose control?

'What you have witnessed today is the process of renewal. Sometimes, like a snake, we must shed our old skin in order to grow a new, stronger skin.'

Someone sobbed loudly near me. I held in a scoff.

'Who's speaking?' Ellery asked.

'Godfrey,' Bas said.

'He's a snake, alright.'

'Yeah,' I muttered, darting through a gap in the crowd. And suddenly, I was on the edge, and an expanse of open space yawned before me. Fifty yards ahead lay the safety of the buildings.

Run for it?

I glanced around. There was a sniper somewhere on the roofs, and I was betting Jackson could call in another shot whenever he wanted. But he didn't know I was here, and even if he did, I doubted he'd risk shooting into the crowd for me.

'Lynx, where are you exactly?' I asked.

'North corner of Prospect.'

I turned until I could see that corner. Ellery was nowhere in sight, but there was a stack of boxes that I assumed he was using as cover.

'No one has anything to fear from this process of renewal,' Godfrey continued. 'The leadership transferral will be smooth, and our union of trust with the Iron Fists and Black Hands will go ahead.'

'I can't reach you,' I hissed. 'It's too exposed.'

'Stay put,' Bas said. 'They've got the entire square covered from the roofs.'

Damnit, damnit, damnit. I slipped back into the crowd. Could I go around the side?

'I will be taking over as the interim mayor,' Godfrey continued. 'I consider it my highest priority to ensure the safety and security of the entire town…'

'Harley!'

Brenda appeared beside me. I pulled her into a hug, relief drowning out my fear.

'You're okay,' I hissed.

'What's going on?' she asked. 'Did you know this would happen?'

'No, but listen.' I pulled back so I could look her in the eye. 'You need to get out of here. Don't get swept up in the crowd. Wait by the buildings until they open the roads again. Then go straight home. And be careful.' I swallowed around a lump in my throat. 'Things are about to get much more dangerous in town. Don't go walking alone at night—and don't let the boys, either.'

'Of course.' Brenda took my hand. 'Will you be okay?'

'I'll be fine. I'm… I have friends who'll help me. Don't worry about me.'

Brenda nodded. 'When will I see you again?'

'I don't know, but soon.' I pulled her into another hug, breathing in the familiar, safe scent of cooking oil, perfume, and soap that made up

Brenda. The scents of home. 'Keep safe,' I whispered.

'You too.'

Then she backed away, swiping a tear out of her eye, and I waved at her to go. I watched her weave between the crowd until she was out of sight.

Now it was my turn. Meandering between the people, I made for the nearest edge of the square. Godfrey seemed to be drawing his victory speech to a close.

'...We will now be opening the exits. We ask you to depart in an orderly fashion...'

There was no applause or any real signal that the speech was over, but all at once the crowd surged towards the edges of the square. I stuck to the line of buildings and made my way towards Ellery, and when I got close, he stepped out from behind the crates.

'Harley!' he hissed. 'Are you okay?'

'Where's Kade?' I asked. 'Did he check in again?'

Ellery shook his head. 'I'm going to move to the RV point. Hopefully, he made it out.'

'Maybe we should look for him,' I said. 'I have to stay anyway. Diego—'

'He'll have bailed,' Ellery said. 'If he was here in the first place. He probably knew.'

Was that why he'd been so reluctant to come today?

'I have to try,' I said. 'I'm going to get to Krani's—I'll double round to the church later.'

The church was our rendezvous point. It was inside the checkpoints, which, with the benefit of hindsight, had been a stupid idea. Would the army shut down the checkpoints? How were we going to get out?

Worries for later.

'I don't like it.' Ellery touched his earpiece. 'Fossa, report?'

'Security has opened up,' Bas said tersely. 'You'll be able to exit via the south, onto River Way.'

'And the hotel?' I asked.

'Jackson and Moriarty have loaded into the cars. The body is still there.'

The body. My stomach did a somersault.

'We're going to have to be ten times more careful getting out than in,' Ellery predicted.

'We need to get out of here,' Bas said.

But at that moment, I caught sight of someone dodging along the line of buildings, heading for the corner that would lead to the hotel parking lot.

Exactly the someone I wanted to see.

Diego!

Ripping away from Ellery, I sprinted across the square. 'OI!'

'Harley, no!' Ellery hissed, but I ignored him, putting on a burst of speed.

Diego caught sight of me and took off like the devil himself was behind him. Down an alley, around a corner. I shot after him. He had a longer stride, but I was fitter—and I'd been training like mad recently. He got tired, and I caught him and shoved him against the wall of a nearby townhouse.

'Oof!' he grunted. 'The fuck, Benoit?' He squirmed. I caught his arms and pinned them against the wall.

'Why'd you run?' I snapped.

'Because I don't need to be seen talking to you after the mayor just got topped!'

'We had a deal!'

Diego managed to worm an arm free and shoved me in the chest. 'Get off me, you mad woman!'

'Shove me again and I'll knee you in the balls.'

'Just let me the fuck go!'

I stepped back, freeing my gun from under my jacket. No chances. Diego blanched, staring at the weapon in horror.

'How the fuck did you get that through the checkpoint?'

'I have my ways,' I kept it pointed in his direction. 'Did you know that was going to happen? To the mayor?'

'Of course, I fucking didn't! You think they'd tell me?'

'I think you have ways of finding things out if you want to.'

Diego rolled his eyes. 'Benoit. I hang around in brothels, fuck men, and fritter my dad's money away on dumb side businesses. No one tells me shit. You think anyone takes me seriously?'

I narrowed my eyes at him. 'I think you'd very much like me to think that no one takes you seriously.'

'You think—' Diego shook his head and ran a hand through his curly brown hair. 'You're a mindfuck, you are. I don't know how Theo ever handled you.'

'Theo didn't have to handle me. I'm a grown fucking woman.'

Diego smirked.

I glared at him. 'What's so amusing?'

'Nothing!'

'Right. Well, any second now Bas is going to get here and paint the walls with your brains. So if you don't want him to know that you recognised me, then get the fuck on with it and tell me what you know.'

Diego looked appropriately cowed. 'Bas is here?'

'Who else did you think I'd be working with?'

'I didn't think…' He paused. 'Of course. It makes sense. He defected around the same time you disappeared. And there's a price on both of your heads. Of course you're working together. Wait.' His gaze sharpened. 'You're fucking, aren't you?'

Great. This, I didn't need.

'We are not,' I said.

'You are.'

For fuck's sake. 'My relationship is none of your business. Nor anyone else's business, so don't you dare get any ideas about gossiping. Or I'll be the one shooting you.'

Diego scowled. 'You can't do that. You need me.'

'I definitely don't.'

'Yes, you do.' He screwed his face up and blurted: 'Theo's alive.'

I froze. For several seconds, my brain struggled to grasp the enormity of that statement. Theo wasn't—He couldn't be—

'How?'

But Diego's expression had shut down. 'Not here. Not now. Neither of us should be seen talking.'

'You can't do that to me!'

'You know I'm right, Benoit. Get out of here. Go back to your man.'

'I want to see him!' I had to see him. I needed to see for myself. 'Where is he?' I'll—'

'No. You need to get out of here. The army is looking for a murderer, and Jackson will be on the hunt for a scapegoat. You want that to be you?'

He was right. I gritted my teeth. 'When, then?' I forced out.

Diego shuffled his feet and glanced around anxiously.

'When?' I repeated.

'I'll contact you.'

'Absolutely not.' He'd disappear off the face of the planet and I'd never get my answers. 'Give me a time and day or take me now.'

'I can't.' I lifted the gun slightly, and his gaze jumped to the barrel, the colour bleaching out of his skin. 'Fine! Fine! Tomorrow. But you better come with answers.'

'When tomorrow? Where should I meet you?'

'I'll pick you up.' He wet his lips. 'At the fuelling station on the Crater's Edge road.'

'That's miles away!'

'Not from where we're going.' Diego glowered. 'Come alone. If you bring Bas, the deal is off.'

There went that plan. But I could worry about how I was going to bring backup later. I had bigger issues right now.

'Fine,' I said. 'I'll meet you there tomorrow morning.'

'Ten,' he said. He looked around again. He seemed more worried about being caught than about the fact that I had a deadly weapon pointed at his chest. Interesting.

Another worry for later.

I lowered the gun and tucked it back into my jacket. 'Don't you dare make me regret this.'

'I'm the one who's going to regret it, you psychotic bitch.' Diego shoved past me and took off. 'Don't follow me!'

I let him go; he sprinted around the corner and vanished from sight, leaving me with a whirlwind of emotions in my chest.

The mayor was dead.

Theo might be alive.

And I had no idea what was going to happen now.

THIRTEEN

WHEN I REACHED THE SAGGING red brick church, with its metal roof, I found Ellery sitting on a pile of crates with the NCC logo on them, waiting. He stood as I approached.

'What the fuck?'

I flinched. 'I can explain.'

'Oh yeah, I'd love to hear the explanation that has you running *into* danger to chase down *Diego Bartholomew*.'

I bit my lip. Put like that, it sounded really stupid.

'He had information about Theo,' I said meekly.

Ellery frowned. 'And how did you know that?'

'Because he recognised me during my fight at the bunker the other night.'

Ellery raked a hand through his hair. 'For fuck's sake.'

He stabbed the button on his earpiece. 'I've got Fennec. Fossa, report?'

'Still on top of the building,' Bas said wryly. 'No sign of Pronghorn?'

'What happened to Kade?' I jumped at the new voice. I'd practically forgotten Laura was on the line, too.

'He ran into trouble with security.' Ellery's lips turned down into a grim line. 'I really hope he hasn't been arrested.'

My stomach lurched. That would be… really, really bad.

'Diego mentioned that Jackson would be looking for a scapegoat,' I said.

Ellery's gaze jumped to mine. Then he said, 'Fossa, can you try and get a visual on Kade? Laura, last position?'

'He was at the entrance to the little street on the corner,' Laura said. 'I think it's called the Slipway.'

'Yep,' I said. 'Bas won't be able to see in from above, though. That street is covered.'

Ellery frowned.

'Okay,' he said. 'Here's what we're going to do. I'm going to try and find Kade. Fennec is going to go and fetch my car and bring it as close to the RV point as she can get.'

'What? I want to help!'

He levelled an absolutely furious glare at me. 'No, you can get the car.'

I was in trouble. I shuffled my weight, feeling about two inches tall. 'Fine, I'll get the car.'

Ellery softened a bit. 'Thank you,' he said in a gentler tone and held out his keys. 'It's parked over by the Hawke and Tern.'

I nodded and grabbed the keys. Ellery gave me one last searching look before he took off back towards the square. I sighed and headed for the checkpoint.

Relegated to fetching the car.

And it was my own damn fault. I never learned.

It was about a ten-minute walk to the checkpoint on Prospect Avenue. I was desperate for news about Kade, so I kept my radio on as I hurried through town, but all I heard was the occasional chatter as Bas and Ellery confirmed their locations. Finally, the checkpoint came into view. I slowed as I approached it; there was a queue of people trying to get out, and I wasn't entirely sure what awaited me.

Were they searching for the shooter? Or had the army been in on the coup? It seemed to be the former—they were frisking everyone with more vigour than usual, and as I watched, a guy was pulled off to the side for a more thorough search. They probably weren't looking for a five-foot-six female, but I wouldn't be able to hide my weapons when they frisked me.

I couldn't see Benny's brother, either.

I couldn't risk trying to go through the checkpoint. I turned and started back towards the square.

And ran straight into a soldier.

'Keep it moving!' he bellowed. 'One-way traffic only, please.'

I tried to dart around him, but he grabbed my arm. 'Thataway, lady.'

'I'm not—I was only looking for someone—I need to—' My tongue seemed to tangle as he steered me into the queue.

'One-way traffic only,' he said. 'We have a lot of people to get through.'

'But—'

'Save it.' He pushed me into the queue between a stooped, white-haired lady and a man with his two teenage sons, then headed off to corral the next unfortunate soul. I looked around for an escape, but there were soldiers everywhere, and they suddenly seemed determined to force all the traffic through the checkpoint as fast as possible.

Did they get some kind of command from someone? To get us all out?

More importantly, could I run for it?

A vehicle rolled up the street and stopped just beside where I was standing. Four more soldiers hopped out, all carrying rifles.

Uh oh.

This was bad.

Heart in my mouth, I shuffled forwards as the queue moved. Every step brought me closer to the checkpoint, and certain arrest. *Fuck.* I needed to get a message to Ellery, but I didn't dare try and contact anyone now. *In fact, I should take my earpiece out…*

The queue moved again. Four groups ahead of me. Three.

What should I do?

Two. One.

I reached the front. A soldier with a green cap casting his face into shadow beckoned me forwards.

'Where you headed?'

'Uh.' Cover story. What was my cover story? 'Um, Freetown.'

'Freetown,' he echoed.

'Yeah. I live there.' *Fuck, fuck, fuck.*

'And you're… walking there?' He raised an eyebrow.

'No… I have a ride.'

'Hmm. Jacket open.'

I swallowed and looked around for salvation. There was none. I opened my jacket to show the gun holstered at my side and resisted the urge to squeeze my eyes shut. If I was about to die, I wanted to see it coming.

The soldier barely reacted. He made a delicate hand signal to his colleagues, and one of them approached. A tall black man whose ankles and wrists poked out of his too-small uniform. I recognised him. Dusty.

'Lay your weapons on the ground, slowly, and take a step back,' the soldier said.

'I have information that might be of interest to you.'

The words tumbled from my lips before I'd fully processed the implications of what I was about to do.

'We don't care. Weapons down or we'll be forced to escalate, lady.'

'About a military deserter.' My mouth kept going, though inwardly I was panicking. What was I doing? This was stupid. 'You asked me months ago, and I said I didn't know, but I know his name and I know where you'll find him.'

Soldier One reached for his gun, but Dusty raised a hand to stop him. 'We've met before, haven't we?' he asked.

'I used to work at the Kranikovska,' I said.

'I remember you. You used to live up this street.' He pursed his lips, then seemed to come to a decision. Jerking his head towards the guard station, he said, 'Over there. No sudden moves. Hands up.'

I complied. What the fuck else could I do? Hands raised above my shoulders, I stumbled over towards the little hut. When I passed the boom blocking the road, I thought my heart would burst right out of my chest. I was through—but how did I get away from the army?

The only thing I could do now was sell the story I'd offered.

A third soldier climbed out of the guard station, a man with blond hair and a square jaw. I vaguely recognised him, too—he'd been with Dusty in the Kranikovska that night they'd asked me about Talbot, right? Probably.

Hopefully.

'What's this?' he asked.

'She says she has information on our deserter,' Dusty said in a significant tone.

'Oh yeah?' Blondie asked.

'Greg Talbot,' I said. 'That's his name.' They seemed to have forgotten about taking my weapons, and I had to keep them talking if I didn't want them to remember. 'Tall guy with red hair and freckles. Blue eyes.'

Dusty exchanged a look with his colleague.

'Yeah,' Blondie said. 'That's the one. How do you know him?'

I had a lump in my throat so large I fully could have believed it was my own heart lodged there. 'He… he's a member of the Aces. The gang. Works in the casinos over in the west. I think he lives out that way, too.'

Would that be enough? *Please, please let it be enough.*

Blondie raised his eyebrows. 'The Aces, eh? Know which casino he works at?'

'No,' I said. 'I know the gang hangs around the Lucky 2089 casino sometimes, though.'

'Hmm,' he said. 'Not a lot to go on. Are you in contact with the guy?'

I bit my lip. 'I… I could be.'

'Could be?'

'He… he's friends with my sister…' I cleared my throat. I needed to sound confident, but my courage had deserted me. I was betraying Savannah, and I knew she'd be furious if she ever found out I had told them about Talbot.

Blondie's eyes sharpened. 'Can you arrange for him to be in a certain place at a certain time?'

'I… I'm not sure.'

He shot me a derisive look. I hunched my shoulders.

'Do you know anything?' he snapped.

'Ease up, Ryan. It's not like she can just conjure the information out of midair,' Dusty said.

'Not much of an informant if she can't actually get us to the guy.'

'I can try and arrange something and then let you know,' I blurted. 'If you tell me when you'll be on this checkpoint.'

'I don't think that's how it's going to work,' Ryan said. 'Do we look like a bunch of lads down the pub? We'll give you a time and a place, and you'll make sure you're there with Talbot.'

'I don't know if I…' What could I say? I'd never intended on going through with the scheme and now they were backing me into a corner. Could I just bail on the meeting?

Worry about it later.

'Alright.' I cleared my throat. 'When?'

'How about we meet on our day off and discuss a plan?' Dusty suggested. He gazed at me with a sympathetic light in his eyes. I snatched the reprieve with both hands.

'When?'

'Sunday. At the Kranikovska?'

I *could not* take that risk. I shook my head hastily.

'Talbot and the Aces have spies in the Kranikovska,' I said. 'Let's meet somewhere else.'

Dusty and Ryan exchanged glances.

'There's the pub on Busker Street,' Dusty said slowly.

'That place is a dump,' Ryan complained.

'The Arsonist,' I muttered.

'That's the one,' Dusty said.

I sighed. We were just as likely to be seen in The Arsonist, and I could get into even more trouble there. I felt like a fly trapped in a spider's web.

'Alright,' I said.

Dusty nodded. An apologetic look crept onto his face. 'We still have to confiscate your weapons.'

'I need them!'

'For what?' Ryan asked. He looked me up and down. 'What do you even do?'

'I'm working on a farm in Freetown,' I said in as snooty a voice as I could muster. 'And I need them to keep myself safe driving back and forth, thank you.'

'And I need to uphold the rules,' Ryan shot back without missing a beat. 'So I'll be taking the gun, thank you.'

Fuck.

Dusty's radio powered to life with a buzz. 'Prospect checkpoint, come in?'

Dusty held a finger up to me. 'Roger?'

'We got a BOLO heading your way. Command says he needs to be arrested discreetly if possible.'

Dusty and Ryan exchanged glances. 'Copy,' Dusty said. 'I'll pass on the message.'

He lowered the radio back to his belt. 'Off you go,' he told me. 'And don't make me regret it.'

'What's a BOLO?' I asked.

'None of your business. Get lost,' Ryan snapped.

'But—'

'Go.' Dusty grabbed my shoulder and steered me down the street. 'Seven o'clock at The Arsonist on Sunday. Got it?'

I nodded and continued walking, even though curiosity was buzzing in my gut like bees. Who was getting arrested? Not one of my friends, hopefully?

Speaking of which…

I switched on my earpiece. 'Lynx?'

'Copy.'

'I'm through the checkpoint. Is everyone alright?'

'So far, so good. What are the checkpoints like?'

'They're searching everyone.' I bit my lip. 'You guys will need to find another way out. They're pulling men aside.'

'Will do. What's your ETA?'

I'd been about to double back and see if I could find out what was going on at the checkpoint. But I changed my mind—Ellery would be annoyed.

'Fifteen minutes?'

'Great. See you soon.'

I sighed and flicked the microphone off again. A glance back at the checkpoint told me nothing had changed. I could stake it out, or I could make sure my friends got out safely.

Easy choice. I set a brisk pace for the Hawke and Tern. Soon enough, the parking lot came into view. This was the pub I'd used to meet Hardwick in, back when he'd had me spying on the Iron Fists for him. It seemed like the distant past, although in real terms it was only a few months. But so much had changed for me since then.

I'd be able to handle Hardwick much better now.

I bit my lip. It was probably a good thing I didn't have to, though. We had enough trouble on our hands.

Speaking of trouble, I probably didn't want to linger here. I made straight for Ellery's car and climbed up. I had to adjust the seat—Ellery was quite a bit taller than me—and as I looked in the review mirror, I froze.

Someone was crossing the carpark. Someone I did not want to see today, of all days.

Savannah.

What the hell was she doing here? This was the second place I'd seen her that she had no business visiting—first the bunker, now here… Savannah didn't know anyone here, did she?

Well, there was Talbot.

My stomach squirmed uncomfortably.

She could be meeting Talbot here—the Aces did occasionally use the Hawke and Tern as a hangout, as far as I was aware. But then again, why not just meet him at her flat? She'd had him over there before.

The other alternative was that it had something to do with work; maybe a function of some sort?

Maybe I should go say hi?

'Fennec, come in,' Laura said suddenly over my earpiece. 'Can you talk? Come in.'

'I'm here,' I replied.

'How far out are you from the car?'

'Just reached it.'

'Right. Lynx wants you to collect the team from the south bank, corner of Main and Docker Roads.'

Why there?

'Copy.' I cast another glance over my shoulder. Savannah had reached the door and was pushing her way inside. If I went after her, I'd be late picking the others up, and Ellery would have even more reason to be annoyed with me. Savannah was my private business, and I couldn't let that get in the way of meeting the others—they were in more danger than she was.

Even though it chafed.

I would just have to ask her about it when I saw her tomorrow— and hope she didn't lie.

I turned the key and put the car into gear, then pulled slowly out of the parking lot. Once I was on the road, I looked back at the pub. Savannah was out of sight. But I could have sworn a curtain twitched at one of the upstairs windows. Had someone seen me? Recognised me?

Nothing I could do anything about now. I accelerated down the side street, heading for the river. When I reached the corner of Docker and Main, Ellery, Kade, and Bas were all waiting there, looking none the worse for the wear. I sighed, tension flooding out of me with the gust of air. We'd all made it out.

'Harley!' Ellery swung the door open. 'Want me to drive?'

'Yeah, alright.' I clambered down. He clasped my shoulder and squeezed it gently. Hopefully, that meant we were okay. I turned to the other two, performing a quick visual check of Bas; he looked as he had earlier. No visible injuries or bloodstains, and his expression was neutral, if a bit tired. He smiled at me when I met his eyes. I turned to Kade last.

'Kade! You're alright! I was so worried.'

'I'm fine.' Kade spared me a smile. 'I got an unexpected assist. I'll tell you when we get home.'

We were going to have the conversation of a lifetime when we got home, and I was in no way looking forward to it. I managed something which might have been a distant relative of a smile.

'Can't wait.'

'This is fucked up.' Ellery slumped on the sofa, his head in his hands. 'Fucked. We are totally fucked.'

Bas stepped over to a chest of drawers and began stripping his weapons off and checking them over. 'Why did Hannover want us to see that?'

'To show us how fucked we are?' Ellery mused.

'He's trying to back us into a corner.' I grabbed a bottle of whiskey and started lining up glasses.

'Pour me one, too,' Laura said suddenly. I glanced at her. Laura didn't usually drink much, but today her face was pale, her skin drawn too tight over her bones. I handed her the first glass I filled.

'Thanks,' she mumbled and took a healthy sip.

I passed the other glasses out. Bas set his aside, but Ellery drained his in a single go.

'If he's trying to back us into a corner, he's got us,' Ellery said. 'The Black Hands and the Iron Fists run the town.'

'They were already running the town,' Bas said. 'Why make it obvious *now*?'

That was a good question. It had always been pretty apparent that the mayor wasn't really in control. Godfrey and Jackson had been pulling the strings all along. Now, they'd brought it all out into the open.

'They obviously don't think they need to hide anymore,' Kade said. 'Something has changed.'

'They've found some way to pacify the army?' Ellery shrugged.

'Maybe the army was listening to Godfrey all along,' I said.

A heavy silence settled over us as we all puzzled over what had happened. Whatever way you looked at it, the mayor being killed was not a good development.

'Hannover has the answer,' Ellery said finally, 'doesn't he?'

'That's what he wants,' Bas said. 'Us to come crawling back to him.'

I felt the burn of curiosity like an itch beneath my skin. We could go back to Hannover and ask what he had planned—but what price would he extract from us in exchange for that information? On the other hand, we could continue on blindly, only noticing the clues after it was too late.

Damned if we do, damned if we don't.

'We can't play into his hands,' Ellery said.

'What's the alternative?' I asked.

'Harley—' Bas started.

'Genuinely!' I sat forwards, whiskey slopping over my fingers. 'I don't want to trust Hannover. But what else can we do?'

Helplessness washed over me. At this rate, Jackson would be able to round us up and shoot us.

'We can't risk it,' Bas said. 'You saw what happened last time.'

'I know, but...' I had no argument. I gripped my knee and stared into my glass. The day was catching up with me; my head felt like it weighed a hundred tonnes, and I wanted nothing more than to crawl into bed.

'We might have another option,' Kade said suddenly. 'When I got caught on the square, Rodney Rochester was the one who bailed me out.'

'Rodney?' I asked in surprise.

'Who's that?' Laura asked.

I glanced at Bas. His mouth had pinched up like he'd tasted something sour.

'Bas's half-brother,' Ellery said quietly.

'You have a brother?' Laura gawked at him.

Bas shuffled his weight. 'What did Rodney want?' he asked sharply.

'He was looking for you,' Kade said. 'It sounded like he'd been looking for a while.'

'No surprise there,' Ellery said cynically. 'Guy doesn't take no for an answer, does he?'

I cringed. I'd been sucked up in Rodney's desperate quest to reconnect with his brother before, too.

I studied Bas; his shoulders were tense, and I could see the tendons in his neck standing out.

'I'm not sure that's a better option,' I said cautiously.

'Safer, at least,' Ellery muttered.

'I could speak to him,' I said. 'It doesn't have to be Bas.'

'No,' Bas said. 'If you go, I go.'

'We don't have to make our minds up tonight,' Ellery said. 'And there might be other options, anyway. Turner, for one. He's been monitoring the Hands because of the slaving activities—he might have seen something else we could use.'

It was a possibility, however small. But we all needed hope right now.

'We can try tomorrow,' Bas said. He pushed off the wall and headed for the door. 'I'm going to bed.'

'Wait,' I started. Bas paused and raised an eyebrow at me.

But the words seemed to evaporate right out of my throat. I was too tired to think, let alone face the condemnation of the others over getting recognised by Diego.

'Can I… can I talk to you? After I've showered?'

Bas nodded. 'Of course.'

'Thanks.'

He left, and after a moment Ellery got up, too. 'He's got the right idea. Let's call it a night and regroup tomorrow.'

FOURTEEN

THE THUMP OF MY FIST on Ellery's bedroom door echoed the thudding of my heart against my ribcage.

Knock-knock.

'Just a sec!' Ellery called. A moment later, the door opened, and I got a face-full of Ellery's bare chest.

'Oh,' he said. 'Not who I was expecting.'

'Who were you expecting?' I demanded. I'd literally told him I was going to come over here.

'Never you mind.' Ellery snatched a shirt and yanked it over his head, then squeezed past me. 'Have at it, then.'

He headed down the hall. A few steps later, he realised I was still watching him.

'I'm trying to give you a moment alone with your boyfriend, Harley. Better make the most of it.'

Heat washed through my cheeks. I turned back to the doorway to find Bas watching me. He was sitting on the edge of his bed.

I'd never been in Ellery's room before. Two twin beds took up most of the room, and a chest of drawers occupied the rest. There wasn't much space. I could tell which side was Bas's without asking—Ellery's side was an unholy mess: clothes jumbled on the floor, shoes lying about haphazardly, and a collection of discarded mugs. Bas had a single bag and a pair of boots sitting neatly at the foot of his bed.

'Hey,' I said awkwardly when the silence stretched too long.

'Hi,' Bas said.

'I… Can we talk?'

He nodded. I eased inside and shut the door behind me—then immediately regretted it. Would people get the wrong idea? Would *Bas* get the wrong idea? Did I want him to get the wrong idea?

Maybe I should leave it open…

Bas cleared his throat. 'What's wrong?'

'Are you mad? That I ran after Diego earlier?' I clasped my hands in front of me, then immediately unclasped them.

'No,' Bas said.

'Really?'

'I expected it.'

Ouch.

'I'm not that bad!'

'I can tell when you're hiding something,' Bas said. 'You've been cagey since you went to the bunker on Saturday.'

I winced. 'I didn't mean to keep it a secret,' I said. 'There just weren't any good moments to discuss it.'

Bas stared at me gravely for a few seconds. Then he sighed.

'Come here. I don't like arguing across the room.'

I crept over to him, stepping daintily over Ellery's mess. When I reached his bed, I stopped in front of him, my knees just shy of brushing his. Bas hooked his hands around the backs of my thighs and looked up at me.

'What did you find out?'

'Uh…' For a moment, I couldn't remember what I needed to say. His dark green eyes were too distracting.

'Harley?'

'Diego… He has information about Theo.' I swallowed. 'He told me Theo is alive.'

'And you believe him?' There was no judgement in Bas's words.

I nodded. 'I had a gun pointed at him at the time.'

Bas pursed his lips in thought. 'Rhett wasn't lying either, though.'

'Maybe someone helped Theo when he was injured,' I suggested. My heart clenched at the thought of Theo, injured and alone.

'Someone like Diego Bartholomew, though?'

I shrugged. When he put it like that, it sounded crazy. Diego was shallow and self-absorbed, and he and Theo had never been friends. And I'd known both of them since our school years.

What was more, Diego and his friends had always seemed to be more allied with the Black Hands than the Iron Fists. Although, now that I thought about it, Diego's closest friend was Louis Godfrey, son of Richard Godfrey, who had just declared himself interim mayor.

Which meant this might be a trap… or an opportunity.

'I'm meant to be meeting him tomorrow,' I said. 'At the service station on the Crater's Edge road.'

Bas's eyes narrowed. 'That's pretty far out of town.'

'I know.' I shuffled my weight from foot to foot. 'He insisted I go alone, as well.'

Bas shook his head immediately. 'Not out into the wasteland. What if something happens?'

'I can handle myself.'

'What if you get a flat tyre? Or break down?' Bas asked. 'What if Diego has an ambush set up? We'd be an hour away. Too far to help.'

I didn't need him to tell me those things; I'd thought of all of them before I knocked on his door. 'What do you suggest then?' I asked. 'He said the deal was off if I brought you.'

Bas glanced down as he thought, tracing his finger idly over the seam of my jeans. I bit my lip. It tickled, and more importantly, my brain kept going places—places like I was in his room, and he was touching me, and we were alone.

How long would Ellery be out?

'You can't take Ellery, Kade, or me,' Bas said. His brain, of course, had remained strictly on track. 'That will put Diego on high alert. That leaves Ms Ellery, Laura, or Claire.'

I bit my lip. 'He specifically said to come alone.'

'The other option is that one of us tails you. But he may well have taken that possibility into account already.'

I weighed the options. Bas was right: driving into the wasteland was dangerous. And unlike Bas, Theo, Ellery… I didn't have the skills to keep myself safe. Sure, I could drive and fight. But that didn't mean I could outrun slavers, nor did I know how to repair a car if something went wrong. Diego could easily post a lookout who could warn him if someone was following my car. Which left Bas's idea: take one of the other women.

Collette, Ellery's mother, was capable and efficient, but I didn't know her very well. She also seemed to prefer not to leave the farm—I'd never even seen her leave Freetown. Laura was unassuming, and Diego probably wouldn't mind her being there, but I wasn't sure how helpful she'd be in a crisis. For one, she didn't know how to drive, as far as I was aware, and for another, I didn't know how much experience she had out in the wasteland—probably no more than me.

And that left Claire.

I sighed.

Claire and I were not what you'd call the best of friends. She was caustic and sarcastic, even to her own family, but she seemed to have taken to me particularly badly. It was probably my fault; we had almost nothing in common, and it wasn't as though I'd made much of an effort to get along with her.

Well, I'd have my chance on the hour's drive tomorrow morning.

Scrubbing my hands over my face, I muttered, 'Ellery's not going to like me taking his sister into danger.

'He'll live,' Bas said. 'Besides, there's always the option of him hiding in the back for the entire trip.'

An inappropriate snort burst out of my nose at that thought. There was no way Ellery could keep silent stuffed in the boot of a car for an hour. He'd bellyache like mad and drive me nuts.

'I'd rather you do that than Ellery,' I said. 'I think we might kill each other.'

'I would if you really wanted me to,' Bas said seriously.

I'd be most at ease having Bas along. But it wouldn't be fair on him when there was an easier solution: Bas was claustrophobic, and I knew being stuck in the boot of a car would be torture for him.

'It's okay,' I said. 'I'll ask Claire. I'm sure we can manage not to kill each other for one car journey.'

Bas smiled, but the expression quickly faded back into his typical frown. 'If Theo is there…'

His question trailed off into nothingness, and I was afraid to prompt him to finish it. The same thought had been weighing heavily on me. What if Theo was there? What would happen next?

I could bring Theo here, but he didn't play well with other people, and besides that, I didn't know if he'd even want to come here or be part of our plans. He'd been pretty eager to leave Bale Rocks behind. Would that have changed?

And what would I do if it hadn't changed?

'I'm not leaving.' I dropped my hands to rest on Bas's wrists. 'I'm committed to our plans. I'm…' Why was this so hard? 'I want to stay with… with you.'

A weight seemed to ease off my shoulders at that confession. It was only a fraction of what I needed to tell Bas, but at the same time, it was the most important thing.

Bas turned one of his hands to capture mine. 'I'm not going anywhere,' he said seriously. 'I'll stay with you as long as you'll have me.'

'Forever?' I asked, my voice small.

'If that's how long you'll have me.'

My heart felt like a tiny bird fluttering against my ribcage. I was sure if I raised my hands to my eyes, I'd see they were shaking. But all I could look at was Bas. I traced the familiar contours of his face: the stubble on his jaw, his high, strong cheekbones, his piercing green eyes. I reached out and brushed my fingers over his jaw. He used his grip on my hand to tug me towards him—down—until he could kiss me.

The world fell away.

Never mind that I was worrying about Theo, that Ellery might come back at any moment, that the mayor was dead and we had no idea what was going to happen next. All I cared about was pressing closer to Bas, tangling my fingers into his soft hair. He sucked on my bottom lip, sending heat rushing through me, and wrapped an arm around my waist to pull me closer.

'Sit,' he murmured into my mouth.

I straddled his legs, my knees bumping the edge of the bed. Bas raked his fingers through my hair and kissed me again, this time with an edge to it. I could feel his need in the way he gripped my shoulders, like I might disappear at any moment, and it made me brave. I ran my hands up his arms, across his shoulders, to the neckline of his T-shirt, and nudged it aside so I could trace his collarbone. He broke the kiss and slid his hands to my waist, working my top out of my jeans.

'Can I?'

'Please,' I mumbled.

He hiked my shirt up, his fingernails tracing lines over my skin. I shuddered. 'That tickles.'

'Sorry.' Bas ran his nail up to my belly button. I tensed.

'Bas.'

He smirked. 'Who knew the great Harley Benoit was ticklish?'

'Shut up!' I yelped. I slid backwards on his legs. He hooked his fingers through my belt loops to stop me.

'Don't go,' he said seriously. 'I was still busy.'

'Busy tickling me!' I grabbed his hands. 'I *will* leave.'

'I'll stop.' Bas tugged on my belt loops, and I let him pull me closer, wrapping my hands behind his neck for balance. We stared at each other, and the moment stretched between us like a spider's web, fragile, yet strong. I didn't want to break it.

'I wish I could stay here tonight.'

Bas laughed, a sudden, deep sound that drew a smile to my lips. 'No you don't. Marco snores.'

'So does Laura. We could put them together and we could share.'

'That would be a bad idea,' Bas said.

'I think it's an excellent idea.'

'Mm.' He traced a line over my stomach again. I realised he was touching the scar I'd received when Briggs had confronted me behind the Kranikovska months ago. 'We'd get distracted, and we have a lot to do tomorrow.'

Distracted.

My cheeks heated again. I scrubbed my hands over them. Bas found me distracting.

That sort of comment shouldn't have got to me; we'd been together for three months. But it did. Heat pooled in my belly.

'I wouldn't mind getting distracted,' I said, biting my lip. Bas reached out and pressed his thumb against my lips.

'We can't afford to slack off now. You know that.' He might have said it, but the fire in his eyes said something else.

'I'm sure we could afford a few minutes,' I said coyly. Sucking in a breath, I gently bit down on the tip of his thumb. Bas's gaze darkened.

'I don't think it would be just a few minutes,' he murmured.

'Really?' I was breathless all of a sudden, as though he'd used up all the oxygen between us.

'I might need longer than that to—'

The door swung open. Bas dropped his hand, and cold disappointment flooded my chest. I twisted to see Ellery standing there.

'My eyes,' Ellery groaned. 'This house is too fucking small.'

I could have died. If a hole had opened up in the ground right then and there, I'd have dived straight into it without looking back. *God.*

'That's what you get for not knocking,' Bas said.

'This is my room. I'm not knocking.'

'Then you get what you deserve.'

'Prat.'

Bas shrugged, a little smile playing on his lips. The moment was over. I clambered off Bas's lap with a sigh.

'Tomorrow,' I said, 'do you think Claire would be willing to come with me on an errand?'

'Depends what the errand is.' Ellery looked at Bas, frowning. A moment of unspoken communication passed between them, and he straightened up.

'Diego Bartholomew has information on Theo,' I said. 'I need to find out what it is. And what he knows about Godfrey's next movements. Someone needs to come with me.'

Ellery nodded. 'I'm sure we can work something out.'

FIFTEEN

WE WERE ALL UP EARLY the next morning, less by spoken agreement, and more from a shared sense that we needed to come up with a plan, and fast, to stay ahead of events in the town. Ellery managed to garner Claire's agreement to accompany me out to meet Diego, though she wasn't too happy about it.

'I do actually have things to do, you know,' she griped as we ate breakfast.

'We've been helping you out on the farm,' Ellery said. 'You can help us out with this.'

Claire scowled. 'Fine,' she muttered, and for the remainder of the meal, she ate her porridge as though it had personally offended her.

Once breakfast was done, we loaded up. Bas and Kade were going to be heading into town to do recon and hopefully speak to Turner at the Hawke and Tern. Claire and I had an hour-long drive ahead. And Ellery and Laura would be holding down the fort, and hopefully coming up with a grand plan to dig us out of our latest hole.

I suspected it was an excuse to do some discreet snogging, but I certainly wasn't going to call them out on it after last night.

Outside the gates, we separated from Bas and Kade as they headed south, and Claire and I cut directly east towards the Crater's Edge road. I had Bas's car, so not only was the driving positively a fun experience, but the radio worked; Claire promptly turned it up loud and spent the next hour staring out of the window.

I had seen the service station on Crater's Edge Road once before, driving past it with Bas on our fateful return to Bale Rocks after Maddock was shot. We hadn't entered, though. Today, as the chain-link fence came into view, I slowed Bas's car. Navigating the slip road was like doing a slalom course between potholes, before we ultimately ended up in the very middle of the road, squeezing between two concrete barriers that were positioned so a car could just pass through. Immediately beyond that, there was a cattle grid on the ground, and the whole car rattled as we crossed it. Then we were inside. The gas pumps were straight ahead, and beyond that, there was a grocery store and restaurant, each bearing faded red and yellow signs. I counted eight cars: two groups of three and one group of two. Most people seemed to prefer to travel the wasteland in convoys. But one other person was here alone.

'Do you know which car is his?' Claire asked.

'I'm guessing it's that one.' I headed towards the dark blue four-by-four that was parked closest to the restaurant. As I pulled in beside it, Claire shifted our gun into her lap.

We needn't have worried. Diego approached from inside the restaurant, his lithe figure obscured by an oversized, clearly well-made black coat.

'Benoit,' he said when I jumped out to meet him. His eyes swept over me, and then over to my car. 'I told you to come alone.'

'You might want to drive the wasteland alone, but I don't,' I said. 'That's Claire. I trust her, and she'll keep to herself.'

'That wasn't our deal,' Diego said mulishly.

'It was her or Bas. I figured you'd prefer this option.' I crossed my arms. 'I'm not risking my life for you.'

'You're risking your life for Theo,' Diego said.

A movement in the restaurant caught my eye. The door swung open, and a tall man with a shaven head, black skin, and muscles for days stepped out and approached us. He was dressed in tactical gear with a gun at his hip.

'You're a hypocrite,' I said. 'You're not alone, either.'

Diego pressed his lips together. 'I didn't say I would be.'

'Claire isn't a threat to you,' I said. 'Either you see this through, or I find another way to speak to Theo and you don't get the information you want from me.'

That was the ticket. A scowl crossed Diego's face, and then he nodded sharply.

'Fine, but she has to be blindfolded. Both of you do.'

You're kidding me.

'How am I supposed to drive blindfolded?' I demanded.

'You don't. You'll be in our car.'

It was official. I was going to kill him.

Claire was even less delighted by the news when I relayed it to her.

'He wants us to leave the car here? What if it gets stolen?'

'Apparently, he's asked the restaurant owner to keep an eye on it,' I muttered. To say I was unhappy about this turn of events was an understatement. 'But you can stay here if you want.'

Claire weighed that offer, tilting her head from side to side. 'No, I'll come with you. Marco will be annoyed if you get yourself shot because you trusted Mr Slimeball over there.'

I wasn't sure whether to smile at the insult to Diego or scowl at the insult to me. I settled on the latter. 'I'm not going to get myself shot.'

'Hey, I have ears, princess.' Claire rolled her eyes. 'Marco's the comedian, Bas is the serious one, you're the reckless one. You think they sent me here because there's safety in numbers? I'm your babysitter to make sure you don't get yourself shot and dumped in a ditch.'

I gritted my teeth. 'I'm not going to get myself shot.'

'Keep telling yourself that.' Claire holstered the gun on her belt and sashayed past me. 'Let's get this over with.'

Stewing with rage, I followed her. By the time I reached them, Claire was already picking her next fight.

'Absolutely not,' she snapped.

'I'm not having you sit behind me with a weapon,' Diego said. 'You'll shoot me in the head.'

'I'm not stupid enough to shoot the person driving my car. If we crash, I'll die too,' Claire said. 'I'm not giving up my gun.'

'Then you can stay here,' Diego said.

'No.'

I was starting to wish I'd brought Laura.

'Might I make a suggestion?' Diego's security guard asked.

Claire raised her eyebrows. 'Suggest away.'

'Remove the magazine, and you may keep the gun.'

'She can still hit me over the head with it!' Diego protested.

'Again,' Claire started, 'why would I—'

'I will be sitting in the back with them,' the security guard said. 'I will ensure your safety.'

I liked this guy. He exuded a sense of calm and competence—and more importantly, he seemed to know exactly how to handle Diego Bartholomew.

'Fine,' Diego said sulkily. 'But search them for any other weapons.'

The security guard nodded and gestured to me. 'Arms out.'

As I spread my arms, I asked, 'What's your name?'

'Warner.'

'Warner,' I repeated. 'Nice to meet you. The knife is strapped to my left hip, under my jumper.'

He nodded in appreciation and retrieved it, but then he continued to search me anyway. Competent and thorough.

Fortunately, I wasn't actually trying to sneak anything past him. It wasn't as though we had an arsenal of weapons at our disposal in any case. Without access to the Iron Fists' weapons, we had to make do with what we had: the guns Ellery and Bas owned, a handful of knives of varying quality, Ms Ellery's hunting rifle, and whatever weapons the Freetown community was willing to let us borrow. And all of them were incredibly precious because we didn't have the funds to replace them.

Once he'd confiscated Claire's knife and the magazine from her gun, Warner blindfolded us and helped us into Diego's car. It was pretty cramped in the back with him sitting between us. No matter how I squirmed, his huge thigh seemed to take up most of my seat. I kept my mouth shut, though.

Because if this whole thing paid off, I was about to see Theo. And if it didn't…

I wouldn't need a gun. I'd claw Diego's face off with my bare hands.

Being driven around blindfolded was amazingly unsettling. It catapulted me back to a similar drive that I hadn't thought about in a long time: when Bas's half-brother, Rodney, had had me kidnapped and driven out of town so we could talk. They had stuffed me in the boot then, and I'd had no idea what was going on. Even though I knew what was happening now, I still felt the same anxiety that made my chest feel tight and my fingers tingle.

I shifted restlessly again.

'How far is it?' Claire demanded from Warner's other side.

'You'll see,' Diego said.

He was enjoying this. Of course he would. I traced my fingers over the seam of my trousers and forced myself to focus on the tiny little bumps, the frayed edge where a hole had started to form—I'd have to patch that… I found the ridge formed by the cargo pocket and traced my finger around that.

We finished weaving from side to side, the car straightening out and settling into a rhythm. We were on the main road, and Diego had merged without having to swing across the road. So that meant we were driving away from town.

I found the cargo pocket on my other leg and traced that one, too, then popped the snaps open and ran my fingers over the soft, frayed edges of the fabric inside.

It didn't take long before Diego slowed the car. I heard the sound of another vehicle passing, and then we rolled across the road, down the embankment, and into the wasteland.

My heart lodged itself in my throat. Where were we going?

We bounced along for what felt like forever before the car stopped abruptly.

'We're here,' Diego announced.

'Finally,' Claire said. I reached up and unwound my blindfold, blinking against the bright daylight. We were parked outside a tall metal fence, beyond which stood a cluster of metal caravans and wooden buildings. I could hear the distant roar of water.

Where the hell were we?

'One of you needs to get the gate,' Diego instructed.

'I'll go,' I said.

'No funny business.'

'I want to see Theo,' I reminded him. Besides, I wasn't going to pull anything out here—Diego was my ride back.

Diego handed me a key, and I climbed out of the car. The gates were secured with a heavy chain, and I had to reach inside to find the padlock. I managed to wiggle the key in and unlock it, then I unwound the chain and slowly dragged the gates open.

'Lock it again behind us,' Diego instructed as he drove past, the car kicking dust up into my face.

'Sure,' I muttered.

Once I'd relocked the gate, I joined the others, who had climbed out of the car. Claire made a show of stretching and cracking her joints, even though the drive hadn't been more than fifteen minutes at most.

Diego led the way between the caravans and buildings, and as we walked, the roar grew louder.

It was the river.

Oh.

That made sense; I was no expert on geography, but I had distant memories of looking at maps of the West Rim when I was at school. The road, river, and railway line all ran more or less parallel to one another from Bale Rocks to Crater's Edge. This had to be some little hamlet that had sprung up along the river—maybe a fishing village?

We passed a few people, and I saw more peering at us from windows, all of their eyes dark with suspicion. Men, women, and children, craftspeople and farmers, and even one woman in some kind of religious robe. Diego paid them no mind as he led us up to a wooden cottage. As we approached the door, I caught sight of the river, down a short bank. It was a raging tumble of steel-grey water, and I found myself keeping to the back of the group so the others were between me and it.

Diego thumped his fist against the door, and a moment later we heard footsteps from inside: heavy boots on a wooden floor. The door swung inwards to reveal a stout woman with wrinkled black skin and greying curls. Her face split in a smile and she stood straighter.

'Dominic!'

Warner pushed past us and scooped her into a hug. 'Hello, Ma.'

She pushed him back and glared up at him. 'You were meant to visit on the weekend.'

'Town's been crazy,' he said. 'I'm here now.'

The woman shook her head and focused on Diego. 'What trouble you got yourself into now?'

Diego gestured to me. 'This is Theo's friend. She wants to see him.'

As if I'd been in a state of shock, my thoughts suddenly cleared again. Forget this strange new facet of Diego Bartholomew's social life. Theo was here, and in a few minutes I'd get to see him.

I took a deep breath to try and steady the sudden racing of my heart.

'Nice to meet you, ma'am,' I said politely.

'Got a name?' she asked.

'Harley. And this is Claire.' I pointed with my thumb to Claire, who stood beside me with her arms crossed.

'Oh, yes, he's told me about you. I'm Grace. Come in. Keep your boots on. Never know what mess has got on the floors.'

Claire and I exchanged uneasy glances. What did that mean?

Grace led us all inside. The cottage was small, the front rooms crowded with furniture. I spied a living room through one doorway, the two sofas so close together that if both were occupied, the sitters' legs would touch. The room immediately opposite looked remarkably similar to the one where Savannah had patched me up in the bunker: a doctor's chair, a metal table, and even a similar doctor's bag. In the corner stood a tall metal cabinet, its doors open to show off bandages, surgical implements, IV bags, and a range of other supplies.

Grace was a doctor.

She led us into the kitchen, which also contained the dining room table. We crowded around it, and Grace put the kettle on.

'I hope you had a safe drive out,' she said. Warner pulled mugs out for all of us.

'It's a mess getting in and out of town,' he said. 'Since the assassination.'

'Yes, Virginia told me about that. Silly business.' Grace tutted. 'You'd think they'd worry about food and medicine and people, but no. All that matters is power and money.'

'I've heard talk that they're trying to get the train line back up and running.' Diego had sat at the head of the table. He held himself upright and stiff, gripping the edge of the table with both hands.

'That would be a big step,' Grace said. 'But will it help?'

'We'd be able to get supplies from Crater's Edge.'

'Oh, yes, of course.' She rolled her eyes. 'More food, more jobs, right? And what's the price? What will we pay for this generous gift from our new mayor?'

The more Grace spoke, the more I liked her. Diego, on the other hand, made a face at the table.

'Isn't it better than how things are at the moment?' he asked.

'Things are never better, just different,' Grace said. She plopped a mug in front of him. 'Herbal tea. Good for your digestion.'

Diego's expression wrinkled in disgust. I received my cup next, and a leafy smell wafted up to my nose.

Grace finished serving us and slid in beside Warner at the table. As my tea cooled, I covertly studied the room. The décor tended towards dark reds, blues, and greens. A painting of a forest hung on one wall, rendered in clumsy brushstrokes. Through the window, I could see the rushing river. A wooden pier jutted out into it. It was lined with old tyres on either side, and a small white boat strained against the rope that bound it to the jetty.

I hadn't even realised that people lived out here in the wasteland. But here was a whole little village that I'd never heard of.

'Your friend is doing well,' Grace said. My gaze jumped to her face, but she was addressing Diego. 'I've started him doing walks around the compound.'

'That's good,' Diego mumbled.

'He gets terribly bored, though. You should come out here more often.'

'I'll try.' Diego seemed to be making a concerted attempt to burn a hole in the table with his eyes.

'What happened to Theo?' I asked.

'I'll leave that up to him to tell you—doctor-patient confidentiality, you know.' Grace winked. I bit my lip. That sounded exactly like something Savannah would have said.

I was practically vibrating with anxiety, but I forced myself to sip my tea and listen to the others make conversation—and resisted the urge to jiggle my legs. Mostly. Once Grace had deemed herself sufficiently updated on the situation in town, she turned to me.

'Would you like to see Theo now?'

I swallowed. 'Yes please.'

'Alright.' She stood.

'Me too,' Diego said immediately, jumping to his feet.

Grace frowned. 'One at a time would be best, I think.'

'I'll go first,' Diego said before I could get a word in edgeways. 'I'm the one he's expecting.'

I ground my teeth together and nodded. I'd rather have spoken to Theo first.

They exited, and I stood, moving to the window. I felt restless. What would Theo say? Would he be angry with me?

Claire joined me. 'How much longer is this going to take?'

'I don't know.' I rubbed my hands on my jeans. 'Can you do me a favour?'

'Depends what it is.'

I shot a glance at Warner and lowered my voice. 'Diego's best friend is Louis Godfrey. Son of Richard Godfrey.'

'Our new mayor?' Claire asked.

I nodded. 'See if you can find out if he knows anything? He won't tell me.'

Diego's guard was up, and no wonder. He and I weren't exactly friends. Claire might have better luck.

She shrugged. 'I'll try. No promises though.'

That was the best I could hope for. 'Thanks.'

Grace joined us again, cleaning the kitchen with the air of someone who wasn't quite sure what to do with herself. 'You're an old friend of Theo's, then?'

'We went to school together,' I said.

'He's mentioned you before. Wanted to get a message to you.'

'Oh.' I didn't know what to say. 'How… how long has he been here?'

'A little over two months. It's been a slow recovery.' Grace turned, a smile on her face, and passed me another cup of tea. 'You look like you need it.'

I grimaced and sipped the leafy concoction. How long was Diego going to be?

After what seemed like a small eternity of small talk and bad tea, Diego finally skulked back into the room. 'He wants to see you, Benoit.'

'Great.' I pushed up from my seat. Grace waved me into the hall and around a corner. We paused at a closed wooden door.

'In here,' she said. 'And take it easy. He's not well, no matter what he tells you.'

'Thanks.'

Heart in my mouth, I knocked on the door.

'Come in,' a quiet voice called.

I pushed the door open and squeezed around it. Immediately, my eyes fell on the bed, and the person occupying it.

Theo.

SIXTEEN

'THEO,' I SAID QUIETLY, LETTING my eyes rove over his form. He was lying propped against a mound of pillows. His face was pale, and he looked much older than he had the last time I'd seen him, as though he'd aged suddenly and unpleasantly.

But when he met my gaze, a smile split across his face.

'Harley!' He pushed himself up. 'You're here!'

'Hey.' I felt a sudden, bizarre pang of shyness. After everything—hunting for him, thinking he was dead, discovering he was alive—suddenly, I didn't know what to say. 'How... how are you doing?'

'Been better.' Theo pushed his blankets down. He had a plain grey vest on, and I could see that he'd lost a lot of weight. He'd always been skinny, but now he looked downright frail. 'How are you?'

'Alright.' I rubbed at my stinging eyes and inched closer to the bed. 'We're staying in Freetown with Ellery. Until... until things blow over.'

'Blow over?' Theo asked.

'A lot has happened.'

He patted the bed, and I sat on the edge of it, careful not to touch him.

'You'll have to update me,' he said. 'Bartholomew never tells me anything.'

'I don't know where to start.'

'Did you and Bas find Maddock?'

That seemed like ages ago. Haltingly, I told him what had happened in Langford and then Crater's Edge.

'So that was it?' Theo asked once I'd run through the whole story. 'Jackson managed to plan the whole coup from the start?'

'And now he has control of town,' I said. 'Him and Moriarty. They had the mayor shot in the middle of the town square.'

'Shit,' Theo said.

'Yeah.' I grimaced. 'That was yesterday.'

'What are you going to do now?'

'I don't know yet.' I nodded to the door and dropped my voice. 'I was hoping Diego might know something about what Jackson is planning. And Bas is asking at the Hawke and Tern in case Turner has any leads on the Hands' movements.'

'You're still with that guy?'

My cheeks heated up instantly. 'Yeah, we're, um…' I'd left out our romantic progression in my retelling. 'We're together. Like, properly.'

Why was this so embarrassing? I'd had no trouble telling anyone else. But with Theo, it was harder.

He scowled. 'I still think that guy's bad news.'

'He's sweet to me,' I said. 'He's never been anything other than respectful.' That may have been stretching the truth. Still, it wasn't as though I was a saint, either. Bas and I had our bad moments, but we were stronger together.

After last night, I was sure of it.

Theo shook his head. 'You're in the honeymoon phase. Bas isn't a great guy, Harley. He's a gang member and a killer. Or have you forgotten that?'

'I'm a killer too.'

'You'll see his true colours soon enough.'

I gritted my teeth. He'd never even seen the two of us together, but that didn't stop him from judging. Why was he so sure Bas would turn on me anyway?

'I don't think you know Bas that well, either,' I said.

'So you admit you don't know him well.'

I clenched my fists in my lap. Ellery had said something similar. Why was everyone so fucking judgemental about my relationship with Bas? 'I know him plenty well,' I said. 'I want to know how well you know him.'

Theo shrugged. 'I know his type.'

I turned away, pressing my lips together. All of a sudden, it was all rushing back: the frustration, coupled with that rebellious resentment that I hated. I didn't want to resent Theo. Why couldn't he listen to me?

'Let's discuss something else,' I said. 'Your turn. Tell me what happened to you.'

'There's not much to tell.' He sounded casual, but when I looked at him, his expression was tight.

'You were hurt,' I protested.

Theo shrugged. 'Yeah, but not that badly.'

I shot him a sceptical look.

'Really! It was the day after I got into town. I was meeting my contact from the army to see what I could find out—someone must have tipped off Jackson, though, because they ambushed me on my way out. Looking for you.'

'Me?' I echoed.

'He thought you might have come back to town.' Theo's lips twisted. 'I took a couple of shots. One in the leg—I couldn't drive. Then Diego pulled up and offered to help.'

Huh. I sat back, studying him. Theo gazed at me, wide-eyed and sincere.

'That... that's not what Rhett said,' I said slowly.

'Rhett?' Theo repeated.

'Yeah, I saw him. He told me you ran into fighting between the army and the gangs.'

A look of confusion crept onto Theo's face. 'Rhett's a liar, Harley. He wasn't even there.'

'How'd he get your car, then?'

Theo opened his mouth—and shut it again. His brow wrinkled. 'My car? I don't know what happened to it. Maybe he found it on the side of the road?'

'Right.' I stared at him, wishing I could see what he was thinking. But Theo remained closed to me, adjusting his pillows and seeming perfectly relaxed.

Had Rhett lied? Or was Theo deliberately downplaying what had happened?

'What... what are you going to do now?' I asked after the silence had stretched on long enough to make me uncomfortable.

'I'm leaving as soon as I'm better,' Theo said. 'Not long—maybe a week or two. You could come with me.'

'With you and... Diego Bartholomew,' I said sceptically.

'Just me.'

'I'd have thought he'd want to come along,' I said.

'It's not... We don't have the relationship you think we have,' Theo said, his voice so low that I had to lean in to hear. 'He'll meet me in Crater's Edge occasionally... That's it.'

'Right,' I said slowly. Had I misread Diego? I could hardly imagine him sticking his neck out for his own friends, let alone someone he didn't care for. 'Well…'

'You should come,' Theo said. 'If things are as you say in town, it'll be safer for you in Crater's Edge.'

'I can't.' I'd known he would ask, but that didn't stop the familiar frustration from blossoming in my chest. 'My life is here.'

'We can fetch Savannah.' Theo rolled his eyes. 'I know you won't go without her.'

'I'm not leaving.' The more I said it, the more certain I felt. 'I want to set things right in Bale Rocks.'

Theo pinched his lips together. 'Why? No one will thank you.'

'I don't care.' And I didn't. I really didn't. 'This is my home. And Bas's home. We're staying here.'

'Oh, so that's it,' Theo said. 'You want to stay with Bas. And he's making you fight for—'

'He's not *making* me do anything.'

Theo rolled his eyes again. 'I thought you were smarter than that, Harley.'

My mouth dropped open as surprise prickled over my skin. 'Excuse me?'

'Losing your mind over some guy who'll get you killed.' Theo shrugged, avoiding my gaze. 'But I guess you really are just like all the other girls.'

I stared at him. A new feeling was kindling in my chest; like a fire, it sparked and then grew, grew, grew. Until it roared.

Betrayal.

'I can't believe you'd say that to me.' Every muscle in my body was tense, but somehow my voice came out calm.

'It's the truth.'

'In that case, this is goodbye.' I stood. 'Even if I had been considering leaving, I won't go with someone who tries to manipulate me into making a decision. Goodbye, Theo.'

I wanted him to apologise, to say he didn't mean it, to say something.

'If you change your mind, you can find me via the Red Rock Inn,' Theo said. 'I'll always help you out.'

He said it like he *knew*. When I looked at him, he smiled like he *knew*. He was right, I was wrong, and I'd end up leaving Bas and Bale Rocks behind.

'That's not going to happen,' I said steadily. 'It was good to see you. I'm glad you're okay.'

Heart racing in my chest, I turned and walked out.

I dragged my heels in the hall, trying to keep my sniffling quiet, but when I entered the kitchen, I still felt as though I had a neon sign on my forehead: *Harley has been crying.*

Diego's little smirk said it all.

'Are you done?' Grace asked quietly.

I nodded. 'Thank you for letting me speak to him.'

'It's no problem, dear. I need to check on Theo, and then I'll walk you out.'

Diego nodded sharply. 'I need to speak to Harley. Before we go.' He met my gaze defiantly and nodded to the door. 'Let's talk in private.'

It was time to uphold my end of the bargain. I pursed my lips and strode to the door; Diego followed me out and shut it behind us.

'I can't tell you anything that would put anyone in danger,' I said.

'You don't get to bargain,' Diego replied. 'I brought you to Theo.'

'Why'd you help him?' I asked.

'Who are you working with?' He met my gaze, his brown eyes unyielding.

'Why ask questions you already know the answers to?' I stepped off the stoop. I wanted distance between me and the riverbank, and the roar made it hard to think.

Diego kept pace with me. 'I want to hear it from you.'

I rounded the edge of the cottage and stopped in the shadow of the overhanging roof. When Diego joined me, I studied him. After everything… The truth was, Diego was practically nothing to me. Whilst I'd been off travelling the wasteland, I'd basically forgotten he existed. He was just an annoying guy who had picked on me at school—not even the ringleader of his clique; that was Brody Cavanaugh. Diego was just a follower. Uncreative, unambitious. And since I'd left school, he had been more of a nuisance than anything else. A rich guy who could have done anything, but instead chose to waste his time entering fights, doing drugs, and messing around in the bunker. Playing like he had such a hard life.

Helping Theo was out of character for him. It exposed him to real danger. As did asking me these questions.

'Who put you up to this?' I asked.

'No one.'

'So, what, you just discovered some rebellious spirit at the age of twenty-five?' I arched an eyebrow.

'Maybe.' Diego crossed his arms.

'I don't believe you.'

'That doesn't matter. You owe me.'

'Go back home and hide behind your walls,' I said. 'This isn't your fight.'

'Maybe I'm tired of watching other people fight,' he said.

'You don't even know what side you're on,' I replied. 'If I tell you my plan, what are you doing to do? Reciprocate? Betray the Godfreys and tell me what's going on? Or are you going to run back to them and point them in the direction of their enemies?'

'It's not like that.'

'Then what is it like?'

Diego squirmed, his mouth opening and closing. 'I…'

'You…?' I glared at him.

He narrowed his eyes, straightening up suddenly. 'I don't need you making fun of me.'

'I'm not.'

'Good.' He crossed his arms. 'If things don't change, Theo's gonna leave again. I'm tired of… of…' He shook his head. 'Never fucking mind. Anyway. Just tell me.'

I stared at him. You could have knocked me down with a feather; I was so shocked, I was sure I could have just floated away.

'You're trying to get Theo to stay,' I said.

'That's what I just said, isn't it?'

'You?' *Shit.* Should I tell him that Theo was almost certainly leaving? If I did, all bets would be off. If I didn't, I might get information out of him now. But then Theo would leave.

But Diego didn't know that I knew that.

'Look,' I said. 'I don't know what you think is going to happen here, but we are not joining forces.'

'Benoit—'

'But you can help us,' I said. 'If that's what you're asking for.'

'I'm asking for information.'

'Sure,' I said. 'You want to know what we're planning so you can step in when there's no risk to you, right? Great way of earning Theo's affections—'

'I'm not trying to earn his affections!'

'I'm not going to let you jeopardise our plans,' I said. Not that we had any plans at the moment. But Diego didn't need to know that. 'We need to know what Godfrey is up to.'

'Of course that's what you want to know.' Diego rolled his eyes. 'I already told you, *and* I told your friend: no one tells me anything.'

Damnit, so much for hoping Claire would be subtle.

'You have to know something,' I said.

Diego scowled. 'Look, it's not like we spend our days camped out around conference tables, gossiping about our plans.'

'That was exactly how I pictured it, actually.'

He glared. 'Even if they did, I wouldn't be invited.'

'And you don't try and listen in? Ask your friends? You're pretty useless.' I rolled my eyes. 'I'm done here. Why would I collaborate with you? You're the most useless person in town.'

I turned to leave.

'Fine. Fine!'

I turned back. Diego scuffed his boots against the ground. 'They've been holing up in the mayor's residence,' he said. 'Louis told me his father moved in there immediately. There are lots of people coming and going.'

'That's hardly news to me,' I said.

'They've been taking deliveries,' Diego said. 'I didn't see what sort, but the trucks were armoured. I'm guessing weapons.'

Brilliant. Just the news I wanted to hear.

'Anything else?' I asked.

Diego shook his head. 'Now it's your turn.' He narrowed his eyes. 'What's your next move?'

I shook my head. 'Uh-uh. I'll discuss your involvement with my team and contact you.'

'You think I believe that? You'll cut me out.'

You bet I will.

But I was going to have to give a bit to get him off my back. I bit my lip. *What to tell him?*

'There's a drop box,' I blurted. 'On Tripp Lane, by the church. You know the street?'

'I think so.' Diego raised an eyebrow. 'What about it?'

'That's how we're passing information,' I invented. 'You can use it as well if you find out anything about Godfrey's plans—and we'll let you know when we start the next step of our plan.'

Diego narrowed his eyes. 'And you'll actually use it?'

I nodded.

'And your plan?'

'Currently, we're working on an in with the Black Hands.' We were not, but Diego didn't need to know we'd refused Hannover's offer. 'They're taking slaves, and we're trying to find a way to break the circle.'

'And that'll help with Jackson and the army?' Diego frowned.

'You can help with that.' I met his eyes. 'You're closer to them than we are.'

He squirmed. This was much more real than he'd ever intended on things getting. So much for Diego's noble goals; I was betting that after a good night's sleep, he'd realise he was safer never contacting me again.

'Fine,' he said. 'That's what we'll do then.'

'Fine.' I held out my hand. He shook it, brisk and businesslike. We'd barely dropped hands when Grace appeared around the corner.

'There you two are. Do you want another cup of tea?' Diego shook his head, stepping out from under the overhang.

'I think we're just about done,' he said. 'Thank you, Grace. I'll go say goodbye to Theo.'

'Alright then.' She patted him on the shoulder.

Diego trooped off. I ought to have followed him and also said another goodbye, but my feet were rooted to the floor.

'Are you alright?' Grace asked.

'Uh… yeah, I'm fine.' I shrugged.

'You seemed upset when you finished speaking to Theo.'

'We disagree on some stuff,' I said. 'That's just how it goes with people you've known a long time.'

'Oh, absolutely.' Grace smiled, the crows' feet around her eyes contracting. 'It's easy to think people will stay the way they are right now. But people can change in an instant. We're constantly growing and changing.'

Was that what had happened? I'd been thinking that Theo and I had just gradually grown apart, but now I realised that the events of the last few months had changed me a lot. Maybe more than I'd realised. More than they had changed Theo. And where once his promises to take me away from everything had made me feel safe and protected… now, I didn't need that anymore. I could protect myself without running away.

'Do you need anything for the road?' Grace asked.

'Oh… no.' I shook away my thoughts. 'It's not far. But thanks.'

We walked around to the front of the house, and a few minutes later Diego, Warner, and Claire joined us.

'Let's go,' Diego said.

Grace walked us to the car. We loaded up whilst she said goodbye to her son, and then she got the gate for us. Diego rolled the window down as we passed her.

'Thank you for everything,' he said.

'Any time.' She waved. Then we rolled away over the dirt track, and once she was out of sight, Warner handed me my blindfold.

'Why so secretive?' Claire muttered sourly.

'Just put it on,' Diego snapped.

I tied mine around my eyes and concentrated on the feeling of the ground beneath the tyres until we met the road again. Not long after that, Diego deposited us at the service station.

'I'll be in contact,' he told me tersely.

'Fantastic,' I replied drily.

Diego scowled. 'And don't you dare tell anyone.'

I saluted him. He glared, rolled up his window, and pulled away from us with squealing tyres.

'You do have a way of annoying people, don't you?' Claire asked.

'Shut up,' I muttered.

SEVENTEEN

A SOLITARY TEAR TRICKLED DOWN my cheek and dripped off my chin onto my jacket. It tickled, but I didn't wipe it away; I was hoping Claire wouldn't notice if I didn't draw attention to it.

She reached over and turned down the radio. 'Fuckin' hate this song.'

'Uh-huh,' I muttered. Having the radio loud had suited me. Now there was nothing to hide my sniffling.

'I thought you were looking forward to seeing that guy.'

Please don't bring this up.

'I was.'

'So, what'd he do? You're not the crying type.'

Fuck.

'I don't want to discuss it,' I muttered.

'What was the point of going all the way out there if you're just going to cry over it?'

'Look, it's complicated.' I swerved around a gaping hole where part of the road was just… missing. What even damaged a road like that? Beyond the broken stretch of road, I sighted a pile of the yellow-gold hay-bale shaped rocks that had given Bale Rocks its name.

''Complicated' is just another way of saying you don't want to explain it,' Claire said.

No shit.

'You really have a way with words,' I muttered. We bounced over an uneven patch of the road. I wasn't taking friendship advice from Claire, anyway. She barely knew anything about me. 'Did you at least manage to get anything out of Diego whilst you two were waiting?'

'Oh, he's one hundred percent smitten with your friend,' Claire said.

'I meant anything about Richard Godfrey's plans.'

Claire shrugged. 'He said he didn't know. All—'

'And you believe him?' I asked snippishly.

'*All*,' Claire repeated, making it clear she didn't appreciate the interruption, 'he *said* is that Godfrey has apparently been holing up in the mayor's house having lots of meetings with lots of people. And the military isn't happy. They don't want to coexist with the gangs; they want the gangs out.'

More or less what Diego had said to me, then. Combined with his mention of arms trucks, it wasn't much to go on.

Better than nothing, though.

As for what would happen next, I was still sure Diego would chicken out and I'd never hear from him again.

And Theo… I had no idea what would happen between me and Theo. Was he really just going to leave?

A fresh wave of tears stung at my eyes. I took one hand off the steering wheel to sniff discreetly into it. Claire glanced at me, but I pretended not to notice.

'He can't be much of a friend if you're crying over him.'

'Can you drop it?' I snapped. 'I've known Theo a long time. And I don't see you swimming in friendships.'

'My best friend was killed by raiders when I was twelve.'

The car bounced over a rock, and I bit my tongue. The metallic taste of blood exploded in my mouth.

'Shit,' I said. 'Sorry. I'm sorry. That must have been…'

Claire shrugged. 'They killed my father, too. That's life in Freetown. Why do you think we have such tall fences?'

A lot made sense all of a sudden. I'd heard stories about raiders, and I knew they sometimes hit the farms on the outskirts of town, particularly the ones to the west, where the terrain was open and unguarded. Freetown was miles away from Bale Rocks and the relative safety it afforded.

'I'm sorry,' I repeated.

'For what? Not like you could have changed it.'

What could I say to that? This felt like it should be a bonding moment, but I sensed that Claire would reject any attempts I made. So, like a coward, I let us lapse into silence. We rolled along the road, eventually turning off onto the smaller, less-well-maintained road that would take us around Bale Rocks and up to Freetown. Here, the first greenery of spring was starting to encroach upon the road, and the wasteland was starting to resemble a green carpet. We were about fifteen minutes out. Would Bas be back yet? Had they found out anything useful?

I had a sudden burning desire to hug Bas and tell him what Theo had said.

'Stop the car.'

I froze up, our wheels bouncing through a hole in the road.

'Harley!' Claire snapped. 'Stop the car!'

I slammed my foot on the brake, sending both of us careening towards the windscreen. My seatbelt cut across my neck and chest with a sharp sting.

'Oof!' Claire grunted.

I sat up straight, rubbing my neck. 'What's going on?' I asked urgently.

'Smoke.' She pointed straight ahead. 'There's smoke on the horizon.'

Now that she pointed it out, I saw it too: thick black smoke was starting to gather amidst the steely-grey clouds obscuring the sky. And it was directly where we were headed; right above Freetown.

A cold feeling stole over me, setting my heart thundering.

Shit.

'That... that's over Freetown, isn't it?' I asked quietly. A thousand scenarios vied for my attention. I couldn't seem to get a full breath. 'Do you think—'

'There's only one way to find out,' Claire said grimly.

I swallowed and reached for the ignition to restart the stalled car. The engine suddenly seemed impossibly loud in the stillness of the wasteland. The tyres on the ground roared like an enraged beast. The smoke thickened on the horizon as we approached, the sky getting blacker and blacker. The car filled up with a thick, sludgy smell.

I kept praying that the smoke would stay on the horizon, but it drew closer and closer, hovering above Freetown like an omen of doom.

The gates came into view, and Claire gasped. The righthand gate had been ripped off its rollers and was half-leaning against the guard tower. I stared at it in horror, as the cold in my chest began to infect the rest of my body.

No.

'What happened?' Claire whispered. 'Where—The guards—'

Her voice seemed to get lost in her throat. I rolled the car to a stop.

'What should we do?'

'We have to go to my place,' Claire said. She grabbed her knees, digging her fingers in so hard her knuckles turned white. 'We have to make sure everyone's okay.'

I swallowed. Were they okay? Bas and Kade might still be out, but Ellery, his mother, Laura…

'Right,' I whispered. 'Do you… think it's safe?'

Claire pulled out the gun and checked it. 'I'll cover us.'

Looking at her face, I didn't doubt her ability to shoot from a moving vehicle. She turned to the window, and I started a slow crawl through the gates and into Freetown.

The centre of town was almost eerily deserted. No children playing, no men and women trading goods, no farmhands at work. I felt as though we were driving through a ghost town. We turned off towards the Ellerys' farm, and my heart sank.

'No,' Claire whispered. 'No, no, no, no—Harley, drive faster, for fuck's sake!'

The engine screamed as I sped up, bouncing over the uneven dirt track, racing towards the horrific sight. Fifty feet short, I stopped. Claire threw her door open and sprinted towards the farmhouse, silhouetted against the blaze.

Flames licked over the building. Even from the car, I could hear them crackling, spitting, hissing. They had consumed the building to its metal roof; if there was anyone in there, they had no chance of surviving.

A fist clenched around my heart.

No. It couldn't be. The only car here was the Ellerys' beaten-up truck. Bas hadn't made it back.

But the others…

I swallowed as Ellery, Laura, and Collette's faces swam before my eyes. No. I had to believe they'd made it out. Even if the car was here, I had to believe it.

A movement on the horizon caught my eye. A person? I squinted. There was someone, far away across the barren fields, over by the next farm. Who were they? Were they coming towards us?

I threw my door open.

'Claire!'

Claire had sunk to her knees in front of her home, her fingers dug into the dirt. She didn't acknowledge me. Gripping my knife, I climbed out of the car and headed for her.

'Claire!'

The heat was immense. It hit me like a wave, stinging my skin and forcing the air out of my lungs. I crouched beside Claire.

'We have to go.'

'I can't!' Claire sobbed.

'We have to. Someone is coming. We might still be in danger.'

Claire shook her head. 'Marco… Mum…'

'They'll have made it out. I know they will.' I had to believe that. 'Please, Claire.'

'I can't!' she wailed.

I crouched down, settling my hands on her shoulders. 'Claire…' I had to find words, but this wasn't my forte. Shouting in anger, witty banter, sparring with arseholes like Hannover… give me those any day. Comforting Claire? I could barely breathe around the lump in my throat.

What would Savannah do?

Savannah had a doctor's touch; she understood humans in a way I didn't. I closed my eyes and inhaled shallowly, trying not to breathe in the smoke. 'Claire, we need to leave. They… they wouldn't want you to stay here.'

'This is my *home*,' Claire hissed.

'We are your home.' Was it arrogant to include myself? Did it matter? 'The people you love. Not the building. I know it's horrible—believe me, I know exactly how you feel.'

Moving out of my childhood home, seeing it repossessed by the Iron Fists… it had cemented my loss in a way that my father's memorial service hadn't.

'But,' I continued after another steadying breath, 'they wouldn't want you to stay here. In danger. Please come with me.'

'I…' Claire brought a hand up and scrubbed at her face. She stared at the ground. 'How… how did you do it? How do you do it?'

I had no idea what she was asking, but that didn't matter either. Her face said she was ready.

'Here.' I took her hand and helped her up. She stumbled, tear tracks glinting on her cheeks. I pried the gun out of her other hand and wrapped my arm around her. Step by step, I led her back to the car. The approaching figure was a dark silhouette on the horizon; we needed to move. I helped Claire into the car, then hurried around to the driver's side and scrambled in. I turned the car on before I'd even shut the door, and navigated us into a clumsy turn that churned the soil in the field beside the road. Then I gunned the engine, and we hurtled along the dirt track, bouncing so viciously we were at risk of taking flight.

A figure ran in front of the car. I slammed on brakes so suddenly that my forehead almost collided with the steering wheel. The figure stumbled back, arms wheeling.

'Jonah!' Claire cried. She threw her door open before I could say a word. I followed her out as she sprinted over to the tall, lean teenager who often guarded the gate. 'Jonah! Jonah, what happened?'

'Claire!' Jonah threw his arms around Claire, and the two hugged each other as though they were the last people on the planet. I held back, feeling like an outsider. Finally, Claire drew back.

'The others—Mum, Marco—'

'I don't know.' Jonah shook his head. 'I thought they had gone out, but—'

Claire shook her head. 'No, they weren't with us.' A sob burst out of her mouth.

'They'll be alright,' Jonah said. 'The passage opens right by your farm.'

Claire clapped a hand against her mouth. 'The passage!' She wheeled around to face me. 'I totally forgot. Harley, we have to go!'

'In a minute.' I focused on Jonah. 'What happened?'

'Armed men,' he said grimly. 'They knew where you guys were staying. They forced their way in the gate—shot Luke—'

'Luke?' Claire cried.

'He's alright,' Jonah said, though his eyes told a different story. 'It was a leg wound. We... we don't know if he can walk still, but he'll live.'

Claire covered her mouth, her eyes glistening with tears.

'Do you know who they were?' I asked.

Jonah shook his head. 'Not the army, I don't think. They weren't in uniform.'

Not the army. But what did that mean? It wasn't Godfrey making a move, presumably. But was it Jackson? Moriarty? Hannover?

'I have to go back,' Jonah said. 'I'm guarding our farm in case they come back. But I saw you drive in, and I wanted...'

His words seemed to fade into nothingness, the same nothingness that was growing inside my chest.

'Thank you for coming,' Claire said. She hugged him again, smothering her sobs in his coat. Jonah patted her back awkwardly.

'Dad's organising a team to come put the fire out,' he said. 'And Greg is keeping an eye on the animals.'

'Thanks,' Claire whispered. She drew back and looked at me, her eyes wild and desperate.

'The passage?' I asked helplessly.

Claire straightened up. 'I'll show you where it is.'

Outside the gates, Claire directed me into the dead zone around the fence, a five-yard-wide area that had been cleared of bushes, trees, and concrete. The weeds tore at the wheels and front of the car, but I cut through them at a faster-than-sensible pace. I had to get to the secret entrance. I had to make sure that Bas had made it out. If anything had happened to him…

Nothing could happen to him.

I refused to entertain the possibility.

Bas and I had come so far. We'd only just found each other, only just found a balance. This could not be it. It couldn't.

Please, please, please, please, please.

'That's it,' Claire said suddenly. 'Just by that copse of trees.'

I slowed down, scanning the land ahead of us. The wasteland to the north of Freetown was dotted with trees, but many of them were dead: either jagged and bleached limbs reaching for the sky… or burnt husks, their branches long gone. The copse Claire was pointing to bore some of the only live trees, their branches withered and tangled. The trees seemed to lean together, as though they were drawing protection from one another.

I turned the car and started towards it, but the ground was rocky and uneven. Theo and Bas had made driving through the wasteland look so easy.

My chest ached. I couldn't think of either of them right now. I stopped the car.

'Let's walk.'

Claire took back the gun. I palmed my knife, and we climbed out.

The stillness was infinite. I couldn't resist glancing back; the cloud of smoke hung above Freetown, and I could just about make out the flames. I forced myself to look ahead instead. We trudged over the debris and bushes and slipped between the trees.

I immediately knew what Claire was after; a giant wooden door was set horizontally into the ground, easily six feet wide and long, painted a mix of brown and green. Dead leaves piled to one side of it. Claire stared at it, her lips twisting through a number of emotions. Finally, she grabbed the iron handle and heaved it up.

'Someone has been through here,' she announced. 'Recently.'

'How do you know?'

'It's usually locked from the inside.'

She dropped the door with a resounding crack and marched back out of the trees. After a moment, she stopped and waved me over, pointing to something on the ground. 'Tyre tracks.'

'Those might not be fresh.' I eyed the tracks. I didn't know enough about cars to identify them. They looked recent, but how recent? 'Your mother's truck was still at the farm.'

'But Bas had Marco's car. He could have picked them up.' Claire gazed at me, and the hope in her eyes made me sick. I wanted to believe… but what would we do if she was wrong? 'They made it out, and he picked them up. Where would they go?'

Where *would* they go?

'I don't know.'

'You know the town better than me.' Claire brushed her hair back from her eyes and glared at me. 'And you know Bas. Where would Bas go?'

I did know Bas. But how well? Where would he go if he was in trouble?

Think, Harley. Think.

And suddenly, it came to me. A long-forgotten snippet of conversation. A moment between us, where we'd thought we might not see each other again.

'If you need to get out of town, or get a message to me, go to the same old factory where we spoke to Rodney, okay? They won't know to look for you there.'

Wasn't that what Bas had said? Before the strike on the distillery months ago? That was where he'd told me to hide.

But would he be there now? Would he remember that he'd told me? It was Bas. Bas would remember. That was who he was.

'Yeah,' I said slowly. 'I think I know where they are.'

EIGHTEEN

'IT'S SOMEWHERE HERE,' I SAID to Claire. I was straining my memory like it was a muscle during my training. It had been months since I'd last been here, and Bas had been driving. But I was relatively certain the factory was off the main road. We'd never turned onto a smaller road.

I hoped.

'Keep a lookout for the RocCo factory,' I said. 'It's past that.'

'I don't even know what that is.'

Claire's confidence from this morning had evaporated. She hunched in her seat, her eyes too wide for her face. I wrestled with the desire to snap at her. She looked so brittle she'd snap in half if I did—but I needed her help if we were going to find this place.

I slowed the car a little as we neared a gate, letting my eyes skim over the logo. Unfamiliar.

'Why are you stopping?'

'I'm just looking at the names.' I took a deep, slow breath and sped up again.

Don't snap at her. She's just scared and upset.

And why wouldn't she be? All the same fears that she was experiencing were also bouncing around in my brain.

We approached the next gate, and I slowed again. Even before we reached it, I felt a shiver of déjà vu. This was it.

RocCo Industries.

'That's it!' Claire cried.

'Yeah.'

'Do we turn off here?'

'No, it's a bit further. Your side. We're looking for a dirt track.'

She sat forward with renewed focus. I kept us at a modest pace. It felt like a crawl—it felt like an eternity, before Claire suddenly said, 'There!'

On her side of the road, I spotted a narrow, overgrown track.

'That looks right.' I swung the car onto it, urging it as fast as I could go over the deep ruts. Yard by yard, we approached the end, where four low brick buildings surrounded a gravel lot. Ellery's car waited for us, parked up against one of the buildings. Claire threw her door open before I'd even stopped the car.

'Claire, wait! It might not be safe!'

She didn't hear me. She hurtled towards the building, and as she ran, the door swung open. Ellery stepped out, followed by Bas, and Claire leapt into her brother's arms.

Relief washed through me, leaving me lightheaded. My fingers tingled. I wasn't even sure my legs would take my weight, but I stumbled out of the car anyway, heading straight for Bas. Bas, who had remembered. Bas, who was safe.

I collided with him. He dragged me against his chest, and then we were kissing. I didn't know who started it—all I knew was that I definitely wasn't ending it. I scrabbled at his jacket until I managed to get my hands under it, against his chest. He gripped my hair, tilting my head back. I could taste his emotions: anger, fear, desperation. I took all of them and gave him mine instead. I didn't pull back until my lungs screamed for oxygen.

'I thought...' I couldn't put it into words. I clung to the lapels of Bas's jacket. 'What happened?'

'Jackson,' Bas said. 'He was looking for us.'

'Did he—The others—'

'Everyone is fine. Kade and I picked them up at the back entrance.'

Another wave of relief washed over me, and this time my knees did buckle. Bas steadied me. 'Are you alright?' He glanced past me. 'Theo?'

'It... it's a long story. It doesn't matter now.' I shook my head. 'I was so scared you wouldn't be here.'

'I didn't know if you'd remember.' Bas's eyes ran over my face, intent, searching. 'I thought you might go to Turner's safehouse instead.'

'I remembered,' I assured him. 'Can we stay here?'

'It won't be comfortable.' A smile tugged at his lips suddenly. 'I'm not sure it's up to your standards of hygiene.'

'Bas!' I shoved his chest. 'You have got to be kidding me.'

'Not entirely.' He smirked. 'Let's go inside and figure out what we're doing next.'

'Alright.'

I let him tug me inside. The building inside had been gutted; the walls were raw brick, and the floor was rough concrete. They'd made a fire under a hole in the roof, and Kade and Laura sat with Ms Ellery on a few abandoned breezeblocks.

'Harley!' Laura sprang up, almost upending the mug she held. 'You're alright!'

'*You're* alright!' I hugged her tight, then turned to Kade, who smiled up at me.

'You made it.'

'We weren't sure whether to leave a message,' Laura said. 'It seemed too dangerous…'

'It's okay. I knew where to come.' I wanted to grin with elation, but one look at Ms Ellery quelled the urge. Her face was pale, and her eyes darted around frantically. I was reminded painfully that she'd just lost her home. I swallowed my joy and sat on the ground beside them. Bas leant against the wall beside me, and Claire squeezed in next to her mother.

'What now?' she asked.

'That's what we're trying to decide,' Ellery said. He turned to me. 'Did you find anything out this morning?'

'Not a lot.' I gave them an abridged rundown of my morning.

'Carsten,' Ellery said when I mentioned the village. 'That'll be Carsten.'

'I've never heard of it.'

'Yeah, I couldn't point to it on a map, but one of their guys comes to us to trade every so often. They're pretty secretive.'

'How did Diego Bartholomew know about it?' Kade wondered.

'His bodyguard is from there,' I said.

'Huh. Didn't see that coming,' Ellery said. 'So what else happened?'

I brushed over the conversation with Theo, my throat aching as I pushed the words out, and then related my conversation with Diego in more detail.

'Meetings in the mayor's house,' Ellery said. 'But not with the army. Who then?'

'The gangs,' Bas said.

'Just like that? Old mayor's dead, and now Jackson and Moriarty are welcome in the top dogs' inner sanctum?' Ellery raised an eyebrow.

Bas hummed. 'Did he say who?'

'No, but I feel like if it was someone he'd have recognised, he might have mentioned them by name.'

'Are we taking Diego Bartholomew by his word now?' Ellery asked.

'You weren't there,' I said. 'I don't think he was lying. I had the upper hand for most of the conversation.'

Ellery frowned. Bas said, 'Harley's good at reading people.'

'I feel like we've had some variant of this conversation before,' Ellery said.

'Yes, and Harley was right about Jackson then, wasn't she?'

I looked between them. 'What?'

'You were the first to say Jackson was a traitor,' Bas said.

'I know.' I just hadn't realised that Bas remembered that, or that he'd discussed it with Ellery. But an odd little feeling blossomed in my chest then: half pride, half something else that I wasn't sure I could name. Bas thought I was good at reading people. Ellery was strategic, Bas was logical, and I had my thing, too. And between the three of us, we could make this work.

'None of that helps us figure out what to do next though,' Ellery said flatly.

I hugged my knees, tamping down on the joy in my chest. We had to plan.

'What did you find out?' I asked Bas.

'Nothing. Turner was as surprised as we were. And none of the feelers he put out to the Aces came back with anything either, so they were cut out of the deal.'

I met his gaze; Bas looked grim.

'I still think the Aces are a potential entry point,' Kade said.

'They won't work with us,' Ellery disagreed. 'We have nothing to offer them. No intel. Nowhere to stay. Nothing!'

He swung around and slammed his fist against the brick, a snarl wrenching out of his throat. I jerked in surprise.

'Marco,' Bas said quietly.

'I'm going for a walk.' Ellery stalked to the door and vanished outside. I glanced at Bas again.

'It's his home,' Bas said quietly.

'I get it,' I said.

We sat in silence for a few minutes before Bas pushed off the wall. 'Come out to the car with me. I want to see what supplies we have.'

I nodded, grateful for the excuse to escape the tense atmosphere.

We headed outside, and Bas opened the back of his car, pulling a bag towards him to rifle through it. I glanced around, but Ellery had vanished from sight.

'You were holding back,' Bas said. 'About Theo.'

'It's not relevant to the group,' I said.

'He said something that upset you.'

I grabbed another bag. Bas had a lot of gear back here—I suspected we were about to be grateful for his foresight.

'It's just what I expected,' I muttered as I thumbed through the contents of the bag: a tent, sleeping bags, a collection of enamel mugs. 'Theo wants to leave. He wanted me to come with him.'

'Maybe you should have gone.'

I shot a look at Bas, but he was focused on his bag. 'Is that what you want?'

'No,' he said matter-of-factly. 'But things are about to get hard.'

'I'm in this with you.'

Bas kept searching. I grabbed his arm to get his attention. Finally, he looked at me. His face was carefully blank.

'I'm in this with you,' I repeated.

'I know,' Bas said quietly. 'But Jackson has made his move now. He brought the fight to us. We have to fight back, or we'll die.'

All of a sudden, I felt as though the air was pressing in on me. I had thought things were real before, but I'd been wrong.

This was real.

This was all too real.

'Do you think we can do it?' I asked Bas.

He pulled a metal case towards him and flipped it open, revealing a rifle that had been painted matte grey. 'It only takes one person in the right place to kill someone,' he said. 'Maddock proved that.'

He'd said something similar to Hannover. But it wasn't his words I cared about. It was the look in his eyes—fierce and determined. I reached out and took his hand.

'I'm going to help.'

Bas nodded. He shut the case and released my hand, returning to his bag.

'I wanted to ask your opinion on something,' he said in a low voice.

Bas's certainty amazed me. I told him I was staying, and that was it. Conversation closed.

'What is it?' I asked.

'How did Jackson know we were staying in Freetown?'

'I don't know.' But the moment he said it, my mind hurtled down the same paths his must have already travelled. 'I never told anyone. Except Theo, but that was today. Could Diego have heard and got a message to them?'

'Timeline's too tight,' Bas said. 'There's Kayla as well.'

'No way. I trust Kayla.' I shook my head instantly. I'd known her for years.

'Savannah. But you trust her as well.'

'Yeah, of course. But I don't think I ever mentioned to her where I was staying.'

Bas nodded. 'There's no one else.'

'Except us.'

His expression was carefully grim. 'Except us. And I trust the Ellerys with my life.'

'But Kade and Laura wouldn't betray us, either…' I said. 'Could someone in Freetown have done it? Maybe they didn't even see it as a betrayal. Just gossip, or…'

'Freetowners protect their own,' Bas said. 'But it's a possibility.'

'There aren't any other options.'

'No.' He zipped up his bag and moved to open the next crate. 'But Jackson has to have found out somehow.'

I swallowed. He was right.

'Someone could have followed us,' I said.

'I considered that possibility as well.' Bas unpacked a stack of tins, lining them up beside the crate. 'You could have been followed from the bunker. Or Hannover could have followed you from The Arsonist.'

'He wanted to work with us, though.'

'It could have been a trap.'

'Then why give us the tipoff about the mayor's assassination?' I asked.

'To lull us into a false sense of security,' Bas said.

'Maybe.' It didn't feel right, though. But I wasn't surprised Bas suspected Hannover. 'What do you think our next step should be?'

'Ours? Or the group's?' Bas asked.

'Are they different?'

'We need to split up,' he said. 'We've involved too many people in this. You, me, Ellery, Kade—we're the ones who need to finish it. The others… We'll take them to Turner's safe house. Claire and Collette can defend themselves. They'll be safe there for a few days.'

I nodded. 'And us?'

Gravel crunched, and I spun around to see Ellery approaching. A glance at Bas said he wasn't surprised. He looked up, tapping his fingers against the top of a tin of beans.

'We're going to take out one third of the dream team,' Ellery said.

Bas nodded. 'Moriarty?' he asked.

'He's the weakest link,' Ellery said.

'How are we going to do that?' The idea felt too big for my brain to hold.

'By getting one person in the right place with a gun,' Bas said. 'And making sure this time I don't miss.'

NINETEEN

'NO,' LAURA SAID STAUNCHLY. She stood opposite Bas, her arms crossed. 'I want to stay.'

'It's too dangerous,' Bas said. 'For one, camping here isn't safe. Nor is it comfortable. The safe house will be—'

'Safe, yeah, I got that.' Laura rolled her eyes. 'I'm staying with you guys. I want to help. I'm not hiding whilst you fight.'

'You don't even know how to shoot,' Ellery said.

'So, teach me.'

'Laura…' I started carefully. I honestly hadn't expected this from her—I'd thought she would be grateful to be safe, after barely escaping a burning building. Apparently not. 'We… we don't know how things are going to go down. It would be better for you to stay somewhere out of the firing line.'

'You aren't,' Laura said. 'I'm not going either.'

Ellery sighed and raked his hair back from his face. 'This isn't some… adventure. We could all die tomorrow.'

'I accept that risk.'

'Let her stay,' Kade said. 'She's helped us out on comms before. We can use her skills.'

I exchanged a glance with Bas. We'd hacked out the beginnings of a plan earlier by the car, but it was beyond dangerous. I wasn't the only one who hated it. Having Laura there would be an added risk.

'Alright,' Bas said. 'Laura stays. Harley can catch you and Kade up on the plan whilst Ellery and I move Claire and Collette to the safe house.'

I shot him a surprised look; I hadn't expected him to agree that easily. Bas nodded to me. 'We won't be long. Be ready to leave when we get back.'

'Alright.'

For this evening, we were splitting into two teams. In order to strike at Godfrey, Moriarty, and Jackson—whom Ellery had taken to affectionately calling the 'Dream Team'—we had to find out where they were staying and figure out what their movements would be in the immediate future. Ellery and Kade would be heading to the Iron Fists' compound to see what they could glean there. Bas and I were going to be spying on the Black Hands.

I relayed the plan to Laura and Kade whilst we busied ourselves putting out the fire and hiding the traces that we'd been there. After being routed once, we weren't taking any chances that our enemies could track us down again. When we heard the car returning, Kade headed to the door to make sure it was them. He returned with Ellery and Bas in tow.

'Ready?' Ellery asked.

'Yep.' I stood, zipping up my jacket.

'Alright. Laura, you're with us. We don't have radios, so we have to use other signals. I'll run over them in the car.' Ellery strode off.

I caught Bas's eye—something about meeting his gaze had become physically reassuring. Yes, we were still on the same page. He jerked his head towards the car, and we all headed out. Ellery paused by Bas's car and clapped Bas on the shoulder.

'No risks. Not tonight.'

'I know,' Bas said. 'You too.'

'Right.' Ellery's gaze flicked between Bas and me. 'Keep safe, both of you.'

'And you,' I said.

Ellery nodded and headed for his own car. Bas closed the boot of ours and went around to the driver's side. A moment later, we rumbled out of the gravel lot. The air in the car was tense, reflecting the churning fear in my chest. If this plan worked, we would be a step ahead of Jackson and his cronies for the first time since returning to Bale Rocks. We really needed that.

But could we do it?

I glanced at Bas. He looked as he usually did: steady. Ready for anything. If anyone could pull this off, it was Bas.

Except that Bas abruptly slowed the car, a long way before the turnoff that would take us south to the Black Hands' compound.

'What are you doing?' I asked as he pulled into the gate of an industrial site. The name on the sign was a hundred percent familiar to me. 'Why are we stopping here?'

'We're not going to the Black Hands' compound just yet,' Bas said. 'We have another stop to make first.'

'What's going on?'

'Don't tell any of the others.'

'What, Ellery and Kade and Laura? Why don't you trust them?' I felt as though I'd missed a step going down the stairs—except this was a step in Bas's logic.

'For now,' Bas said, 'this stays between us.'

He rolled down the window. A security guard had approached.

'This is a restricted area.'

'My brother will see me,' Bas said.

'I'll be the judge of that,' the guard snapped, adjusting his jacket to better show off the RocCo company logo. 'Papers?'

'I don't have them,' Bas said. 'Just tell Rodney Rochester that Sebastian is here.'

Sebastian. The name shivered over my arms like a cold breeze. Bas never called himself that.

Disgruntled, the security guard stalked back to his hut. Through the window, I could see him making a call on his radio. Four or five minutes passed before the gate rolled back and we were able to drive through into the complex.

It looked much like it had the last two times I'd been here. A concrete parking lot was surrounded by low buildings, all painted white. Beyond the furthest structure, I could see the towers and chimneys of a manufacturing plant. Bas stopped us outside the main office.

'I'll be back in a few minutes.'

'Okay,' I said. 'But what's going on?'

'Rodney helped Kade for a reason,' Bas said. 'He'll help us for the same reason.'

'He wants to speak to you,' I guessed.

Bas nodded. He pushed his door open and jumped out, leaving the car idling. I watched him enter the building, the door shutting behind him. My stomach was twisting itself into knots. Why didn't Bas want me to tell the others?

I trusted Ellery, Kade, and Laura. Didn't I?

Of course I did. None of them would betray us.

Yet, Bas had insisted that I go with him this afternoon, even though

Ellery had initially suggested partnering Bas and Kade. And there was my chat with Bas earlier. He hadn't said he suspected any of our group to be traitors. But he hadn't said he *didn't* suspect them, either.

But they were our friends.

And yet... I thought of Theo. Sometimes, friends weren't who you thought they were.

But that was different. Theo and I had grown apart. We hadn't turned on one another.

I shifted against my seat, the back of my neck prickling with unease. If we couldn't trust Ellery, Kade, and Laura, then who *could* we trust?

Bas. I have Bas.

And at that moment, Bas emerged from the office building with Rodney in tow. Not for the first time, I was struck by the similarities between the two brothers. Both were tall, with had red-brown hair and olive skin. Both had the same fierce green eyes. Somehow, today they looked even more similar. There'd been a shift in Rodney since I had last seen him. Was he standing taller? Or was it his expression? Something felt different.

They walked right over to the driver's side of the car, where Bas's door was still open.

'...don't have long,' Bas was saying.

'You always were impatient.' Rodney's cool gaze settled on me.

'Yes, it runs in the family,' Bas said flatly. He realised where Rodney was looking and shifted so his back was to me. 'Don't look at her. You're talking to me.'

'You two are still hanging around together,' Rodney said, his voice taking on a smug air. 'I knew she meant something to you.'

'To me, yes. To you, no,' Bas said. 'You stay away from Harley. I don't want you to hurt her.'

'I'm sure she's capable of looking after herself,' Rodney said.

'And I'm sure she'll have an easier job of it without the taint of the Rochester family around.' Even from behind, Bas radiated anger. 'Harley is irrelevant to this agreement. Can you do it or not?'

'You're asking a high price,' Rodney said.

'I was a slave for fifteen years.' Bas's voice was harder than granite. 'There is no price too high.'

A cloud of shame fell over Rodney's features. He cast his eyes towards the ground for a moment, before looking up—and there it was.

The familiar air of desperation that he used to wear like a cloak.

'I'll do it,' he said. 'Whatever it takes.'

'Good,' Bas said. 'We'll be in contact.'

He climbed up into the car.

'Thank y—' Rodney's words were lost in the slamming of the door. Bas put the car in gear and, with a single dismissive glance at his brother, started towards the gates.

'What's going on?' I asked, twisting to watch Rodney. He stood behind the car, watching us in return.

'Rodney is going to create the opportunity we need to kill Moriarty,' Bas said.

My stomach dropped to rest somewhere around the wheels of the car.

'How?'

'That's up to him,' Bas said.

'What are you trading in return?' I asked. Everything was a trade with Rodney, and the price for this favour would be steep.

'Exactly what he's always wanted,' Bas replied. 'The opportunity to get to know his brother.'

Stakeouts, it turned out, were boring.

I'd had high hopes for finally getting to see the Black Hands' compound, but all we did was hike a few hours through the wasteland and then hang out in a ruined building, watching the goings-on behind the tall fence through a pair of binoculars. Absolutely nothing of note happened.

'We're not going to get any information by watching through the fence, are we?' I asked Bas once we'd hiked back to the car. I turned the heating up to warm myself up—turned out, stakeouts were cold, too.

'We did learn a few things,' Bas said. 'They've increased security considerably.'

'How will Rodney get us in there?'

'Hopefully, he won't. He'll draw Moriarty out.'

'Oh.' That possibility hadn't even occurred to me. But now, a range of options opened up in my mind. If Rodney had the power to draw Moriarty out, then our risk lessened considerably. We could plan where and how we took out Moriarty.

'Is this it?' I asked suddenly before I'd even really finished the thought in my own mind. 'We're going to assassinate the gang leaders?'

'Moriarty has to die,' Bas said. 'That's the only way to end the slaving ring. If we leave him in place, it won't matter what we do—he'll just move his operations.'

'Hannover, too,' I said.

'Yes.'

He'd thought of that already, I realised. Where Moriarty went, Hannover was sure to follow. Which meant we could kill both of them with one strike.

And Bas would have his revenge.

I swallowed that thought. Revenge wasn't the main point here—breaking the alliance between Godfrey, Jackson, and Moriarty was. If we brought them down, we might be able to restore things in town.

'What are we going to do about the army?' I asked.

'I'm not sure yet,' Bas said. 'First, we'll have to see how they respond to Moriarty's death.'

He said it so calmly, it sent a shiver down my spine. Even after everything that had happened, it was still hard for me to just discuss someone dying. Even if those people were Moriarty and Hannover, all-around bad guys.

Hannover! Abruptly, I recalled a comment he'd made when we had met with him. *'Haven't you ever wondered what the military wants with our washed-up backwater?'*

'If we could find out why they're here, maybe we could give them what they want and get rid of them that way,' I suggested.

'The army isn't just going to tell us why they're here, Harley.'

'No, but Hannover seemed to know.'

Bas tensed, his knuckles turning white as he clenched the steering wheel. 'We're not speaking to Hannover again.'

'I can go on my own, if you want.'

'Harley, no.'

'What if that's the answer?' I pressed. 'The clue we need?'

'Hannover's games are too dangerous,' Bas snapped.

'Okay.' I could tell from his voice that pushing him wouldn't help, so I let the conversation lapse. But the thought still lingered in the back of my mind.

What if Hannover did hold the answer?

We had agreed with Ellery that we would rendezvous the following morning. They were going to try and stay with Laura's family for the night, and Bas had picked a spot for us. The spot turned out to be a tall, narrow house on the south bank of the river with a sign in one of the front windows.

Rooms to let, fully furnished

We parked in a tiny lot at the back of the house. Shaking off the residual tension of having to sneak through the checkpoint yet again, I climbed out of the car and stretched out my back. 'Can we afford this?'

'It comes prepaid,' Bas said in a sarcastic tone. 'Rodney owns the building.'

I goggled at him. Bas held up a small silver key. 'Shall we?'

'Did he give you that?'

'Yes.'

Rodney was either amazingly trusting or planning on betraying us. He might have been one of the only people in town for whom I was more inclined to suspect the first option.

'Spending the night in proper bed? Count me in.'

Bas snickered quietly. As he rounded the car to fetch a few things from the back, I heard him whisper, 'Princess.'

'Git.'

'Yes.' He tossed a bag my way and grasped the rifle in its case. 'Let's go.'

The key got us in the back door. The building was as narrow inside as it had looked from the outside; we entered into a long, thin kitchen, and from there into a stairwell with doors up only one side. Each one led to a room, I assumed. Bas checked the number on the key and led me up the creaky stairs to a door on the first floor. The room beyond was square, with a large window looking out onto the parking lot, and comfortable furniture. No bathroom—that must be shared with the rest of the building. I shuddered to think what the rent on a place like this was: shared kitchen, shared bathroom, but an address right on the river? More money than I saw in a year, probably.

I sat on the bed and kicked off my shoes. 'So, what now?'

'Food and sleep,' Bas said.

'Is there a shower?'

'Should be.' He vanished out of the door and returned a moment later to report: 'It's just next door.'

'Thanks.'

'You can go first. I know you like being clean.'

I was being mocked. I rolled my eyes and made a show of sniffing my sleeve. 'Well, if you like the smell of smoke, I suppose I could always skip it for tonight…'

'Go.' Bas pointed to the bag I'd brought in. 'There are clothes in there. Borrow what you want.'

Fresh clothes and a shower sounded heavenly, and I didn't even care how much he teased me for it. I rifled through the bag and found a T-shirt and a pair of men's underwear, then went to do my ablutions. When I came back, Bas was sitting on the bed, methodically checking over the rifle. I dropped my clothes on a chair in the corner.

'Bathroom's all yours.'

Bas looked up, and a shiver rippled through his shoulders. For several seconds, he just stared. Awkwardness settled over me like a cloud.

'I… Uh… My jeans are dirty,' I muttered. I felt naked in just his shirt; it barely brushed my thighs.

'Right.' Bas cleared his throat. 'Shower.'

He set the rifle aside, grabbed his stuff, and fled the room.

Great. He'd just run away from me, and no matter that now really wasn't the time to be thinking about… sex stuff, I couldn't help but be hurt. I abandoned my plan to go and examine the kitchen and crawled under the bed covers instead. It was heavenly, of course. Maybe the nicest bed I'd ever slept in. Rodney Rochester sure didn't skimp on quality.

I turned onto my side, staring at the wall, and let out an enormous sigh. So much had happened today, I felt as though I could sleep for a week. Finding Theo. Losing him. The attack on the Ellerys' farm. Rodney. Staking out the Black Hands' compound. The potential traitor.

It was too much.

I rolled onto my back again, my eyes following a hairline crack in the ceiling. My brain felt too full to process any of it anymore.

When will this end?

But there was no answer to be had. I was in a tunnel, and there was no end in sight.

The door cracked open, and Bas crept in. His hair was dripping onto his shoulders, wetting his shirt. He dropped his dirty clothes with mine, then came over to the bed.

'Do you want anything to eat?'

'No,' I said. 'I'm tired.'

'Alright.' He picked up one of the pillows and dug a blanket out of his bag. After a moment, I realised what he was doing.

'We can share.'

Bas looked up from where he was laying the bedding out on the floor. 'What?'

'The bed. We can share.'

'I don't want you to feel uncomfortable,' Bas said, the words about as meaningless as if he'd said them in some foreign language.

'Why would I feel uncomfortable?'

Bas fiddled with the blankets on the floor. 'I don't want you to feel pressured into anything.'

'I don't.' In fact, I felt as though a thread had pulled taut in my belly, and any second it might snap and unleash something. I didn't know what, but I knew I was ready to find out. After everything that had happened, I wanted to find out.

The universe owed me this.

Bas approached cautiously like he was scared I might get spooked. Finally, he sat on the edge of the bed.

I touched his thigh, and he tensed.

'Do you feel pressured?' I asked.

'No.'

'Good.' I sat up and cupped his cheek. His stubble was rough and scratchy against my palm. Turning his head, I kissed him.

Bas responded instantly, as though he'd just been waiting for permission. He pulled me close, tangling our legs together, then tugged my hair until I tilted my head back. His tongue ravaged my mouth; his nails dug into my shoulders. I could taste his desperation—the same desperation I felt.

Today had been too close. There had been a moment there where I'd thought that I'd lost him.

All of that fear came out now, twisting together with Bas's. He rolled me onto the bed, his leg settling between mine. I pressed myself against it as heat pooled in my belly. *This.* This was what I wanted. I found the hem of Bas's T-shirt and dragged it upwards, raking my nails over his chest, and he made a noise into my mouth that sounded rather like a growl.

Fuck yeah.

He broke the kiss, dipping his head to suck at a spot on my neck. I gasped.

'Bas…'

I clawed his back, playfully at first, but then he tensed, and I did it again. Less playfully this time. Bas groaned against my neck, and I felt his teeth dig in.

I gasped. Bas chased the pain away with his tongue, then moved to kiss a steady line down to my collarbone and the top of the shirt I was wearing. His fingers found the hem, and he slid it slowly up my belly.

His fingers tickled.

I squirmed, too sensitive to bear it. Bas pressed a hand against my abdomen, hot and heavy, holding me in place.

I was going to explode with want. Any second now.

On a whim, I scratched his back and moaned, 'Sebastian.'

Bas tensed.

Fuck. I'd ruined the moment.

'I'm sorry,' I said.

He remained stiff and unmoving under my hands for what felt like a million years, thought it was really only a few seconds. Finally, he murmured, 'I don't mind.'

That felt worth exploring. I twisted my fingers in his hair and gently tugged his head back until I could meet his gaze.

'Why don't you use your full name?'

'It feels strange.' Bas's eyes skittered to my lips, my neck. 'Let's not discuss this now.'

'I like your name.'

'No one calls me that anymore.' His voice was husky.

'Sebastian.' I traced a finger playfully over his arm.

'Just Bas.'

'Why? I like the idea that I'm the only one who calls you that.' I shouldn't push him, but I'd found that sometimes Bas liked to be pushed. Sometimes he actually wanted to be pushed. And I could always stop if he pushed back.

He caught my finger. 'It's cumbersome.'

'It's your name.'

'Mmm.' He sighed and shifted so he was resting his weight on his elbows and looking down at me. 'If I call myself Sebastian, then people expect a full name. Sebastian Rochester. But I don't want that man's name. I don't want anything from him. So it was easier to let go of it and just be Bas.'

'I don't know. I rather like the idea of saying 'Sebastian'…' I leant in, hardly able to believe my daring. 'Whispering it into your ear whilst you use those clever fingers on me…'

I was halfway to imploding with embarrassment—but Bas's gaze dropped to my lips, and then lower, and suddenly it felt totally worth it.

'What sort of things would I do with my fingers?' he whispered back.

'What sort of things would you want to do?' My heart was going to burst right out of my chest any second now. I was terrified that I was going to make a stupid mistake and shatter the moment.

'What about this?' He shifted back onto his knees, so he was sitting between my legs, and twisted one hand into the fabric of my shirt, pulling it up. His gaze was as focused and intent as it always was… but now he was focusing on me, and my heart raced in anticipation. Slowly—so slowly I thought I'd die before he touched me—he lowered his other hand and swiped his index finger against my centre.

My entire world narrowed to that single touch as pleasure rushed through me.

'Bas,' I mumbled. And then, because he had just given me permission, '*Sebastian.*'

That seemed to spur him on. Still with the same look of concentration, he dipped his head and kissed me through the briefs I was wearing. Every muscle in my lower body tightened. I grabbed the bedsheets, digging my fingers in.

'Shit. Bas, please!'

'Please what?' Bas whispered, mischief dancing in his green eyes.

'Don't tease.'

He hummed—a tiny, playful sound that heated my blood. He brought a hand up, tracing a line over my thigh, before tucking his fingers under the waistband of the briefs and easing them down. Every movement was calculated, deliberate, and torturously slow. I wasn't sure if I wanted to push him away or pull him closer. Beg or scream.

Both, maybe.

I brought my legs up so he could get the briefs off, and finally, he tossed them on the floor and settled himself more comfortably on elbows and knees between my legs. I squirmed. His entire attention was focused between my legs. What if he didn't like what he saw?

He used his thumbs to part my labia and blew gently against my clit.

I shuddered, my thoughts evaporating.

'Oh God!'

Bas smiled and lowered his head.

'Bas—' I started, half-protest, half-plea, but my words were lost as I felt his tongue touch my core. He licked slowly from bottom to top, and it was as though his touch was rewiring my body. I arched my back, pressing closer to him, and buried my hands in his hair.

Bas hummed, sending little jolts of pleasure through me. He adjusted his position, and then I felt his finger sliding slowly into me—long and uncomfortable and way, way too much, until suddenly it wasn't enough, and all I could do was plead for more. I clung to Bas, an incomprehensible prayer tumbling from my lips as he drove my pleasure higher and higher. How did he know where to touch me? It was as though my body was an instrument that he had been learning to play for years. His fingers and tongue guided me ever closer to a peak that I desperately needed to reach—

It hit without warning. Bas sucked my clit into his mouth, and I tumbled over the edge, gasping and arching my back as pleasure rushed through me.

The spasms seemed to last forever, hours and days of golden pleasure, before finally it subsided, leaving me drained and limp. Bas pulled away and collapsed onto the bed beside me, a gentle smile that I'd never seen before on his face.

'Wow,' I whispered.

'Glad you enjoyed it.'

'Uh, yeah.' I had no idea what to say. I shook myself a bit. 'Think I'm still recovering.'

'Mm-hmm? I'm confident you'll get there.'

I gave his side a playful little shove. Bas grabbed my hand, holding it against him. Then he worked the covers over himself and me.

Was he going to sleep?

'Do…' I cleared my throat. 'Don't you want me to reciprocate?'

Bas seemed to hesitate. '…Not now.'

'Are you sure?'

'I'm sure.' He rolled onto his side and put an arm around me, tugging me close. 'That was enough for now.'

'Okay.'

I wanted to push him, but I didn't know how. I stroked his long fingers where they rested against my abdomen. 'When you're ready, I'll be here.'

Bas hummed into my neck, making my hair flutter. 'Go to sleep,' he whispered.

'Alright. Goodnight.'

'Goodnight, Harley.'

I was dreaming, and then I was not. I sat up abruptly, the duvet tumbling off me.

'Fuck.'

'What is it?' Bas scrambled up beside me, his hand reaching for his gun.

'Savannah,' I said, my stomach lurching as though I'd missed a step going down the stairs. 'I forgot to meet Savannah.'

TWENTY

I WANTED TO GO TEARING off to find Savannah the moment I woke up the next morning, but unfortunately, circumstances conspired against me. Rodney was sitting in the kitchen when we descended the next morning, wearing a suit and drinking coffee, looking for all the world as though he belonged there.

I drew up short, and Bas grabbed my shoulder. 'Harley?' he murmured.

'Rodney,' I whispered from the corner of my mouth.

'Good morning,' Rodney said.

Smoothly, Bas shifted past me, putting himself between me and Rodney.

'What are you doing here? This wasn't the plan.' He strode in and grabbed the pan of coffee, peering at it.

'That's fresh,' Rodney said. 'Help yourself. I came to tell you that everything is arranged.'

Bas looked up sharply.

'Already?' I asked in surprise.

'What?' A wry smile played on Rodney's lips. 'Didn't think I could do it, Miss Benoit?'

'Talk to me, not her,' Bas said darkly.

'You know, if we're going to be rekindling our relationship, I'm going to have to speak to your girlfriend eventually.'

Girlfriend. Despite the tension suffusing my body, I caught myself smiling. Last night had washed away the last vestiges of uncertainty. Bas and I *could* make this relationship work. We *were* better together. All it took was patience. Trust.

Bas narrowed his eyes.

'It's fine.' I touched his arm. 'I can handle Rodney.'

Bas tensed. 'My brother,' he said lowly. 'My problem.'

Perversely, Rodney smiled. 'At least you're acknowledging our relationship.'

Of all the times to be smug! Bas slammed the pan down on the stove, slopping coffee onto the counter.

'Get out,' he said.

'I'm here to give you information.'

'Then give it to me and leave.'

'This is my property,' Rodney said placidly. Couldn't he see that he was riling Bas up more and more? Or was that his goal? 'I thought we might breakfast together.'

Bas kept his back to the room, retrieving mugs with jerky movements. 'No. We're going out as soon as you leave.'

Rodney frowned at Bas's back. 'That's not what we agreed on.'

Bas's shoulders were practically up by his ears. 'I don't remember agreeing for you to invade my personal space or get in the way of my prearranged plans.'

For a moment, neither of them spoke. I gripped the doorway, trying to figure out what to say or do to ease the tension. The last time Bas and Rodney had faced one another, Bas had decidedly had the upper hand the whole time. But today, he seemed off balance. Because he'd agreed to try and make up with Rodney? Or was it something else?

Bas finished pouring the coffee and turned to hand me a mug. I cradled it between my hands and smiled at him.

'*Okay?*' I mouthed.

He nodded. Rodney looked between us a few times, before pushing to his feet.

'Sunday,' he said as he strode past us. 'They will be visiting us for a late lunch. Expected arrival is two PM. The strike must take place before they enter the property, is that understood? I don't want a mess on my hands.'

'I'm sure that can be arranged.' Something told me Bas was fighting not to roll his eyes.

'I'll expect an amelioration of your attitude, as well.'

'You'll get what you get. You're lucky I'm even talking to you.'

For a moment, tension crackled between the two brothers. Both wore identical angry expressions. Neither seemed to want to look away.

Rodney caved first. He cast his gaze downwards, then turned.

'I hope we can change things,' he said. 'That's all I've ever wanted.'

He turned and walked away. Bas didn't relax until we heard the front door slam.

I was a bundle of anxiety as we made our way to our rendezvous point. Before I could head to the clinic to meet Savannah, we had to meet Ellery. Savannah, as Bas had pointed out, wasn't exactly going anywhere. Nor could I just barge in on her whilst she was working.

He wasn't wrong, but I still felt as though I had to fight to squeeze my breaths down my throat.

Bas didn't want to risk driving, because we were less likely to stand out travelling on foot—and it was easier to duck into side streets to hide. Besides that, our current residence was quite close to where we were meeting Ellery, on a small street named Kilter Passage. We made our way over in silence, but as Kilter Passage came into view, Bas said quietly, 'Harley?'

'Yeah?'

'Don't mention Rodney or the plan to them. Not yet.'

I nodded, even though my stomach churned at the thought of hiding it. If we couldn't trust Ellery and Kade, who could we trust?

We slipped into the alleyway. I'd never been here before, but I knew Kilter Passage by reputation. Once upon a time, there had been a tattoo parlour here that was known for helping escaped slaves. Until the Black Hands had gutted the place. The remnants were still there; the painted façade peeling and grimy, the windows boarded over. I'd heard that the owner had been shot, and the shop had been left empty as some kind of strange memorial. As I stepped closer, I noticed that people had painted on the boards: names, dates, and a variety of symbols. I recognised one of them—a silhouette of a bird taking flight. It was the same tattoo that Bas had on the inside of his wrist, covering up his old slave mark.

I traced my fingers over it. Were these marks left by people who had been freed?

I glanced at Bas, but before I could speak, a shuffling sound at the end of the alley caught my attention. Bas drew his gun, and we pressed our backs to the wall as someone entered the alley.

'Don't shoot,' Ellery called. 'It's me.'

He had a hat pulled low over his head, and his jacket was buttoned up to his chin. Bas lowered his gun, and Ellery dropped his hands.

'Where are the others?' Bas asked.

'I came alone,' Ellery said. 'I thought it would be safer.'

Bas nodded and tucked his weapon back into its holster.

'What did you find out?'

'Jackson's not in the compound anymore.' Ellery shot me a half smile in greeting before turning back to Bas. 'Looks like he moved out when the deal with Godfrey went down; at least, we overheard a conversation to that effect.'

'Makes sense.' Bas's eyes moved constantly as he kept a lookout towards both ends of the alley. 'Any idea where he's gone?'

'Not yet. Kade and Laura have gone ahead. They're going to try to tune into the radio chatter from the compound today..What about you? Anything new at the Black Hands' compound?'

Bas shook his head. 'I might have an in, but it needs more work. We're heading back to the Black Hands' compound this afternoon.'

Ellery nodded sharply. 'I suggest we RV again this evening.' He shifted his weight, also looking back and forth—down the alley, and at Bas and me. 'We need to strike whilst the iron is hot.'

He was on guard, I realised. And not just because we were in the open.

Because he, like Bas, had realised that we might have a traitor.

'Not here,' Bas said. 'Somewhere else.'

Ellery nodded. 'Hustle Highway, the west end. Where the Lounge is.'

'That'll work.' Bas clasped Ellery's hand. 'Keep safe.'

'And you.' Ellery gave him a long, searching look, before turning and taking my hand as well. 'I'll see you later.'

He pulled away and loped off down the alley. I stared after him, my stomach squirming.

'Let's go,' Bas said. 'We shouldn't linger.'

I hastened after Bas, a single thought swirling in my head.

No one seemed to trust anyone anymore.

We returned to the car to enact the next phase of Bas's plan, which took us to the Rochesters' mansion. When we finally stopped across the road from the gate, I stared in awe at the huge house. Painted white, it sat at a distance from the road behind a tall wall. Two wings extended from either side of it, and there were more windows than there had been in my old block of flats. It even had a garden.

It looked like a little island of paradise amongst the desolation of our town. I couldn't even imagine what it must be like to live there.

When I looked at Bas, he had wrinkled his nose, as though he smelt something bad.

'This is where Rodney and your father live?' I asked.

'And *his* wife,' Bas said in distaste.

'Your father's wife?'

He nodded. I swallowed. It had never occurred to me that Jonathan Rochester might be married.

'We need to find an ambush spot,' Bas said. 'As close as possible to the gates.'

'Rodney said to keep it away from them.' Not that I thought Bas had forgotten, but he was wearing a strange expression.

'He said not to do it on their property,' Bas said. 'That's it.'

'Right.' I glanced around uneasily. Bas started the car again, and we headed away from the house.

'This is the route they'll take coming from the compound,' he said. 'It's the shortest route. They'll probably travel in two cars—Moriarty and Hannover in one, with a driver, and a security team in the other. The security car will be in front.'

I nodded along, my stomach stirring uncomfortably. The more real this plan became, the worse I felt about it.

'Are you going to tell Ellery? Won't we need him as backup?'

'You're my backup,' Bas said.

'Of course, but—' His meaning caught up with me. 'Wait, you want to ambush him *alone*?'

'I have to. I'm not risking putting you in the line of fire.'

'You have got to be kidding me.' Except he *wasn't*. Bas looked utterly serious.

'No,' I said. 'I'm staying with you. If you face this, I do too.'

'Absolutely not.'

My unease coalesced into realisation. 'You're losing sight of our goals, Bas.'

'I'm not.'

'You are. This is—' I hesitated, the words jamming up on my tongue. No matter how far we'd come, I was well aware that there were lines I couldn't cross with Bas. But if I couldn't cross them with him, then what was our relationship worth? 'Is this about helping our town, or is it about your revenge?' I asked quietly.

Bas tensed. 'I know what I'm doing, Harley,' he said coolly.

'Do you?'

'Of course.' He stopped abruptly and nodded to a pair of huts, one on either side of the road. They looked to be some kind of guard huts, abandoned, but well maintained. 'Those will do.'

He opened his door and jumped out, approaching the nearest hut. I watched him open the door and examine the interior before he crossed in front of the car and headed for the other to check it as well. When he returned, I asked, 'What are they for?'

'I think there used to be a police checkpoint here,' Bas said.

'And will they work?'

'Yes.' Bas indicated the closer one. 'You'll wait there. I'll be on the other side. You should be able to see out without being visible from the road. Don't come out unless I signal to you.'

I swallowed. The whole plan seemed appallingly flimsy. 'Will you be able to take them all on your own?'

'As long as the security car is in front, I should be able to,' Bas said. He started up our car and turned us back towards the centre of the town. 'I'll have enough time to shoot Moriarty and Hannover before they manage to stop and get back to us.'

'And then?' I asked.

'Then I take out the security team.'

Just like that. My stomach twisted itself into another knot. I glanced at Bas's profile. His features were set with determination.

'So long as you're sure,' I said quietly, 'that you're planning this for the right reasons. Because it sounds… so risky, and—'

'I'm sure,' Bas said.

'Alright.' I swallowed. 'I'll help.'

TWENTY-ONE

FOOD HAD BEEN SPARSE ON the ground recently. Bas raided the back of his car, and I used the communal kitchen to cobble together something resembling lunch. Another resident, a well-dressed woman, came in whilst I was cooking and eyed me like I was some kind of bad-smelling vagrant whilst she fetched something from the fridge, but she refrained from speaking.

After we had eaten, I said quietly, 'Do you mind if I walk over to the clinic on my own?'

'I'd prefer to come with you,' Bas said. 'There's safety in numbers.'

'I know. It's just…' I chewed my lip. 'I feel like everything is about to change, and I just need a moment to… process, I guess. And Savannah will be happier to talk if I go alone.'

'I can walk part of the way with you,' Bas said.

'Please.' I injected a bit more force into my voice. 'I need this, Bas.'

Bas frowned. My chest ached like someone had scooped out my innards and left a hollow cavern behind. I hated putting pressure on him like that, but I really did need time alone.

'Alright,' he said finally. 'But if you aren't back in three hours, I'm driving over to fetch you.'

I nodded. I didn't like putting a time limit on my conversation with Savannah, but if that was what I had to do, then I'd do it.

'Thank you,' I said.

I returned to the room to grab my jacket, then headed out. As I walked towards the bridge over the river, I glanced back. Bas was watching me from the open doorway. I waved to him and lengthened my stride.

Five minutes later, I was across the bridge and the building was out of view. I reached into the deep pockets of my borrowed jacket and pulled out Bas's radio. He'd kept it since leaving the Iron Fists, and whilst he'd been out at the car, I had stolen it out of his bag. Hopefully, it still worked. More importantly, hopefully, Ellery had his on him.

The last time Bas had used it that I was aware of, it had been to speak to Ellery. Which meant that all I had to do was switch it on and press the talk button.

As soon as I flicked it on, chatter emanated from the speaker. '…got a delivery incoming. Boss needs you to…'

'Roger.'

Shit, what did I do now? I hadn't accounted for other people using the same channel.

No way but forwards. Well aware that I was about to do something extremely risky, I hit the talk button.

'Lynx?' I cleared my throat. 'Lynx, come in.'

Silence. The chatter vanished.

'Lynx, come in,' I repeated.

'H—Fennec, Jesus Christ.' Ellery's voice was the best thing I'd heard all day. 'What the fuck are you doing?'

We were on borrowed time. Not just that, we might have already been caught. 'I need to speak to you,' I said. And then, as cryptically as I could, I added, 'My sister. Get to her. As soon as you can. I'll meet you there.'

'What? Are you crazy?'

'Please!' How could I get the urgency through to him? I cast my gaze about for ideas, as though inspiration might be waiting in the cracked façade of a nearby building. 'It's a matter of life and death.'

Before Ellery could respond, another voice cut in. 'Unidentified station, identify yourself. Over.'

Fuck. Shit. What did I do now? I had no idea how to respond.

'This is Charlie two-six, over,' Ellery said.

'Copy.' A brief pause ensued before: 'There's no Charlie two-six. What unit are you? Over.'

'I'm with Hannover's team. Access requested to—to confirm tactical collaboration.'

Silence. I was so tense, I felt sick to my stomach. What was going on? Were we caught out?

'Access denied. All stations this net, roll comms. Be prepared for radio check and respond in sequence. Zulu, out.'

Abruptly, my radio went silent. Only Ellery and I were left.

'What… what just happened?' I asked carefully.

'They switched channels,' Ellery said. 'We can't spy on them anymore.'

Fuck.

I was a few streets over from the clinic when Ellery pulled up beside me in his car, cut the engine, and rolled the window down.

'Get in,' he said tersely.

I scrambled up into the passenger seat and glanced into the back. 'You're alone. Good.'

'"Good'?' Ellery quoted. 'What the fuck are you doing, Harley? We were using that channel to spy on the Iron Fists, and now we're out and I have to waste time trying to figure out what new channel they're using.'

'I needed to talk to you.' I couldn't look at him. I gripped my knees, digging my fingers in. This had been a stupid idea, but I had no idea what else to do. 'Something's wrong, and—'

'What?' Ellery demanded. 'What happened? Where's Bas?'

'That's what I need to speak to you about.'

Ellery's brow furrowed. 'What's going on?'

'I...' Now that I was here, the words stuck in my throat. 'I'm worried about Bas.'

'Bas?' Ellery echoed. 'Has something happened to him?'

'No.' I shook my head. 'It's more... how he's behaving.'

'Spit it out,' Ellery snapped.

I swallowed.

'Firstly...' I hesitated over my words. 'Bas thinks there's a traitor. Who let on that we were staying at your place in Freetown.'

Ellery frowned. 'I considered it,' he said. 'But I think it's more likely that Hannover has been following you for longer than we realised. Maybe even when you were fighting at The Arsonist.'

That was an option that Bas and I hadn't considered—but it was definitely a possibility.

'Since we discussed it, he's been different,' I said. 'He went to... to see Rodney. And he asked me to keep it a secret.'

'His brother?' Ellery gaped at me. 'You're joking.'

'He asked Rodney to lure Moriarty out.' It only took me a few moments to outline the broad strokes of Bas's plan. Because, in fact, I only had the broad strokes. He hadn't even shared most of the plan with *me*. As I talked, Ellery's expression shifted into a worried frown.

'And then you called me?' he finished, more a statement than a question.

'Yes,' I said. 'Sorry, I know it was stupid. But I didn't know what else to do.'

'No,' Ellery said. 'I'm glad you did.'

Abruptly, he buried his face in his hands and heaved a deep sigh. When he lifted his head, he looked exhausted. 'I should have expected this,' he mumbled.

'It's because of his father, isn't it?' I asked. In retelling, everything was starting to come clear. 'Because he wants revenge.'

'No,' Ellery said. 'It's because of *you*.'

'Me?' What the hell did I have to do with this?

'He's trying to protect you, Harley. In his own way.' Ellery shot me a grim look. 'He's afraid of losing you.'

'He's not going to lose me!'

'There are no certainties in life,' Ellery said. 'You know that.'

I scowled. 'I'm not going to walk away from him.'

'That's not what he's afraid of.'

No, he's afraid of me dying.

Of course he was. He'd even told me what had happened the first time he'd faced Moriarty.

I hugged my legs to my chest, fielding a pointed look from Ellery for putting my feet on the seat. 'What do we do?'

'Show him he can rely on us,' Ellery said. 'What time did you say Moriarty was arriving?'

'Two.'

'Alright, so you and Bas will have to be in place before that. Let's say by eleven, to be safe.'

It seemed too early to me, but Ellery was right—Bas wouldn't take chances on the time. I nodded.

'We're not going to be able to communicate,' Ellery said. 'Not now that we've lost the transmission station in Freetown. So I'll make sure to be at the guard station before you.'

It only took us a few minutes to create the outline of a plan, but in those few minutes I felt as though a weight lifted off my shoulders. I had been worrying about Bas, more than I'd even realised. But Ellery's calm confidence helped. He was Bas's best friend. I was Bas's girlfriend. Together, we'd help him. We'd get him through this.

Once we'd run out of things to discuss, Ellery asked, 'Do you need a lift home?'

'No. I need to walk over to the clinic. I forgot that I was supposed to meet Savannah yesterday.' My stomach squirmed again with guilt. How could I forget my own sister?

'Okay. I'll drop you on that street.'

'Yeah, alright.'

Ellery pulled us off the kerb and we headed for the clinic. When we turned onto that road, we found the way blocked. Ellery had to hit the brakes, bringing us up short of two grey four-by-fours that were turned sideways to block the road.

'What's going on?' he asked.

But my gaze had already jumped to beyond the blockade—to the clinic, where uniformed men were swarming the property. My heart lodged in my throat, and a cold sweat formed on my back. I grabbed my door handle in clammy hands and threw the door open, hurrying to the blockade.

'Hey!' a man shouted. 'Halt! Miss! Halt!'

Someone stepped in my way, and I drew up short.

'My sister—my sister's in there—'

'You can't enter this area, miss. It's been closed off for a criminal investigation.'

'What?' I couldn't remember how to form sentences. My head felt as though it was filled with buzzing flies. 'I—But—What—'

Ellery strode up beside me. 'What's going on here?' he asked.

'Federal investigation.' A tall man with a pockmarked face and windswept hair held up a badge:

Walter Schone
Brackfields Police, Investigative Unit

I stared at it. The buzzing in my head was getting louder and louder.

'I'm afraid I'm going to have to ask you to leave,' Schone said. 'This area is restricted until we've completed our investigation.'

'But this is our only medical clinic,' Ellery said.

'My sister's in there.' I wasn't even sure if I'd spoken aloud. My lips moved, but I couldn't hear my words over the buzzing in my ears. I couldn't be rightly sure I had heard Ellery. Schone's lips moved, but his words were also lost.

My fingers tingled.

What was this? What was happening?

At that moment, another person strode up. His words cut through my brain, the familiarity punching me like a fist in the gut.

'What's going on here? Get rid of them.'

'On it,' Schone said. He brought a radio up to his lips.

I swayed, unable to take my eyes off the man who had joined us.

Blond hair. Tall, weedy figure. Cold blue eyes. But he was in a uniform I'd never seen before. Gone was the generic black of the mayor's security team, replaced by an expensive and professional-looking uniform, complete with body armour. He looked at me like I was dirt beneath his feet, before an expression of recognition crept onto his face.

'Harley Benoit.'

It was Evander Hardwick.

My breath jammed in my throat. Hardwick. What was Hardwick doing here?

'Unconscionable! We're doctors!' A rough cry rose up in the distance. Schone whipped towards it, but all I could focus on was Hardwick's cruel smile.

'It's time for you to leave,' he said.

'What have you done?' I whispered.

Someone yelled, and I heard the clap of flesh on flesh. Another bellow.

Ellery gasped.

That was the sound that made it through the fog. I turned to him and followed his gaze.

And there she was. Looking so small, so vulnerable, so terrified, between two massive soldiers.

Savannah.

Her hands cuffed together, she was led across the road towards a truck.

At once, the world rushed into hyperfocus. I took two steps forward, then broke into a sprint. Savannah! I had to get to—

I slammed into someone with such force that the air rushed out of my lungs. Winded, I wheezed.

'This is a restricted area.'

I'd slammed into Schone. I fought furiously, twisting and clawing, but his grip was unyielding.

'SAVANNAH!' I screamed. 'SAVANNAH! NO! THAT'S MY SISTER!'

Schone threw me backwards, and I crashed onto the asphalt, grazing my hands and sending pain jolting through me.

'Back off, lady. These people are under arrest for aiding and abetting slavers.'

My vision blurred. 'NO! My sister never had anything to do with the slavers.'

'That's not up to you to decide.'

'You're making a mistake!' I scrambled to my feet. 'I know everything—Savannah's not one of them. It's Clairmont!'

Schone shook his head. 'The investigation will determine that,' he said. 'If you have evidence, you can contact my superior—'

'I don't care about your superior! I need to speak to my sister!'

I swayed, feeling as though I was about to float away. A feather in the wind. I had no feeling left in my body.

Not Savannah. Not my sister.

Schone shook his head. 'Leave, or you'll be arrested, too.'

If they arrest me, at least I'll be with Savannah.

Ellery cut through that thought with a cool voice, 'Come on, Harley.'

'No! I have to help Savannah.'

'You won't help her by getting arrested.' Ellery took my arm, tugging me away. 'Thank you for your time, Officer Schone.'

Schone nodded, gazing at me with an expression of pity. I felt sick. I wanted nothing more than to run to Savannah—fuck anyone who tried to stop me—but instead, I let Ellery pull me away.

'Yes, off you go, Harley.'

I whipped around at Hardwick's whisper. His smug, white face leered back at me. I took a step towards him, balling my fists, but Ellery tightened his grip on my arm.

'I hope you never lose a sibling,' Ellery said. 'You might not find the experience as funny as you think.'

Hardwick glared at us. Ellery put his arm around my shoulders and steered me to the car.

'Come on,' he whispered. 'I'll drive you home.'

TWENTY-TWO

IF PRESSED, I DOUBTED I could have related a single thing about the car ride back to the house where Bas and I were staying. It passed in a blur, and I only surfaced from my daze when Ellery said, 'Harley, you should probably walk from here.'

'Yeah,' I croaked. 'Thanks.'

I reached for the door, but Ellery's voice held me back.

'Listen,' he said. 'Don't do anything reckless. We're going to figure this out.'

'Alright.'

'I mean it, Harley.' His brown eyes were wide and sincere, but his words seemed to pass right through my brain without sticking.

'I need to go lie down,' I muttered.

Ellery sighed. 'Alright. I'll see you tonight.'

'Yeah.'

I trudged across the bridge and back to the house, feeling like I was dragging an enormous weight behind me. Every step was a slog. The stairs were an insurmountable obstacle. I knocked on the door, and when Bas opened it, I sagged against him, wrapping my arms around his torso.

'Harley?'

At once, the tears came. Thick and fast, they tumbled down my face, soaking into Bas's T-shirt. I sniffled. He pulled me close, smoothing a hand against the back of my head.

'Harley,' he repeated, lower this time. 'What happened?'

'Savannah… She… They… I couldn't…' My words get lost amidst the tears. I pressed my forehead into Bas's chest, as though that would stop them, but there was no stopping the flood. All I could do was cling to Bas and hope that I absorbed some of his never-ending strength to get me through the storm.

After untold minutes, my sobs subsided into hiccoughs. Bas rubbed my back and head, humming—I couldn't pick out what, but I felt the rhythm in his chest, and that seemed to help more than anything. Eventually, the tears dried, and I leant back, feeling wrung out and weak.

'Ready to talk?' Bas asked.

'I… They arrested Savannah,' I blurted. I had to get it out as fast as possible, or I'd cry again. 'And all the doctors. For the slavery ring. But Savannah's innocent!'

Bas's expression darkened. 'When?'

'Just now. Whilst I was there.' Another sob escaped my chest and wrenched out of my mouth. More tears welled in my eyes, and I buried my face in his chest again.

'Shh,' Bas murmured. 'Harley—'

Abruptly, he cut himself off, his body going stiff. Footsteps thudded up the stairs, and I turned in Bas's arms to see Rodney walking towards us.

Uh oh.

He stopped short, frowning at the two of us.

'What are you doing here?' Bas asked. 'I thought I told you not to keep coming back here.'

'My apologies for interrupting.' Rodney adjusted his jacket cuffs, looking anywhere but us.

'What is it?' Bas snapped.

'I…' He studied a spot on the wall. 'Is there anything I can help with?'

'No,' Bas said, his hands tensing on my shoulders.

Rodney shuffled his weight. He seemed about to protest, but then he changed tack. 'I've just received word that Godfrey's going to be giving a speech on the square this evening. It occurred to me that you might not have heard.'

I twisted out of Bas's grip. 'About the arrests?'

'Arrests?' Rodney echoed.

'You don't know yet.'

His brow furrowed. 'I'm not sure what you're referring to.'

'The Brackfields police have arrested the doctors at the clinic in connection with a local slavery ring,' Bas said. 'You wouldn't happen to know anything about that, would you?'

Rodney squirmed, his mouth opening and closing.

'Of course he knows. He was in the original meeting with the mayor and his father when I learned about it.' I shot him a pointed look. Rodney's gaze drifted off to one side.

'I'm aware of a local ring,' he said. 'I don't approve of it.'

'Your lot approves of anything that makes them money,' Bas said darkly.

'That's untrue.' Rodney straightened his tie.

'I don't see you putting a stop to it.'

'It was Father who agreed to this, Bas. I don't have that kind of power.'

Bas glared. I squeezed out from between the two of them, who were suddenly standing very close together. 'What time is the speech?'

Rodney glanced at me. 'Five PM. If you leave now, you should still make it.'

'Good.' I turned to Bas. 'I want to go.'

Bas frowned. 'We don't have a plan in place. How will we get in?'

'I can help with that,' Rodney said.

Rodney's help made things much smoother than ever before. We entered the checkpoint in his car, and no one even searched us for weapons. It was probably a good thing because I could barely focus on my surroundings, my entire brain redirected to a single problem which I turned over and over.

How was I going to help Savannah?

I didn't even know where she'd been taken, let alone how I was going to get her out. If I *could* get her out. Why hadn't I asked more questions?

Rodney parked around the corner from the square and instructed his driver to stay with the car. We walked the rest of the distance, and one street over, he said, 'This is where I leave you. I'll meet you back at the car once it's over.'

'We can make our own way,' Bas said.

'It'll be easier for you to get in and out of the checkpoint.' Rodney's eyes lingered on Bas's jacket, underneath which his gun was concealed.

Bas made a non-committal noise in his throat and turned to me. 'We should get going.'

'Yeah.'

'I'll see you later,' Rodney said, before heading off down the road.

I slid my hand into Bas's, squeezing his fingers. My stomach was churning with a potent combination of fear and nausea. What was I about to hear? Would Godfrey reveal what Savannah and the other doctors' fates would be?

When we reached the square, I paused in surprise. There were more people there than I'd expected, considering the short notice. Word about the arrests must have spread fast. The square was buzzing, and worried faces abounded.

There was also more security than the last time we'd been here. That didn't surprise me—clearly Godfrey wasn't going to risk meeting the same fate as his predecessor.

Keeping my grip on Bas's hand, I eased us into the crowd. We stuck to the edge of the square, and Bas's gaze roved around, searching for danger.

'Marco,' he said in surprise.

I glanced at him, before following his gaze. Ellery was pushing his way through the crowd towards us.

'Harley, Bas!' he called. 'What are you doing here? Weren't you heading to the Black Hands' compound?'

'Change of plans,' Bas said. 'What about you?'

'Jackson is here. We followed him over,' Ellery said. 'Any idea what this is about?'

'They arrested the doctors,' Bas said. A pang of hurt jolted through my chest, and I turned away from them as my breathing grew ragged.

It's okay… You'll help her. You have to.

I squeezed Bas's fingers, and he pulled away and wrapped his arm around me instead.

'…going to do about medical facilities for the town?' Ellery was asking. I'd missed Bas's explanation about the arrest, not that I was sad I had. I had lived it.

Bas gestured to the hotel steps. 'I assume we're about to find out.'

Security guards were buzzing around outside the front doors of the hotel, with one notable absence: Evander Hardwick. Whenever the mayor was out and about, Hardwick had always been with him. Maybe Godfrey had fired him?

Or had he finally fulfilled his purpose in town and vanished back under whatever rock he'd come from?

He'd been in a police uniform at the clinic earlier. Had he been working for the Brackfields police all along?

'Harley?' Ellery asked. I looked at him, and he raised an eyebrow.

'Sorry, I wasn't listening,' I mumbled.

'How are you holding up? Do you know where they've taken Savannah?'

I shook my head, swallowing around the lump in my throat. 'I only know what you know.'

Ellery frowned. At that moment, microphone static filled the square, and we all turned to the hotel. Godfrey had stepped outside, flanked by two huge bodyguards carrying heavy rifles. He definitely wasn't taking chances.

'I'd better get going,' Ellery murmured. 'Figure out where Jackson's at.'

'See you later,' Bas said.

'I'll catch you before I leave.'

Ellery slipped off into the crowd. I turned my attention to Godfrey, who cleared his throat noisily into the microphone.

'Thank you for coming, ladies and gentlemen,' he said. 'I'm sure some of you have already heard what has transpired. For those of you who haven't, with the help of the Brackfields police force, today we have taken an important step towards securing the future of our town and driving out those who would exploit us for their own personal gain.'

Uncertain applause filled the square. I kept my hands by my sides. Savannah had never exploited anyone for personal gain.

'Many of you may be worried about our town and your future. Let me assure you as your mayor that I am here for you. I will hear all of your concerns and address them. For now, I would like to reassure you that we are working on an interim solution to get the clinic up and running again…'

Some bumped into me from behind. I stumbled into Bas. He righted me, and I twisted around to see what was going on. 'Hey—'

The words died in my mouth as I saw who was standing behind me. The hairs on the back of my neck rose.

'Begging your pardon.' Hannover smirked.

'You!' I hissed. Bas tensed against my side.

'Harley Benoit, you have gotten yourself into trouble this time, haven't you?'

'Get away from me. I don't want to deal with you right now.'

Hannover smiled. 'It seems to me that you might benefit from my help right now, actually.'

I froze. What did he know?

'Definitely not,' Bas said.

'Does it bother you, Sebastian?' Hannover's gaze shifted to Bas, his voice taking on a sing-song quality. 'That this is an issue you can't help her with?'

'I don't know what you're talking about,' I said. My voice shook, my attempt at keeping cool falling short. 'Why would I need your help?'

Hannover stepped closer to me, invading my personal space. My breath shuddered in my throat as I tensed, ready to run.

'You know exactly what I'm talking about,' he whispered. 'How's your sister these days?'

My heart seemed to skip a beat, before making up for it in double time. 'How do you know—'

He knew. Not just about the clinic, but specifically that Savannah had been arrested, too. How could he know that? Unless he'd been there—or was involved somehow.

Abruptly, rage began to simmer in my chest. Of course he was involved. Because it was him—and the rest of the Black Hands—who had set up the whole slaving operation.

'This is your fault,' I snapped. 'You're the one taking the slaves in the first place.'

Hannover tsked. 'You should be careful with those accusations… I'd hate for anyone to think you'd been conspiring with your sister.'

'My sister is innocent!'

Hannover laughed. 'Innocent, guilty,' he mocked. 'Do you really think that matters?'

I ground my teeth together. He was playing games—of course. That was what he always did. And I couldn't allow him to rile me up.

'Just tell me what you know,' I said.

'Oh no, that's not how it's going to work.' Somehow, despite the people milling around us, Hannover looked perfectly collected—almost smug. 'It's your turn to give a little.'

'We're not agreeing to anything,' Bas said coldly. 'Get out of here.'

But my mind was churning. I'd wanted to find out what Hannover was after, and here was my chance.

'What do you want?' I demanded.

'Harley, no,' Bas said.

I didn't have time to convince him of my plan. I was going to have to just go for it—and hope Bas trusted me.

I met Hannover's gaze. Hannover smiled.

'What you want and what I want are very well aligned,' he said slowly. 'You want your sister free. I want the army out of town. They're getting in the way. We can achieve both with one blow.'

'I don't see how the two are related, actually,' I replied.

Hannover spread his hands. 'Look around you. There's no prison in our town. Your sister is being held in the only place she can be—the military camp north of town.'

His words made sense—too much sense. But I couldn't see how his plan would come together. What could possibly free Savannah and get the army out of town?

Suspiciously, I asked, 'How do you know?'

'Let's say a mutual acquaintance told me.'

Did he mean Hardwick? I stood straighter. I'd seen Hannover and Hardwick together before—but now it didn't make sense. Surely they weren't allies?

'Who—'

'That's for me to know.' Hannover's eyes narrowed.

I frowned. 'Even so, getting the army out of town won't free Savannah,' I said.

He was playing with me. Did he really think I'd be stupid enough to go along with whatever he had planned?

'With the right bargaining chip, you can do both,' Hannover said.

'Don't believe him, Harley,' Bas warned quietly.

'I don't.' I kept my gaze on Hannover, whose smug mien didn't slip an inch. 'There's no such thing. Let's go, Bas.'

'Do you really want to trust your sister's fate to the military's woefully biased justice system?'

I turned back. 'I don't want to trust it to you, either.'

'I can give you the power to help her.'

'I can help my sister on my own.' I crossed my arms. 'Why would I trust you? I know full well you have your own agenda.'

And he'd shoot me, given half that chance. It wasn't as though I hadn't given him a reason to.

'The army wants something,' Hannover pressed. There was a strange light in his eyes that put me on edge. All of a sudden, I wanted to walk away.

'So you've already said,' Bas sneered. 'But we all know you have no intention of telling us what it is.'

He pulled away from me suddenly. 'Harley, come on.'

I hesitated, and in that brief moment, I lost Bas in the crowd.

Hannover chuckled. 'Trouble in paradise, I see.'

'That's none of your business.' I rounded on him again. 'Tell me, or I'm leaving too. Tell me straight. You need something from me, and I'm tired of your stupid games.'

Hannover stared at me, as though weighing the dilemma, before he finally said, 'The bunker is built on multiple levels. You know how to access the others, don't you?'

I had no idea what he was talking about, but I certainly wasn't going to admit that.

'What's that got to do with anything?'

'The second level contains an old military armoury. It's sealed off. Jackson knows how to access it—of course—but why would he share? He plans on using the weapons to take over the town once and for all—declare himself mayor.' He met my gaze. 'But if someone were to remove the weapons first, that would put a wrench in his plans, don't you think?'

'Why are you telling me this?'

Hannover examined his fingernails. 'It seems to me that whoever takes the weapons has the power to determine the fate of this town. Use them—or hand them over to someone else who will use them.'

He was right.

'Why tell me?'

'Jackson isn't watching you. You could stop him, save your sister, and persuade the army to leave.' He mimed throwing something. 'Three birds, one stone.'

I stared at him. It could not be that easy. This was a trick, without a doubt.

But... that didn't mean it couldn't work.

If we could find the weapons—which was no guarantee.

'Why don't you do it yourself?' I asked.

Hannover shrugged. 'I don't know where the entrance is.'

'Then how do you know about the weapons?'

He quirked an eyebrow. 'The one thing men in power love more than all else is the opportunity to brag. I'd have thought you'd know that, Harley.'

That was a non-answer. I frowned. All of this was just too convenient.

'I'm not agreeing to this. You think I don't realise this is a trap? You'll shoot me in the back and take the weapons for yourself.'

Hannover tsked. 'Harley, Harley, Harley, do you really think you can walk away from me?'

I froze, awareness trickling down my spine.

'You see, now you know, and I'd hate for you to get noble ideas about using the weapons against me. It wouldn't be the first time, would it?'

Against my will, I felt my cheeks heating. He meant mine and Theo's plan to kill him.

'I won't use the weapons against you,' I insisted. 'I have zero interest in your quarrel with the army.'

'I can't take that risk.' Hannover stepped closer, crowding into my personal space. 'I know you well, Harley Benoit; you aren't good at keeping your word. No... a little incentive is needed. And as it so happens, the police have provided the perfect one, haven't they? Your sister... a sitting duck in her cell... I'd hate for something to happen to her.'

My breath caught in my chest, and my body felt as though it had turned to ice. He wouldn't *dare*...

But of course he would.

Hannover patted me on the shoulder. I wrenched away, bile rising in my throat.

'I'll see you soon, Harley.'

He smiled and walked off.

Fuck, fuck, fuck.

What the hell was I going to do now?

TWENTY-THREE

'WHAT KIND OF WEAPONS?' ELLERY ASKED. Bas, Ellery, and I were standing in a little huddle under the awning of a restaurant on the edge of the square.

'I don't know. He didn't say.'

'I told you not to speak to him.' Bas leant against the water-stained wall, his arms crossed. 'This is a complication we didn't need.'

I bristled. I'd already explained to him why I had forged ahead with Hannover—to find out what he wanted. He didn't need to rub in the fact that I had missed Hannover's trap.

'I don't know,' Ellery said, a pensive look on his face. 'This *is* valuable information. Harley's right.'

I shot him a grateful look.

'I'm still annoyed,' Ellery added. 'Don't get me wrong.'

I sighed. 'I didn't realise he would—'

'—make things worse?' Bas interrupted. 'That's what he does, Harley.'

I cringed. Put like that, it seemed obvious.

'There was nothing stopping him from just blackmailing us into helping him,' I argued. 'At least this way, we have some control over our own actions.'

'Until he betrays us and leaves us in an even worse position,' Bas said flatly.

'So we don't let him! We find the weapons first and remove them before he can take them!' I insisted. We at least had to try.

Ellery and Bas exchanged glances.

'Hannover will have thought of that,' Bas warned.

'If we moved quickly, we might still be able to pull it off,' Ellery said.

'I doubt it's going to be that simple.' Bas shook his head.

'Look,' I cut in, 'we all agree that we don't want the weapons in

Jackson's hands, right?'

'Right, but we don't want them in Hannover's hands either,' Ellery said. 'And currently he can't access them.'

'So he says,' I said. I didn't believe his reasoning for sending us after the weapons—it didn't make sense. My going theory was that he wanted to use us as a scapegoat somehow.

If only I could figure out *how.*

'We don't even know if there are weapons,' Bas said. 'This could be a trap.'

'If there aren't weapons, then what's on the second level of the bunker?' I asked.

Silence reigned as we all looked at one another. It was a good question. I'd already figured out why Hannover thought I knew— Maddock. Somehow, he had reached the conclusion that I had either helped Maddock, or had figured out how Maddock got through the bunker to the compound. And he was right: Maddock was the one who had clued me in. It just hadn't been intentional. I'd seen the notes on the wall of his flat in Crater's Edge.

'That's a good question,' Ellery said.

'There's only one way to find out.' I glanced at Bas. 'Will you help us?'

Bas was the deciding vote. If he refused to go along with this— which he might—then I'd have a choice to make: support Bas or go my own way.

Not the choice I wanted to make.

It seemed to take forever before he finally spoke. 'I'm not letting you go alone,' he said in a low voice.

My insides, which had been twisting themselves in knots, relaxed abruptly as relief flooded my veins. We were still aligned. Somehow, someway. I took Bas's hand.

'When do we go?' I asked.

'Now?' Ellery replied. 'There shouldn't be anyone in the bunker at this time, but we'll have to be quick.'

'We can take the other entrance. You know,' I caught Bas's eye, 'the one we used after Maddock shot Sayle.'

Bas shook his head. 'There's an easier way.'

Ellery nodded. 'Let's find Laura and Kade and get going.'

He led the way to a side street, where we found Kade leaning against a wall, keeping a wary eye on the entrance to the square.

'Ellery.' He straightened up immediately. 'Harley, Bas!'

'Hey.' I smiled. It was good to see him again. After spending so much time living together, it had felt weird not having Kade's calming presence around for the last day.

'Where's Laura?' Ellery asked.

'We got separated on the square,' Kade said. 'But she knows we're meeting here.'

Ellery frowned. 'Maybe we should—'

But at that moment, Laura came jogging into the alleyway. 'Sorry,' she panted. 'I thought I saw someone I knew. Harley!'

She threw her arms around me. I squeezed her, grinning. 'Hey.'

'How are you?' Laura pulled back. 'What's the plan?'

'We're heading over to the bunker,' Ellery said.

'Why?'

'Because we might have a lead. I'll catch you up in the car.' He glanced at Bas. 'See you there?'

Bas nodded and turned to me. 'Come on.'

I had to hurry to keep up with Bas's brisk pace, but I didn't complain. It was just gone four, so if we were fast, we could get into the bunker this afternoon still. But time was against us: it was Friday, and in a scant few hours the first of the bunker staff would start arriving to set up for the fights.

And if we got caught, we were almost certainly done for.

Rodney was waiting for us at his car. When we arrived, he pushed off.

'I almost thought you weren't coming.'

'I almost didn't come.' Bas pulled open the door and climbed in. 'Make it quick.'

Rodney scowled but climbed into the car as well.

It didn't take long to drive back to the house where we were staying, but I felt every second tick down as though there was a clock embedded in my chest. Finally, Rodney dropped us in front of the building.

'I'll see what I can do for your sister,' he told me. He darted a glance at Bas.

'That's the bare minimum you can do, seeing as it's partly your fault she was arrested,' Bas said stonily.

Rodney flinched. I took Bas's hand and squeezed it, but his hand remained limp in mine.

'I'd be grateful,' I said. Rodney's help wouldn't hurt, in any case.

Rodney nodded to me, before shooting a wistful stare at Bas. Bas just reached for his door and clambered out. I sighed and followed him, muttering a 'thanks' to Rodney as I went.

The drive over to the bunker was similarly uncomfortable. Bas was silent, obviously stewing in anger. As we left town, I finally scraped together the courage to apologise.

'I'm sorry for speaking to Hannover,' I said quietly.

Bas's knuckles whitened where he was gripping the steering wheel. 'Hannover can throw you off course with just a few pretty words.'

I frowned. Maybe I shouldn't have spoken to Hannover—but did he really think I was that stupid?

'Have you ever considered that your 'off course' is just me looking at things differently to you?'

'We *had* a plan,' Bas snapped.

'We still have that plan, and I'm still committed to it!' I took a few deep breaths, trying to reign in my anger. 'But I don't remember you listening to my hesitations on that, either.'

'I do listen to you.'

I pressed my lips together and breathed slowly. 'I have to help Savannah, Bas. Not as an afterthought. Hannover knows where she is— if he catches us going after Moriarty, he can retaliate against her. I can't risk that.'

'I would have helped Savannah,' Bas said. 'You didn't give me a chance to come up with a plan.'

I stared out the window. 'You have that chance now.'

'Now you don't need me. You have Hannover's plan.'

I dug my fingers into my knees. 'Don't be petulant. I thought we were in this together.'

Bas drove in silence. I turned to look out the window again. We were driving towards Freetown.

'You're right,' Bas said.

I glanced at him. He was focused on the road ahead.

'I can't... think clearly when Hannover's around,' he said in a tortured voice. 'I never have been able to. But Harley... I don't want you getting too wrapped up in his machinations. He'll get you killed.'

'I don't care about his plan,' I said. 'All I needed to know was where Savannah was.'

Bas nodded. 'We'll figure something out,' he said. 'We'll find a way to get her out. Tonight.'

'Thank you,' I said quietly.

The silence in the car felt more tolerable after that. A few minutes later, Bas pulled off the road and drove up to the burnt shell of a small, square-ish building. Ellery's car was already there, and when we stopped, Ellery jumped out of his car, followed by Laura and Kade.

'Ready?' he asked as we joined him. He clicked on a torch, and I glanced at the sky. It hadn't started getting dark yet.

'Let's go,' Bas said.

The reason for the torch immediately became obvious: amidst the rubble of the building, we found a staircase leading down into the basement. Ellery went first, gun in hand, and Bas brought up the rear. At the bottom of the stairs, we squeezed into a small room which was dominated by a vault door, rather similar to the one that barred the bunker's entrance in the bottling plant.

'How many of these doors are there?' I asked.

'I think this is the only other one,' Ellery said. 'But there could be others we haven't found.'

He passed the gun off to Kade and the torch off to Laura. 'Bas, lend me a hand here?'

Unlike the other vault door, which I'd never seen closed, this one required quite a bit of huffing and heaving to open. Finally, Ellery and Bas managed to turn the wheel and the door opened with a scream of metal hinges and a puff of dust. The hall beyond it was totally in darkness—none of the floor-level emergency lights that lit the other tunnels. I felt like I was staring into the gaping maw of some prehistoric beast.

I shuddered.

'Wow,' Laura whispered somewhere near my shoulder.

'Spooky,' Kade remarked.

'Let's go,' Ellery said, hoisting a leg over the lip and into the tunnel. 'No time to waste.'

He led our procession. Our boots were impossibly loud in the corridor, and the torches cast strangely shaped shadows on the rounded walls. We walked around fifty yards, rounded a corner, and came to a halt.

The way was blocked by a wall of rubble.

'It's blocked,' Laura said, her voice echoing the disappointment bubbling in my chest.

'Do we have time to turn back?' I asked.

'There's a way through.' Ellery turned to the wall, grabbed a metal handle, and heaved. A panel slid up out of the way, revealing a second, smaller tunnel.

Beside me, Bas tensed unhappily. I took his hand.

It didn't take me long to realise why he didn't like that particular tunnel. It was long, zigzagging, narrow, and seemed to go on forever. Without lights, it was impossible to see more than a few yards ahead. And the ceiling was low, so we had to walk in a stooped single file. Finally, we reached the end. Ellery signalled for us to wait a few feet back, then carefully lifted the sliding panel and stepped out, gun first.

I held my breath, listening, but there was no sound of people or gunfire. Finally, Ellery reappeared.

'All clear,' he whispered. 'Come on.'

He helped Laura out, and the rest of us followed. I stretched and looked around—I recognised where we were now: near Carlos's office.

'The entrance is in your dressing room, right?' Ellery asked.

'That's the one I know of,' I said.

He nodded and set off. The bunker was much creepier than I'd expected out of hours. Our footsteps seemed to echo much louder; every rustle of clothing and every breath we took seemed louder. The hums and ticks and bangs of the different tech systems were much more intrusive than usual. I couldn't help but twitch at every noise. At one point, we had to hastily hide in a storeroom when two members of the Iron Fists passed by on patrol.

When we reached my dressing room, I stepped forward and twisted the handle, opening the metal door.

Crrrrreaaaaak.

I jolted in shock, gasping for breath. Ellery clapped a hand on my shoulder.

'Alright?'

'Yeah, fine,' I muttered. My cheeks burnt. Ugh, embarrassing. I should have remembered the creaky door.

'Let's go,' Bas said urgently. 'We need to be through before the next patrol passes by.'

I nodded and pushed the door fully open. My dressing room was empty and silent. The cupboards and dress racks loomed out of the darkness, and the chairs and tables became an obstacle course. Worst were the mirrors, which reflected flashes of torchlight into my eyes, blinding me. I squinted as I led the way to the back corner, and what had once been my dressing table.

'Shine the torch at the ceiling, please,' I instructed Ellery.

I climbed onto the table and heaved at the ceiling panel.

It stayed put.

'Fuck,' I breathed. 'They've bolted it down.'

I turned to the others, who all wore identical *oh shit* expressions.

'Should have seen that coming,' Ellery muttered.

'Are there other ways in?' Kade asked.

'At least one.' I clambered off the table. Bas put out his hand to steady me. 'In the office. But that one is screwed down.'

'There have to be others.' Ellery shifted, running the torch along the ceiling.

'If it were me, I'd have bolted them all down,' Bas said. 'Not worth the risk.'

'One has to be open,' I said. 'Otherwise, how did they get in and out to bolt them down?'

We exchanged glances.

Ellery opened his mouth.

'We can't check every room,' Bas said. 'We don't have time.'

Ellery shut his mouth, his teeth clicking. 'I wasn't going to suggest that.'

Bas shot him a pointed look.

'How many rooms are there?' I asked. I knew the front-facing area of the bunker, and the warren of back rooms we were in now, but there were tonnes of other corridors that I'd never been in—areas that were restricted access, had been blocked off or caved in…

'A lot,' Ellery admitted. 'Fine, we can't check every room. Then we have to figure out which room they left open. What would you do?'

He looked at Bas. Bas frowned, examining the wall. I could practically see the cogs turning in his head.

'A room that's easily defensible,' Bas said.

'Somewhere close to the compound, then,' Ellery said. 'In one of the restricted areas.'

'Possibly.' Bas paced across the room and back again. 'One of the offices, maybe? Or the armoury?'

I leant against my dressing table and glanced at the ceiling. 'How far away is that from here?'

'Half a mile,' Ellery said. 'Maybe more? It's in a separate network of tunnels.'

'Then it's not there,' I said. 'No one would crawl that far in these tunnels. I'm not even sure it's possible—It's a maze up there.'

'She's right,' Bas said, starting another tour up and down the room. 'It's too far. There has to be an entrance in this sector.'

'But Maddock got from here to the compound,' Ellery said.

'I thought of that,' I said. 'He might not have gone the entire way through the ceiling. Hannover said this place has more than one floor, and I think, from the blueprints we saw at Maddock's place, that he knew that too.'

'So he accessed a separate floor?' Ellery asked.

'And got through to the compound that way,' Bas finished. He glanced at the ceiling. 'Makes sense.'

'Doesn't help us find the entrance here,' Ellery said.

'The office would be defensible,' Kade offered.

'But we know that one is sealed,' I said.

'You're sure?' Bas asked.

I nodded. 'I saw it.'

'We could check anyway,' Ellery said.

'And risk getting caught?' Bas shook his head. 'Where else is there?'

We lapsed into silence, all trying to think. After a few moments, Ellery approached the table.

'Let me get up there and see.'

I stepped away, and he climbed onto the table, fiddling with the hatch.

'We might be able to get a crowbar in here,' he said.

'We don't have one,' I pointed out.

'We could make do. Or there might be one in the maintenance room.'

Realisation struck me.

'That's where it's open,' I said.

They all looked at me.

'Think about it!' I continued, brimming with excitement. 'Maintenance has to be able to get in to keep things running!'

'She has a point,' Kade said. 'And no one would think to look there.'

Ellery was looking at Bas, silent communication passing between the two of them. After a moment, Bas nodded.

'Let's check.'

The maintenance room was on the other side of the big hall. We made it to the hall without running into another patrol, but when we got there, we all stopped just inside the tunnel.

'Run for it?' Ellery suggested.

'Keep to the walls,' Bas said. 'You and Kade go first. Once you're across, the rest of us will follow.'

My heart seemed to lodge itself in my throat. I watched with growing apprehension as Ellery and Kade crept along the wall towards the other side of the room.

And then I heard the footsteps.

'Bas,' I mumbled.

He nodded sharply. 'Go. Quickly.' He waved to the hall.

Every part of me wanted to run. It was physically difficult to fight that urge and take slow, cautious steps along the wall. Every step, I looked back. Three-quarters of the way across the room, I saw the torchlight out of the corner of my eye.

The patrol.

'Run!' Bas said.

I grabbed Laura's hand and broke into a sprint, towing her along. We pelted into the corridor, the shouts and footsteps of the patrol following us.

'In here!' Ellery hissed.

I staggered past him, through a doorway and into the maintenance room.

'Where's the hatch?' Kade cried.

'Ceiling,' I said. Ellery shone his torch up and we all looked around. I stepped back, my shoulder bumping into a metal cabinet mounted on the wall.

'There!' Laura pointed. 'That's it.'

Relief flooded me—I'd been right. *Thank God.*

'Great.' Ellery grabbed a ladder and towed it over to the corner of the room. In a trice, he was up and had heaved the panel out of the way. He scrambled up and reached out a hand. 'Laura, come on.'

Laura scrabbled up and Ellery helped her into the ceiling. Kade followed.

Just Bas and me left. Bas pushed me to the ladder, and I hurried up, my feet slipping away from underneath me. Ellery caught my hand and helped me up the last bit, and I crawled into the ceiling.

Which left Bas.

He was watching the door.

'Bas, come on!' I hissed.

He hurried to the ladder and started to climb.

The door flew open.

'HALT! GET BACK HERE!'

'Come on!' Ellery grabbed Bas under the arms and hauled him up. He twisted around, gun in hand, and took aim.

BANG! BANG!

The gunshots sounded incredibly loud, and the aftershock reverberated through my soul. For a second, the five of us just sat there, breathing loudly. Nothing moved below us.

'Did you get them?' Ellery hissed.

Bas nodded. Then he reached down and knocked the ladder over with a loud clatter.

'Shut the panel and let's go,' he said.

TWENTY-FOUR

ANY SECOND NOW, SOMEONE WAS going to follow us into the ceiling, and we would be dead.

The thought circled my head and pounded through my veins. And yet, I was forced to move slowly through the crawlspace, ducking under pipes and around ventilation units. Every sharp pant of breath disturbed the dust. Every shuffled movement made splinters snag on my clothes.

I kept moving. My gaze roved around, following the torchlight, searching for signs of an entrance to another level.

'Any other clues you have would be really helpful right about now,' Ellery muttered.

I grimaced. 'We're at the extent of my knowledge.'

'The stairs have to be in one of the blocked tunnels,' Kade theorised. 'So we need to find one of those.'

'And hope the panel hasn't been sealed,' Ellery muttered. 'And that there's a way back.'

I swallowed and glanced at Bas, crawling silently beside me. We'd created a lot of problems for ourselves in a very short time.

Kade solved the first one.

'We should be above the blocked tunnel in the west now,' he said.

'You think?' Ellery asked. 'I don't think we've gone far enough.'

'I'm pretty sure.'

Kade shone his torch on the ceiling beneath us, sweeping it in slow lines until he found a panel with a handle on the inside. 'There we go.'

It took a few minutes to work the screws out of the panel, using makeshift screwdrivers. Finally, Kade got it up and shone his torch into the hallway below. Like the one we'd entered by, it was totally dark and covered in dust.

'Looks promising,' Ellery said.

'I'll go first.' Nimbly, Kade lowered himself down and dropped to the ground. We all watched, hardly breathing, as he moved around below us, checking nearby doors. A few moments later, a faint 'aha!' floated up to us.

'Found a staircase!' Kade jogged back over. 'There's definitely a lower level. Possibly even two.'

'Thank fuck,' Ellery said. I sagged in relief, reaching for Bas's hand. It was there. That was the first hurdle survived.

Now we just had to see if there really were weapons.

One by one, we dropped out of the ceiling and landed in the dusty corridor. It was immediately obvious that no one had been here in years. The entire place had the feeling that it had been abandoned to time; tree roots had grown through the ceiling, mould and damp covered the walls. Dust and slime mixed to make a gross sludge under our feet.

Kade led the way to a door, and we descended a flight of stairs to a second level that was cleaner—but no less abandoned—than the first. A sign hung just outside the door.

LEVEL ONE
Atrium
Cafeteria
Common Room
Administration
Classrooms

LEVEL TWO
Dormitories
Training Centre
Sports Facilities
Swimming Pool
Medical Bay

LEVEL THREE
PERSONNEL ONLY
Maintenance
Recycling Centre
Electrical and Water Department
Security

'We need to go one level further down,' I said quietly. It felt wrong to speak too loudly down here for some reason.

'What's that?' Ellery asked, turning away from where he was examining something on the wall.

'Guys, look at this!'

We all turned towards Laura. She was standing in the doorway of a room about fifty feet down the hall. Ellery broke into a jog, and the rest of us hurried after him. I passed through the doorway last and stopped dead.

It was a living room.

That much was obvious: very old, very broken sofas, some kind of frame on the wall, though the space where the picture was meant to go was black. Some other device hung on another wall, facing the sofas, looking rather like the sort of thing Declan had in his shop—a thin metal rectangle with black glass in the middle. Laura was standing in another doorway. She turned to us, holding something. A very worn, fragile-looking teddy bear.

'Do you think people lived here?'

'I think that's what it was for,' Ellery said.

'What happened to them?' Laura asked.

We were all silent. None of us had an answer.

'That… this stuff is ancient history.' Ellery shuffled his feet. 'We need to focus.'

Laura's brow wrinkled in a frown. She disappeared into the other room and came back without the teddy.

'Yeah,' she said. 'Let's not disturb this stuff. It… it feels wrong.'

A shiver ran down my spine. Suddenly, I wanted out of that long-abandoned living room, where people had once lived. Underground. Hidden away.

From what?

But there was no time for questions. We headed back to the stairs, where Ellery pointed out what he'd been examining: a map.

'We're on the middle level,' he said. 'The floors are labelled in descending order. And it looks like we want to be here.' He pointed to a spot on the far side of level three labelled *'Security. Restricted Access.'*

'So, down and across.' Kade squinted at the map as though he was trying to imprint it into his brain. 'Right, let's go.'

Kade, it turned out, was an exceptional navigator. Based solely on his memory of the map, he brought us across level three and to the door we needed.

Level three held fewer ghosts than level two because the rooms were dedicated to all manner of machinery: water filters, air purification, food production, and a whole host of other things that I didn't understand, such as the 'cryogenic facility' and the 'pathology laboratory'. We passed by all of those and finally arrived at a sturdy metal door with peeling letters:

RESTRICTED AREA — MILITARY PERSONNEL ONLY

'This is it,' Kade said.

Ellery tried the door handle.

'Locked,' he said.

We all stared at the door. Then Ellery turned and headed down the hall, letting himself into another room. A moment later, he was back with a ladder. 'If I've learnt one thing about this place,' he declared, 'it's that everything has a back door.'

Ellery turned out to be correct. After another short sojourn through the ceiling, we arrived in the restricted area.

It wasn't a single room like the map had implied. There was a whole separate complex down here which hadn't been marked on the map.

Fortunately, the Pre-Crash builders of the bunker had provided us with another map.

'Look at this.' Ellery tapped a point on the map.

'Escape hatch,' I read.

'That's our exit point,' he said. 'Saves us the trip back through the bunker.'

'We're out of time, anyway,' Bas said. 'By now, they'll have found the bodies.'

We exchanged grim looks.

'Let's get moving then,' Ellery said.

'Where are we going?' Kade asked.

We all peered at the map. It was littered with labels, but none of them made any sense to me. Control Room One, Control Room Two,

Communications Centre, Technical Support, Silo One, Silo Two, Silo Six…

'Shall we start in the control room?' Ellery asked.

'There's also a storage room,' Bas said.

'Let's split up and meet in the control room,' Ellery said. 'Harley and Bas, check the storeroom and these two silos. We'll work our way around the other side.'

I nodded. Bas and I headed off down our corridor, leaving the others to their side. We moved quickly and silently, checking rooms as we went: some kind of dormitory, a maintenance room, a room filled with weird devices.

'We're going to need Declan to decipher this stuff,' I said.

Bas hummed in agreement. The next door was labelled 'Silo One'. He twisted the handle.

Locked.

'Do you think we can get in through the ceiling?' I asked.

'Let's keep moving,' Bas said. 'We can always try later.'

I nodded and strode to the next door. 'Silo one maintenance.' I pulled it open and found a staircase leading down.

'There's another floor.'

'What?' Bas asked sharply. He strode over, nudging me out of the way. I followed him down the stairs, and we came out into a strange room: perfectly round, with a metal staircase winding around the outside. The middle was taken up by a strange metal cylinder.

'What the hell is this?' I asked.

Bas ran a finger over the metal, staring at it with a frown.

'I think…' He trailed off, his lips twisting. 'I think this is the weapon.'

'Really?' I immediately took a step back from the thing. I'd been picturing racks of rifles and guns and whatever else the military had. I had no idea. But this thing—it was huge. Unfathomable.

'What does it do?' I asked.

'I've only heard rumours.' Bas cleared his throat. 'They can blow up entire cities with these.'

'Holy fuck.' I had no words. Well, I had a lot of words. But none of them were polite. 'We cannot let Hannover get hold of these.'

'No,' Bas agreed. He straightened his shoulders. 'Let's go meet the others.'

We found them in the control room, which was one of the rooms with glass screens, and metal and plastic boxes of all sizes covered in buttons and dials and connected by myriad colourful cables. How I wished Kayla were there to try and get them running, but Laura had made a concerted effort; she'd figured out how to get one of them on and was reading the words that appeared on the screen.

'Did you find anything?' Ellery asked.

'These are missile silos,' Bas said.

'Yeah, that's what I thought. No wonder the military wants it.' Ellery grimaced. 'This is dangerous shit.'

'We can't let Hannover have it,' I said.

'Absolutely agreed,' Ellery said. 'I think we need an expert in here.'

'Declan,' Bas said.

Ellery nodded. 'If we drive over there now, we can be back here within an hour. Assuming he agrees to come.'

'One of us will need to stay here,' Bas said. 'Just in case.'

'I was thinking you and Kade. The rest of us can—'

'I have to get Savannah,' I blurted.

Both of them looked at me.

'Harley,' Ellery started. 'This is dangerous shit. Hannover could erase the entirety of Bale Rocks with just one of these.'

'She's my sister.' I swayed under the weight of their gazes. 'And Hannover already threatened her.'

I felt as though something in my chest was wrenching apart. Weapons. Savannah.

'I can go to the military and let them know this is here and be done with it,' I said. 'I could do that right now.'

'Or we could use this to end things,' Ellery said. 'There's enough firepower here to wipe out the Iron Fists complex five times over. If we could get this system working, we might be able to take out all of our enemies in one blow.'

I shook my head and looked at Bas. He met my gaze, frowning.

'You said you'd help,' I whispered. Weapons, Savannah. Weapons, Savannah. Save the town or save my sister.

'Someone has to stay here,' Bas said.

I swallowed. I felt like puking.

'That someone doesn't have to be me.'

'No,' he agreed. 'It has to be me.'

So if I went for Savannah, I went without Bas. Urgency filled me, a bubbling feeling that had nowhere to go. Hannover might have been bluffing about Savannah. But I couldn't take that risk. And how long would it be before he realised we had found the weapons and intended to use them against him? How much time did we have?

'I have to go,' I said. 'I have to help Savannah.'

'Don't make a rushed decision,' Ellery said. 'Savannah's safe where she is.'

'You don't know that.' My heart ached, as though just keeping itself beating was incredibly hard, tiring work. 'I… I can't take that risk. Savannah needs me.'

I'd put other people ahead of her. Time and again, I'd done that. I hadn't even realised I was doing it. But right now, Savannah needed me. I had to put her first. I couldn't allow Hannover to hurt her.

Ellery pursed his lips. 'Bas, have you got your radio?'

'It's in the car,' Bas said.

'Fine. When we get back to the car, I'll tune the two radios to the same channel. You won't be able to communicate with us if we're down here, but if one of us is above ground, we'll be able to talk.' He glanced at Kade. 'What do you think? Will the escape hatch get us out near where we left the cars?'

'I'd guess we're about five hundred yards away,' Kade said. 'Maybe a little more.'

Ellery nodded.

'Let's go.' He looked at Bas. 'I'll fetch Declan and come back. You lot see if you can get this thing working whilst I'm out.'

Bas nodded. Then he turned to me. 'Good luck.'

'Thanks.' My lips trembled. 'You too.'

And then I left. I didn't want to, but I had to. Every step carried me away from Bas and towards Savannah.

And I was terrified that this would be the last time I saw him.

TWENTY-FIVE

KADE'S PREDICTION PROVED ENTIRELY CORRECT; we hiked for less than ten minutes before the car came into view.

Whilst we'd been underground, the sun had set. The horizon in the west glowed pink with the last light.

At the car, Ellery pulled out the two radios and spent a few minutes tuning them to one another, before handing me one of them.

'I wanted to speak to you before you go,' he said, his tone uncharacteristically serious.

'Yeah?'

'If Declan can get the missiles up and running, there might be a chance we can stop Bas from going after Moriarty,' Ellery said.

'Oh.' That was a nice thought.

'But he'll fight us on it,' Ellery added.

'Why?' But then I answered my own question. 'His dad.'

Ellery nodded. 'Just keep that in mind. Whatever you do tonight, you have to make it back to Bas. I'll need your help to… to help him.'

I nodded. 'Okay. Thanks.'

Ellery clasped my shoulder. 'Good luck. Don't do anything stupid.'

'I won't.'

I took Bas's car, and Ellery took his own. I followed him through the wasteland and into town, and we separated at Declan's shop. I had the beginnings of a plan to help Savannah, but it was very basic, and I had no idea how I was going to pull it off.

Or even if I could line up all the pieces.

But damned if I wasn't going to try.

I drove to Prospect Avenue and parked outside my old flat. Straight ahead of me, just outside of the circle of light from the headlights, was the checkpoint. I could make out the two soldiers who were manning it, smoking underneath a streetlight.

No one else was around.

Taking a deep breath, I started the car up again and drove over, stopping at the sign. The soldiers straightened up, and one of them approached, a hand resting on his rifle.

I rolled the window down.

'You got permission to enter?'

It was Dusty.

I leant my elbows on the door. 'I don't want to get onto the square,' I said. 'I want to help you arrest a traitor.'

'What?' he stared at me. 'Wait, Harley? Didn't even recognise you! You can drive?'

'Mm-hmm.'

'We agreed Sunday.'

'Sunday doesn't work anymore,' I said. 'I need to do it tonight.'

Dusty eyed me suspiciously. 'Can you get Talbot to us?'

I nodded. *Hopefully.*

'Fine.' He seemed to weigh his words. 'Ryan should be back at the base already. I won't get off duty for another hour. Can we meet then? In an hour?'

That gave me an hour to solidify my plan of how the hell I was going to lure Talbot out.

'Should work,' I said. 'Where should I meet you?'

'Here. I'll radio base and tell them to send Ryan here.'

'Okay.'

Dusty returned to his colleague, and I reversed up onto the pavement to turn the car. Then I headed home.

One hour later, I returned to the checkpoint. I had changed into Savannah's clothes and pulled a hat on to hide my hair. Hopefully, it would work. It only had to fool Talbot long enough to get him to the car. After that, it didn't matter if he realised I wasn't Savannah.

Dusty and Ryan were waiting for me. Dusty waved me out of the car and handed me a mug of coffee.

'We'll have to talk in our car—there isn't space in the hut.'

'Alright,' I said. Now that I was here, actually doing this, the nerves were starting to take over. I followed the two men over to their car and climbed in the back.

'So.' Ryan turned to me, frowning sceptically. 'You know where Talbot is at?'

Savannah was much more organised than I was. I'd found a notebook with people's addresses in her bedside table drawer, and helpfully, Talbot's had been there.

'I know his home address,' I said. 'If he's not there, he's at the casino. The Lucky 2089.'

I took a sip of the coffee and wrinkled my nose. It was stale.

'Fine,' Ryan said. 'Seems simple enough. We drive you over there, you do what you have to to get him out to us, and then we do the rest. Got it?'

I nodded and took a deep breath. Time for my spiel. But before I could start, Dusty said, 'How are you going to get him outside?'

'I'll pretend to be my sister.'

Ryan squinted at me. 'And you can pull that off?'

'Seeing as we're identical twins, yes,' I said. Probably. But I didn't have to fool him for long.

'Fine.' Ryan turned to Dusty. 'Time to go, then?'

'Before we do,' Dusty said, 'what made you change the plan, Harley?'

Dusty was smarter than I'd given him credit for. I clamped my hands around the mug, trying to draw its warmth into my body. 'My sister's been arrested. I want to arrange a trade.'

'Absolutely not,' Ryan said. 'We don't release criminals.'

'She hasn't done anything,' I said. 'It was a mistake.'

Ryan snorted. Dusty asked, 'Who is your sister?'

'Savannah Benoit. She's a doctor,' I said.

'Oh, I see,' Ryan said. 'One of the ones that the Brackfields lot arrested this afternoon.'

'Exactly.'

'We can't release her. She's accused of conspiring with slavers.'

'She's didn't! She's innocent.'

Dusty frowned. 'Can you prove it?'

I opened my mouth. Shut it again. *No. Yes. With difficulty.*

'I can tell you everything I know,' I said. 'I've been following the slavers for a long time.'

Dusty and Ryan exchanged glances.

'Start from the beginning,' Ryan said.

It took me a while to run through everything I'd found out about the slaving ring, from spying on the NCC office in town to following the truck to the Black Hands' compound, to visiting the office in Crater's Edge. I squirmed through the whole thing. The clock was ticking, and I wanted to be moving. When I was finally done, Dusty exchanged another glance with Ryan before turning back to me. 'How much of this does your sister know?'

'None of it.' I sat forwards, willing them to believe me. 'I asked her about it, but she didn't know anything.'

'Yet *you* know an awful lot,' Ryan said, the beginnings of a sneer in his voice. 'Almost too much, for some little village girl.'

'Of course I know a lot,' I snapped. 'None of the authorities were helping us, so me and my friends had to do something about it ourselves.'

'Doesn't look to me like you've done much at all.'

I gnashed my teeth. Before I could muster an appropriately scathing reply, Dusty intervened, 'Come on, Ryan. This is valuable information.'

'If it's true.'

Dusty turned his gaze on me. 'Would you make a statement to my superior about this?'

'Um…' The thought made me squirm. But for Savannah… 'Yes. Sure.'

'In that case, once we've verified your story—'

'No!' I cried. 'You have to release Savannah tonight, otherwise I'm not helping you get Talbot.'

'We can get him on our own,' Ryan said. 'All we need is his address.'

'If you could get to him on your own, you'd have done it by now,' I said. Which begged the question—why hadn't they? 'But you're his team, and he recognised you, right? He knows you're in town, so he hunkered down.' They both looked away, and I knew I was onto something. 'You can't get close, but I can. He won't suspect me.'

'This isn't a negotiation,' Ryan snapped, crossing his arms over his chest.

'Okay.' I put my coffee mug down on the seat and reached for the door handle. This was a setback, but I'd find another way. Maybe I could blackmail Talbot.

'Wait,' Dusty said. 'We can arrange the trade.'

'Dusty—' Ryan hissed.

'It wouldn't be the first time we've done it,' Dusty said. 'By her account, the main players in the NCC are the higher-ups. If I had to choose between having Talbot behind bars or having her sister behind bars, it's Talbot.'

Ryan pinched his lips together, but I could see that he was on the verge of agreeing. Finally, he nodded. 'Fine, I'll radio base and warn them.'

He climbed out of the car, but when I made to follow suit, Dusty stopped me. 'Where are you going?'

'I'll drive in my car,' I said. 'You can't exactly pull up in front of Talbot's house in a military truck.'

Dusty frowned. 'Alright, then,' he said reluctantly.

Talbot's place was grungy. I wrinkled my nose as I parked across the road and surveyed the street. He lived in a low block of flats, one of the newbuilds in the south of town, with the landings wrapping around the outside of the building, so that everyone who lived there left all manner of laundry, furniture, and junk outside their doors. Even though the building couldn't have been more than five years old, it was dirty and stained with water damage.

Hopefully, Talbot was here.

I ran over the plan once more in my mind before climbing out of the car and making my way to the stairs. Talbot lived on the first floor, which complicated matters somewhat. I was going to have to get him downstairs before Ryan and Dusty could arrest him.

Savannah… Savannah… Savannah…

She was the one I was doing this for. But also, I had to get myself into her head. And considering I could count on one hand how many times I'd seen Savannah together with Talbot, that wasn't too easy.

What would Savannah say?

I drew myself up, tilted my chin, and took a deep breath.

Then I rang the doorbell.

Ding-dong.

'Coming, coming!' Heavy footsteps sounded, and then the door swung inwards. 'What—Oh.'

A smile split Talbot's face, and he brushed a hand over his messy red hair to smooth it. 'Hey, Sav. Wasn't expecting you. Did you walk all the way down here?'

'I—I caught a taxi-truck,' I said. Savannah often caught taxi-trucks, didn't she?

But Talbot's brow drew together in a frown. 'I thought you didn't use them anymore.'

'I—' *Fuck.* My mind raced. 'It… I—I just really wanted to speak to you!'

I reached out and grabbed his hand, making my eyes wide as I gazed up at him. His expression cleared. 'Aw. Alright, babe. We can talk about whatever you want.'

He leaned to kiss me. I turned my head at the last second, and his lips brushed my cheek.

'Babe?' he asked, drawing back.

My stomach roiled. 'I—I'm not feeling well,' I fabricated.

'You should have stayed in bed.'

'I just *really* wanted to see you.' I was going in circles. *Come on, Harley, think!* I traced a finger over his arm and tugged his hand to me. 'I missed you.'

A little smile crept over Talbot's face.

'Come in, then.'

'No!' I blurted. Talbot shot me an odd look. I took a deep breath. *Calmly, calmly.* 'No, let's go for a walk.'

'You want to go for a walk?' He waggled his brows. 'I thought you wanted to…'

Oh God. My cheeks were so hot I thought my face would explode. 'No… I really do want to talk.'

'Aw, come on. We haven't had sex in ages.'

Gross! Don't tell me that!

'Maybe later,' I said. 'I want to talk to you first.'

Talbot rolled his eyes. 'You never want to have sex anymore. Fine. Let's talk.'

He grabbed a jacket and shoved his feet into a pair of boots that was sitting just inside the door and stepped outside, bending over to lace the boots up. I eyed him. Was he armed? I was going to have to find a way to check.

We descended the stairs—part one of my plan over. Now for part two.

I casually slung an arm around Talbot. He slouched a bit against me.

'What did you want to talk about, then?' he asked impatiently.

Good question. 'I—uh… I'm worried about… Harley.'

'Harley? Babe, I told you to just forget about her.' Talbot pulled away from my hand, with which I'd been trying to find his gun. 'She just causes you stress.'

'She's still my sister.' I couldn't stop the defensiveness from creeping into my voice.

'You can't keep letting her drag you down,' Talbot said. We reached the edge of the road, and I tried to covertly glance around for Dusty's car. 'Come on, let's go back upstairs and we can find a way to relax you.'

He caught my arm, tugging me back towards his building. I couldn't risk that. Time for plan B.

Sorry, Bas.

I went on tiptoes and kissed him.

Talbot kissed like a fucking dying fish. His hands locked around my shoulders, and his mouth opened as his tongue slobbered at my lips. I shuddered, my stomach tossing like a boat in a storm.

Focus.

I had to make sure he was unarmed.

I moaned into the kiss, pressing myself closer, and snuck my hands under his jacket. All he was wearing underneath was a thin T-shirt, and I could feel the heat of his body.

I was going to puke.

No, focus.

I slid my hands down to his waist and felt around the back. *There!*

Talbot broke the kiss and wrenched back from me. I hastily put my hands behind my back, tucking the gun into my belt. He stared me up and down, a searching look in his eyes. 'What are you doing?'

'Kissing you?' I asked. 'I thought that was what you wanted.'

'You're not Savannah.' His eyes narrowed. 'Harley.'

He reached for his gun, except, of course, it was currently tucked into the back of my trousers. When his hand came up empty, his expression shifted into pure rage.

'You!' he snarled.

'Sorry,' I said. 'Savannah is more important than me.'

'You little bitch!'

I took a step back. Where was Dusty?

'Don't do anything rash,' I said.

'You fucking traitorous bitch.' Talbot spat at the ground. 'Of course. You and your sister both. The bloody Benoit sisters.'

'What the fuck are you talking about?'

He laughed, high and angry. 'You mean you don't know?' Talbot snorted and shook his head. 'You here trying to help her, and she's probably off with the blond guy from the mayor's office who she's been fucking around with.'

Who? What?

'Savannah would never!' I hissed. 'You take that back!'

'You bloody naïve—' Talbot's head whipped to the side, and I realised Dusty was approaching. *Finally—*

And then Talbot lunged at me. I didn't have time to react before he was on me. My back hit the ground, and I lay there, stunned, as he wrapped his hands around my neck. All I could see was his rage-filled face. My lungs burned, and I clawed at his hands as black spots started to take over my vision. Air—I needed air.

Metal hit flesh with a crack as Dusty clocked Talbot over the head with his gun.

'Oh.' Surprise flickered over Talbot's face, and then he keeled forwards onto me. His hands went limp, and I dragged in a rasping breath, so fast I started to cough. Dusty hauled Talbot backwards and discarded him on the ground.

'You alright?' He held out a hand. I grabbed it and let him pull me up.

'O-okay,' I muttered. My throat throbbed in time with my heartbeat, and the world seemed distant and out of focus. 'I'm… I'll be okay. Can we get Savannah now?'

Dusty and Ryan exchanged glances.

'Yeah,' Dusty said. 'You can follow us out in your car.'

I nodded.

The drive seemed to take forever, and yet it was over far too fast. Soon, we pulled up to the gate of the northern outpost, a collection of low buildings surrounded by a tall wall. I had to park outside and walk in, and then I had to wait in an office building with extremely uncomfortable metal chairs for what felt like forever.

I tapped my foot. I drummed my fingers.

What were Bas and Ellery up to? Had they managed to make their plan work? Had they been caught by the Iron Fists?

No. They'll be okay.

I stood and paced back and forth a few times until a uniformed woman behind the desk on the far side of the room shot me a glare.

Message received. I sat again.

Where were Dusty and Ryan? Had they tricked me?

Should I ask someone what was going on?

Finally, a door on the far wall swung open, and Dusty appeared with Savannah in tow. I shot to my feet and sprinted over to them.

'Savannah!'

'Harley?' Savannah stared at me, her eyes glassy. 'What are you doing here?'

'Taking you home.' I threw my arms around her. 'I'm sorry I was late, but I'm here now.'

Savannah's shoulders trembled. 'I didn't think I'd ever see you again,' she sniffled.

'I'm here. Shh. I'm here.' I squeezed her tighter. 'We can discuss everything else at home.'

'A-alright,' Savannah whispered.

Over her head, I caught Dusty's eye. He nodded.

'Give your address to the assistant.' He gestured to the lady at the desk. 'We'll be in contact about the statement you'll be giving.'

'Okay.' I chewed my words, before forcing them out. 'Thank you.'

'You're welcome.'

Dusty escorted us—via the assistant's desk—to the door, and out towards the gate. We climbed into the car, and I turned around to wave bye to Dusty.

'Whose car is this?' Savannah asked.

'Bas's.' I started it up and turned us in a clumsy circle to get out of the parking lot, and in that moment, the headlights lit up the front courtyard of the military base, along with the three people walking across it: Ryan, another soldier in uniform, and Talbot.

'That's Greg.' Savannah leant towards the window. 'He's—Have they—They've arrested him!' She whirled around to face me. 'We have to help him!'

'We can't help him, Sav,' I muttered. A deep feeling of shame was creeping through my veins.

'What do you mean?'

I started the car, manoeuvring us towards the gate. 'I did what I had to do.'

'What did you do?' Savannah hissed.

'It was him or you. I chose you.'

'You turned him in?'

I nodded.

'How dare you!'

The gate slid open.

'HOW DARE YOU!' Savannah screeched. 'TAKE ME BACK! HARLEY!'

She scrabbled at the door handle, but I accelerated, carrying us into the darkness.

TWENTY-SIX

BY THE TIME I MANAGED to coax her into our flat on Prospect Avenue, Savannah was barely holding in her rage. Like a bubbling saucepan, she overboiled.

'How dare you!'

I had used the drive back to fortify myself, but any walls I had built crumbled in an instant.

'I had to help you,' I said.

'By sacrificing my boyfriend?' Savannah paced over to the kitchen counter, stopped, and whirled around. 'You had no right.'

'I wasn't going to leave you in prison.' My voice sounded pleading to my own ears. Squaring my shoulders, I added, 'I don't regret what I did.'

'You're sick,' Savannah snapped.

'*Sick?*' I hissed. 'For getting you out of prison?'

'They wouldn't have kept me there!' Savannah shook her head. 'I didn't *do* anything, Harley.'

'You think anyone cares?'

'Of course they do!'

'It might have taken months for them to even hold a trial!' I cried. 'Hannover was already threatening you—'

'He couldn't have done anything! I was in prison.'

'Couldn't he? You have no idea how far his reach extends.'

'Of course I do,' Savannah said. 'I met him in the bunker, remember? He's all talk.'

I shook my head. How could she be so naïve? 'Hannover is dangerous!'

'My God, Harley.' Savannah threw her hands up. 'Do you even hear yourself?'

'He knows exactly who you are, and he told me what he planned on doing!' I took a step towards her. Why didn't she understand how urgent the situation had been?

But Savannah laughed and rolled her eyes. 'And you believed him!'

What the hell?

'Of course—'

'You believed him,' Savannah continued, 'so you went rushing off to do something stupid.' She shook her head. 'The only person bringing danger into my life is *you*, Harley.'

I clenched and unclenched my fists. This couldn't be happening.

'I'm trying to keep you safe,' I tried.

Savannah laughed bitterly. 'You have got to be joking. Nothing you've ever done has kept me safe. All you do is gallivant around with boys… do whatever you want. You're selfish. And whilst you're off living your best life, I'm the one who has to make hard decisions to survive.'

A cold fury filled me like nothing I'd ever felt before. After everything I had done for her, everything I had been through…

'The only selfish person here is you,' I snapped.

It felt good. It felt so fucking good, I wanted to repeat it. I wanted to scream it to the heavens, announce it to the world, paint it across the façade of our building. *You. You are selfish, Savannah. You.*

'*Me?*' Savannah demanded, with that same dark laugh in her tone. 'You're ridiculous. All this time, all you've ever cared about is men and dancing, whilst I've worked and—'

'—cared about being a doctor?' I interrupted. My hands shook from the adrenaline rushing through me. 'Followed your dreams? Your dreams had a fucking high price.'

'Oh, here we go.' Savannah rolled her eyes. 'Wah, wah, right? You didn't get to be some dancer in a troupe in Providence, and I actually achieved something—'

'I quit school so you could *'achieve something'*!'

'You hated school!' Savannah said.

'That's not the point!' I sucked in a deep breath, trying in vain to calm myself. My heartbeat roared in my ears. 'Who do you think paid off your medical school bills?'

'Dad—'

'—left us thousands in debt to Sayle! I paid that off, Savannah. Me.'

Savannah stared at me.

'But—'

'But what?' I sneered. 'But it doesn't fit your narrative where I'm selfish and reckless? You think I chose to work in the bunker because I *like* having people groping on me and all that crap? I could write a book about the things you don't know about me, you selfish bitch.'

It was so fucking satisfying. All the things I'd never said, all pouring out of my mouth at once. And I wanted to say them. I wanted to hurl the words at her like rocks and hurt her and finally make her see.

And she saw. I could see it in her eyes. She opened her mouth and closed it again, caught her breath.

'But… but why did you never say anything?' she asked in a small voice.

'Because it was all you cared about! Medical school. Making Mum and Dad proud.' I sucked in a breath. 'The first thing you said to me after we found out, well, at least I'll have a good job one day. You're going to have to quit dance. It won't support you.'

I scowled as the familiar old anger came back. 'You hated the fact that I danced. You couldn't stand that I found a little bit of joy in life. No. The world sucks, we all have to be miserable. Well, guess what? I was miserable. I was miserable for years keeping you in medical school, and us in a flat and fed. There was never an ounce of gratitude. I should have quit years ago. I hate you!'

I was breathing hard by the time I finished, my hands shaking as I blinked back tears. *Don't cry. Don't cry.*

Instead, Savannah's eyes began to look glassy. She stared at me, open-mouthed before a sudden transformation came over her. The emotion washed out of her face, and she stiffened her shoulders.

'So what, then? You left. You abandoned me. You got your revenge. I get it, Harley. You're amazing and I suck, and you got the last laugh. I'll just fuck off out of your life then.'

Savannah's cheeks glistened with tears, and I realised that I had finally done it: I'd gone too far. I'd pushed her over the edge, and now there might not be a way to bring her back.

'Savannah, I—'

'Oh, spare me,' she gasped, somehow still finding the energy for sarcasm. 'Let me guess: you're sorry? You told the truth, Harley. Now leave me alone.'

Abruptly she shoved off the kitchen counter and stalked towards me. I wavered on the spot—what the hell was she doing? But she walked right past me, opened the door, and let herself out.

'Sav—'

The door shut with a resounding *slam!*

I was alone. *Fuck.*

It was as if all of my energy had flooded out of me all in one go. I slumped down onto the sofa, staring around me at the once-familiar flat. I had lived here… and yet, now it felt foreign. As though it had belonged to someone else, a different Harley Benoit.

I wasn't her anymore.

Slowly, I pushed myself up off the sofa and traipsed to the bedroom. My side of the room was untouched, a thin layer of dust covering everything. My bowl of cheap jewellery on the bedside table, my old scarf discarded on the pillow, my box of dance clothes under the bed. I sat on the duvet, sending a cloud of dust wafting up.

'Achoo!'

Grimacing, I covered my face and picked up the scarf. Mum had made this for me before she died—one of the few mementoes I had of her. It had kept me warm through many a winter since then.

Now, it was wearing thin in patches, holey in other places. Just like my memories of Mum. If I closed my eyes, I couldn't quite picture her: an outline, the broad strokes, but nothing more. The way her long brown hair had tickled me when she kissed me goodnight. How bony she had felt when I'd hugged her. The way she'd never seemed to be able to get warm in winter. Her singing. The sound had faded, but I could still remember how I'd felt. The way my cheeks had hurt from smiling.

Would she be proud of where I'd ended up?

Would Dad?

Dad had always advocated for a peaceful life. *Keep your head down. Don't attract attention.*

But then, he was also the one who had started all of this. He was the one who had borrowed money from the Iron Fists and not been able to pay it back. He was the reason I had ended up dancing in the bunker… met Ellery… wound up at the Kranikovska… met Bas. Everything had spiralled out from that one decision my father had made.

Everything about my life. My relationship with Savannah. Everything that had gone down with Maddock. Everything.

I wouldn't be here if it wasn't for that decision. Where would I be?

I'd probably have left town with Theo years ago.

Theo. Another person I couldn't seem to make things right with.

I slumped back onto the bed, staring up at the cracked and water-damaged ceiling.

'I can't do it, Mum.' The words were a tiny whisper, but they still sounded loud in the silence of the flat. 'I can't look after Savannah. I can't save the people I love.'

The silence seemed to press in on me, stifling even my breaths.

Savannah was free. She would come back after she had cooled down and processed everything, and we could have a reasonable conversation. Maybe now, she would finally see that she needed to leave—that we needed to leave.

And once I'd convinced her, we could run.

But that meant abandoning Bas. And I couldn't do that—he was standing on a precipice; the same precipice I'd thrown myself off for Savannah. And like me, Bas would throw himself off to save the people he loved.

Like me, he might not survive the fall.

But Bas had been there with a net to save me in the past, and I needed to do the same for him. That was what it meant to be partners.

'So I stay,' I said aloud. 'And see this through to the bitter end.'

But what if I couldn't save him?

'If I don't try, then I definitely won't succeed.'

Even if it scared me, I had to try. For Bas. For Bale Rocks. For the life that I had always wanted, but never been able to grasp.

I sat up, feeling like a fire was sparking inside me. Okay, so maybe I was afraid. Terrified. But staying was the right thing to do.

It was time to go home.

Bas opened the door on my third knock. His face went through a range of expressions before turning carefully neutral.

'You came back.'

'I did.'

He stepped back to let me in and shut the door.

'What about Savannah?'

'Savannah has to figure out her own path,' I said. 'I left her a note in the flat.' I realised I'd left out half of the story. 'I managed to get her out, but... we fought, and she stormed out. I left her directions to the safehouse where Claire and Collette are staying. She'll be safe there.'

Bas nodded slowly.

'What about you?' I asked. 'Did you—Ellery mentioned... He said he wanted to try and get the weapons systems up and running. So we could... end this.'

I hadn't had the headspace to consider the implications of that whilst I was worrying about Savannah, but now they hit me full force: people would die. Maybe a lot of people. My stomach churned.

Bas shook his head. 'Our plan goes ahead,' he said.

I bit my cheek. Bas's plan set my teeth on edge.

'Can't we use the weapons in the bunker to take out Moriarty and Jackson?' I asked.

'Those missiles have a range of six hundred miles.'

I frowned. 'They don't need to go that far—only a few miles.'

Bas shook his head. 'That's their minimum range. They can't travel less than that.'

'Oh.' I sat down heavily. I'd been hoping... I wasn't precisely sure. Ellery's plan might have been extreme, but it would have ended things. And now... 'So, tomorrow...'

'The plan goes ahead,' Bas said. 'If we eliminate Moriarty, it will leave Jackson and Godfrey scrambling. If we move fast, we might be able to take out the other two. Ellery and Kade will be in position.'

That *directly* contradicted my arrangements with Ellery. My stomach squirmed. Did that mean he had changed the plans without telling me? Was Ellery going to leave me to handle Bas's plan alone?

'Harley?' Bas asked, and I realised I had been silent for several moments.

'Yeah,' I said. I took a deep breath. 'Alright. Do we... Are we prepared for tomorrow?'

'Yes.'

'Okay.' Another breath. The walls were pressing in on me. 'I... I think I need some fresh air.'

'If you don't want to come tomorrow, I can manage it on my own.'

'No.' That was the last thing I wanted—Bas facing Moriarty, and potentially Hannover, on his own. 'No, I want to help. I just need to get some air. Today's been... a lot.'

Bas nodded, though he was studying my face as though trying to read my thoughts. I pushed up off the bed and headed to the door, slipping past him. Down the stairs, out through the kitchen. The chilly spring air breeze cooled my cheeks and blew the cobwebs out of my head.

I needed to speak to Ellery.

I'd left the radio in the car. Our room didn't look out on the back, but I still positioned myself behind the car, so I'd be hidden from view if he came to the kitchen and looked out. Then I switched the radio on and hit the talk button.

'Ellery? Ellery, come in.'

For a long moment, I thought he wouldn't respond. Then he said, 'I'm here.'

I sighed in relief. 'Bas just told me—He said… you guys changed the plan.'

'Sorry,' Ellery said. 'I wanted to discuss it with you, but… Did you help Savannah?'

'Yeah, I got her home.' I leant against the car and tucked my free hand under my jacket to keep warm.

'Good.'

'What's happening tomorrow?'

The radio was picking up interference—voices on the other end. 'Hold on a second,' Ellery said.

'Okay.'

I waited a minute or so in silence, the dark pressing in on me. Finally, he said, 'Right. Tomorrow. Bas told you the missiles were a no-go?'

'Yeah.'

'He's going ahead with his plan tomorrow—at least, I assume so. He was cagey. He wants Kade and me ready to take shots on Godfrey and Jackson.'

'So you won't be able to help us.'

'No,' Ellery said. 'I'll be there. Kade will take the shot on Jackson. We have to hope that's enough.'

I swallowed. I wanted to feel relieved, but I was too overwhelmed. This was all happening so fast, and I wasn't prepared at all. I was in over my head.

'Harley?'

'Yes,' I said. 'Sorry. That sounds fine. So we'll meet tomorrow morning, as agreed.'

'Yes.' Ellery cleared his throat. 'Get some sleep.'

Conversation over. Just like that. All of my worries swirled around my brain with nowhere to go.

'I will. You too.'

'Wilco.'

I lowered the radio, my heart pounding against my ribcage. No, it wasn't enough. I wasn't okay with it. But what could I do? Ellery and Bas wanted to end this—truth be told, so did I. And objectively, I knew that the faster we moved, the better a chance we had.

Sighing, I returned the radio to the car and headed back upstairs. Bas was in bed, with the lights off, leaving the room in darkness. I washed up quietly, then crawled in beside him.

'Are you alright?' he asked softly.

I jerked in surprise; I'd thought he was asleep.

'Yeah,' I mumbled.

'You've been distant the last day or so.'

I lay beside him, wrestling with what to tell him. Should I explain that I was afraid he wouldn't come back from this mission?

I chewed my lip.

'It's just been hard these last few days,' I said. 'And Savannah... I knew she wouldn't be grateful for what I did, but...'

Bas reached out and touched my shoulder. 'She'll come round.'

'Yeah.' *Probably. Maybe.* I covered his hand with mine, and a sudden longing for physical contact filled me. 'Bas...'

'Yes?'

I rolled onto my side, dislodging his hand. Although the room was dark, I could make out the broad strokes of his features in the dull light sneaking between the curtains. His eyes glittered darkly.

'Can I kiss you?'

'Of course.' He touched a hand to the back of my neck. I wriggled closer until I could feel his breath on my face. I closed the gap and pressed my lips gently to his.

Then I pulled back.

'Harley?' A thread of amusement crept into Bas's voice.

I kissed him again, a little deeper this time. My tongue brushed his lips. And then I eased back.

'What are you doing?' Bas's voice had dropped a little.

'Kissing you?'

'I see that.'

I leant in again and brushed my lips against his again—this time, Bas's grip on my neck firmed, and he stopped me from pulling away. He licked my lips, then took the bottom one between his, biting it gently.

I gasped.

Bas pulled back, gazing at me with dark eyes. 'Okay?'

'Yeah.' My voice was a breathy whisper. 'More than okay.'

We were on the same page, clearly. I put my hand on his chest and pushed until he rolled to lie on his back, staring up at me.

'What now?' he asked.

'Now...' I threw a leg over him, straddling him. 'I want something better to think about than what a selfish bitch my sister is.'

'I could accommodate that,' Bas said slowly.

'But...?' I stared at him. It definitely felt like a 'but'.

He stared at me.

Stared.

Stared.

'Bas?' I asked, unease crawling down my spine.

'There's no but,' Bas said.

'I don't want to do something you don't want.' He knew that, right? Above all, that had to be clear. I loved Bas. I could never ever hurt him.

I loved him.

The force of the feeling hit me straight in the gut. I loved Bas in a way I wasn't sure I had ever loved anyone before. With all my heart, all my mind, all my soul.

And now I really wanted him to give me the chance to show him that.

But he was still hesitating.

'I do want it,' he said softly. 'I want you.'

'Then what's the problem?' I asked gently.

'I... don't know,' he said haltingly. 'I don't know if I deserve you.'

What?

'Of course, you deserve me!' I protested.

Bas traced a finger over my hip, sending a thrill through my skin. I pushed the feeling away. He was avoiding my gaze, and I knew we couldn't move on until this was resolved.

'Look at me,' I said, and his eyes snapped to mine. 'You deserve me. You are the single best thing in my life.'

'I'm not,' he said.

'Of course you are.'

'I want to deserve you. So badly.' Bas looked away again. I wanted to reach out and hug him. I wanted to shake him and scream that I loved him as though that might drive the words into his skull.

Instead, I fought for calm. 'You already do.'

Bas shook his head.

'You do.' I ran a finger over his forearm. 'I swear.'

Bas stared at a spot near my left thigh. 'I told you before. Hannover raised me. I—He tainted me, Harley. I might hurt you. And I don't want you to give me something you can't get back.'

What the fuck?

'Give you something?' I asked.

'Yourself. Your heart. I… I don't know.' He turned his head away, frustration colouring his voice.

'You already have me,' I said. 'Do you think sex will change that?'

'Of course it will.'

'Don't be silly,' I said. I grabbed his hand and pressed it against my ribcage. 'You have all of me. Every part. Whatever you want. Whenever. It's not like… I'm not holding anything back.' I had no idea what to say, so I just babbled it all out. 'I'm not worried about Hannover. I like you for you. Despite who raised you. Because of who you are today. That's what's important. Us. Here. Today.'

I took a deep breath. Bas was looking at my face again, but I wasn't sure if that was progress or not.

'I've hurt you before,' he said softly.

'I've hurt you, too.'

'It's not the same.'

'Yes, it is,' I said firmly. 'I'm an adult, right? Sensible. I'm capable of making my own choices, right?'

My eyes bored into his, daring him to respond in the negative.

'Of course,' he said.

'Then I choose you.'

'I don't want you to get hurt,' he said. 'I don't want to hurt you.'

'That's for me to worry about,' I said. 'I'm the only one who can bear the consequences of my decisions.'

Bas stared at me, a war playing out behind his shadowed eyes. I tried for patience, failed, and put my hands on his shoulders, pressing down.

'I'm going to kiss you,' I announced. 'If you really don't want to have sex with me, then tell me now. I won't judge you if you're not ready. But I want you to know that I would very much like to have sex with you. Actually, I've been waiting for ages.'

Bas grabbed my wrists, and my breath caught. He was going to push me away. I swallowed.

'Kiss me,' he said, his voice husky.

Triumph exploded in my chest like fireworks. I leant in and pressed my lips to his, putting my entire weight on him. I tangled my tongue with his, battling him, as though I could force him into submission that way.

He gave as good as he got. In a swift movement, he took hold of me and rolled us so that I was underneath him, and he was crouched over me. He broke the kiss, panting, and I stared up at him.

'You're sure?' he asked.

'Yes.' I'd never been more certain in my life.

'Alright.' Bas dipped his head to my neck and nipped a sensitive spot beneath my ear, sending a little jolt of pain through me. I gasped. He licked the spot to soothe the hurt, then moved down my neck, nipping and sucking. I tipped my head back to give him better access. He shifted so his legs bracketed mine and he was hovering with his head over my chest. Meeting my gaze, he grabbed the bottom of my T-shirt and tugged it up.

I lifted my upper body so he could work it over my head and toss it away. Then I lay back as Bas drank in his view of my upper body. He took his time examining me, tracing my skin with his fingers. Each touch sent a little frisson of heat through me, straight to my core.

His fingers brushed the curve of my breast.

'Bas!' I gasped.

He dipped his head, mouthing at my nipple. I arched my back, trying to encourage him, but then his hands were on my shoulders, holding me down.

'Patience,' he murmured, his breath brushing my breast and sending jolts down my spine.

'I am not patient,' I groaned.

'I know.' He chuckled. 'But I want to enjoy this. I've waited a long time for this, too.'

Slowly, ever so slowly, he kissed his way over my breast, into the valley between them, and up the other. He kissed my nipple then sucked it briefly.

'Fucking tease,' I hissed.

His teeth dug into my hard peak, and a strangled noise escaped my throat. 'Fuck!'

Laughing, he soothed the hurt away with a kiss. 'I told you to be patient.'

'Git.'

Bas hummed against my skin, resuming the sucking and kissing until I was sure I'd go mad from the stimulation. 'Bas, please!'

He dropped a hand between my legs. 'What do you want?'

'You.'

'Me?'

'Yes, you,' I panted, shifting my hips to try and get his fingers where I wanted them. He pulled away. 'Bas, come on!'

'Patience.'

'I'm not going to be patient,' I said. I wriggled against his other hand, which was still restraining my shoulder. 'Maybe I'll get on top of you and tease you, and we'll see how you like it.'

'I might like it very much.'

Even in the darkness, I could see his cock straining against his briefs. I very much doubted his resolve—but it did give me an idea.

'Okay, then.' I lifted a hand and palmed him through his briefs. Bas stiffened.

'Harley,' he groaned. *Shit.* I'd never heard my name spoken like that before, like he was in literal pain.

'Yeah?' I teased. 'What do you want?'

Bas opened his eyes and shot me a dark look. 'Fine, you win.'

'I do?'

Abruptly, he ground his palm against my centre. I moaned, pressing down against him—I could feel how wet I was. Bas shifted his hand, and I felt a long, slender finger pressing up into me.

'Ohhhh,' I muttered.

He thrust it in—out—in—out—then added a second one.

'Bas!' I was losing my mind, it was official. I was losing my mind, and I wanted him to lose his, too. With me. *Sebastian.*

Bas pulled away, leaving me cold and shivering.

'Hey!'

'Patience.' He smirked as he stepped off the bed and worked his briefs off, freeing his cock. It sprang to attention, hard against his abdomen. 'You are really impatient.'

'One of my finer vices.' I arched my back, determined to tempt him back onto the bed. He crawled over me again, settling between my legs. I swallowed, suddenly nervous. He seemed awfully big, awfully present…

Bas ran a hand over my cheek, brushing my hair back, and kissed me again. My worries evaporated in the wake of the heat pooling in my belly. I lifted my hips, grinding against him.

'So impatient,' he whispered against my lips. He pushed me down, and then I felt the head of his cock brush against me. *Oh.*

He did it again—again—

'More,' I whispered. 'Please.'

This time, he didn't mock me. I could see in his eyes that he was feeling rather impatient, too. He shifted against me, his dick sliding into me an inch. I shuddered.

'Yes, God.'

Slowly, so, so slowly, Bas began to thrust back and forth, slipping deeper with every pass. It was agony. I clutched his shoulders, scratched his back. 'Please,' I cried. 'Faster.'

But no matter what I said, he kept that same pace, until finally his hips bumped mine. He hovered above me, staring into my eyes.

'Okay?'

'Yes, God. Please move before I die.'

Bas smiled. He braced his arms beside my head and pulled out to the tip—then thrust back in. *Hard.*

I yowled as pleasure rushed through me. 'Yesssss.'

Bas jerked his hips, picking up a punishing pace that I was certain would break me apart. I could feel him deep inside me, so deep I swore he had infected me, put fire in my veins and heart. I moulded myself to him, wrapping my legs around his thighs and squeezing. My heart was like a drum in my ears, and he was all I could see.

Bas, Bas, Bas.

The pleasure rose higher and higher until I was sure I was going to shatter into a million pieces. Bas dropped a hand, working it in between us until he found my clit. His breathing grew ragged, his strokes erratic. He brushed a clumsy finger over my clit, once, again—

I didn't so much tumble over the edge as I dived off the cliff into a sea of pleasure. I clung to Bas's shoulders, kissing him messily, and he swallowed my cries and gasps. A moment later, he stiffened against me, grunting as his cock hardened even more, and I felt a rush of wet heat inside me.

'Shit,' I whispered. 'Fuck. Bas, that was…' But I had no words. I wrapped my arms around him, pressing our sweaty chests together. Bas buried his face in my neck, and we stayed like that for seconds, minutes, until finally he sighed and rolled away.

I lay back, breathing hard, but feeling utterly satiated and relaxed. Bas collapsed beside me, panting in harmony with me.

'Thank you,' I whispered. I reached out across the bed until I found his hand. Bas grabbed my wrist and used it to pull me into his arms.

'Any time,' Bas replied, nuzzling my shoulder. I sighed into his neck as I felt sleepiness wash over me.

Now we just had to survive whatever tomorrow would bring.

TWENTY-SEVEN

MY HEART SEEMED TO HAVE lodged itself in my throat, and no amount of swallowing would get it out.

Sunday was a bright, clear day—the weather almost perversely good. The sun was strong enough to break through the clouds and warm my cheeks. I wanted to tip my head back, close my eyes, and just enjoy it.

Instead, Bas and I were making our way down to the southwest side of the town, where we planned on ambushing and killing Moriarty.

It took much shorter than I wanted it to for us to arrive. By then, the sun was already high in the sky, and the sparse woodland around the Rochester property seemed to be coming alive. We hid the car amongst the trees and walked back to the two guard stations that flanked the road.

'Are you sure about this?' I asked Bas quietly.

He glanced my way. 'Positive.'

That was that, then. In a few hours, either we'd have killed Moriarty and Kade would have taken out Jackson… or we might all be dead. I just had to pray it would be the former.

I kissed Bas one last time before he pulled away.

'Wait for my signal,' he murmured.

I nodded. He crossed the road and entered the hut on the other side. I opened mine.

Ellery wasn't there.

I stared at the small space. Metal folding table and chair, a few scraps of paper discarded on the floor. And nothing else. Ellery had said he'd be here waiting.

But he wasn't.

Fuck.

A car engine rumbled, and I hastily entered the hut and shut the door, crouching down so I could see into the window of Bas's hut, but hopefully be invisible to any passing vehicles. The car passed us and vanished from sight.

Where was Ellery?

Maybe he'd been delayed? But if so, what would we do? Our plan hinged on him being able to get close enough to stop Bas from doing anything risky. But he wouldn't be able to approach without Bas seeing or hearing him.

Fuck.

Had he changed the plan? Gone after Godfrey after all?

But why would he lie to me?

Unless he's the traitor.

But he couldn't be. Ellery and I might have had our differences in the past, but he'd never turn on Bas.

At least, I hoped so.

He'll turn up, I thought desperately.

But I was wrong. Minutes trickled by, turning into hours. My legs cramped, and when I shifted to sitting, my bum grew numb. The clock ticked ever onwards as I grew sick and sweaty with worry.

I was going to have to face this alone.

Me, Bas, and the gun I had holstered at my hip.

One o'clock passed, and the countdown began.

One-fifteen.

One-thirty.

One-forty-five.

Two.

No car.

It should have gone through by now.

Ears perked and eyes on the window of Bas's hut, I waited. Five more minutes passed, then ten. Fifteen.

Still no car.

They weren't coming.

Finally, Bas signalled to me to leave the hut. I stumbled to my feet and had to grip the back of the chair as my body got used to being upright again. By the time I stepped outside, Bas was already across the road.

'Come on,' he said briskly.

'Where are we going?' I fell into step beside him.

'The Rochester house.'

'But Rodney said—'

'I don't care about what Rodney said,' Bas cut across me sharply. 'Not when he's the one who betrayed us.'

'Rodney?' I asked. The thought hadn't even occurred to me.

'He was the only one who knew.'

Except that wasn't true. Ellery knew because I had told him.

My stomach twisted itself into a knot. I had told him… Had he betrayed us?

But Bas trusted Ellery. And I trusted Bas's judgement.

'What are you going to do?' Bas was walking so fast I had to jog to keep up with him. The car came into view, and he marched over and threw his door open.

'What I should have done in the first place.'

I did not like the sound of that.

We drove at the limits of the car's abilities back to the road and then along towards Rodney's house. All the way, my stomach twisted itself into an ever more complex knot. What were we going to find when we got there?

Someone had evidently warned Moriarty not to use the road we were on—which was the most logical access route between the Black Hands' compound and the Rochester home. Did that mean he hadn't come at all? Or had he taken another route? Or had the meeting been moved?

If it had, the house would be empty.

If it hadn't…

I swallowed and pushed the thoughts away, focusing on the moment. Bas stopped the car on the side of the road and sprang out, and I hurried after him.

'How are we going to get in?'

'Staff entrance,' he grunted without breaking his stride.

There was a staff entrance. Bas knew where it was. That spoke of a depth to this plan that I really didn't like.

A short walk brought us to a door set into the high walls. Bas listened at the door for a minute or two, before twisting the handle and opening it.

'Wait here.' He slipped in, and a moment later I heard a grunt and a thud. Then Bas reappeared, pulling the door open wider.

No one was in sight.

An expanse of green lawn stretched ahead of us, more grass than

I'd ever seen in one place in my entire life. It was gorgeous. It looked more like a carpet than something nature had created.

'Wow,' I muttered.

Bas surveyed the property before nodding towards a line of trees. 'That's probably our best bet. We'll work our way along the wall and then approach in the shadow of those trees.'

'Okay.'

I reaffirmed my grip on my gun and checked for the knife in my belt. My stomach had given up on knots and seemed to have sunk to take up residence somewhere around my boots. My every step felt heavy and clumsy, and I was sure we were going to be discovered any second now.

But we didn't see a single living soul, except for the one guard Bas had already knocked out. We reached the trees and darted from one trunk to the next, making our way slowly over to the large house. Finally, we were in the shadow of the walls. I pressed my back against it and breathed a sigh of relief.

'What now?'

'We need a window or door.' Bas's eyes scanned the environs restlessly. 'This way.'

He started down the wall, testing each window we came to. The first looked in on an empty room filled with cupboards and cabinets—some kind of storage. The second was a bedroom that I assumed belonged to the staff because there were two small, narrow beds shoved into the tiny space. At the third, Bas and I had to duck down hastily, because there were three women in the room, all dressed in smart blue uniforms with aprons around their waists, chattering together.

We inched along the wall on our haunches until we were safely out of sight of the window.

'I don't think they saw us,' I murmured.

Bas nodded, but I could see that he was tense. Worried. I reached for his hand, but he was already on the move again, heading for the next window.

Swallowing, I followed him. The next room was another bedroom, and the window was cracked open. Bas worked his fingers into the gap and pulled it wide.

'Here we go,' he said. 'Do you need a hand over?'

I nodded. Bas grabbed my hips and helped me up onto the sill, and

I dropped down the other side. I turned back to face him—and he slammed the window.

'Bas!' I yelled.

Bas turned his back to me, raising his hands. Had he been seen? Caught? A man in tactical gear came into view, and I ducked down hastily, watching from behind a chest of drawers as a security guard took Bas's weapons and prodded him in the back with his gun. He led Bas out of my view, leaving me crouched on the floor, my heart pounding in my throat.

Fuck. What was I going to do now?

I had to help Bas. But how?

I definitely couldn't stay here. A quick glance around told me that this was another staff bedroom. I rifled through the drawers and found a uniform which, from the size, probably belonged to a man. I pulled it on over my clothes—not enough of a disguise to fool anyone up close, but it might give me a chance if they saw me from a distance.

Taking a deep breath, I opened the door.

I was in a narrow, unfinished corridor. Bare concrete floors, plain white walls, and a low ceiling. Doors lined either side of the hall, but I knew that I wouldn't find Bas in here. I followed the main corridor to the end until I found a door that looked different to the others, more ornate, and made of dark wood. I pushed through it and found myself in a totally different part of the house.

This corridor was dark and ornate, with a thick brown carpet underfoot, dark green wallpaper on the walls, and gold-framed mirrors and paintings set at regular intervals. All the doors in this hallway were open, which made it easy for me to check room after room: all of them full of fancy furniture, all of them empty of people.

Where was Bas? Where would they have taken him?

Was he even in the house? Maybe the guards had a whole different building?

Worry squeezed my neck like a vice, restricting my breath. I moved from one room to the next, unable to contemplate what would happen if I couldn't find Bas—what they would do to him.

'Hey!'

I paused in the doorway of some kind of lounge, complete with a bar counter and two enormous leather sofas.

'You.' A short woman was hurrying over to me, her grey hair frizzing about her face. 'What are you doing?'

'I—uh—' I sucked in a breath and stood up straighter. 'I was asked to clean up in here—by the head of staff...' Was that okay? *Please be okay.*

The woman shook her head. 'That will have to wait. Get this to the dining room.' She thrust a bottle of wine into my hands. 'And straighten your clothes!'

Then she was gone, leaving me clutching a bottle of wine that probably cost more than the Kranikovska had paid me in a year.

Dining room.

That was probably where Jonathan Rochester was—and if I were him, I would want to know that my illegitimate son had broken into my house. Hopefully that meant I'd be able to find something out there.

I made a concerted effort to straighten my stolen uniform in front of one of the many mirrors, then set off in search of the dining room.

The dining room was at the front of the house. I straightened the uniform once more, ducked my head, and entered.

There were five people in the room, sitting around a large, sturdy table: Jonathon Rochester at the head, looking stern and austere. Rodney sat to his left, Moriarty to his right. Hannover sat beside Rodney. At the far end of the room, a fire crackled in the hearth.

What brought me up short, though, was the fifth person in the room: a petite girl with long red hair in a ponytail, wearing a knee-length green dress.

I had seen her once before, on the night when Theo and I had tried to kill Hannover, and her presence here, now, sent a pang of fear through my chest.

Rionach. Moriarty's daughter.

What was she doing here?

Before I could even theorise, Rochester noticed me and clicked his fingers. 'You. Is that the wine?'

'Yes, sir,' I murmured, still keeping my head ducked. There was a very good chance that Hannover and Rodney were going to recognise me, and I needed to delay that for as long as possible.

'Good. Pour it for us.'

This, at least, was something I could do. I uncorked the bottle and set about pouring for the four men.

As I bent to fill Moriarty's glass, two security guards hustled Bas through the open doorway. He looked like he had been roughed up—a bruise was starting to form beneath his left eye—but his features were set in determination.

Rochester immediately looked up.

'What's this?'

'We found him trying to get into the house, sir,' the guard reported.

Jonathan Rochester's eyes narrowed. I couldn't read Moriarty at all, his face impassive. But Hannover's eyes glittered with malice, and Rodney looked worried and afraid.

'Sebastian,' Jonathan said, and Bas shuddered.

Beside me, Moriarty said sharply, 'Pour and leave, girl.'

'Sir,' I murmured. I went back to filling his glass, then moved around the table to do Hannover and Rodney's.

'Remove him,' Jonathan said. 'He's not welcome here.'

'Of course, sir,' one of the guards said.

Hannover covered his glass to stop me from pouring. 'Not for me.'

'Sir.' I set the bottle down and headed for the door. My gaze met Bas's. One of the security guards grabbed his shoulder and started to haul him backwards—and then Bas shifted his weight, as quick and predatory as a cat, and kicked the guard's legs away. Twisting, he planted his boot in the other guard's chest. The first one tried to stand again, but Bas grabbed his collar and whacked his head against the doorframe, before letting his body crumple to the ground.

Jonathon Rochester shot to his feet. 'What is the meaning of this?'

'I'm not leaving.' Bas snatched a gun out of the holster on one of the guards' belts. He lifted it and took aim at Rochester. 'I've been waiting for this moment for a long time.'

Rochester's face had gone chalk white. His gaze darted around the room, searching for salvation. 'SECURITY! GUARDS!'

Beside him, Moriarty drew his gun. Bas turned to aim at him.

'Do you really think you can take on all of us alone?' Moriarty asked.

I drew my gun and pointed it at Hannover. 'He's not alone.'

Moriarty turned to me, a dismissive twist to his lips. 'A servant?'

'She's not a servant,' Bas said coldly. 'She's the woman I love. And the last person you'll ever see.'

He lowered his aim, shifting it to the cowering figure beside

Moriarty. 'Drop your weapon, or I'll shoot your daughter.'

A sudden silence engulfed the room, so thick I felt like I could have cut through it with a knife. Slowly, ever so slowly, Moriarty lowered his pistol and set it on the table.

'You have no quarrel with Rionach,' he said. 'She's just a child.'

'When you bring children to the table with criminals, they're the ones who bear the consequences of your actions,' Bas said. His eyes were cold and icy—so cold that I felt like if I met his gaze, I'd freeze. 'Tell her. Tell her what you did.'

'I insist you leave,' Jonathan said.

'You, shut up,' Bas said. 'It's not your turn.'

He looked back at Moriarty. 'Tell her.'

Moriarty cleared his throat. 'The boy was one of my slaves.' There was a smug, defiant note to his voice, and it hit home. I saw Bas flinch. 'One of many, and not especially talented, either.'

Bas's hand faltered. Moriarty snatched up his gun.

BANG!

For a moment, fear obliterated my thoughts—Moriarty had shot Bas. He'd shot him. *No, no, no.*

Then Moriarty crumpled forwards, almost in slow motion, blood welling from a perfect hole in the middle of his forehead.

His body hit the table.

Rionach screamed.

Bas turned his gun on Jonathan Rochester.

Rochester's face had turned ashen. 'What do you want?' he asked. 'Is it money? Is that it?'

'I want my mother to live the life she should have had,' Bas said.

Rochester shuddered. 'I can buy you a house,' he said, a pleading note to his voice. 'Land. Whatever you want. We can put this behind us.'

'That's not going to happen,' Bas said.

'Then what? There has to be something that can make this right.'

'*Make this right?*' Bas's rage was so strong, I thought it might singe me. 'There's no making this right! The only thing that will make anything right is your death.'

'You think that will change anything?' Rochester asked, and I could see the same cold fury in his eyes as in Bas's. 'Your mother will still be dead. And you will still have been a slave. There's no changing that.'

'At least she'll rest easily knowing the man who betrayed her is dead,' Bas snarled.

'Betrayed her?' Rochester scoffed. 'You think I ever cared one whit for that woman? She threw herself at me, and in the end, she got what she deserved. And so will you.'

I saw the words strike at Bas, saw the resolution in his gaze, saw him squeeze the trigger.

This time, I was prepared. But the gunshot still reverberated down my spine and made my teeth rattle.

Then it was over, and Rochester collapsed. Dead. But Bas didn't relax. His expression didn't change. There was no peace, no relief.

And then he twisted around to face Moriarty's side of the table, where something had moved in the corner of my eye.

Because whilst we hadn't been watching, Hannover had vanished. And now, he popped up on the other side of the table and pulled Rionach into his arms. She clung to him, white-faced and terrified, and I saw Hannover's plan unfolding before my eyes. To kill him, Bas would risk shooting Rionach.

No.

But Bas turned his gun unerringly on Hannover.

'Here we are,' Hannover mocked. 'The last rung on your ladder to revenge, Sebastian.'

'Let go of her and face me like a man,' Bas said coldly.

Hannover backed himself and Rionach towards the corner of the room—where, I realised suddenly, there was another door. I hadn't even noticed it before.

Fuck.

Shoot him, risk hitting Rionach. Don't shoot him, risk him escaping.

My hands slid against my gun, too sweaty to keep a proper grip.

'Then again,' Bas said, 'you always were a coward.'

'I've been called worse,' Hannover said. 'Are you going to shoot the girl, Sebastian? It's your only chance to finish this.'

'No!' Rionach screeched, shaking her head again and again.

'Yes,' Bas said. I whipped around to face him. He stared at Hannover with an expression carved from stone.

'Bas, no,' I said.

'I have to, Harley.'

'No!'

Hannover laughed. 'Me or your lady friend, Sebastian?'

Bas's hands trembled. I grasped for something, anything to say.

'Please,' I whispered. 'I know you want revenge, Bas, but this isn't the way. You're better than this.'

Hannover was shuffling ever further backwards. Bas tracked him with both eyes and weapon.

'He can't be allowed to escape,' he said.

I touched Bas's shoulder. 'You can't shoot a child. Please, please don't do that to yourself.'

He'd never live with the guilt. I knew that without a doubt. For all he hated Hannover, he would never be able to live knowing he'd killed an innocent child.

Bas's hands shook, and I knew I was getting through to him. I massaged his shoulder gently. 'Let him go,' I whispered. 'Let them go.'

'That's right, Sebastian. Let us go,' Hannover sang.

'You shut up,' Bas snarled. The gun came right back up, anger shoving out whatever vulnerable part of Bas's soul I'd managed to reach.

Fuck.

I did the only thing I could think of. Holstering my own gun, I put my arms around him and my hands over his. His body trembled under my hands; his shoulders were taut. I stroked the backs of his knuckles with my thumbs before sliding my hands into place so my finger was also on the trigger.

'If you're going to make this decision, we'll do it together,' I said. 'I won't have her blood on your hands alone.'

Bas tensed. I could feel the indecisiveness like I could feel his ribcage expanding with his every breath.

And then, miracle of miracles, he lowered the gun. 'I can't,' he rasped, low so only I could hear. 'You can't.'

CRASH!

My head jolted up in time to see Hannover hurl a glass into the fireplace. It must have been alcohol, because the flames flared higher and began to lick over the carpet. Hannover threw the door open and sprinted out, dragging Rionach behind him.

The door slammed.

And Bas sagged against me, a muted sob escaping his mouth.

TWENTY-EIGHT

I SQUEEZED BAS'S SHOULDERS, TRYING to lend him my strength. Everything in his life had built to this single point, and now here we were: two men dead, Hannover gone, and his revenge incomplete.

'I should have shot him first,' Bas whispered.

'It's okay,' I said. 'I love you. It's okay.'

He shook, leaning heavily against me. There were no words, but I didn't mind. He needed me much more than I needed him right now.

'FIRE!'

I jerked in shock.

Rodney unfroze abruptly, leaping into action. He grabbed one of the fancy, tassled cushions and whacked it against the carpet again and again, before casting it aside and stamping on the flames. By some miracle, he managed to put them out.

He turned to stare at us.

Time seemed to stand still.

And then Bas rounded on Rodney with a fury like I'd never seen before. I didn't have time to speak, to move, before his fist connected with Rodney's nose.

I flinched. Rodney reeled backwards. Bas went in for another blow.

'BAS!' I grabbed his arm. He strained against me, his every muscle tensed. 'Stop!'

'Traitor!' Bas snarled. 'You! You told them about our plan!'

'What?' Rodney asked, his voice muffled by the hand clutched to his nose.

'You must have thought it was such a good idea.' Bas stopped trying to escape my grasp, clenching his fists at his side. 'Set the whole plan up and then betray me? Too bad it didn't work out for you.'

'Are you insane?' Rodney dropped his hand. Blood covered his mouth and chin, turning him into something out of my nightmares. 'Why would I do that? Why would I do anything that would jeopardise my life? MY FATHER'S LIFE?'

'He was scum,' Bas said.

'He was my father.' Rodney balled his fists. 'I *helped* you.'

'And then you betrayed me.'

Rodney hissed, a wordless exclamation of anger, regret, frustration. He turned away. 'I didn't fucking betray you.'

'Then who did?' Bas snapped.

Rodney stared at the burnt patch of carpet, still smoking gently. The silence stretched on for minutes that felt like hours, before I finally said, 'We need to go.'

'We need to deal with this traitor,' Bas said, but his voice was less fiery than before.

'What if he's not the traitor?' I asked. 'Have you checked in with Ellery and Kade?'

Bas spun to stare at me. 'Marco is not the traitor.'

'I arranged with him to meet us here.'

Bas frowned. I met his gaze, even though I wanted to cringe away from the accusation lurking there.

'You told him,' Bas said quietly.

'I had to.'

'No. I asked you not to.'

'You asked,' I said. 'But that wasn't what was best—for either of us. If Ellery had been there—'

'—he would have stopped me,' Bas said.

'He would have protected you because he's your friend.' I nodded to his belt. 'Radio him. Find out why he didn't come.'

Bas's eyes narrowed. Not looking away from me for a second, he lifted the radio to his mouth. 'Lynx, come in.'

Nothing.

'Lynx, come in. Pronghorn, come in.'

Nothing.

'Rodney's not the traitor,' I said. 'There's no way he could have known where Kade, Ellery, and Laura were to get to them.'

Bas's lips thinned. He turned to Rodney. Rodney spread his hands. His nose was still bleeding, and deep lines furrowed his brows. He looked ancient and exhausted.

'I didn't betray you,' he said, and I sensed he was talking about more than just today. 'You're my *brother*.'

Bas stared at him, and I could see the indecision in him. Go after Rodney, finish his business here. Make sure Ellery and Kade were alright and finish things with Jackson.

If we still could.

Because if Ellery had missed his meeting with me, there was a good chance that Kade was also MIA.

'Let's go,' I said.

Bas turned to me. I held out a hand. *Choose me. Come on. You know I've always supported you.*

'I just wanted to make sure we all made it out alive,' I said quietly.

Bas took my hand. I swayed, suddenly lightheaded with relief.

'I'm not done with you,' he told Rodney. 'Not by a long stretch.'

'The feeling is entirely mutual,' Rodney said coldly, but I got the feeling it was a façade. He'd put a wall in place, and behind it, he was crumbling.

I felt the same way. Half of me wanted to just collapse in relief that Moriarty was dead and Bas and I had survived.

But I couldn't, not until we were sure that Ellery, Kade, and Laura were alive.

I tugged on Bas's hand. Slowly, he moved to the door. Out into the ornate hallway. Outside, onto the grass.

Rionach had vanished. *Thank God.*

We had to get to the car, and from there, across town. Bas took us straight to Laura's brother's house, in the east of town, near where I had lived before my father died. No time for a trip down memory lane, though. At the house, he parked, and we threw ourselves out. Ellery's car stood neatly in front of the house, apparently unmoved. Bas went straight to the door and banged on it.

No response.

The seconds dragged on.

'Maybe they took a different car?' I said.

'We can retrace their steps, but we need to check here, first.' Bas examined the lock. Then he signalled to me to round the side of the house. I went left; he went right. I clutched my gun, my palms sweating.

Bas trusts Ellery and Kade. And I trust Bas. That's all that matters.

Which meant they'd run into trouble somewhere.

I reached the back a shade behind Bas, my heart pounding like a drum in my ears. He shot me a questioning look, and I shook my head.

Nothing amiss.

Bas nodded. Then he kicked the back door, his foot landing with a crash against the wood. Again. Again. On the third strike, the flimsy wood shattered, and Bas was able to pry it loose and reach in to twist the lock.

Thud.

It was the quietest of sounds—I almost missed it, but Bas held up a hand and swung his gun to point into the back room. I stilled, on high alert. We couldn't shoot, could we? What if Ellery and Kade were in there?

The seconds stretched out as I held my breath, afraid to move a single muscle. Nothing stirred inside the house. Finally, Bas signalled for me to wait and took a cautious step inside.

No shots. No voices.

I followed him at a distance. The kitchen was small, but the large windows provided good light. We rounded an old wooden table and approached two doors. The first was locked when Bas tried it, and the second led into a hallway with robin egg blue walls. The house was clean and well-kept, and I halfway expected Laura to step out at any moment and offer me a drink.

Bas held up a hand to tell me to wait, then edged around a doorway to look into the room beyond. In short order, he'd checked all three of the downstairs rooms.

'All clear down here,' he murmured, his words barely a whisper. 'I'll go upstair—'

THUD!

All of a sudden, a litany of bangs and crashes exploded from behind us, before falling silent again just as quickly. I whipped around, bringing my gun up, but there was no one there. The kitchen remained empty.

'There must be a cellar,' Bas said. He approached the locked door and studied it. 'Cover me.'

I stepped back into the kitchen, keeping my weapon firmly on the locked door. Bas stepped back and landed a kick against the door. The wood groaned. He kicked it again.

This door held on for longer than the back door had, but finally the wood broke. Bas holstered his gun and braced himself against the wall to kick it one last time. His foot broke through, sending shards of wood tumbling to the ground.

He backed off, pulling out his gun again, then put pressure on the wood with his hands. It had broken more or less from top to bottom, and he was able to swing one side of the door open, whilst leaving the lock intact.

A dark hole yearned beyond. Bas pulled out a torch and shone it in, illuminating a flight of stairs.

'I'll go first,' he said.

'Alright,' I murmured, swallowing around the lump in my throat.

We descended into the cellar. No matter how quietly I walked, my footsteps seemed impossibly loud. My breathing sounded like a windstorm and my heartbeat was like a drum.

Bas reached the bottom and swept his torch across the space.

It was a small room with raw brick walls. Two metal shelves sat against the far wall, bare except for dust.

Ellery and Kade sat in the middle of the room, gagged and with their wrists tied together. There was no sign of Laura. Kade was on a wooden chair; Ellery was on the floor, his chair knocked over. He lurched upwards when he saw us, and immediately fell back.

Bas holstered his gun and hurried towards them.

'Got you,' he said, pulling a knife out and working on the ropes at Ellery's wrists. I moved around to Kade and unwound the cloth from his mouth.

'What happened?' I asked. 'Where's Laura?'

Kade coughed a few times. 'Laura,' he croaked.

'What?' I crouched down to work on the ropes, but my fingers kept slipping, so I moved to ungag Ellery instead.

'Where is Laura?' Bas asked.

The knot came loose. As I pulled the cloth free, Ellery caught my eye.

'Laura betrayed us,' he said hoarsely.

For a moment, I forgot how to breathe. Then it came back, along with a roar in my ears. I stumbled back a step, watching as if through a tunnel as Bas finished sawing at the ropes. Ellery and Kade both stood, rubbing at their wrists.

Laura.

It didn't seem possible. Laura was our friend. She'd been with us from the start.

Ellery was talking to Bas, but I cut in. 'Why? Why would Laura…?'

I trailed off. I had no idea how to phrase it.

They turned to me.

'No idea,' Ellery said, rolling his shoulders to get rid of the stiffness. 'She wasn't very…'

'Coherent,' Kade filled in.

Ellery nodded. 'She kept talking about someone named Jack.'

'Her husband, I think,' I filled in. 'He died. Before she moved to Bale Rocks.'

It hit me suddenly how little I knew about Laura. I couldn't even confidently say that was her husband's name. I didn't know how long ago he'd died. How long they had been married. I wasn't even entirely sure how old Laura was.

The silence stretched on. Finally, Bas asked, 'How did it happen?'

Kade's gaze jumped to Ellery, who suddenly looked a little sheepish. 'I—uh—It was my fault,' he muttered. 'We were… yeah. She took my gun. Made me tie Kade up, then she did me.'

'You were…' Bas prompted.

Ellery's cheeks flushed. 'You know.' He gestured between me and Bas.

I didn't know whether to laugh or curse.

'Why did she lock you up?' Bas pressed, looking desperate to move on from the exchange.

'From what I could gather, she was supposed to interrupt something,' Ellery said.

'The strike on Moriarty?' I asked.

'Seems likely.' Ellery turned a serious look on Bas. 'Did Harley tell you what we planned?'

Bas's expression closed off. 'Yes.'

'I'm sorry.' Ellery clapped him on the shoulder. Bas's expression remained stony for several moments, before he nodded jerkily.

'I understand,' Bas said.

'Did you take the strike?' Ellery asked quietly.

Bas's gaze slid away, his shoulders tensing. None of us spoke, as though by unspoken agreement we all knew we had to give him a moment. Finally, he steeled himself and looked back at us.

'It's done. Moriarty is dead.'

'And your father?' Ellery asked in a careful tone.

'Also.'

'Hannover?' Kade asked.

Bas was silent. I reached over and took his hand, squeezing it gently.

'He escaped,' I murmured.

'Fuck,' Ellery said.

Bas's fist clenched under my hand. I stroked the back of his knuckles, trying to lend him my strength. He took a breath, then relaxed and opened his hand to weave our fingers together.

'Why would Laura want to interrupt the strike?' Bas asked.

'No idea.' Ellery paced restlessly across the room, searching the corners as though they might hold clues. 'She stayed here with us for a while, and then she… changed her mind, maybe? She left.'

'How long ago?' Bas asked.

'An hour, maybe?' Ellery pursed his lips in thought. 'You didn't see her?'

'No,' I said.

'Did she say anything?' Bas glanced restlessly around the room.

'A lot of somethings,' Ellery muttered sardonically.

'She ranted a lot,' Kade explained.

'It didn't make much sense,' Ellery added. 'I think she mentioned meeting someone, but then she also mentioned looking for someone. And when we asked her to let us go, she kept saying it was too late.'

'Too late for what?' I asked.

Ellery shrugged. 'Just 'too late'. She'd already told him everything, and it was too late.'

Already told who?

I didn't know what to do with that, and neither did the others, so it seemed. We lapsed into silence, each lost in our own thoughts. Finally, Kade said quietly, 'What now?'

'Jackson,' Bas said. 'We need to finish things.'

'We should consider that Hannover got away,' Ellery said. 'That means the weapons in the bunker are still in play.'

'Except Hannover doesn't know where they are,' Kade said. 'Unless someone told him or he had some way of following us, or…'

Unless someone told him.

And it clicked.

'Hannover,' I said. Hannover had known I was Sierra. And he and Moriarty had known to drive a different route to the Rochesters' house today. Conceivably, he could have set the fire in Freetown as well—or at least arranged it.

'Hannover?' Ellery asked.

'He's been a step ahead of us the whole way through,' I said. 'Since long before I got into the bunker. Almost as if he knew what we were doing. What we were planning.'

I could see the moment the light came on for the others, the dawning realisation in their faces.

'You think Laura was reporting to Hannover?' Ellery asked. 'Why would she do that?'

'I have no idea,' I said, 'but—'

'I might know,' Kade cut in. I glanced at him in surprise, less because of his words, and more because he'd interrupted me. Kade was usually so reserved. But now he was frowning, and he continued urgently, 'Laura came to me at one point to ask if I knew anything about the gang activity in Crater's Edge. She was looking for information about a gang member there.'

'What did you tell her?' Ellery asked.

'I couldn't tell her anything,' Kade said. 'It was never my area of expertise. I told her she needed to find someone who travelled to Crater's Edge regularly, because they'd know the lay of the land. She never brought it up again.'

His words triggered a memory for me—a moment I'd basically forgotten amidst everything else. Months ago, right before the strike on the distillery, Laura had asked me the same question.

'She was looking for the person who killed her husband,' I said. 'She asked me about it, too.'

'Why ask you?' Ellery asked.

'She knew about my father.' My chest ached, but the hurt was old. I pushed it aside for later. We had to focus now. 'What if Hannover got to her at some point?'

'It would have to have been before she came to Freetown,' Ellery said. He paused. 'Although, thinking about it, I always did think that it was a bit strange that she was so happy to come with me. I mean, she has a family in Bale Rocks...'

'Did she?' Kade asked. 'We never met her brother.'

I glanced around the empty cellar. When we'd had our own house, our cellar had been filled with all sorts of things. Mainly preserved food, which we stored for winter. But there had also been children's toys, old clothes, cooking fuel and a camping stove, weapons...

Everything we might need to keep ourselves safe in a crisis.

This room was empty.

'Does she really have a brother?' I asked.

My question fell like a stone in the room. All of a sudden, I was hyperconscious of the echoey bareness. It felt wrong, like I was treading somewhere I didn't belong. Walking on a grave.

I wanted to leave.

'Who knows,' Ellery said. He seemed to share my feelings, because he pushed towards the door. 'We should go.'

'I don't think we're going to find her,' Kade said.

'No, but we need to check on the bunker. If she was working with Hannover—If she told him about the weapons…'

The thought robbed me of breath.

Never mind that she had betrayed us. If Laura had told Hannover where the weapons were, then we might have a much bigger problem. What kind of destruction could Hannover wreak with those missiles?

I turned to Bas, and saw the same determination in his eyes.

'We have to stop him,' I said.

Bas nodded.

TWENTY-NINE

THE WASTELAND SEEMED TO STRETCH on forever while we made no discernible forward progress. I leant forwards in my seat as though I could physically urge the car on faster.

Go, go, go.

Go.

We have to get there before Hannover.

I had no idea what we would do when we got there, but we had to get there. Because the idea of Hannover getting his hands on missiles with a range of... I couldn't even fathom a range of hundreds of miles, let alone thousands—it was unthinkable. It would be the end of the world.

Go, go, go.

I kept my thoughts locked up in my head, though, because I didn't want to distract Bas. He was driving with a look of fierce concentration on his face, pushing the car to the absolute limits of safety across the uneven wasteland. We bounced over roots and swerved around rocks, but I didn't complain or comment.

Go, go, go.

In the back of the car, Kade and Ellery were similarly silent, apart from a few terse directions from Kade.

'You need to head a bit further south.'

'We're about half a mile out.'

Finally, he said, 'That's it.' Not that any of us hadn't immediately zeroed in on the small building when it appeared on the horizon. Bas put on another burst of speed, then slammed on the brakes, bringing us to a lurching halt beside the building in the scree. We all clambered out, unholstering weapons as we went.

'I'll take point,' Ellery said. 'In case he's down there.'

'I can—' Bas started.

'No,' Ellery interrupted. 'You bring up the rear. The last thing we want is to get trapped down there. Kade—stand guard up here.'

Ellery tossed him a radio. Kade nodded sharply.

'Rifle's in the back of the car,' Bas said. 'Don't hesitate to shoot him if you see him.'

Kade nodded again and circled the car to the boot. 'Good luck.'

We headed into the building. It was squat and sturdy, and obviously built to weather all manner of disasters. The walls appeared to be made of solid concrete and were as thick as my forearm was long. The only thing in the room was the metal vault cover, propped back to reveal the shaft in the ground. I'd never thought of myself as being afraid of heights, but standing at the top of the ladder made me dizzy, and I had to squeeze my eyes shut for a moment.

I opened them again when Ellery's boots clanged against the rungs. 'Count to twenty before you follow,' he said.

'Alright,' I murmured.

I watched him descend out of sight. *One… two… three…*

The sound of his boots hitting the rungs grew distant. *Nineteen… twenty.*

I glanced at Bas. 'Me next?'

Bas nodded. 'Keep alert. This might be an ambush.'

'I will.' I went up on tiptoes and kissed him—short and tense. He grabbed my shoulders and pulled me closer, deepening the kiss. His tongue swept against my lips, and then he moved to kiss my cheek.

'I love you,' he murmured.

It was barely a whisper, but it sent a jolt through me that set my fingers tingling.

'I love you, too,' I whispered back.

Bas pulled me into a hug, squeezing tight. Then he eased back. 'Go.'

And it was my turn. Keeping my eyes fixed straight ahead, I climbed onto the ladder and started to descend. Rung by rung, I let the earth swallow me. Somehow, I'd never realised how deep underground the bunker was.

The belly of the beast.

My hands grew sweaty, my shoulders ached, and my thighs burned. Just as it became unbearable, the soft glow of the safety lights reached me.

'Harley?' Ellery called up to me.

'Yep,' I confirmed. 'All clear?'

'It's clear.'

I reached the bottom and stumbled off the ladder to stand beside Ellery, breathing hard. He had his gun in hand and was frowning.

'What is it?' I asked.

He held something out to me: a small metal screw. I stared at it.

'What's that?'

'I'm not sure.' Ellery shrugged. 'I found it on the floor.'

It went without saying that it hadn't been there before. Aside from the dust, the floors in this section of the bunker had been pristine. But now the dust was scuffed by boot prints and scrape marks. Were they ours? Or Hannover's?

'Did you guys get the lights on?' I asked.

'That was Declan. He rerouted the power from the main hall.'

I sent a silent thanks to Declan. At least the place wasn't so creepy with the lights on.

Bas joined us a moment later, jumping off the ladder and stretching before pulling out his gun. 'Ready?'

Ellery nodded.

We fell into formation, Ellery checking ahead, Bas guarding the rear, and me keeping an eye on the shifting shadows to either side of us. The corridors looked different in the light—the layout made more sense now that I could see the bigger picture. Doors at regular intervals, an internal logic to what went where. We reached the first silo, and Ellery left us to stand guard whilst he went down to scout.

He returned a few minutes later.

'Untouched,' he reported.

'It would take pretty significant machinery to move the missiles,' Bas said.

'This is Hannover we're talking about,' Ellery said. 'He probably had a plan all along.'

'Are there other weapons here?' I asked.

'Not that we found.' Ellery signalled with a jerk of his chin to keep moving. We made our way down the halls, checking each room we passed, until we arrived at the control room. Ellery pressed his back against the wall and opened the door with one hand, then swung around the doorjamb to point his gun inside.

'What the fuck?' he hissed.

'What?' Bas demanded, tensing up.

Ellery beckoned. 'Come look.'

We crowded into the doorway behind him. I felt my jaw dropping as I surveyed the room.

The entire room had been gutted.

Ellery stepped over to one of the walls, as though taking a closer look might make it make sense. But all that remained was a mess of cables, screws, and damaged paint. The screens and terminals and other Pre-Crash devices that had been here before were gone.

Hannover hadn't wanted the weapons—he'd wanted the system to run them.

The tech.

But that didn't make any sense.

'Why?' I asked.

'Hannover,' Bas murmured.

'I know, but...' I couldn't think what to say. I'd been worried that Hannover was going to wipe our entire region off the face of the Earth. And instead he had wanted... Pre-Crash tech?

'Hannover doesn't make sense,' Bas said grimly. 'He never has.'

'There's a good market for tech in the cities,' Ellery said. 'And this is military-grade and still functional. He must know something about it that we don't.'

I traced a finger over the scars on one of the walls. 'What do we do now?'

'No idea,' Ellery said.

We all stared at one another. I tried to rally, to pull my scattered thoughts back to where they needed to be. Hannover had to have planned this from the very beginning. Could we chase him down? Or should we go after Jackson?

Ellery cleared his throat. 'Let's... Let's get back above the surface, and—'

His radio buzzed with a sudden burst of static.

'Lynx, come in,' Kade said. And then, 'Lynx? Urgent. Repeat: urgent. Multiple vehicles incoming.'

'Fuck,' Ellery cursed, fumbling his radio off his belt. 'Pronghorn, what's going on up there? Are you hidden?'

'They can't see me,' Kade reported. 'Five vehicles, military for sure. You guys need to get out of there.'

Ellery turned his pale, frightened face to Bas and me.

'We might be able to open the door to this section from the inside,' Bas said.

'Let's go.' Ellery nodded sharply.

We sprinted through the hallways, heading for the door out to the rest of the bunker. When we reached it, we stopped, panting. Ellery spoke into the radio again.

'Pronghorn, come in.'

No reply.

'Fuck,' Ellery said.

'He might just not be able to answer discreetly,' I said.

'Maybe.' Ellery turned on the door and yanked the handle. Locked.

'We need to go through the ceiling,' Bas said. 'Boost me up.'

The ceiling panel we'd crawled through before was still open, but we didn't have a ladder to hand. Ellery braced himself and gave Bas a boost, but he could barely get his hands around the edge.

'We need to hide,' I said.

'Where?' Ellery asked.

'The silos?' I suggested.

'No way. They'll check there.' Ellery frowned, his gaze roving around restlessly. 'There's a weird maintenance room. Come on.'

The room Ellery chose was directly opposite the control room, its door reading 'Server Maintenance Room'. We shouldered through the door just as heavy footfall reached us down the hall.

It was empty.

Several large cabinets stood against the walls, their glass doors hanging open. Their contents, however, were gone.

'Hannover.' Ellery uttered a string of curses. 'We can find somewhere else.'

I had my ear pressed to the door. Out in the hall, the footsteps had drawn level with our hiding place. 'It's too late.'

'If they look in here—'

'There's no time,' I hissed. I squeezed into the corner between one of the cabinets and the wall. Bas did the same directly opposite me, and if I craned my neck, I could see Ellery crouched underneath a table. Out in the hall, I could hear muffled shouts.

'—gone—'

'What?'

'—other rooms—'

More footsteps, this time louder. Someone running. Then the door to our room flew open, and my jaw dropped as Jackson pelted inside.

What was he doing here?

Three other men followed him in: an older man in a medal-bedecked military uniform, a man in black who was obviously some kind of private security, and Godfrey in a pinstriped suit, his hair neatly combed. One of them flipped a light switch, bathing the room in bright artificial light.

I squinted.

Please don't look over here. Please. Please.

As my vision cleared, Jackson moved into the middle of the room. He was looking around with an expression of dawning horror.

'It was here. Sayle was certain.' He swiped a hand over his bald head, where sweat was gleaming in the white light.

'And now it's not,' Godfrey said.

Jackson wrung his hands, looking pale and washed out. 'I—' he started. 'We—I'll start a search.'

'No need,' Godfrey said. In contrast to Jackson, he looked perfectly calm.

'But…'

Godfrey nodded to the security guard beside him, nothing more than a slight jerk of his chin. Then he turned to the military man. 'I assume your men can take control of this facility?'

'It would be our pleasure,' the man responded in a gravelly voice.

'Perfect. In that case, we can be done with the matter.'

'Done?' Jackson squawked. 'That wasn't our deal.'

'I'm putting a new deal in place.'

The security guard shifted, and I realised he was holding a pistol, hidden just behind his leg. Jackson spun around.

The guard raised the gun.

BANG!

The noise was deafening. I jerked, my head slamming against the wall. My ears rang, and all other sound faded to a distance. Jackson tumbled to the ground, and Godfrey clicked his fingers, summoning more security guards to remove the body. He turned to the military general, his mouth moving, although I couldn't hear any of the words over the sound of my own heartbeat.

Jackson was dead.

Godfrey had betrayed him.

How long had he been planning that?

A shadow fell over me, and before I could even think of reacting, the security guard plunged a hand down and snatched my arm, hauling me upwards. I stumbled out into the open.

'Found an intruder,' he said.

Godfrey wheeled around to stare at me. Ellery scrambled out of his hiding place, Bas following suit, both of their hands in the air.

'What is the meaning of this?' Godfrey demanded. The security guard pushed me into the middle of the room and herded Bas and Ellery to stand near me as well.

'It was Dean Hannover,' Ellery said. 'He removed the computers—last night or this morning.'

Godfrey's eyes narrowed. 'How do you know that?'

'Because we were here yesterday, trying to prevent him from finding them,' Ellery replied.

Behind Godfrey, several other soldiers entered the room. At once, they surrounded us, their rifles trained on us. I stiffened, my heart pounding in my throat. I wanted, more than anything, to reach out and take Bas's hand, but I didn't dare move. The six inches between us felt like an unbridgeable chasm.

'Who are you?' Godfrey demanded.

'Uh…' Ellery hesitated, then cleared his throat. 'Marco Ellery, Harley Benoit, and… Sebastian Rochester.'

At Bas's name, Godfrey's eyes narrowed in recognition.

'You're the ones who killed Moriarty.'

'Um.' Ellery didn't seem to be sure whether to answer yes or no. I swallowed. It could go either way. Godfrey *had* just had Jackson killed. Finally, Ellery said hesitantly, '…Yes.'

Godfrey waved a hand dismissively. 'You did me a favour, I suppose. Even so, I'm afraid this is a restricted area, and I can't have you talking about what you found here.' He nodded to one of the military guys—by the many badges and stripes on his jacket, I assumed he was important. 'Arrest them. Get them above ground whilst we finish up here.'

The other man nodded and issued a few brisk commands to his men. My head was buzzing too much to focus on them.

Arrest… arrest… arrest.

We were so fucked.

One of the soldiers kept a gun on me whilst another patted me down for weapons. Then he steered me out into the corridor, where we met another group of men.

'What are they doing here?' a soldier asked.

'Search me. Boss says to get them to the prison.'

I was transferred into the supervision of the new group, along with Bas and Ellery, and they marched us towards the hatch.

'Fancy seeing you here.'

I jerked at the soft, unfamiliar voice. Twisting my head, I met the gaze of the soldier who was leading me. Shock jolted through my stomach. I might not have recognised his voice, but I did know him—he was Benny's brother, Raf. The one who had got us through the checkpoint on the day the mayor was shot. He met my gaze and offered me a little wink.

I swallowed. I wanted to ask him what was going to happen now, but surrounded by soldiers, I didn't dare.

The walk through the corridors seemed to last forever. Finally, we reached the escape hatch, where we had to rearrange so they could escort us in single file up the ladder. Bas was sent up first, then Ellery, and then me, each with a soldier before and after us. At the top, we ended up squeezed into the small building.

'Right-ho,' Raf said when he emerged from the ladder, the last one up. 'Off you go, then.'

My jaw dropped. *What?*

'We're meant to be arresting them, sargeant,' one man said tentatively.

'Seems a bit excessive,' Raf said. 'They've done us a favour—or two'—he winked at me again—'so I think we can let this one slide. So long as you keep your mouths shut about this place. I'll get an NDA sent your way.' He nodded to me.

I had no idea what an NDA was, but I was absolutely not going to disagree with him.

'You're letting us go?' I asked, just to be clear.

'I am,' Raf confirmed. 'Give Ben my regards, yeah?'

'Thank you,' I breathed.

'You'd better go quick. Before the pencil-pushers get here.' He waved to the door. 'Don't worry, if I know politicians, they'll have forgotten about you within a week.'

I sure bloody hoped so.

'Thanks,' I said once again. I caught Ellery and Bas's eyes.

'Right,' Ellery said, taking the lead to my extreme relief. 'We'll be on our way.'

He stepped out the door, and Bas and I hastened after him. As Kade had warned us, there were now five big military vehicles parked outside, alongside our car. Two men were guarding our car, one of them with his gun on a scowling Kade.

Raf followed us out.

'Good job, men,' he called. 'You can let him go now, I think.'

'Sir?' one of them asked.

'Don't worry. This one's on me.' Still smiling, Raf waved us all over to our car. The two soldiers there fell back, one of them with a suspicious look in Kade's direction. For a moment, we all stood there in confusion. Then Raf broke the tension.

'Right. Well, I'll be seeing you.' He waved. 'Gents, let's get back downstairs. See if there's anything to be salvaged.'

He headed back for the building, leaving us by our car. We all climbed in in stunned silence, and Bas started the car.

'They still have our weapons,' I muttered.

'I'm not asking for them back,' Ellery said. 'Let's just go. We're lucky to be alive.'

I didn't like that; having a gun had become like a safety net. But I also didn't want to face Godfrey and risk him changing his mind and executing us, too. I kept silent as Bas manoeuvred the car out from between the military vehicles and turned us towards town.

'Where to now?' Ellery asked.

'I don't know.' A wave of exhaustion washed over me suddenly, all-encompassing and deadening. My limbs felt like they were weighed down with bricks. 'What's left?'

'Did you see Jackson in the bunker?' Kade asked. 'He was with Godfrey.'

'He's dead,' Bas said.

'Godfrey had him shot,' Ellery elaborated.

Kade whistled. 'So Godfrey comes out on top?'

'Looks like it,' Ellery said.

'He played a long game, if this is what he's been planning from the start.'

'More likely, he seized the opportunity,' Bas said quietly. He steered us onto the road, the noise from the tyres ebbing as we moved from wasteland to asphalt. 'With Moriarty and Jackson gone, he's probably hoping he'll be able to cement his power before the gangs pull themselves together again.'

'Could just about work,' Ellery said. He sagged back into his seat, as though he'd suddenly run out of energy. 'What are we going to do now?'

'We need to lay low,' Bas said.

'What about Hannover?' I asked.

'He'll be gone,' Bas predicted darkly. 'He isn't going to stick around now.'

'But...' I suspected he was right, but the niggling fear wouldn't stop gnawing at me.

'Bas is right,' Ellery put in. 'The Iron Fists and the Black Hands are going to be looking for someone to blame. We need to keep a low profile for a while.'

I chewed the inside of my cheek.

'Let's go home and regroup,' Kade suggested. 'Will Rodney mind if we all go there?'

'I'm sure he'll find it in his heart to be generous,' Bas muttered sardonically.

After that, we drove in silence. An odd atmosphere permeated the car. I felt as though the tension had vanished so suddenly, it had left behind a void. I had no idea *how* to feel.

'Listen,' Ellery said suddenly, 'can you drop me back at Laura's? I want to grab my car and drive out to check on Mum and Claire.'

'Alright,' Bas said. We were already in town, so he turned off on the next street, redirecting us towards the outskirts of town.

By the time we reached Laura's house, I was practically asleep. I jolted awake when Ellery spoke.

'Looks like no one's here.'

'We'd better check, to be safe,' Bas said.

'I'll go.' Ellery climbed out of the car and vanished around the back of the house. Less than ten minutes passed before he returned.

'She's gone,' he reported. 'Looks like she cleared her stuff out.'

'Skipped town, then,' Kade mused.

'Yeah,' Ellery said. 'I'm going to drive out to the safehouse. See you at seven?'

Bas nodded. Ellery headed to his car, climbed in, and peeled out of the driveway. Once he was gone, Bas turned the ignition. 'Where do you want to go, Harley?'

'Um...' I stifled a yawn. Where did I want to go? To sleep, really.

But there was something I had to do first. 'Back to Rodney's, I think,' I said. 'But do you mind stopping at my flat on Prospect Avenue on the way? I want to… I want to apologise to Savannah.'

'Of course,' Bas said.

'Thanks.'

Bas turned the car and started towards the centre of town. On a whim, I reached out and brushed my hand against his arm. He glanced at me from the corner of his eye, and I smiled.

We were safe. I had no idea what tomorrow would bring, but as Bas returned my smile, I found I didn't care. We were safe, and that was all that counted.

EPILOGUE

Three weeks later

'HERE.' ANNA SLID ME A GLASS of whiskey, the good stuff from the top shelf that Tom reserved for the gangs, the rich boys, the politicians. I accepted it with a smile.

'Feels weird to be on this side of the counter,' I said. Obviously, as a waitress, I'd manned both sides of the counter. But today I wasn't wearing an apron and flaunting my wares and flirting with customers. The Kranikovska's bar was empty; the lunch shift would start in half an hour. Tom, the owner, had asked me to come in for a meeting, and I'd decided to stop in and chat to Anna and Kayla on my way out.

'Maybe you'll be back behind the bar with us again soon,' Anna suggested.

'Probably,' I demurred, taking a sip of my whiskey and relishing the smoky taste.

Tom had offered me my old job back, and I was probably going to accept—at least for the short term. But it had been with great pleasure that I told him I had to check with my partner before I agreed to anything. Because that was what Bas and I were. Partners.

Unfortunately, we were partners without jobs or permanent living arrangements. The Kranikovska was familiar and would allow me to keep up to date with the news around town, so it worked for me.

I leaned against the counter, surveying the room.

'That would be good,' Kayla said. 'Without you and Laura, I've had to pick up double shifts here.'

'Sorry.' I hid a grimace at the mention of Laura.

For the sake of letting sleeping dogs lie, I hadn't told anyone what Laura had done—or why. There was no point in tarnishing her name to her colleagues and friends. It didn't matter anyway; she was gone. As best we could tell, she had skipped town along with Hannover—no amount of searching had turned up hide or hair of either of them.

'Well, it wasn't your fault,' Kayla said. 'But also, don't do it again.'

Anna and I giggled.

'It would be nice to have you back,' Anna said. 'You have a knack for handling drunk patrons.'

'I concur,' Kayla said as she went back to doing prep for her shift. I watched her head bobbing as she hummed along to the music. Kayla and her father had come out rather well from the whole affair. In spite of Declan's distaste for the army, he had agreed to help them try to salvage the equipment in the bunker now that the Iron Fists were out. Apparently, his price had been steep—and he'd been promised that he could take anything the military didn't find useful for himself. But Kayla had pointed out that the faster it went, the sooner the soldiers would be out of town, which was a benefit for all of us.

'Besides, Dad loves tech more than practically anything else in this town,' she'd added.

It seemed like things were finally dying down, at least.

I lingered with my friends for a few more minutes, letting Anna fill me in on the town gossip whilst she filled water jugs and counted bottles. Business was booming since the barricade around the centre of town had been lifted.

'Although the people who put in the effort to get permits to drive through the centre are disappointed,' she explained. 'They were taking money from people to run deliveries.'

'There are always people who profit off of bad situations,' Kayla said cynically.

'They'll live,' I said. I slid my empty glass back onto the counter. Before I could say my goodbyes, though, someone entered the bar.

'Hello, hello!' Brenda called out. 'Thought I'd pop in and say hi—Harley! What are you doing here?'

She hurried over and pulled me into a hug. I squeezed her tightly. 'Brenda! How are you?'

'Good, good,' she said. 'Boys are running me ragged. As usual. But what can you do?'

She pulled back. 'What are you doing here?'

'Hopefully, accepting her old job back,' Kayla said.

'Oh, that will be good for you.' Brenda grinned. 'Still got your fella?'

A secretive little smile pulled at my lips. 'Yeah, still got him.'

'Oooh,' the others all chorused. I felt my cheeks heat up.

'Shh,' I mumbled.

'Oh, look, she got shy.' Kayla smirked. I rubbed my cheeks.

'Have you still got the dog?' I asked Brenda to divert attention from myself.

Brenda huffed an exaggerated sigh. 'What do you think?'

'I might know a place for it,' I said, thinking of Claire and Collette Ellery. They were staying with one of their neighbours whilst they worked on rebuilding the farm. Fortunately, most of the property had been untouched by the fire—only the house had been damaged. They were homeless, but they still had the fields, the animals, their livelihood. And Ellery, who was splitting his time between town and his home, helping his mother.

'Nah, that's okay.' Brenda shook her head. 'The boys have got attached. We'll make do somehow.'

'Alright, then.'

'It seems weird how quickly things went back to normal,' Anna said.

'Tell me about it,' Brenda agreed. 'Nice not to have to detour around the square on my way to work anymore, though.'

I had meant to leave quickly, but I ended up staying for another fifteen minutes, chatting with my friends. It was nice to be able to do that again—just hang out without having to look over my shoulder all the time.

'How are things out at the casinos?' I asked Kayla in a quiet moment.

Kayla raised an eyebrow. 'Not a lot happening, why?'

'Same as up north, then,' I murmured.

'I suppose so.' She shrugged. 'Time will tell how things change. I think everyone is keeping their heads down for now.'

I nodded.

Moncrief—Jackson's main competition for leadership—had taken over the Iron Fists, but he was a decidedly weaker leader, and without the bunker, they had lost their main source of income. I'd heard a rumour that Moncrief was trying to strike a deal with The Arsonist to use their facilities, but considering how small the pub was compared to the bunker, I doubted much would come of the attempt. It looked like the Iron Fists would be fading into the background. The Black Hands were also gone; between Moriarty's death and Hannover bailing, most of them seemed to have decided to jump ship—a wise decision, considering that the army's last act before leaving had been to raid their compound. The reason? An 'anonymous tip-off' informing them that the Black Hands were holding slaves.

That only left Percival and the Aces, but they were keeping their heads down at the moment.

As for Godfrey, I certainly wasn't going to be trusting him soon—but one mayor was just the same as another, as far as I was concerned. He was working on reopening the train line, which most people around town seemed to think was a good thing.

Finally, it was time for the bar to open. I said goodbye to the others and headed out into the lobby. Benny was sitting on a plastic chair just inside the front door.

'Oh, hi Harley.' He offered me a toothy grin.

'Hi,' I returned.

'Haven't seen you in ages. Tom said you were going to come back and work for us.'

'I might do,' I said cautiously.

'That'll be fun,' Benny said. 'S'not the same without you and Brenda.'

I smiled. 'Thanks. I've got to be off—but can you do me a favour?'

'Sure thing.' Benny waggled his eyebrows.

'Can you tell your brother I said thanks next time you see him? He'll know what for.'

Benny's eyebrows vanished under his mop of brown hair. 'Yeah, alright,' he said. 'Can do.'

'Thank you.'

I said my goodbyes and headed out the door, walking along an old, familiar path towards the Prospect Avenue apartment where I was currently staying. Bas had headed back to Freetown to help out the Ellerys, but I hadn't felt comfortable doing the same—even though they had invited me. Fortunately—and much to my surprise—Savannah had invited me to move back in with her temporarily. After taking her time to cool down, she had reached out, and a wild tale had emerged— of how Hardwick had convinced her to help him root out the slavers in the NCC clinic, and how that had ended with her getting the job in the bunker to spy on Markus Clairmont.

It wasn't at all what I'd expected, but I was glad to have my sister back, even if a certain amount of awkwardness remained between us after my harsh words to her.

The checkpoint on Prospect Avenue was gone, although the concrete barriers hadn't been moved yet. Someone would probably repurpose them into building materials eventually. For now, they sat on the side of the road, gathering rubbish and dead leaves at their bases. I passed them and let myself into my building, climbing the stairs to the top landing, where a neat row of buckets and tins captured the water that was leaking through the roof again.

Some things never changed.

I let myself in cautiously, because these days I never knew what Savannah's mood would do. She was one of only three doctors now working in the clinic, and she alternated between insanely stressed, sobbing over Talbot, screaming at me, and sleeping.

But when I opened the door, she was doing none of those. The lounge was in disarray, several crates sat in the small open area in front of the sofa, two empty and the third filled with an assortment of books and knickknacks. I could hear noises from the bedroom, so I made my way in that direction.

'Savannah?'

'In the bedroom!'

Evidently.

I poked my head in, and my stomach lurched.

'What are you doing?' I asked in a small voice, not that I needed confirmation of what my eyes had already told me.

Savannah was packing.

And not just a few things. Not just an overnight bag.

She was packing everything she owned.

All the books. All the clothes. Her medical scrubs and doctor's bag. An assortment of whiskey bottles and a small knife that I hadn't realised she owned. It was all laid out on her bed and shoved into various crates and bags that were squashed into the floor space between her bed and mine.

'Packing,' Savannah said.

'Yes, but… why?' My voice had faded to a whisper. I'd never seen this coming. Why would Savannah leave now? After everything?

'I'm going with Theo.' Savannah turned to me and fixed me with a smile. 'When he leaves for Crater's Edge.'

I stared at her. She was *what*?

'You're… going with him?' I asked.

Ultimately, Theo's recovery had taken longer than he'd expected. Not that I'd spoken to him again, but Diego had kept me updated — reluctantly. He was leaving this week.

'Yes.' Savannah was still smiling at me. The expression looked strange. I actually couldn't remember the last time she had looked happy around me. But she was happy now, standing taller, her eyes crinkling. 'I need a fresh start. Away from the NCC. Crater's Edge Hospital is hiring.'

'But…' Words failed me.

Savannah's smile faltered. 'I thought you would be happy about this. You wanted me to leave. Besides, it frees you up to go and live with your… whatever he is.'

After everything, Savannah was still weird about talking about Bas. I shuffled my weight, before edging past the boxes to sit on my bed.

'You can call him my boyfriend.' I swallowed and fiddled with the hem of my shirt. 'I never meant for you to leave without me, you know.'

Savannah hunched over a bag, rifling through the contents. 'Well, you don't have to leave anymore,' she said in an unreadable tone. 'Now, I do.'

The thought shocked me. I'd never considered leaving without her… but now she was leaving without me.

And yet, maybe this was what she needed. I had left. And come home. Savannah would leave and come home, too. She had to.

And if she didn't… maybe it was time to accept that we needed different things in life.

'I…' I cleared my throat and continued thickly, 'I'll miss you.'

Savannah shot me a weak smile. 'I'll miss you, too.'

My eyes prickled, and I had to look away. I stared at my bedspread, swallowing hard.

Knock-knock-knock.

Savannah and I both turned to the door.

'Are you expecting anyone?' she asked.

'Uh… no.'

Savannah stood, rolling her shoulders. 'I'll check who it is,' she called over her shoulder as she exited.

I stared after her, my stomach churning. Savannah, leaving. Leaving me. For Crater's Edge.

'Harley!'

I took a deep, shaky breath. 'Yeah?'

'It's Bas.'

I jumped up and hurried through to the main room. Sure enough, Bas was standing in the doorway, smiling a little uncomfortably.

'Bas!' I slipped past Savannah to throw my arms around him and press a kiss to his stubbly cheek. 'I wasn't expecting to see you today.'

'I wanted to talk to you.' His voice had a wonderful calming effect on me these days. After everything we had been through together, there was something reassuring about being able to hug him, kiss him, talk to him.

'Sure.' I drew back. 'Do you want to come in?'

'I…' Bas cleared his throat. 'I'd rather go for a drive.'

'Oh. Sure.'

I turned to Savannah, and at once a pang went through my chest. She was leaving. I ought to spend what time I had left with her. 'W-will you…'

'I'll still be here when you get back.' Savannah rolled her eyes. 'I'm leaving the day after tomorrow.'

'Oh.' I squared my shoulders. 'Okay. See you in a bit then.'

Bas had parked outside my building. We both climbed into his car, and he started us towards the north of town.

'Where are we going?' I asked.

'You'll see.'

I'd never been the greatest fan of surprises, but I forced myself to be patient. We made small talk as Bas drove us out of town, and by the by, he turned us off the road and we bounced through the wastes.

'Tom wants me to come back and work at the Kranikovska,' I said.

Bas hummed. 'Will you?'

'I think so. But I wanted to discuss it with you first.' I glanced at him, taking in his handsome profile. Smooth, olive skin, slightly messy brown hair, piercing green eyes. And all mine. 'See whether you had any plans.'

'Uh huh,' Bas said noncommittally.

'Do you?' I prompted.

'Not so far.'

I chewed my lip. 'Savannah's leaving town,' I blurted. 'She's going to Crater's Edge.'

'Is that so?'

'Yeah.' I stared at him. Was he going to make me ask?

He glanced at me. 'I suppose we could find a place to live together.'

'Yeah.' All of a sudden, my voice had gone husky. 'I'd like that.'

'For which we'll both need proper jobs.'

'I'm pretty sure lots of people would love to hire you,' I said.

'Without any qualifications?' Bas shot me a smile. 'We might be living off of your salary.'

'Not for long,' I said. Bas was hardworking and competent. Someone would hire him. 'Where would we live?'

'Where do you want to live?' Bas asked.

I shrugged. Not a subject I'd thought too much about. 'In walking distance of work, I guess.'

'We could get you a car.'

'We could.' That would open up new possibilities. 'In that case, somewhere quiet.'

I turned to look at Bas again and caught him smiling.

'That sounds nice.' Then he nodded towards my window. 'Look.'

I turned—and gasped in surprise. It was as though the whole wasteland had lit up with colour. Flowers. They'd been popping up all over the place, but out here, they were everywhere, crowding densely together in an explosion of pinks, blues, and yellows for as far as the eye could see.

'Oh, wow,' I said.

Bas stopped the car, and we climbed out.

'I wanted to show you,' Bas said. 'This part of the wasteland is particularly beautiful in spring.'

I kept staring, trying to imprint the memory into my brain. It was without a doubt one of the most beautiful things I had ever seen.

'This is amazing,' I whispered. 'Thank you for bringing me here.'

'I've been planning this for a while.' There was an undertone to Bas's voice that made me glance at him. He had a thoughtful look in his eyes like he was miles away. He continued: 'I wanted to have this conversation before we discussed housing, but this is okay too.'

'What… what's going on?' I asked, suddenly nervous. I wiped my palms down on my jeans. Was he breaking up with me?

Bas took my hands, squeezing them gently as he looked me in the eye.

'I know I haven't always been the person you deserve. I know I might not always manage to be that person in future… but I'd like to try. Will you… Would you… Will you marry me?'

I stared at him, my mind oddly blank.

Marry him?

I'd never imagined getting married—not to Bas, not to anyone. I'd always thought I'd be fighting alone.

But the past few months had proven to me that there was a better option.

Bas's face fell, and I realised I'd been staring gormlessly at him.

'If you don't want to…' he started.

'Yes,' I said. 'Yes, I do want to. I would like that very much.'

Bas sighed in relief. I pulled my hands away from him and threw my arms around his shoulders with such force that he actually stumbled back a step. Then we were kissing, our tongues tangling together. Heat surged through me as I fused my body to his. *Closer. More!*

And Bas seemed to read my mind, because he kissed me harder, held me tighter.

When I pulled back, my smile felt so big it could barely be contained on my face. I tugged Bas towards the car.

'We can go back to my place,' I said. Then I changed my mind. 'Actually, no. Let's stay here.'

'What?' Bas asked.

'Savannah's at my place, and Ellery is at yours,' I said. 'And I want to do something that I've actually wanted to do for a while now. Climb in the back.'

Bas, confused but willing, clambered into the back seat. I moved the front seat forwards, then got in the back with him and settled between his legs.

He stared down at me. 'Harley? What are you doing?'

'Reciprocating.' Grinning, I put my hands on his crotch. 'The same thing I'm going to be doing for you—hopefully—for the rest of our lives.'

THE END

WHAT'S NEXT?

Dear reader,

Thanks for giving The Iron Fists Series a chance! I hope you enjoyed reading about Harley's adventures as much as I enjoyed writing them.

I'd love it if you could take the time to leave a review on my Amazon and Goodreads pages. Reviews are the best reward an author can receive.

If you want more from this world, please join my mailing list. You will receive a free short story, as well as updates about my writing, sneak peeks at new projects, and freebies from other series.

And if you want to explore my other books, check out my website.

You can also follow me on my socials to learn more about me.

See you in the next book!

Hunters are supposed to hate vampires—but everyone will betray their people for a price. Nathan is about to discover his.

Nathan is a vampire hunter on the cusp of graduation. He's been training for this his entire life: the moment he qualifies and joins the rest of his family in their noble calling.

If only it were that simple.

His grades are a mess, his social life is a disaster, and what's worse, his best friend is a witch! Add to that, his vampire uncle is back in town and his crush might just be supernatural too, and you have one big melting pot of potential parental disapproval. Nathan doesn't think he can take much more, and then the dark mages come to town.

As bodies begin piling up in the streets, Nathan finds himself pulled deeper into political intrigue and a deadly plot that will pit him against his own family. When the girl he likes comes under threat, Nathan races against time to solve the mystery... well aware that with every step he takes, he comes closer to his father exposing all his secrets.

ACKNOWLEDGEMENTS

Finishing a series is a heady feeling. Twenty months after penning the first word of Rise, here we are with four books in the world. It's a wild achievement—there were times when I honestly wasn't sure if I could see it through.

But I did manage, and that is in large part thanks to the team I had helping me along the way.

Firstly, to my alpha reader Chuck, who read every chapter seemingly as soon as I had written it, and also provided invaluable feedback regarding the military and weapons for the entire series: thank you, thank you, thank you. I hope that I am able to provide you even a fraction of the help and support you have given me (even if I never keep up to date with my critiquing).

To the rest of my Discord group, thank you for the emotional support, the laughs, the chats about writing technique—and most importantly, for the feedback about the different meanings of words between British and American English. TIL. Thanks, also, for providing the call signs for Harley, Bas, Ellery, and Kade.

To my editor, Cameron: thank you for catching the myriad comma errors, and also for weeding your way through the mess I made of the middle of this book. We got there in the end!

To my family, for all of their support this last year. To my dad, who promotes every single one of my posts on social media. To my brother, who lent me his flat (and his cats) during the early stages of writing Revenge, when I was struggling to gain momentum.

To my kitties, Smoky and Snowy, who always picked the very best moments to sit on my keyboard.

And last, but never least, to my mum: formatter, proofreader, cheerleader, emotional support, and so much more. Thanks for battling your way through last-minute laptop shenanigans to pull this together. Thanks for holding my hand as I sobbed and said I couldn't do it. Thanks for the hugs and the laughs and the 'business meetings' over coffee and cake. I couldn't have done it without you

Margot de Klerk is a British author who writes fantasy and science fiction for teens and adults, with a bit of comedy, a dash of romance, and a whole lot of plot. She is most often found in her favourite coffee shop typing furiously on her computer with an iced latte at hand. When not writing, she enjoys photography, travelling, sewing, and various sports.

Follow her on social media, subscribe to her mailing list, and get information on new books:

www.ingramcontent.com/pod-product-compliance
Lightning Source LLC
Chambersburg PA
CBHW060651190726
48289CB00002B/354